Monarch Of The Dragon

MONARCH of the DRAGONS

Katelyn Sheddy

Monarch Of The Dragons

First edition originally published 2020

Summary: Edwin gets taken to a land called Xolf, where they have dragon knights who are both dragons and humans working together to protect the allied kingdoms.

Paperback Print ISBN: 979-8-9948606-0-1

Hardcover Print ISBN: 979-8-9948606-1-8

Ebook ISBN: 979-8-9948606-2-5

CONTENTS

ACKNOWLEDGEMENT

Thank you, dear reader, for picking up my book and giving my story a chance. I hope it was a fun read. If not, maybe the book can be good fire fuel?

Some of you may or may not recognize the title, for I wrote and published this story back in high school. Since then, I have returned to the story in my maturity and revised it. I took the time to refine the world and characters, along with, thanks to the encouragement of my husband, returning to some story points I was scared of doing in the first draft, which eventually led to its hiatus. But no more! Here is the start of the series, “Monarch”, new, improved, and ready to tell the entirety of Edwin’s story!

I hope that you like the tale I have to write. Edwin and this book mean a lot to me as it represents not only my growth as a storyteller but also is a memento of me as a survivor. In high school, I was not in a good spot, and so to help live through it, I turned to writing this book. Thank you, Edwin, Merlin, Skypris, Terro, Demmis, Empress, and all other characters for being my friends in my darkest hours. I hope that they have the opportunity to help you in a time of need, even if it is only a simple smile!

I want to take a moment to really thank those who have supported me throughout my life with my art and stories, whether it be financially or just encouragement. Your engagement means the world to me. Thank you so much for supporting me and, in turn, supporting my starting family!

A special thanks to my external family for being the best cheerleader and inspiration for my creative work. Especially my parents! And a big thanks to the friends in my life, even the ones who have come and gone. Thank you to my editor, Jennifer Rees, for managing to keep my whacky voice in the story yet help perfect it!

A loving thank you to my daughter for being my muse.

A phenomenal thank you to my husband for being my number one supporter in everything I do! For always pushing me to give the best of my work, and for being an awesome soundboard and developmental editor for this story.

Also, babe, if you're reading this, take out the trash, please, I got a saga to write!

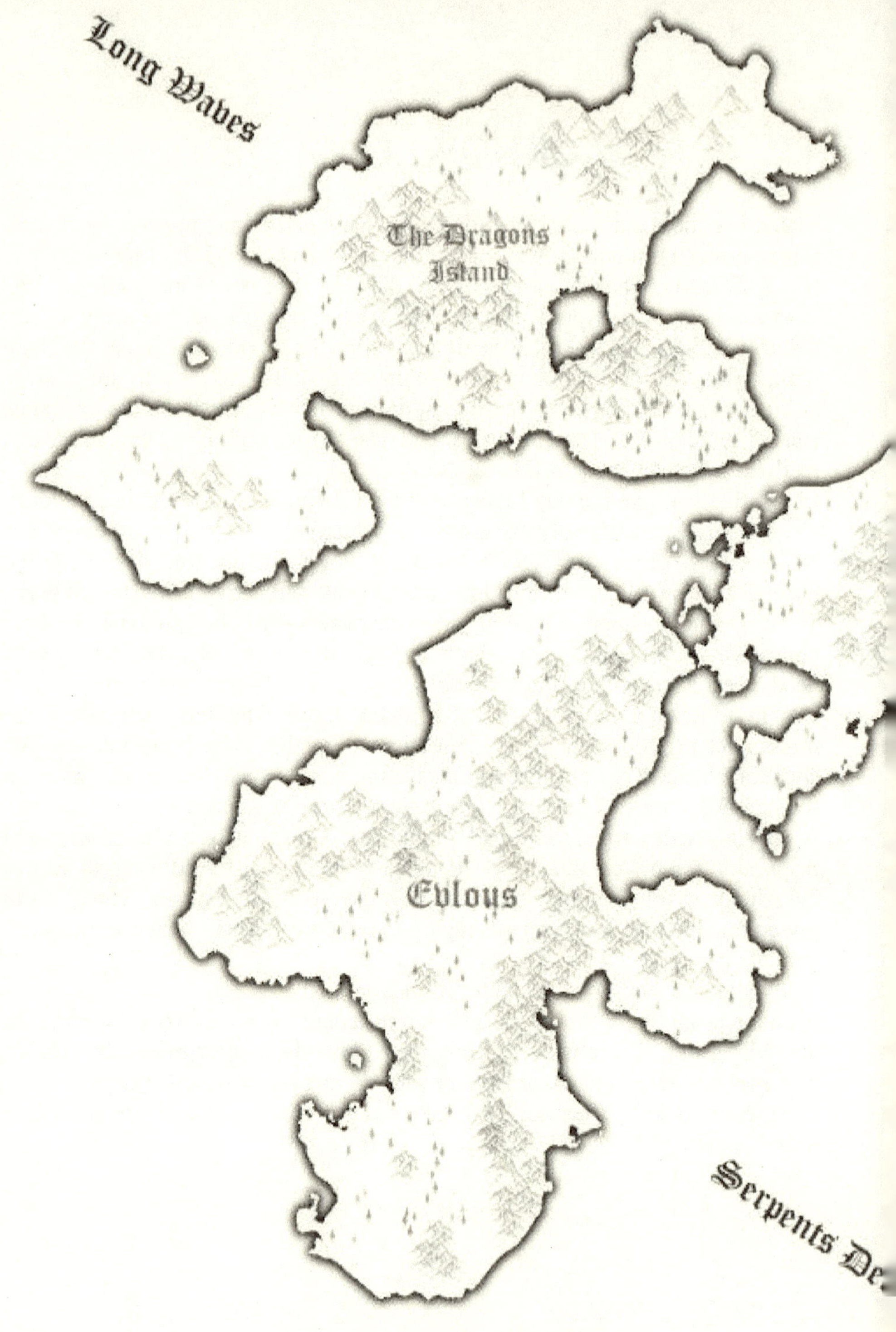
Long Waves
The Dragons
Island
Evlous
Serpents De

poseidon's Land
Brosh's Capital
The Gorish Empire
The Kingdom of Alena
Xolf
Thrist Kingdom
Ishmia
Ryjah Kingdom
Laxor Kingdom
Exwear Kingdom
ents' Deep

Chapter One
Coming Of Age

Thud!

THUD!

The colossal monster stomped. Its weight forced the cave ground to crack with each step. The cave reeked of sulfur and of charred bodies. Hiding behind a large boulder, Knight Lockwood tried to catch his breath as sweat beaded down his brow and drenched his body as if attempting to cool its owner against the hot metal armor he wore.

That fire was hot!

Lockwood turned to his left and saw the princess hiding behind another form of cover. Her dress had once been long and flowy.

However, it had been shortened due to the flames that had gnawed the ends. She looked just as distressed and sweaty as the knight, yet her beauty did not sway. Was she worth fighting this great beast for? She looked to Lockwood with pleading eyes, and he knew the answer. He signaled to her with a hand to wait. He tried to make his expression as confident as possible to reassure her. Lockwood didn't hear the footsteps of the monster for a while, so he peeked over the boulder, and the moment he did, he ducked immediately as scalding flames erupted around the cover. The princess screamed for her hero. The knight shook off the heat. If it wasn't for his experience and the rock to shield him, his hero's journey would have come to an end.

A big bellowing sounded in frustration at the knight's quick reflexes. Covered in a thick hide of scales, the creature's eyes were the color of rubies that burned with hatred. It inched closer, and then...

And then...

"EDWIN!"

Edwin hastily closed the book that had pulled him out of reality. He jumped to his feet and stumbled back to the ground, making the chickens cluck and flap as they avoided getting crushed. The teen boy winced mostly from embarrassment rather than pain.

The boy had long facial features that matched his lean body. His hair was brown, and his eyes were a lighter version of the color. However, in the correct lighting, they sometimes reflected gold. The clothing he wore fit him well. They weren't as ragged as most of Gorish's subjects. He wore a long-sleeved tan shirt and trousers with a darker, worn vest over top.

Around him, instead of being in a cinder-filled cave, he was in nothing more than a barn that, in his opinion, looked more like a rusty old shack. The smell of cow and chicken dung filled his nose instead of the mildew cave smell he would have welcomed instead. It wasn't too bad, though, once he adjusted to the stench.

Taking a slower approach to standing, Edwin avoided slipping on the straw again. The cow mooed at him as though laughing. Edwin glanced up at his uncle, who glared with rage. He shouldn't be scared, yet his uncle was a giant, intimidating man who took up nearly half of the barn's entrance. Even though the barn was on the smaller side—needed only to support a single cow—still, it didn't make his uncle's looming to cause Edwin's chest from tightening any less.

His uncle's hair was messy blond with a darker-shaded full beard that Edwin could only dream about growing one day. His uncle had a tummy, yet it didn't remove his intimidating demeanor. He wore his baking apron, which was covered in flour dust, and smelled of fresh bread and…sweat? Edwin found it hard to tell over the barn stench. His uncle's clothes were nothing special, just a bunch of dull colors like Edwin's. He supposed he should be thankful that because of his uncle's successful profession as a baker, they didn't have to wear rags like most common folk in the country.

"Wit are ye doin, lad?!" He grabbed Edwin by the shoulders and tossed him toward the entrance, his grip harsh against the boy's collarbone.

"A-A wis just reading." Edwin tried to sound confident despite feeling as if he'd been caught in a sinful act.

"Ye dinnae have time to jest! No today af aw days!"

"A wiznae!" he protested, slipping his book into the inner pocket of his vest. "A finished ma chores!"

His uncle glanced around, seeing a basket full of eggs, the cow's stall clean, and a few tins of milk while the cow chewed on its cud. He huffed at the sight. "Well then, let's no waste yer time reading." He reached into his pants' pocket, pulled out a small sack that rattled, and handed it to his nephew. "A need ye to gae into toon and buy fifteen pounds af flour."

Edwin wanted to say no and kick himself for not taking longer on his morning chores. He wished he had pretended none of them had been done and just taken the scolding! He really wanted to read and escape. It helped Edwin to relax and forget about what today was—even if he didn't understand every word in the book. Taking too long to answer to his uncle's liking, the guardian gave the boy a challenging look.

Edwin evaded his eyes from his uncle's. "Dae ye want me to buy the flour from Zilener?"

"Ye're gonnae have to. No other shops will be open today," Edwin's uncle scoffed. "Cowards. The lot of 'em!"

"Or just smart," Edwin wanted to say, but held his tongue.

"Zilener might be a boggin. However, he's a brave one, especially if coins are involved," the man finished before shooing Edwin away with the back of a hand.

Edwin nodded as he turned and walked out of the fickle barn. Behind him, his uncle called out, "And hurry!"

Hastening his pace, Edwin continued his journey by walking once he was out of his uncle's sight. He was in no rush to get to his destination. However, on his way home, he did plan on running. Passing two farmers' lands, he took note that neither the workers nor the owners and their families were anywhere in sight. Edwin could usually hear loud sheep, pigs, and cows, and yet the pasture was silent with the livestock safely tucked away in sheds or barns—depending on how profitable the farm was—staying instinctively quiet. On one acre, it seemed like someone had started to harvest wheat yet stopped in the middle of it. In the field was a wagon and some sickles near a bunch of harvested and tied stalks. Edwin swallowed hard, guessing that they had forgotten what day it was. No. How could anyone in their right mind forget about this horror fest? They had more than likely started chores just to end them early, not wanting to take any risks. Edwin didn't blame them.

Finally making it into town, unlike the farmer's lands, the marketplace was particularly crowded. It was an odd outcome once you realized most of the shops and booths were closed and boarded up by multiple layers of wood. Not even the tax collectors or coachmen were to be found. Some of the shops had signs that kindly told anyone who passed by that they were welcome to come tomorrow, while other signs were more raunchy, saying things Edwin didn't want to linger on.

Why did the streets feel so claustrophobic then? Well, all the stores were closed except for the bladesmith's forges. That's where the entire town's attention was at—and by the entire town, it was really mainly the men, the boys around Edwin's age, and maybe some of their older or younger brothers. As Edwin passed by the bladesmiths, he tried to peer into the shop to join the majority. However, he wasn't able to see anything other than hands and the exterior of the wood and stone-made shop. The crowd started in the forge and then finished ten feet out, leaking into the marketplace's walkway. The boy finally gave up trying to spectate and continued walking, trying his hardest to weave through the bodies that wouldn't budge. The sound of hammering metals meeting and the hissing of quenching oil faded into the murmering of the crowed as he approached a stand that didn't have its own identity. The only way Edwin was able to tell it was his destination was the fact that the storekeeper's owner didn't have any signs saying to come back another day.

Edwin's stop was a wooden booth shaped like a square with a missing side so that customers could walk in and out. The booth displayed potatoes and other vegetables that grew in the earth. Crates were set up under the farthest table, making the booth seem neat. The keeper, Zilener, was busy selling a bag of radishes to a young man with a scowl on his face. Yep, this was definitely the right booth.

Zilener was an older man who did his best to clean up as he wore a clean, white puffed long sleeve shirt with a dark vest and pants to match, which to nobility made him look like a stable boy, yet to the common folk it showed how well off he was what with being one of the main sources of vegetables in the town.

As his last customer took his leave, Edwin approached. "Well, look who we have here!" His voice almost came off as mocking. "Mordecai's second mistake…"

Edwin hesitated when he heard his father's name, especially in such a disrespectful tone. This wasn't an unexpected reaction, though. Zilener was a rival to Edwin's family. He'd hated Edwin's father for some reason, yet he used to be best mates with Edwin's uncle before he married Edwin's father's sister, then that relationship shattered.

"Wit brings ye here?"

"A..." Edwin took a deep breath. "A want to buy fifteen pounds af flour from ye."

"Disnae yer uncle have his own flour?" Zilener puffed up, acting like a child who had won an argument. Edwin didn't understand why he was so smug. The only reason he had flour was because his farm had some planters that his father planted that returned every season. It wasn't even his main sell, nor was it Edwin's family's. It's not as if they were in any business competitions with each other.

"We were short and dinnae have time to process more. Ma uncle wants to sell this batch tomorrow morning."

"Weddnae he be planning a funeral tomorrow?" He smiled at the boy with yellow crooked teeth that clashed with his pristine outside appearance.

Edwin's throat went dry, and he stayed quiet.

"Ye are af age, no?" he pushed, sizing Edwin up.

"Aye." Edwin felt cold, like the blood had drained from his face.

"Tell me, dae ye miss yer father, boy? Are ye excited to be joining him soon?"

Edwin could feel his bottom lip starting to quiver. Weight pushed on his chest. He couldn't tell if he was going to cry or punch the booth owner's face. He stammered, "A-are ye passing up a business deal?"

The man seemed to enjoy Edwin's anxiety.

"Give me the coins and take yer flour!" He snatched the sack from Edwin, causing the boy to yelp, which made Zilener laugh hard. "Dinnae pretend to be brave, boy! Denying one's nature only gets a man killed."

Edwin quickly grabbed the flour sack and pivoted on his foot. His body shook more than the coins he had given up. His arms felt heavy as he fought for breath. He had to escape. He had to feel safe. Edwin needed to calm down. He couldn't let his fear kill him before the monsters even had the chance, though dying from fear seemed far less gruesome than getting ripped apart. Edwin started daydreaming about his book, and what was going to happen—how was it going to end? Even though he had already read the book five times over now, Edwin still made himself focus and wondered about different outcomes and possibilities. He pondered if he would be able to slay his beast like Knight Lockwood had done in the book. Edwin began to think about his father and how his life was taken—how he was taken from Edwin by the same creature he was destined to face later that day. The boy's heart sank to his stomach as he started to realize that he probably wouldn't be seeing tomorrow, when CLASH!

Pottery flew across the walkway as Edwin stomped his feet to find stable ground. Unfortunately, his foot had been in a large pot, and the bottom shattered as Edwin tried to prevent himself from falling. A cloud escaped from the sack of flour as it hit the ground. "*Am such an Eejit!*" He cursed himself for not paying better attention. Lifting up his foot, he was grateful for his thick trousers to help against any cuts to his skin that the jagged ends of the pottery might give. He sighed with disappointment.

Before he had time to react, he heard a door open and slam shut, followed by an enraged voice, "Wit are ye doin'?!"

An elderly woman hobbled over from a shop that presumably had living quarters above it. Her hair was short and messy, her face wrinkly with a lazy eye caused by age. She had stains all over her clay-colored dress. Not only was the situation making Edwin feel uncomfortable, but the woman's appearance and hostility didn't help.

"A-Am so sorry! I'se clean it up!" Edwin started to gather and stack the knocked-over bowls, vases, and other pottery around him.

Collecting everything, the older woman started to nag at him about how this was her living, and clay wasn't cheap. Even though he deserved to be scolded, Edwin tuned her out the moment his mind gave him the chance. The boy didn't want his embarrassment to grow anymore. It already felt as big as his family's cow! Finally, the older woman threw her hands in the air and wobbled back inside the shop. Edwin heard wood shifting as she shut a giant latch to barricade the door from the inside. If Edwin's mind wasn't occupied, it would have been funny and concerning that she thought that alone could stop the horde of monsters if they wanted to attack. Bending down to collect the last of the pots, Edwin heard girlish giggling. Looking over to his right, he saw a woman passing by with three younger girls, his age.

Of course.

The only girls out today, and Edwin just humiliated himself in front of them, he felt like a Court jester. His entire face felt hot as he grabbed the last of the cracked pottery. He placed the clay over by the shop's booth where they had originally been before. Staring at a completely shattered vase, his stomach tightened. He should have been paying attention, even if the older woman had placed her pottery in the walk space. Reaching into his pocket, Edwin felt a hole in the bottom of it. He relaxed once he found a single copper coin in his other pocket. It wasn't enough, though it was all the boy had. He placed it into one of the cracked bowls, hoping it was positioned for the elderly woman to see and not just a struggling passerby.

Grabbing the flour sack, Edwin tossed it over his shoulder. A cloud puffed, turning his clothing white. He touched his cheek closest to the sack and could feel that flour had covered it.

Edwin started his trek home, deciding that he wouldn't be running back, after all. The last thing he wanted to do was draw attention to himself, and running with a flour sack on his shoulder, half of his face almost as white, was just screaming, *"Hoi Look at this fewl."* He might as well slather the rest of his body in the powder and took up the role as the King's Jester.

Passing by the smiths' shops, Edwin's attention drew back to the weapons they had forged. He saw a lot of fathers and sons testing out finely crafted swords. Edwin couldn't help but stop and admire a few of them. They were a pleasing distraction until his mind started thinking about what they were going to be used for. Why hadn't his uncle taken him to retrieve a weapon? He was going to need one today! A shield, too! All the knights in the stories had one for good reason.

Now thinking about it, Edwin's uncle didn't seem to prepare him at all for this day. Even though, legally, his uncle wasn't supposed to train him specifically for today, he could have at least taught the boy how to hunt. Edwin looked at all the boys his age and took note of how muscular they seemed to be compared to him. They were a loaf of bread, while he was only a leaf! They were sons of farmers and other practices that naturally build muscle. He was at a huge disadvantage, wasn't he? He was reading stories while he should have been exercising. Why didn't his uncle do something?! Why didn't he teach Edwin to hold a sword at minimum! Was he setting his nephew up for failure on purpose? What was he supposed to do, throw bread at the beasts?

After hearing a commotion that had a more hostile tone, Edwin scrunched up in alarm, realizing he had buried himself in his head again.

Looking over, Edwin saw some King's knights harassing an older man. The older man had barely anything on. His raggedy clothes were tethered. His hair was stringy and thin. His bones were almost visible, his hands and ankles were bruised and bloody from the shackles he wore. Edwin knew that he must be someone from the land of Elvous—a spoil of war.

The Elvin was on his knees, his hands together raised, pleading with the knights around him. A knight clearly demanded, "Shut yer gub!" before backhanding the man over onto his side, where the rest of the *noble* knights started to kick him. The Elvin was in a ball, his arms protecting his head as much as possible while his knees failed to protect his stomach.

What was Edwin supposed to do? Step in and stop the knight? Protect the man and his honor, that's what Knight Lockwood would do. Defend those who can't defend themselves!

The reality was that he not a hero. He couldn't do the right thing. It was too risky. Too scary.

Besides, this wasn't a fairy tale. Was what the knights were doing honestly so wrong? The Elvin's land had been conquered; they had lost, and with that they had also lost their identity as something to be respected. That's what his uncle and most of the kingdom thought, or he supposed at this point it was more of an empire than a kingdom. His aunt was the only person he had seen who thought differently. She didn't say she did; however, Edwin could tell. Every time someone from Elvous was treated like so, she couldn't watch; he also saw her giving bread to the starving beggars—it had been moldy, which was going to get fed to the pigs anyway. Still, the principle stood. Edwin didn't know what was right or wrong. He never knew what to think when his heart would meet his stomach.

Edwin looked away as he slouched, trying to make himself seem submissive so the knights didn't harass him.

As Edwin approached the bakery he called home, Edwin stopped to take a deep breath before he had to face his aunt and uncle, face anything about today. Edwin stared at the two-story building as smoke rose from the stone-crafted chimney. The bottom floor was the bakery where they made and prepared goods to be sold, the only homely items allowed on the first floor were a small table, fireplace, and storage room which kept mainly resources to make dough, while the upstairs doubled as living quarters, which contained three cots, a bookshelf that was empty except for a few family items, a chest, and a bathroom of sorts. Edwin turned his attention behind him, where over the treetops and the roofs of the town, he could barely make out the castle walls in the distance. Ever since Edwin was younger, he dreamed about visiting the castle at least once before he passed away, just to see the magnificent structure; yet, Edwin was really doubting he would live past the end of the day, his childhood dream never to be fulfilled.

Knowing Edwin was too close to home to daydream comfortably without getting interrupted by an angry caretaker, Edwin broke his concentration and started moving forward, staring at his next step, downcast.

Coming out of the bakery was his aunt, tossing her head around in a panic as though she was looking for something. Once she saw him, she hastily started to head in Edwin's direction, lifting the bottom of her dress so she didn't step on it. Her hair was tied up in a sloppy bun with a purple tie. The hair tie was the only colorful piece of clothing she wore, mainly because it was the only one she owned. Edwin's uncle had given her the hair tie last year. He sold half their chickens, their second cow, and most of their bread money just to get that little ribbon. Edwin almost starved because of it.

"Ah, Edwin!" His aunt, with a stern tone, approached him. "There ye are! Wit in the king's name tewk ye so long?!"

"A—"

"No excuses!" She ushered the boy into the bakery, patting the flour from his face. "We need to get this dough proofing by tomorrow!"

Entering the doorway, Edwin could smell the strong scent of yeast, followed by bread goldening in the oven. Edwin's uncle was at a table needing dough; he stopped and wiped his hands on his apron before turning his attention to his nephew. "Ye sure tewk yer sweet time, lad. Did Zilener give ye a hard time?"

As his uncle spoke, Edwin looked away, trying not to show frustration toward his guardian. "No, the streets were just crowded because everyone is getting their young men ready. Ye ken, swords, shields, armor?"

The large man, who didn't take the hint, was oblivious as he took the flour from Edwin's shoulder. "A shud have ken that wedd be the cause, wedd have sent ye earlier if ye didnae have been slacking aff."

Setting the flour on the table, he opened the sack, scooped up a handful, and rubbed it on the dough and tabletop. Edwin didn't want to be forward with him. If he did, his uncle would take it as accusatory and become defensive. If he could buy Edwin's aunt a ribbon, surely, they could put in the effort to get him a dagger. Edwin hoped they didn't expect him to slay a beast with a peel. Then again, maybe the creature would die of laughter.

"A dinnae ken why ye still bother with that man, Aldo," Edwin's aunt said as she checked on the fire in the oven.

"A dinnae unless it is a necessity."

Edwin directed his attention to the display of memorabilia on the bakery's wall. There were multiple scales, fangs, nails, and a stuffed scale toe roughly half the size of Edwin's forearm. These were all trophies of the beasts his uncles had slayed over the years. He wasn't the only one, either. All the men in Edwin's homeland, Gorish, kept reminders of every monster they conquered. Twice a year, large migrations of the beasts would fly over the land of Gorish. When the migration was heading west, anyone could participate in slaying them. Yet on their way east, returning from their migration, it was customary for only fourteen-year-old boys to hunt the beasts to earn their manhood.

"Edwin," his aunt said, grabbing the peel and sliding it under the baking bread, "cud ye go and retrieve firewood?"

Edwin nodded. "Aye."

Just as Edwin stepped through the exit, the wind picked up just like it always did, causing his bangs to aggressively tousle in his face. Using his hand as a block, he watched as what was once a gentle breeze quickly turned into gusts of powerful forces of nature. The trees rustled as the leaves fled from their original home. Edwin heard their cow and chickens sounding the alarm. Edwin's aunt and uncle followed Edwin out of the bakery.

Edwin and everyone who could experience the sudden change in weather knew exactly what it meant—the beasts were here, and his time was at its end.

Edwin's throat hurt as he swallowed. All he was able to do was stare at the sky, waiting for the thing of every fourteen-year-old boy's nightmare to reveal itself. Edwin glanced off to the horizon, where the forests lay.

"They'll kill ye if ye run," Edwin's uncle said as he stood behind him with arms folded and his face scowling.

Edwin and his aunt pretended like he was referring to the beasts Edwin was about to face, but they knew he was talking about the king's knights. Edwin tightened his jaw as his uncle nodded his head in the direction of the town. However, before he could take a step, Edwin's aunt intervened, "Haud for a wee moment." She lifted her dress and disappeared inside.

Not long after, she emerged with something long, wrapped in cloth and yarn. Edwin was able to take a deep breath and wash away most of the tightness in his body as he guessed that he was going to be given something more than a stick to poke the scaly animals with after all. Untying the yarn, the cloth came easily undone. The sword belt dangled, as his aunt held out to him a sheathed sword. "This wis yer father's. When he passed, A kept it safe until yer coming af age." Her eyelids were low as she stared at the sword of Edwin's father, her late brother.

She took in the weapon for a moment with what Edwin thought to be tears forming, then looked up at Edwin and smiled. "It will protect ye like it did for him during his hunts."

Edwin picked up the sword and unsheathed the blade. It probably didn't seem so manly of Edwin to have his mouth hanging open as he awed the sword. The handle was black with a textured leather grip, the pommel had a red gem embedded into it, and the blade was a dark metal with a beautiful pattern skillfully crafted into it, not a hint of nips on the edge or rust to be seen. The sword seemed to have been only crafted yesterday despite its history.

Gazing into the blade, Edwin saw nothing more than a simple boy who was getting confident. Dangerously confident.

Edwin let the flat of the tip of the blade fall into his hand, and Edwin continued to stare, letting his mind drift on the fact that this was his father's.

His father.

Memories danced in his head of his father's warm embrace and the feeling of belonging he gave the boy. His face had become unclear to Edwin now. However, he remembered that he would always pick him up and scratch his beard against Edwin's cheek when he would come home from hunting when Edwin was a small boy. A kiss on Edwin's cheek pulled him away from his sweet memories, as his aunt then cuffed the spot she kissed with her hand. Their eyes met, and Edwin could see all the love and worry his aunt felt for him in that moment.

"Thank ye," Edwin said and placed his hand overtop her's. "Wit's the sword's name?"

"Ma brother gave it no name," his aunt informed. "He said ye shudd name it yersel based on the first creature ye slay with the blade."

Maybe Edwin could survive this challenge? His father and many more had before him, and all Edwin had to do was get something of the beast. It didn't necessarily—

"A lot af good that knife did him in the end," Edwin's uncle retorted, earning a warning glare from his wife. "Come on! We shuddnae delay any longer or the knights will think ye a traitor to the king."

Edwin's aunt hugged her brother's sheathed sword as Edwin fixed the belt to his hip. It made Edwin's uncle think about how scrawny Edwin seemed for a baker's boy. Sheathing the sword, Edwin and his family continued the rest of the walk in silence. He felt like he was a mouse being watched by a barn cat, as he would occasionally glance up at the sky. It was a challenge to breathe, let alone make any noise. Edwin's uncle's footsteps sounded like dinner bells being rung.

Going towards the town's entrence, a few other families of trade that lived in the farmlands started to shadow them. Entering in, it became instantly crowded. However, instead of it just being men and their sons, it was men, women, children—everybody—the entire population was making their way to the center. The crowd in front of them slowed down, and Edwin began to shuffle with the others as the crowd became too large to move in full steps. He felt almost like one in a herd of sheep. Ahead of them, going against traffic, making its way to the center, was a large wooden tower being wheeled out by multiple Elvous slaves.

Eventually, the shuffling stopped as everyone settled into position around the placed tower. For a crowd this large, the noise volume was surprisingly low. Like Edwin, everyone seemed too scared to talk or bring their voice higher than a loud whisper. Edwin caught others' eyes, wondering up at the sky or anxiously glancing at the knights who encircled the crowd. Edwin brought his attention to the tower. Edwin wasn't able to see the herald until the man got to the last five steps up to the top. Edwin was too far away to make out any distinct facial features. All the boy knew was that he wore the colors of the king's house—red and silver.

The herald unraveled a scroll, and with that cue, a trumpet blew, silencing even the verbally bravest in the crowd. The king's messenger walked up to the corner of the wooden structure where a bullhorn was mounted. "Hear ye! Hear ye!" His voice was loud and sung with confidence. "Our beloved King, Borin Anthony Gaulish the Fifth, addresses his kingdom on this momentous ceremony:

"Ma loyal subjects. The time calls upon our sons again to prove their devotion to this land. They must take on the mantle af no only manhood but also honor their families' legacies! Lineages! Aye, this task is difficult and yet necessary. We can no allow the beasts to see weakness, no even in our bairn. If these monsters see us as vulnerable, they will no hesitate to invade this land, destroy our homes, our families, our entire livelihood, just as they did in the times af auld. Our young men must show their devotion to our kingdom by taking something from the beasts, if no its life, then it must be a momentum of their fierce battle that would make the creature fear the land af Gorish. This trial will end at dawn. Please, ma people, prepare yer sons af age and let us send them aff so there is no delay."

Edwin didn't feel encouraged by the King's words at all, like he was expecting. Wasn't his ruler supposed to cause a spark in him?

Something that would fill his motivation with hope? Instead, Edwin's stomach gnawed at itself at a sickening pace, even worse than the time Edwin rode in a wagon on a bumpy trail.

"Go," Edwin's aunt urged him.

"Honor us!" his uncle added. "Pass the trial or dae no bother returning home."

Edwin wished the speech hadn't ended. It was a good way to distract himself from the nerves he felt. Edwin threw up in his mouth, then swallowed, as gross as that was. Edwin didn't want anyone to know just how scared he actually was. Looking around, Edwin saw the boys making their way toward the wooden tower. Knights began to seek out those who were hesitant, giving them a little more stimulation. Edwin took a deep breath, his aunt took a sharp one. Edwin looked around and saw that a knight had locked in on the boy, not being pleased with Edwin's pace. Instead of moving forward, Edwin froze.

Closing his eyes tightly, he felt the sweat of his brow drip. As the knight drew closer, a sudden gust of powerful wind shook the wooden tower and knocked over some unprepared townsfolk. Edwin took this chance of opportunity and stumbled forward with help from the wind. Out of view of the knight, Edwin turned his attention to the sky when a roaring bellow pierced it. Everyone quickly threw their eyes up to the heavens as if to expect rainfall during a drought. Edwin's throat went dry, his eyes teared up, and his face turned cold as a giant winged creature flew overhead, casting a shadow as it momentarily blocked out the sun. Edwin wasn't able to make out any strong features, yet he was able to tell that the beast had the body of a true apex predator—not of a bear, but more like a cougar, although Edwin was not going to second-guess the monster's strength. The creature had four limbs, a long tail and neck, and a wingspan larger than its entire body length.

As the beast made its way overhead, it angled its wings, causing itself to elevate higher as though it had only dropped in flight to be close enough to intimidate the townsfolk. It gave another mighty roar, which was then followed by a thunder of noise erupting in the distance as an entire flock of the flying nightmares approached. They were far enough away at the moment that they looked no bigger than birds. However, soon they would be overhead.

“Gae now!” the herald shouted at the top of his lungs, barely louder than the crowd. “Gae now and prove yer allegiance to yer kingdom!”

Edwin started to breathe faster. It was challenging getting the air through his chest, as if he were swimming in thick mud. Drowning in it. Watching the creatures when Edwin was younger was terrifying enough! Now he had to face one! Would his sword even make a dent? It would most likely be like a mosquito bite to it. Edwin’s mind was too numb to describe the fear he felt.

“Wit are ye doin’?!” Edwin’s uncle hollered. “Move!”

Edwin shook, then tapped his temples with his palm, which worked to snap him out of the trance. However, it now caused dizziness. Nevertheless, Edwin pushed through the crowd, making his way to the forest outside of the town, with some of the last boys leading his way. Once Edwin was away from the gathering, he took off running, his sword slapping against his thigh. Edwin could feel a pounding in his head like drums of war. His chest was tight as he continued to run, yet Edwin wasn’t stopping for anything, even though it took every bone in his body not to duck for cover as he heard the scary beasts flying overhead, roaring.

Chapter Two

On The Hunt

Out of breath, Edwin came to a stop, placing his hands on his knees, panting, which probably made the cramping in his side hurt worse. However, that was the least of his concerns. Edwin collapsed on his rear and rubbed the back of his neck. How was he going to handle this without getting hurt or worse? Distract a beast? Wait until one is asleep? Should he just not try at all and shame his family? Edwin imagined his guardians losing the bakery and becoming nothing more than beggars for the king's Ishtar to have their fun with, like the people of Evlous. The thought of his uncle having this lifestyle didn't bother him as much as the thought of his aunt enduring it.

Edwin sighed with an overwhelming sense of dread as though there was ice in his veins. Glancing at his father's sword by his side, Edwin couldn't shake the doubt of what a failure of a son he turned out to be. Edwin wasn't even brave enough to face the things his father once did or even try for the sake of his sister—the woman who had taken care of him since the moment his mother had passed.

How was Edwin even going to get close to one? Edwin's breath started to have weight to it as a shadow covered the sun. Looking up, beasts passed overhead, their wings creating powerful winds. Edwin held his breath, as though if any of the air escaped it would alert them.

"Hoi…"

Edwin flung his eyes all around him, trying to locate the hushed voice. "Ye shudnae be oot in the open like that." Edwin noticed two shaded figures hiding in the dark area of the forest.

That was a good point.

Being weary of his lapse in judgment, Edwin staggered to stand. Once he did, he shuffled over to join the protection of the treetops. Now being close, Edwin was able to discern that the figures were two boys his age. Edwin recognized the blond one as Aland, even though he had never met him personally. Aland was the bladesmith's son, and it was easy to tell that his father had been training him in the trade by his build. Being the son of a smith was the dream for this trial. Aland was dressed in a chest plate along with shoulder guards, shin and arm guards. To top the armor off he, of course, had a newly forged shield and sword. Edwin would kill for a shield.

Edwin didn't know anything about the boy Aland was with. He had thin brown hair and long features, was shorter and yet had a strong stature of a farmer who threw hay bales around all day. He wore a chest plate and carried a newly crafted battle axe with a blade on both sides, one of them having a longer point as though it was designed to stab. Edwin was naked compared to them! He didn't even have an apron on! Not as if it would be anything more than a handkerchief to the beasts.

A loud roar rumbled around them. They all froze as they watched the creature fly directly above them and land about fourteen acres away. The treetops shook as the creature landed.

"We shud go," Aland's friend decreed. "A doubt that they'll be here longer than they need to."

Stepping down from a rock he had used to hide in some of the tree's lower branches, Aland nodded. "That wedd be wise."

Aland turned to Edwin as the two boys got closer. "Yer parents own the bakery, right? Wit's yer name?"

"Edwin," he replied. "And they're ma aunt and uncle, actually."

Edwin noticed a twinge of curiosity in Aland's eyes. From that, Edwin was able to tell he wanted to know how Edwin's parents had died yet was aware this wasn't the proper time to ask that question. He then introduced himself and his brown-haired friend as Bramwell.

"Nice to meet ye," Edwin nodded, not knowing if a handshake would be seen as too proper.

Edwin didn't exactly know how to socialize with others his age or in general. He was more of a recluse. After the bakery and doing his chores, Edwin would hide away and read the only book he had. Edwin would get lost in his imagination of a better, more adventurous life. Yes, he did have imaginary friends on his adventures.

"Aye." Bramwell frowned. "Although A wish the circumstances were better."

They took a second to let the wave of trepidation wash over them. Finally, Aland broke the ice. "Wedd ye like to join our group?"

Edwin was a bit embarrassed that he couldn't hide his feelings as he got an adrenaline rush of hope shining on his face. Or it could have just been sweat from the heat. Either way, this was the perfect opportunity! If they worked together, they were to at least get a scale each. Maybe even kill a beast!

No, Edwin definitely was getting ahead of himself with that anticipation. As Edwin was about to accept, a tightness entered his chest as thoughts popped into his head. "Haud, are we allowed to team up?"

His question arose from the rule that no one was allowed to train anyone for this coming-of-age tradition because that would be helping. So wouldn't teaming up be the same?

"The King never said 'no'," Aland smirked. "Besides, who's gonnae ever ken?"

"Dinnae worry, ma father teamed up with some mates during his trial. A for one am no facing a beast alone, ye've seen the size af them!" Bramwell retorted.

"Look, are ye comin' with us or no?" Aland's tone felt a little guarded, as though he was starting to think Edwin would possibly alert the king's knights about his and Bramwell's alliance.

Edwin moistened his throat. "Af- af course am!"

"Great!" Aland's face lit up with relief as he started to lead Edwin and Bramwell off. "Let's go."

As light and darkness shifted above them ever so often, Edwin didn't care that he crushed the overgrowth beneath his feet. The wind rustled the leaves enough that the sound covered anything quieter than it. Edwin was about five steps behind when Aland turned to face him and Bramwell. "We want to make this fast. The beasts migrate across the ocean to their island of desolation. So Gorish is their only opportunity to fill their bellies before the trip. They arenae dumb, so they're going to be quick, so their chances af survival are higher."

"Wit we need is a definite resource they need, so we can wait and ambush," Bramwell plotted.

Aland and Edwin thought for a moment. Edwin personally couldn't think of anything. It's not like they could tie a pig out in the woods and trap them that way… Or not for the trial, at least. Luckily, Aland thought of something. "There's a pond no too far from here, ma father takes me fishing in. It's a perfect place for the beasts to quench their thirst!"

Edwin stayed quiet and let them continue planning without him. They seemed to have a lot more understanding than he did. As Edwin tried to force himself to think of something, his mind instead swam into imagining what would happen best-case scenario. Edwin could see himself on top of a dead beast, holding up his sword with Aland and Bramwell by his side—

"Edwin!"

Edwin blinked frantically as though he had dirt in them. Once they saw they had his attention, they gestured to him as if waiting for his input. Edwin wiped his nose with his forearm. His cheeks were warm, and he wanted to hide. Edwin hoped he hadn't been making a goofy face while he daydreamed. "Ah…" he wondered, "cud we use more members in our group?"

"We cud, yet am worried we dinnae have enough time. The beasts cud leave the region or the good game cud get taken while we recruit others." Aland shook his head.

"Okay then, we"—Edwin cleared his throat—"we shud go." Edwin wanted to change the conversation fast. However, his face felt cold, realizing what the end meant.

Leading the way, Aland wasn't too careful about making sound until they got closer to their location. With the wind whistling through the vegetation, any small sound, like the crunching of leaves, was covered by the noise caused by the beast's wings. The wind, once strong, had almost completely died down by the time the boys arrived at the pond. Edwin decided to share a tree with Bramwell and hid on the other side of the stump. Everyone had their eyes to the heavens. "How long will it take?"

"It shuddnae take long." Bramwell lowered his voice, the wind around them being nothing but breezes.

"Aye." Aland tossed his head to the side. "Let's pray that it dinnae."

Edwin then became aware of the weight that one not showing up had. Edwin's throat became dry at the thought. However, Edwin had to stop his body from shaking at the idea of if one actually did. What were they going to do if they couldn't find one? Were they going to spend all this time doing nothing when they should have been trying to get a beast with a different method?

Before Edwin could spiral out of control with "what ifs," close wing beats made his mind go blank. After waiting for what felt like too long for comfort, finally, something in his nightmares arrived.

A beast that was a little bigger than his neighbor's workhorse glided down like a duck landing in water as its weight flattened the long grass. Edwin's muscles tightened against his will. Edwin didn't try to move. He dared not. However, he recognized the mannerism. This is what his body did when it was frozen with fear. Edwin glanced over to Aland, who took a calculated step to the right and signaled with his shield for Bramwell and Edwin to go left.

The brown-haired boy gently reached behind his back and grabbed where his axe's handle and blade met and brought it to his side. Aland drew his sword and tightened his grip on the straps of his shield. He shook to hype himself up. "Get ready."

Edwin didn't draw his sword—it felt as if he was in a trance. His jaw dropped… there—in front of him—was a creature so powerful it could tear him apart without effort, and yet there was something so gentle about its appearance. Its eyes were wide with awareness like a doe as it scanned the area for danger. Once it felt safe, it approached the water to drink. Two horns at the top of its head had a slight curl at the tip, along with two smaller ones at the end of its jawline. The ears were long and droopy, almost rabbit-like. It had white fur going down its spine, and the wings were bat-like, halfway extended like it was getting ready to take off. The colors of the beast were emerald green with a tan underbelly, and its skin resembled that of keeled snake scales. It shook its head as if to shake off water, and it then looked over its shoulder. For a second, it seemed as if it was looking straight at Edwin; however, its eyes didn't show any recognition of him.

The beast returned to its watering hole. Bramwell called for Edwin's attention by taking a step forward, getting ready to charge. "This one's a wee beast," Bramwell observed. "A bet we can kill it."

And Edwin thought *he* imagined a lot. Edwin took another look at the beast to see if that was even possible. He noticed that the end of its tail was chewed off and scared. Either another of its kind did that, or it had fought off a predator that was probably scarier than the boys could ever be.

Aland stuck his shield out to halt Bramwell and Edwin. “Wait. For. Opening,” Aland mouthed.

The forest was silent, other than the sound of his heart, until suddenly Edwin heard a beast bellowing in the distance. It drew everyone’s attention, even the beast drinking in front of them. The roaring soon turned into a… woman screaming?

Some poor woman must have been taken or wandered into the woods and was now paying the price.

“It’s distracted!” Bramwell charged.

Aland followed after his friend. They were right. The beast was distracted by the distant cries, and its back was away from them. It was the perfect moment to strike, so why wasn’t Edwin moving? His ears rang with echoes of the woman’s screams, and Edwin was appalled that he was the only one who seemed to be affected.

Was this how things just were? When someone was facing their death, they didn’t even bother to acknowledge it? Maybe even this coming-of-age trial wasn’t even supposed to prove loyalty to the kingdom; maybe it was some sick game the nobility played to help keep the population in line.

A bloody slash followed by a bellowing pain knocked Edwin out of his overwhelming thoughts. When his eyes focused ahead of him, Edwin saw the emerald green beast grabbing the side of its neck. The creature roared and reared up. It looked over to see Aland trying to recover his sword from the monster’s thigh. The once innocent eyes of the beast narrowed in hatred, and it pounced away, giving Aland the leverage he needed to pull his sword out. Edwin almost heaved at the gore. The beast used its tail to swat at the Smith’s boy. However, Aland blocked it just in time with his shield, the force knocking him to the ground. The beast didn’t come down fast enough, giving Bramwell the chance to slice. Its emerald side was now turning red. Edwin heard a young woman cry out in anguish mixed with the beast's roar. For a moment, it sounded as if the scream came from the monster itself. It backed away slowly as it looked at the boys who surrounded it. The creature extended its large bat-like wings and bent down.

"It's gonnae take aff!" Aland warned.

"A ken!" Bramwell called as he ran to flank the beast. "Edwin, where are ye?"

Edwin tightened the grip on his sword's handle as sweat dripped from his brow.

Move, he told himself. *Move!*

Edwin couldn't swallow the lump in his throat. At that moment, he couldn't even register that he was breathing! He had to move, he had to help, or else he would have to go in alone to face a beast by himself or shame his family. *Move!*

Rearing up, the green animal twisted around in a frantic whirlwind, and Bramwell ducked as he avoided the tail hitting him in the head. Aland came from the beast's blind side and stabbed the sword directly in the monster's hip, holding onto it for dear life, trying not to get flung off. Crying in anguish, the beast rolled over on its back, yet Aland wouldn't let go, and instead the sword lodged deeper into the beast's scalded skin.

"Help!" Edwin heard a woman's wail jolt him out of his paralysis.

Where was that voice coming from? Edwin scanned the area to see if there was a maiden nearby, yet he didn't see anyone besides the two other boys.

Suddenly, as Aland and Bramwell continued to draw blood, a thundering sound appeared from the sky. Everyone and everything, including Edwin's heart, halted and looked up. Coming out of the clouds revealed another large beast approaching from the direction in which the monsters had been heading.

Chapter Three
Begging For More

The large, oncoming beast leveled its large wings and swooped down, ripping Aland from the green creature's hips and slamming itself onto the ground, pinning the boy between the grass and its talon. Aland struggled to break free, however, the monster just leaned more weight on him. Aland groaned in pain, though his armor was protecting him well.

The small, green one locked eyes with its savior, which snarled and swayed its head toward the sky—toward the direction from which it came. "I'll rejoin you and the others momentarily," a powerful feminine voice rippled the once still water.

Edwin looked all around, his chest racing in his ears! Where—who?! Was he losing it? Did it finally happen? Did he crack from all the stress?

Edwin turned his attention back to the clearing in time to see the green beast open its wings, staggering to get lift, wincing in pain. Once it found itself, the creature didn't stop gaining momentum even with its injuries as it flew east.

Bramwell charged up to the large remaining creature that still had Aland pinned with its talon. He tried to stab it with the long point of his ax; however, the beast's tail swept the boy's feet out from under him. Hitting his back hard against the ground, Bramwell gasped, then got up fast. He took his axe and hacked into the tail as it came back toward him. A weak groan came from the monster's throat, then a snarl as it looked at the boy in utter annoyance.

The creature backhanded Bramwell, causing the boy to slide through the grass and hit his head on a rock. Bramwell stirred and winced before going limp.

"Bramwell!" Aland cried for his friend as his struggles to break free became more urgent. "Free me!" he demanded the giant monster. "Edwin, help us ye cowardly eejit!"

Edwin gritted his teeth in distress. Why had Bramwell called for him? He had given him away, and—Edwin stopped. Surely the animal wouldn't be that aware. Edwin inhaled deeply when he saw the creature scanning the forest for any signs of life. He was scared to move, yet Edwin had to do something! Anything! However, what could he possibly do against that thing?! It seemed to be smart on top of being a force of nature. Edwin had to run away. He didn't care about the consequences. He waited until the beast returned its gaze to Aland, where it made a low rumbling sound, using its tongue to moisten its scaly lips.

Instinctively, Edwin started backing away carefully, then stopped when he saw Bramweel lying still. His stomach ached with guilt.

Mind going blank, disturbing thoughts ran around like a wild horse, and his instincts took over. Quietly, Edwin unsheathed his father's sword and held it in both hands, trying to steady his trembling grasp. Continuing to make it out of the shelter of the trees—against his better judgment—and into the open. Edwin was going slowly for a second until he understood that the beast hadn't seemed to notice him as Edwin moved along behind it.

He picked up his speed over to Bramwell, then dropped to a knee, noticing a small amount of red where Bramwell's head and the rock connected. Edwin placed his finger on the knocked-out boy's neck until he felt a pulse.

Thank the heavens! He was alive.

Suddenly, the hairs on the back of Edwin's neck stood on end as a gurgling growl produced hot air engulfing him from behind. *Don't look up, don't look up!* He convinced himself that dying would be easier without seeing what was coming.

Edwin couldn't hold his breath any longer and gasped for air. After not meeting his death, he turned to face the beast glaring down on him. His light brown eyes connected with the monster's fire-patterned ones. Maybe it was his fear or just the creature's rage, but he swore the fire pattern was moving like an actual flame. Edwin watched as the beasts' slit pupils enlarged into thicker diamonds. Edwin brought up the courage to stand and walk cautiously away from Bramwell, its eyes not leaving his for a second.

"Strike it doon!" Aland called from the monster's grip.

Take down this beast? Was Aland going mad? Did he realize how huge this thing was?! Its head alone was the size of a cow. He's fortunate it's giving him as much movement as it was!

Edwin didn't know what to do! If he distracted it long enough, then maybe it would let release Aland, then he could grab Bramwell and run off? Maybe Edwin should just get Bramwell and leave Aland? Or get Aland and run off, leaving Bramwell? Edwin groaned in frustration. There was no way he could distract or alarm this monster for that long.

The creature's eyes went to his shaking hands as they rattled the sword he held at the ready. "Put your sword down, boy, and I won't hurt you!" The same powerful feminine voice from earlier struck his eardrums.

The voice was so striking Edwin yelped, dropped his sword to the ground as he lay prostrated, shielding his head with both his arms—as if they would do much—his heart slamming against his ribs in its attempt to leave his chest to where it was painful. "P-PLEASE… MURCY!" Edwin begged.

"Wit are ye doin'?!" Aland called furiously, trying to break free. "FIGHT IT, COWARD!"

Edwin looked up just in time to see the monster take Aland up into the air and toss him from its claw into the pond. After a large splash, Aland came up gasping for air, his armor giving him some grief, yet he was managing. The monster gave him a roar and a warning snap before returning its attention to Edwin. The beast's eyes were wide. It almost appeared to be surprised. "Can you understand me, boy?" it asked, its once raging voice now filled with curiosity.

Edwin's eyes darted everywhere. First, on Aland in the water, who seemed to be shooting him a glare, then he was finally able to peel his eyes away from the forest to the monster, where Edwin took in its appearance.

Like all the others, it—more like she—had a long body with toned muscles like an apex predator. Her coloration was a black that oddly shimmered with the different colors of a rainbow in the correct lighting, especially her underbelly, where the colors were on display most. Her muzzle was horse-like, and her head was crowned in sleek, simple horns that resembled the smoothness of a cow's. Her spine was slightly elevated, going along her neck to the top of her tail, where she had an arrowhead-shaped scale. Her hide was soft and had the scale patterns of a simple garden snake.

Edwin didn't want to speak. His voice was so dry, he didn't even want to bother. However, he was afraid that not answering her would cause her to switch back into being hostile, so the boy nodded in response to the beast's question, his lips thinned to a line.

"Speak!" Her tone lacked patience. "I know you can."

Edwin sat up, uncovering his head. Edwin tried to talk, but no words came. He looked away from the beast, yet he could still feel her eyes on him, waiting with a growling scowl. "Aye," Edwin finally squeaked out.

"You and your friends were going to kill one of my subjects?" she questioned.

"A wiznae gonnae—"

"Yes, you would sit back and watch as your comrades did the hard work for you."

"No, that's no—"

"So you were going to help them kill that dragon?"

Edwin stopped. She was obviously toying with him. He didn't know what to say without breaking the eggshells he was walking on. What was that? A dragon. Maybe it's the name of that smaller one? "A never wanted to," Edwin shook his head. "Am being forced to by ma kingdom. Slaying yer kind or claiming an ornament af victory shows ma loyalty to ma country. A need to in order to become a man and to protect ma family from shame."

"I am aware of your people's foolish customs!" she snapped. "How could you think that way?"

"A dinnae!" Edwin knew her question was rhetorical, yet he didn't care. "If A dinnae, ma family will lose everything!"

"So you would kill or cripple one of my kin and return to your comfortable life rather than return home with a few hardships and the feeling that you granted mercy?"

"Everyone expects me to, or I'se be a coward till a dae take yer kind's life! A dinnae have a choice!" Edwin said, his body shook uncontrollably.

"Young boy, you always have a choice. You chose to stay back and let your friends get defeated. You had a choice to let them hurt my subject."

No matter what Edwin would say or do, he wasn't going to win with her. "Am sorry."

"For which one?"

Edwin hung his head, his body still quivering every now and then. Would he have had the actual strength to slay a monster? These dragons? As he thought about it, the more the scenario drifted. No, of course, Edwin wouldn't be able to. He was incapable of even moving because he was so afraid of just the small one. "A dinnae ken. A wish there were more options for me."

He wiped an escaped tear from his cheek and glanced over to Aland, who had swum to the other side of the pond, trying to get away from the looming threat above Edwin. Maybe it was a good thing Edwin was about to die. He couldn't show his face at home now, especially after Aland saw him act so cowardly… "Am such a coward," Edwin said under his breath.

Edwin prayed that Aland wouldn't tell others about his behavior, that he chose to talk with a beast instead of killing it. Edwin hoped to spare his family from any consequences. If he had died while trying to slay a beast, his aunt and uncle could keep their livelihoods.

Picking up his father's sword, he slid it back into its sheath. His heart was in his ears, and he squeezed his eyes closed, bracing for his end. Edwin heard the creature in front of him move and shift. Edwin opened his eyes when he heard something that sounded like a sheet flapping in the wind. Edwin witnessed the beast stretch out its enormous wings. Then the next thing he knew, the beast's talons were wrapping around him. She turned her body and hopped a few steps, splashing the pond water, before jumping toward the sky, beating her wings, creating enough wind to pull the trees from their roots, then soon gained momentum.

Edwin desperately called out for help to the point where his lungs and throat started to ache. He watched the ground get farther away from his feet and then finally disappear under the clouds. Was this it? Was this how she was going to kill him, dropping him to his death? That sounded a lot worse than just being eaten alive! Maybe she was taking a snack for her long trip? "Wit are ye dinnae?" Edwin called up to her, his voice being muffled by the wind.

"Taking you!" She flapped her wings hard and then glided in a circle back around and headed east.

The air was cold and moved past his face strongly. Edwin had to close his eyes to shield them from being attacked by the wind when the beast picked up speed. He was able to finally open his eyes when she began flying smoothly and steadily. Her grip on him was tight.

"Where?" Edwin asked, looking for more detail.

She didn't say anything else to him and just repositioned him into her other talon. Edwin decided not to scream or talk anymore, trying to keep as much air in his lungs as possible. It was almost impossible to breathe naturally. He had to force himself to take clear breaths. He didn't know if it was because his heart was twenty feet under him or if the air was just thicker.

The sun was setting as its light kissed the top of the ocean on the horizon. Mentally, Edwin wasn't comfortable at all. He couldn't stop the anxiety of the anticipation that the beast would eat him at any given moment. Edwin kept turning over in his head the ideas of what it would feel like to be dead or to die. Would it be painful to get eaten alive? Or should Edwin request for her to kill him quickly, then eat him? Maybe she would be willing to give him that mercy—she got her meal no matter what; unless the beasts think it makes the meat tastier if they are living? Edwin wondered what was after this life. Would he get to see his mother and father in heaven, or was there nothing? Would it just be eternal darkness with his mind numb?

Thank the heavens Edwin got distracted from his thoughts when he noticed a smaller dragon passing by under the one who carried him. The smaller beast under them was having a difficult time flying. It had long, floppy ears that flipped back in the wind. Edwin recognized the beast as the emerald green one that Aland and Bramwell had tried to slay. The larger one, holding Edwin tucked in her wings, drifted down next to the injured creature whose front legs glided through the ocean's surface.

"I know you are tired. Nonetheless, you must fly higher," the larger beast gently instructed. "The waters are not safe, even for us."

The small, long-eared beast bared its teeth in pain and turned the front of its wings up. Gradually, it soared to a higher position thanks to the wind. The little one was breathing heavily through its nostrils like a horse that had just plowed for two days with no end.

The boy saw the wounds inflicted on the doe-eyed creature. Most of them had stopped bleeding, yet the scales around the area were stained scarlet. His throat dried. He was happy this beast didn't know he was there while it was being attacked, or it might have wanted to take revenge. Still, he must also admit that seeing any animal in this much pain was cruel. It reminded him of one of the only memories he had with his father. When Edwin was younger, he watched sons beat a captured rabbit as the fathers cheered them on, saying, "Now this is how a real man daes it!"

Edwin could distinctly recall his father covering Edwin's eyes and telling him to hurry back home. Horrified at what the others were doing, Edwin did as his father told. Later, when his father returned, he had brought that very same rabbit, on the brink of death, home. Edwin's aunt was furious that he'd brought it into the cottage, yet his father still placed it in a bed he made for it by the fireplace, gave it a good meal, and gently patted it until it died. Instead of eating it the next day, they buried it in the woods under the biggest tree they could find.

Would his father show that much kindness to this beast? Probably not because he would have been seen as a traitor to Gorish. He was a hunter after all, which made him not understand his father's actions towards the rabbit, and Edwin didn't think he ever would.

“We have almost caught up to the thunder. By morning, we should arrive home,” said, the large black beast, soothing the smaller one.

Home?

So she wasn’t going to eat him? Edwin figured if she was, she would have done so by now, right? You eat the snack in between meals, not right before. Maybe the beast had other plans for his fate? Livestock? A slave? An offering to an even bigger monster?

Edwin struggled to break free. He would probably drown in the ocean, yes, but wouldn’t that be a better end? The monster squeezed him, not enough to hurt, but more so to let him know she was aware he was trying her grasp.

The next thing he knew, his eyes were getting droopy, and he blinked only for the day to be night. Edwin looked around, seeing the moon high in the sky. His drowsiness continued, and he dozed off from time to time despite fighting to stay awake. He felt like he wouldn’t sleep for long, and when he woke up, he was in shock because he kept having this dream that he was falling. It would end with him getting either eaten or ripped apart before even hitting the ground. With his heart racing, Edwin looked all around, hoping to find the green injured beast. He couldn’t find it anywhere, but he froze when he saw that behind the large beast carrying him was a thunder of them. Edwin came back to front-facing, his eyes squinted shut as he tried not to scream in alarm. He kept on breathing in and out, building up the oxygen in his lungs, hyping himself up as though he was about to pull out a needle from his skin. Glancing back underneath himself, behind the large beast, he saw maybe twenty others, all with different features, yet their body types remained similar: terrifying.

While his attention was on them, he heard murmuring off to his right. After some searching, he could see two beasts whispering back and forth the best they could with their distance apart. They reminded Edwin of when he would help his aunt with washing their clothes down by the stream. The woman there would always gossip with one another about anything they could, whether it was their business or not. Edwin cocked his head and continued to look at the beasts, seeing if he could make out what they were saying. One of them darted their eyes at him, then looked full on towards him once they realized he was staring. It then didn't take long for their friend to join in. Were they talking about him? One of the animals then connected its eyes back to their friend and bobbed its head away from its direction. The two soon followed the new route, leaving Edwin behind.

Edwin was aware that all the other beasts knew he was there. Edwin could see them staring or glancing at him from the corner of their eyes, trying to hide their interest. Edwin looked up at the beast that held him, realizing that she was the largest of the group. He wondered if that made her their leader?

His eyes threatened to close. Edwin wished he had gotten better sleep. He didn't know what was going to happen or what his fate was going to be with this monster, so Edwin would have liked to be more rested for it. Finally, he couldn't fight the heaviness anymore and let his eyes slowly shut, only for them to fly back wide open when he heard the loudest roar rumble from the large beast holding him. The other beasts behind her started roaring as well, in unison. It didn't sound like a dangerous roaring, more like a happy purr. The noise banged against his eardrums, hurting at first, but then he soon adjusted to the sound.

Edwin searched frantically around him to see why the beasts had called. When he looked ahead, he found it. There, in the distance, was an island waiting for the animals' arrival.

Chapter Four
Arrival

Usually, the smell of the ocean air would ease King Clayus's nerves. Not this time, though. He attempted to distract himself by taking in the scenery of his kingdom, hoping that would be enough to settle his stomach. The sun was just rising over the horizon, bringing a new day as the night finally slept. King Clayus watched as, in the distance, waves crashed against the cliffs near the beach, rushing in as they drifted to shore. Making whirlpools as they got dragged back to sea. He took in the lavish, green forests filled with towering trees from ancient times as he stood on the railless balcony of his castle that belonged to his kingdom, the Kingdom of Alena.

Yes, the castle was magnificent. It was gigantic, designed so that multiple dragons could pass in the halls and perch with their knights wherever the knights may go. Clayus then rested his eyes on the city below the castle, where he could see the specks of civilians moving about their daily tasks.

Scales rattled as a large dragon shook his neck. King Clayus's dragon, Cerberus, was larger than any steed. He had heavy scales, which stuck out down his spine with a beard of rough spikes covering his jawline and chin. He was green with darker tones forming strips. His tail and underbelly were drenched in hard scales that were layered on top of each other. His main horns grew out of his bottom jaw, facing forward instead of on his head, growing back. Finally, he had the Dragon Empress trait, one that all her children shared: a triangular plate at the tip of his tail. Yawning, Cerberus returned to rest his lizard head on his forearms like a canine as he snored into a deep sleep.

"At it again, I see," an elderly voice mused.

The king turned to see an elderly woman whose beauty had not been taken by age. She wore a white, hooded robe with a golden trim long enough to drag behind her. She made sure her hood was down so that her expressions were clearly shown.

"The dragons will be here this morning. I want to be the first to greet them when they arrive," King Clayus explained.

"My King, isn't that why you have the Royal Guards on the lookout?" She smiled kindly, taking note of his muscle tension, giving away his strained feelings. "To inform you when they do come? You trust them to be on the lookout for the other kingdoms' caravans."

"I suppose you're right, Latona. I just feel so uneasy."

She chuckled. "Clayus, are you sure you're not just nervous about your son starting his training?"

Closing his eyes, King Clayus shook his head gently with a grin. "Am I really that readable? I should put this energy to something more useful, I suppose."

"That would be wise."

"I need to prepare my son for when they come, along with the rest of the becoming knights."

"I'm sure they're feeling anxious about the choosing themselves. I remember when it was your time to receive a dragon. You got so angry as your elder brother mocked you for being so antsy." Latona raised her hand to his shoulder. "I see a lot of you in the young prince."

Smiling warmly at the older woman, he nodded, excusing himself from the conversation. He turned, making his way across the balcony. "Come, Cerberus!" he said firmly to wake the dragon from his snoring.

The slumbering dragon raised his head and yawned, exposing his sharp, alligator-like teeth. Smacking his scaly lips, he stood up in a similar fashion a horse takes after rolling on the ground. He strolled behind as Clayus made his way back into his rooms, out of the bed chambers, and into the entertainment room, where he strolled over to a coat rack where he kept his royal robe. Throwing it over his shoulders, he clipped the golden chain on the collar to the other side, as he slipped his arms through the sleeves. His royal robe was red with a brown trim that matched well with his brown trousers and furred-trimmed boots. His white undershirt made the other colors in the outfit stand out on their own. As King Clayus tied his brown hair up into a short bun, he made his way out of his rooms along with Cerberus, going into the halls of the massive fortress.

The castle was lit by sunlight as it came through the many thin vertical windows, making the off-white marble of the palace light up almost like freshly fallen snow, yet not as glaring. The flooring was mainly covered by a long black rug. Tapestries hung as decorations on the walls between the windows, adding more story to the halls. Most tapestries were artworks that depicted a Golden Dragon or Dragon Empress. Occasionally, there was a unicorn or griffin on the wall. Vases filled with beautifully picked flowers were potted and placed on stool-like tables, adding color and wonderful smells as the open windows carried their scent with the outside air. Decretive swords and shields were well placed throughout the halls, complementing the overall design. Maids and staff bustled around the castle, attending to their morning duties, sweeping, and polishing the marble. Some of the maids switched out the dead flowers for live ones, and the tapestries were swapped out to be dusted. So much more was being done, and King Clayus couldn't keep up. As he and Cerberus passed, the staff all stopped and turned to them, bowing until they were well away from them. King Clayus made sure to give respectful nods to them in return whenever they could see, and when they couldn't, he would make a comment about the work they were doing, always something positive.

Turning a corner, King Clayus and Cerberus approached a certain maidservant dusting behind a tapestry. She was humming a sweet melody, easily getting lost in her vocals as she gracefully moved the feathered cleaning tool. Clayus stood straighter and groomed his beard with a hand, making sure he was more presentable than if he were at a conference. As Cerberus and the king made their way, he didn't want to look at her head-on, so he followed her with his eyes until she disappeared into the corner.

"Oh, my grace! I didn't see you!" Her voice was soft.

Clayus stopped in his tracks, perhaps faster than he desired, and pivoted around to face her. She curtseyed to her lord, and he took a deep breath, happy that he was presented with an opportunity.

"No harm done." Clayus gestured for her to stand. He looked into her gorgeous green eyes. "My dear, what is your name?"

"Emma."

"Emma..." King Clayus looked around the hall and gave a kind smile. "Everything's looking exceptional."

"Thank you, Your Majesty." She curtsied again.

"Well, I must be off. My son will be getting his dragon today."

"I wish the prince good fortune!" With a warm smile, she dipped her head respectfully, and Clayus did likewise before turning back and heading on his way.

He often took this hallway because it was the one Emma was in charge of cleaning around this time. It always made his day better when he got to hear her humming and see her beautiful appearance, and he now knew her name.

Going through some more hallways and down quite a few flights of stairs, Clayus reached his destination. Walking out of the castle, he found himself in an elongated pavilion that connected two archways dividing the castle in half. Making his way through the pillars instead of going to the end of the pavilion, Clayus found the courtyard with the Golden Dragon Fountain, where two teenagers dueled with wooden swords. Terro, his eldest son, swung his sword toward his childhood friend, Skypris, as she used hers to intercept his, creating a hollow sound as they clashed. Skypris stumbled back as the two swords clashed again; this time, Terro used more force. The duel carried on with the young girl mainly blocking the young boy's strikes. Every so often, she was lucky enough to give her own.

Having an opening, Skypris swung her sword, aiming for Terro's head, forcing him to duck. She took her chance and jumped onto the rim of the fountain's main pool as rushing water gushed in. Terro followed her and swatted the wood at her knees. She evaded the blows by moving back or blocking with her wooden weapon. Stepping down to the tile, she continued to face the boy who was better at the sport than her. Terro laughed as he swiped the sword down at Skypris's feet, resulting in her losing balance and falling back on her butt, yelping in more alarm than pain. Before she had time to recover, she was blocked by the tip of Tero's weapon right in her face.

"Ha!" Terro boasted. "I win again!"

"I don't like this game," the girl declared in a pouting manner.

"It's not a game, it's practice! And when you compare your losses to my wins, for you… it's necessary."

"Can we take a break? We literally had breakfast less than an hour ago," she asked, brushing off the passive insult.

"Why? We're having fun!"

"I thought you said it wasn't a game?"

"Training could be fun," Terro informed her, taking the wooden sword away from the girl's face.

"Maybe for you," she murmured.

King Clayus walked out to Skypris's side, helping her to her feet, while Cerberus went to the fountain to quench his thirst. "Can't you go easy on Skypris?"

"I could; however, if I did, how would she learn? If she is to become a Dragon Knight, she needs to know how to protect herself, and I doubt that any enemy would go easy on her." Terro rested his sword on his shoulder with a cocky expression. "It's not my fault if she's beneath my skills."

Clayus smiled in amusement at his son's tone, which reminded him of his elder brother at his age. Skypris gritted her teeth in frustration. "Well then…" Clayus called to the boy's attention, taking the sword from Skypris, calming her down. "Let's put your *'skills'* to the test."

The King assumed a fighting stance, moving his robe behind his right leg so he could extend it. His son's smile vanished. "Are you sure?" he said with uneasiness.

"I'm sure, Terro." Clayus smiled brightly, trying not to appear too amused.

Shrugging his shoulders, Terro readied himself. Skypris moved to Cerberus as he finished drinking to greet her with a gurgle. The young girl stroked his nose and guided him away from the fountain to give the males more room, yet not so far that she couldn't see the action. "Shouldn't you take off your cape? It might slow you down," Terro questioned as they started to circle one another.

"No need, this will only take a moment," the king replied, swinging his sword around in a showy manner.

Terro lowered his brow, not liking the comment. He hastily stepped forward and made an attempt for the king's gut, but the king evaded his advances, resulting in Terro stumbling. When Terro turned to face Clayus, the king made sure Terro saw him counting coup. This only seemed to make his son angrier as their swords clashed with each other one time after another. King Clayus started to see the sweat on Terro's face dripping as he blocked and lunged, relying on strength rather than balance. This was the first time he had ever seriously dueled with his son, so Clayus was expecting Terro to try and show off a bit, yet now he could tell dueling with King Clayus had made him choke as he was forgetting the basics. If they were still that little boy and father playing sword fight, Clayus might have lightened up. However, things were different now. Clayus tripped Terro up with his matured talent, making him lose his grip and stifling him to the ground, where the boy cursed under his breath.

Walking over with a bright smile, Clayus picked Terro's wooden sword off the ground. "Not bad for your first real fight against me."

Clayus moved his hand down to the blade of the sword and then offered the handle to the boy. After a moment of Terro doing nothing but pouting on the tile, Clayus gave the weapon a little shake. "Aren't you going to take it?"

Grudgingly, Terro stood and took the wooden weapon. Skypris came skipping up to Terro with a smug smile on her face. "Don't be too disappointed, Terro! It's only training."

Terro's face turned red, and Skypris's playful mockery only seemed to make it intensify. King Clayus put his arm around his son's shoulder and gave it a little shake. "Cheer up! You put up a stronger fight. You just need to remember to stay focused on your opponent, no matter what they say or do, and don't forget your basics. It's all about balance, not strength."

Tilting his head back, Terro's tone filled was with disappointment. "If you say so."

"Don't worry, you'll have plenty of time to work on your fighting skills once your training begins. Are you nervous?"

"I'm not!" Skypris chimed in. "I can't wait to get my own dragon. I have been dreaming about this day for so long, and now it's finally happening. It doesn't feel real!"

Clayus asked, chuckling with amusement, "Have you come up with any names for your dragon?"

"Not really, I'm going to wait until I've seen them."

"I was planning on naming my dragon Scaltor," Terro said, looking at Cerberus with excitement as the dragon approached them, trying to pick his nose with his forked tongue.

"That's a good name," Clayus says, disgusted by Cerberus's uncivilized manner. "A name for one's dragon is a very powerful thing."

"Any rehearsals for tonight?" Skypris wondered, trying to look at the dragon.

"No, not for this. You know how it works. It's not very complicated—don't let the other arrivals from the kingdoms scare you."

"When are we going to gather everyone?" Terro asked.

"Once a guard alerts me that the other kingdoms' caravans are approaching."

Cerberus raised his head, eyeing the direction of the sea beyond the courtyard's wall. The humans followed when, at the same moment, a Royal Guard shouted, his armor rattling, "My King, my King!" The guard had the voice of a young man, his features hidden by a helmet.

"Have they arrived?"

"Yes, the scouts reported seeing the Dragon Empress on the horizon!"

"What of the caravans?"

"We got a bird with the report that they passed the closest checkpoint nearly half an hour ago. They should arrive when the dragons finish nesting."

"Right on time as usual!" King Clayus headed into the pavilion with Cerberus leading the way through the archway back into the castle, the guard by the king's side as the teens shadowed them. "Thank you. Please instruct Latona and General Archesilaus to meet me by the shore."

"Yes, Your Majesty!" The Royal Guard bowed before running off to perform the orders.

Terro ran up to meet his father's pace, Skypris doing likewise. “May I come with you, Father?” Terro asked.

“No, Son, you must stay here.”

“Why can’t I?”

“Because the female dragons will be starting to nest as they prepare to lay their eggs, and they can become very aggressive while this is happening. I want as few people down there as possible.”

“Even if I’m the future king?”

Turning down a hallway, King Clayus could tell Cerberus was getting antsy as the gear room got closer. “Indeed, you are. However, since you are getting a dragon today, the Dragon Empress will see your visit as though we are trying to rush the events of today.”

“That’s stupid!” Terro exclaimed.

“Not to an expecting mother who is giving her child away.”

After a flight of stairs and down the last few hallways, they found themselves in the saddle room, where racks of saddles hung along with other Royal Dragon equipment. Clayus took off his robe and handed it to a staff member, who walked away with it. Another staff member grabbed a saddle off its stand that had already been polished and checked for the day. Cerberus bent down until the staff tossed the saddle, placing it over the shoulder, right before the wings protruded. Cerberus stood up as the help fixed the straps under the dragon's belly, chest, and around his front legs as if it were a vest, fitting them to him so the saddle couldn’t move.

“Maybe next year,” Skypris suggested, putting her hand on Terro’s shoulder.

“That would be good, actually." As the staff moved out of the way, Clayus placed his foot in a strap and hoisted himself up on his Dragon, feeling him shake in excitement.

Terro folded his arms and jerked his shoulder away from Skypris’s hand. “It’s still stupid.”

“Don’t be like that,” Clayus lectured, gathering his wits and holding onto the gullet that was made into a hand’s grip.

Cerberus turned once his rider gave him the signal. The dragon exited the room through an archway that led out to a giant landing platform. Worried they might get blown away by any wind Cerberus' takeoff created, Terro and Skypris only came out of the room so much. Not being able to wait a second longer, Cerberus ran to the edge and jumped off, pumping air with his wings vicariously as if he had a predator chasing him.

Clayus called out in surprise at the rough takeoff, “Whoa, Cerberus, I know you’re excited to see your mother, but you can be a little steadier, I almost lost my crown!” The king laughed, holding onto his symbol of authority.

Cerberus roared with glee as he flew over the city. The dragon and rider approached the beach where a mile of igneous rocky cliffs stood strong. The rocks were strong enough to host adult dragons as the thunder headed inland, and the others deeper in the island made it outland to the rocks to greet their friends and family. Cerberus called again, and this time the bellow was echoed by many others who were equally as excited. Cerberus straightened his wings, gliding down, enabling him to land gracefully onto the dirt of the forest directly before the cliffs of the ocean shore. He clawed at the ground to keep himself distracted, like a horse egging its rider to hurry. Clayus turned to him with a smile, thinking that a life of pampering had made him impatient. Cerberus returned his own toothy grin. Yet they both waited, facing towards the castle. Soon, Clayus saw who he had been waiting for.

The king's most trusted general’s dragon, Skilidous, landed and advanced toward them. Skilidous seemed as eager to greet the other dragons as Cerberus was. Skilidous had a thick, orange hide with an even thicker tail. His underbelly was dark orange, and he hung his head low to the ground as his knight, Archesilaus, and his guest rider mounting off. Archesilaus held Latona’s hand as she found her footing and walked up to meet King Clayus. “Your Majesty,” said the general, bowing.

The man was about Clayus's age with green eyes, black sideburns, a scar on his face with a damaged nose, and a body resembling an individual who often enjoyed bouldering. His outfit was the typical Dragon Knight armor. However, it had some polished gold embroidery used to frame each section of the leather stitching. His underclothes were a nice velvet to show his status.

Skilidous moved ahead of them, trotting over to greet the newly arrived dragons. They wrapped their necks around each other as though in a hugging embrace. It wasn't too much later when more dragons from the city came for the reunion.

"Hello, General," King Clayus acknowledged, taking over for being Latona's guide. "I hope you weren't in the middle of reports when I summoned you."

They made it deeper into the thunder of dragons, many of them finding and making nests from the rocks. "Not at all! I usually try and keep my schedule open on this date if I can help it, just for this occasion."

"A wise decision," said Latona with a smile.

The three of them came to a stop once they reached the center of the dragons. Cerberus met them halfway with a large dragon next to him, her black scales shimmering a rainbow glow in the light, her chin high with her wings tucked, pride ringing with every calculated step she took.

Clayus led the bows. "Welcome, Dragon Empress."

The Dragon Empress's gaze was soft as she bowed deeply in return, then rose again.

Latona narrated, "She greets you in kind."

"I hope the journey wasn't too troubling for you." Clayus's tone was filled with remorse. "It appears you only lost six on this journey."

The mighty dragon closed her eyes as though she were feeling the pain of those lost. Reopening her gaze, she turned her long neck behind her and bellowed gently as though she was calling someone over. An emerald green, floppy-eared dragon limped toward Latona. "Oh my!"

Her hand went to her mouth as she started to move quickly to meet the weeping dragon halfway.

Latona held the dragon's head in her hands as the rest of the dragon's body shook, threatening to collapse. "Gorish," Latona said, yet Clayus wasn't able to tell if it was to report or if she said it in anger.

General Archesilaus narrowed his brow, clenching his hands. "How could they do something so disgusting?! The savages didn't even have the decency to grant her mercy after inflicting so much pain."

"Latona, will you be able to heal her?" Clayus stepped up to the young female dragon, looking long at her injuries.

"I will do all I can. However, it will take time," she said, stroking the young dragon's nose.

"She will be okay," King Clayus reassured the Dragon Empress. "Was she the only one who was inflicted this badly?"

The empress nodded.

"Very well, is there anything else we can do for you at this time?" Clayus gestured with an open hand with a slight bow.

The Dragon Empress's brow raised. She then bellowed again toward a red dragon behind her, who seemed to have been waiting for the order. It walked a few paces to the right and reached its head down in a crack between the rocks.

"P-put me doon!" a shaky voice contradicted the attempted demand.

The red dragon lifted the owner of the voice out of the crack. A young boy hung by his leg in its jaws, the dragon being careful not to draw blood with its teeth. Moving in front of the empress, the dragon dropped the boy at their ruler's claws and took their leave. Latona, Archesilaus, and King Clayus all watched in awe as the boy got up, keeping a nervous eye on both of them. His hair was a brown mess, more than likely caused by the flight, and his facial features were long and had only started to mature. He was lean, and being around the same height as Terro, who came up to Clayus's chest, making him guess they were about the same age. The clothes he wore weren't of the best quality, yet for a Goreon, they were the quality of a well-off family.

Clayus then directed his attention to the sword strapped to the boy's waist, and Clayus wasn't the only one.

"He's from Gorish!" General Archesilaus drew his sword with an angry ring in his voice. "He must have been the one to injure the young dragon!"

Without another word or signal of approval from the proper authority, General Archesilaus lunged for the boy, who squashed his legs and arms to his core, tucking his head and bracing for impact. Before the blade could meet its target, a large, scaled tail slammed down between the boy and the general, shaking the ground, halting General Archesilaus, and causing the boy to fall back. She growled, baring her teeth at the adults.

"What is the meaning of this?!" Clayus stomped forward. "Why would you bring someone from Gorish here?! Knowing what they are taught—knowing their traditions!"

The empress lifted her chin away from the king, putting her fangs to rest.

"Do not question her!" Latona walked over, leaving the injured dragon. "She has wisdom beyond even my years!"

It took King Clayus a second to come to his senses, pushing back the anger. Clayus cleared his throat, putting his diplomatic training to the test. He looked down at the boy, who shook in fear. Clayus's heart clenched as the boy reminded him of his own children, who had been scared many times in their lives. Clayus straightened himself out, locking his hands together behind his back, looking down. "My apologies, your grace. It was out of line for me to question your judgment without fully understanding your intentions."

The Dragon Empress turned her head back and gave a nod with a soft expression.

The young boy looked up at her and then back to the rest of them as she moved her tail away from the situation. General Archesilaus sheathed his sword and finished his reach to the boy as he grabbed his arm and hoisted him to his feet, taking the weapon from his waist. "Hoi!" the boy protested with a strong Gorish accent.

"Quiet!" the general growled. "My deepest apologies." General Archesilaus bowed to the Empress. "I just wanted to avenge the injured dragon."

The brown-haired boy tried to fight the grown man's grasp. Directing her gaze, the Empress and the boy stared at each other for a long moment, which caused him to stop struggling. He slumped his head towards his feet, gritting his teeth as his body shivered.

Latona put a hand on Clayus's arm, patting it as she returned to the injured dragon who waited patiently.

"General," King Clayus called for his attention. "Take this boy to the upper levels of the dungeon on your way back to your daily duties."

"As you wish," Archesilaus answered and began to lead the boy off the igneous rocks, whistling to call over his dragon.

Galloping to his rider, Skillidous bowed, letting the man mount him, leaving the boy from Gorish unattended. The Goreon tried to take the opportunity to bolt into the woods. However, his grand escape was cut short when Archesilaus's dragon stood on his hind legs and grabbed him with his two front talons. Skilidous snorted and was able to lift without much effort to get into the air, using his powerful hind legs to push off the ground as his wings gained momentum, making sure to pump his wings in a different direction so the remaining people did not get hit by his wings. It didn't take long for the general and his dragon to reach the castle.

"Clayus, we should take our leave," Latona suggested.

Clayus looked around to see all the female dragons nesting and lying down in the rocks, sending most of the males and dragons who belonged to a knight away with a kind nod or hissing and snarling. "Agreed." Clayus nodded and waved for Cerberus to come.

He nuzzled his mother's nose one last time before trotting up to Newla and Latona. The old sorceress mounted onto Cerberus as he bowed for her to do so.

"I am sorry for how I acted." Clayus turned to the empress one last time before mounting her son. "We will keep the boy with us until you give the order on what to do with him, and I will make sure the young dragon gets treated."

The empress nodded. Cerberus trotted away and, with a leap off the rocky cliff, he was winged into the air. The young, injured female staggered to follow after her altitude loss.

Chapter Five
Choosing

Skypris couldn't contain her excitement, or at least not anymore, yet who could blame her?! She'd been waiting patiently all day for this, and finally, she was going to get her own dragon! Skypris was going to become a Dragon Knight like her parents were. She waited almost irrevelently with Terro, King Clayus with Cerberus, Latona, and two other teens as they stood at the castle's entrance. Terro smirked at the squirming girl. Skypris playfully rolled her eyes, as if he wasn't as impatient, or even more so, than her. He was just better groomed to hide it.

Luckily, the other kingdom caravans soon arrived. The Laxor Kingdom came by carriage, escorted by a single Dragon Knight, whose name was Xavior, who was to be the trainer of the fourteen-year-olds he guarded. This year, they had six trainees to receive their dragons. The Kindoms Thrist, Ryjah, and Exwear hailed from the island of Ishnia, so they had to escort their new trainees by air, causing them to bring one Dragon Knight per two teens. Luckily, they only had four to-be knights, making a total of two dragons from the island.

King Clayus greeted the Dragon Knights hosting the youth at the entrance of the Dragon Empress's castle with Cerberus and Latona by his side. Skypris didn't talk much aside from simple exchanges. The fifteen young teens in total got acquainted with one another before everyone started to trek down to the dragon's nests at the shore.

All the knights watched the teens from the sky, Latona riding with King Clayus on Cerberus as they all circled the young group, not wanting to go too far ahead. At the forest's dirt path's end, the sand of the shore started. Skypris and the rest made it to the rocky cliffs and started to hike up the wet rocks effortlessly in their youth. At the top, they found Clayus and the other older dragon riders waiting for them, all giving proud and encouraging smiles as the teens looked on with their own smiles, some nervous and others excited. Beyond the adults, were many dragons lying on the igneous with their brood of eggs. At this point, they weren't so territorial, allowing other wild dragons to bring gifts to the mothers and to admire the eggs they had borne.

Skypris tried to fight the wide grin growing as she stared at the wild dragon mothers caring for their cluster. She knew that everyone was feeling the same way—well, most of them at the very least. Skypris took a deep, calming breath to still her heart and watched the sun make its way behind the mountain, wondering how much longer it was going to be until they started. Terro stood next to her after laughing with a few other boys from Ishnia. Everyone else did a single-file line once they got onto the rocks.

After the last of the group arrived, King Clayus approached. "I know you have been waiting for this all day…"

“More like a week,” Richard, a boy from the Kingdom of Alena, murmured.

“I am happy to say the wait is finally over. Today you will have your dragon,” the king finished.

“Please remember to stay calm. Mothers won’t give their eggs away to somebody who they think will drop them,” Latona chimed with a wheezing chuckle.

Skypris wondered if the reason why Latona mentioned that was because, in the past, a foolish teen actually did.

“Now, I assume you all remember from your classes as a younger youth how this ceremony goes?” Latona scanned the group.

Maro, a scrawny boy at the end of the line, barely waved his hand to grab the king's attention. Skypris didn’t know him personally, even though he lived in the castle. Skypris would see him roaming the halls of the palace, mainly entering the kitchen, where the staff would give him food. Other than that, he might as well not have existed. His hair was jet black, with eyes almost as dark. His clothes were baggy, leaving more room to grow. He had a belt on that tightened to the last loophole, probably keeping his pants from falling off his thin waist. His skin was pale, as if he rarely saw the light.

Maro sucked in his lower lip, timid from all the eyes on him now. “Uh… could we get a reminder?” His voice cracked. “Do we choose the eggs or are they given to us?”

Latona looked to Clayus before continuing with a nod, “You will all walk up to the dragons in their nest, and if they choose you, then they will personally give you an egg. Remember your manners and thank them in kind when receiving one.”

“Are there any other questions before we start?” King Clayus asked before continuing. “Once you have gotten your egg, you will wait here with the Dragon Knight who escorted you, understood?”

The teens all nodded, too excited to verbalize a reply.

"Are there any more questions?" King Clayus asked. Once there was no reply, he waved a hand toward the dragon behind him. "Then go find your dragon!"

The group dispersed, each taking a route toward their first female dragon to test if she would yield an egg to them. Skypris didn't hesitate to ask, nor was she shy, in going up to the first mother dragons, and she wasn't worried when she was denied an egg, nor the second or third. Before carrying on, she turned back to see that all the knights and the king were distracted by three teens who had already found their eggs, showing them off and getting congratulated by the adults. It made her feel better that none of them were from their kingdom. She decided to stop going around the rim of the land of igneous and ventured into the center. Farther into the flock of roosting dragons, none of them glanced at her. This is when Skypris's throat dried.

It wasn't common. However, it would happen to the unluckiest of the Dragon Knight's bloodlines. It was possible that no dragon found her family worthy anymore, that she wasn't worthy of a dragon. The fear of that possible reality weighed heavily on the young girl's chest. Her shoulders, once full of pep, now slumped. Perhaps she was too excited and scared them, making them think she would drop the egg. She shook the thought out of her head, how ridiculous! Surely, the dragons were used to seeing young, upcoming knights. Pushing on, she refused to allow herself not to be a knight.

Terro went quiet as he stood next to his father, trying to seem as mature as an already-crowned king. He looked on as each teenager returned with an egg. By now, almost everyone had been given their future dragon, all except for one, and they were the one he cared about the most. Going on his tippy toes, Terro peered around to see if he was able to spot Skypris. However, in the thunder of dragons, he wasn't able to spot her reddish-brown hair. King Clayus took his son's shoulder. "Shall we go and see the Empress now?"

"Shouldn't we wait for Skypris?" Terro wondered, feeling a bit stupid to want to delay what he had been preparing for his entire life.

His father gave him a warm smile with slight amusement. "Don't worry, she shouldn't be much longer—we'll just get started."

He led his son away from the assembly and toward the center of the dragon's nests. There at the center was the Dragon Empress; even lying down, she still towered over the other mothers. She watched as Terro and his father approached. Lifting her chin up, she held such an manner that Terro couldn't tell if she was being cold or reserved. The Empress didn't look at them or return their bows. Clayus had an unsure expression, recognizing this wasn't her typical behavior. Terro looked to his father with equal concern, wondering if this is normal. He had never met the Dragon Empress until this moment. "Go on," the king encouraged.

Terro gulped, now feeling how heavy his limbs had become. Stepping forward, he set his eyes between her two talons in front of her chest, where a campfire was lit. Getting closer, he realized that it wasn't an actual flame at all, but her egg with the coloration of one. Taking a last step, the Dragon Empress moved her claw over her egg and hissed toward the young prince, making him flinch in fear. After recovering, the boy furrowed his brow in shock. "What?!" he exclaimed.

King Clayus got closer. "What's wrong?"

A cold stare rested on Terro, before she flicked her head away, uninterested. Confusion was plastered on Clayus's face. Terro tried to take another step forward, reaching for where the egg had once been exposed. She bared her teeth once and moved her tail to intercept his path. "She's not giving me the egg!"

"Terro," Clayus hushed his son now in front of him, looking to the large Dragon. "Is this egg your next heir?"

She moved her head away as though giving them a childish silent treatment. The king bowed his crown, contemplating what the issue could be, then he looked back up. "Is my son not to have your egg?"

She turned to him, her expression lightened. Terro saw his father lower his eyebrows, not in anger but searching deeply. "If not him, then whom?!"

The question struck Terro's heart as if he had just been slapped, and there was nothing but a sting and an embarrassed pride. He wasn't supposed to have the egg? What foolish joke was this?! Of course, he was. It was his right by birth!

Terro's thoughts were interrupted as the Empress pointed her head and gazed at the castle. He saw his father follow her view and watched as his father's appearance changed to realization. "Father?" Terro asked, hoping he was misreading the situation. "What's going on? Why isn't the Empress giving me her egg?"

"I'm unsure myself, though I have a hunch. Stay here." Clayus retreated to the group. Skypris still hadn't returned from receiving an egg.

Despite his father's wishes, Terro followed along.

"What's the matter?" Latona asked, taking note that the boy did not have an egg in his arm.

"The Empress wouldn't give me her egg," Terro whispered through gritted teeth to the old woman, worried that others would hear.

Latona looked to Clayus with the intention of speaking with him. However, Clayus threw his leg to the other stirrup in Cerberus's saddle, taking grip of the fork of the saddle. With one command, Cerberus leapt off the side of the rocks and then gained momentum, leaving Terro and the others to only wonder.

Chapter Six
The Boy From Gorish

The stone floor that Edwin sat on was cold. His cell was a lot bigger than he would have thought a castle's dungeon cell would be. However, given the actual size of the castle and what he saw of the layout, it should have made sense to him. The space was larger than the upstairs of his family's bakery, yet it hosted a lot less stuff, which Edwin didn't know was possible. He cuddled up in the corner of his cell looking for warmth but couldn't find any. He could use the cot provided, though he didn't know how much help it would be without a blanket and pillow. Besides, the ground made him feel safe. He looked over to the other corner to see a bucket for the waste. Luckily for him, it was empty when he arrived. Another thing to be grateful for was that the man who brought him in hadn't used the shackles in the cell, allowing him to roam.

He hadn't gone through the whole castle, even though part of him wished he had received a tour. The monster rider—or dragon rider—took him through a door in the back of the castle, which was on the ground with no elevation at all, and once in it, he was immediately led to a corridor and then to stairs that led down. The outside of the fortress was something to behold. It was bigger than the castle the king of Gorish owned, even with it being far away, and never visiting, Edwin was able to make that assumption. He wished the prison had the marvelous, white polished stone that the outside of the castle did, yet instead, he was stuck with the boring clay colors of the earth. Maybe the outside of the castle was only an off-white, and the inner structures were done in dull earth? No, that's not possible, or at the very least, Edwin didn't want to believe so. He'd never seen so many towers or bridges in his lifetime, and until now, he probably never would have.

To take his mind off the cold, Edwin stared at his feet as he swished them side to side, as his heel pivoted. He synced them together and then would make them go the opposite of the other, and yes, it wasn't the perfect entertainment, yet it was all he had to keep his mind from self-destructing. Yes, he could read the book he had in his vest's inner pocket, yet he was afraid they would take it like they took his sword. He didn't want to risk that. When was he ever going to read it again if not in the cell? Was he expecting them to set him free? Kill him—at least he got to see an astonishing castle before he joined his parents. He wondered if he should try to escape. Where would Edwin go afterwards? A boat? No, he wouldn't even make it off the coast before being caught.

His feet stopped moving, and the young boy held his knees. The tightness in his chest slowly returned, and he held his breath, trying to keep as much hot breath to himself as possible. To avoid panic, Edwin's thoughts drifted to this place—to where the dragon had taken him. There had been rumors—scarce rumors of people seeing humans riding on the backs of the beasts, and of an island that was populated by people other than Gorish and Elvous. No doubt the nobles and lords probably knew more about this place than the common folk, but even with the hearsay feeding his imagination, Edwin never would have imagined a place like this. He couldn't get it out of his mind how beautifully built the castle was and how the men were flying on the dragons! That didn't seem right. Where are the dark, evil caves where the dragons kept their gold and all the starving, enslaved people that had to serve the monsters? No, this was quite the opposite. The humans at the shore looked happy with the beasts. The man had attacked him, and not the dragon. Edwin was the monster in this situation.

A light illuminated the hallway outside of Edwin's dreary cell. Edwin stood up as the light got brighter. Once he realized the torch was heading his way, he looked on the ground frantically for anything, a loose stone, a twig? Any form of weapon. Maybe the bucket for waste would do? Were they coming to end him? He hoped heaven would be warmer. He would even be willing to go for the other option if it meant he could get some heat.

Edwin walked to the bars and gripped them, peering out as he saw a man come into view. Stopping in front of the cell, the torch he held revealed some features from the shadows. His beard was thick and short, his eyes brown, his facial features almost perfect, his crown shining. He recognized the man from the shore. He had to be a king. "I am King Clayus, ruler of the Kingdom of Alena, High King of Xolf, and who are you?"

Yep, king.

Edwin hesitated, scratching his head to give himself some time to think. Clayus pronounced his words oddly. For one, he said '*I*' like '*aye*,' so it took Edwin a second. He had to stop his hands from shaking, "Edwin."

King Clayus squinted his eyes, making them disappear in shadow. "Where do you come from exactly?"

The boy hesitated to speak. At the shore, they'd almost killed him because they assumed he was from Gorish. What would they do if he confirmed it?! It seemed pointless to lie. King Clayus already knew and was just being polite, "A-" Edwin's mouth was dry.

"Are you from the land of Gorish?"

Swallowing, Edwin nodded slowly, making the king's gaze harden. "Why have you come here? How did you get here?"

Edwin wondered why the King was asking questions he already knew. Perhaps he was testing Edwin in some way to see if he would try and lie. "A dinnae ken."

"Lies!" The king banged his fist on the barred cell.

The young boy crouched down, covering his head. "A dinnae ken a swear! A wis taken by that big mon- dragon—that big dragon!"

"You mean the Dragon Empress?" King Clayus corrected. "Why would she bring you here?"

"She didnae say why."

"Say…" King Clayus placed his hand on his chin, trying to figure out if the boy was being sarcastic or if he had genuinely expected a verbal answer from the Empress.

The dungeon went silent.

Pulling out a set of keys, the king unlocked Edwin's cell, opening the creaking gate. "I don't know what the Empress is thinking, bringing you here. However, she is wiser than my oldest adviser. She must see something I'm not."

"Ye're letting me go?"

"No," King Clayus rested a hand on his sword handle that was strapped to his side. "I'm taking you to her. If you try anything, I'll cut you down where you stand. Do you understand me?"

"Aye."

Edwin stepped out with King Clayus leading the way. Edwin thought it was odd that a grown adult with a stature like King Clayus would see him as a threat. He could barely pull his weight with flour, and he wasn't fast either. Recalling a time a chicken was angry with him and chased him down, and how he wasn't able to outrun the fowl. As they walked, Edwin noticed the king had Edwin's father's sword on the other side of his hip. The urge to try and snatch it came to him, yet this was a king! He must have years of professional training and experience. Besides, if Edwin tried to use the sword, he would end up doing himself in. "Ye have ma father's sword," Edwin's voice squeaked, a tone of remorse knowing that he might never see it again.

"It's a fine weapon, forged very well," King Clayus admired. "Are all Gorish weapons like this?"

"Some probably, but no aw. That's ma father's. It wis passed doon to me when—" Edwin caught himself. "A become af age."

"How old are you?"

"Fourteen years."

King Clayus nodded, playing with his lips as he thought out loud, "That might explain it."

"Explain wit?" Edwin tilted his head.

"I have a hunch, and to be honest, I hope it's wrong."

Distracted, Edwin thought about the dungeon's structure. It appeared to be designed like a labyrinth with a bunch of passageways that forked and branched out with a lot of roundabouts. Edwin couldn't even remember where they turned or how many they did exactly to reach the stairs he was led down not too many hours ago. On his way to his cell, he passed by many that already had occupants in them. Most of them seemed normal, though there was a certain man who really made him uncomfortable. The man seemed old and was shirtless, so you could see his bones. He didn't see the old man or many other prisoners walking the path that the king took, which made Edwin know there had to have been multiple routes to get to where he was being held.

Edwin stopped at the foot of the staircase, wondering if King Clayus would take the lead. He glanced over his shoulder once up the first few steps to make sure Edwin was following. He was. After about twenty-five steps, the two arrived at a wooden door. Taking out his copper key set again, the lock clicked as he pulled out the key and opened the door. The wooden doors creaked loudly, giving away their age. "After you," the king gestured.

Edwin stepped out into a room, being cautious. The stone was the same as the dungeon's. Edwin looked to see another staircase leading up to another door. Behind the door, under the stairs, was a table with dealt playing cards. Guards were standing, gripping their spears, looking at Edwin. The boy feared they would run him through, thinking he was escaping, when King Clayus stepped next to him, closing and locking the door. He nodded to the guards as they bowed respectfully, sharing a few words between each other. Then Edwin and King Clayus made it up the second staircase and out the door; all the while the guards were watching, no doubt going back to their card game once the king was unable to see.

Now out of the dungeon, Edwin blinked, adjusting his eyes to the daylight the window let leak in. The stone was now white, exactly like the outside of the castle. Edwin's jaw hung as he looked around at the castle's decor. He looked up to see that the ceiling of the castle was just as tall as the sky. Quickly, he noticed that King Clayus was a few paces ahead of him. Running to catch up, Edwin slowed to a walk with the king, who watched Edwin closely as the boy did so, making sure he wasn't trying anything, though his expression and body posture showed no sign of his concern.

Edwin wasn't able to keep track of how many stairs and hallways they made their way through. It got to the point that his legs were starting to tire. Knowing he could never memorize where he was heading, he decided to keep his attention on the decor of the castle and stare at servants and guards who would pass by. Edwin glanced back at a suit of armor, unable to tell if it was fake or an actual guard. Probably empty armor because the design did not match the palace protectors he had seen already, and it was way too shiny with no wear at all.

"This way," the king said, moving past an archway into a large room, each wall drenched in saddles.

"Where is the Empress?" Edwin asked, approaching a saddle that a servant was in the middle of polishing and checking the strength of the straps.

The staff member was a young man. He didn't speak but looked up at Edwin, an eyebrow lifted. Noticing the man's judgment, Edwin's cheeks felt warm. Now that it was brought to his attention, even the servants of the castle had cleaner, more affluent clothing than those who would have the same status in Gorish. "She is where you last saw her. Down by the shore, like the rest of the roosting dragons."

Edwin felt a bolt of nausea when he heard those words and when he saw the dragon in a saddle approaching Clayus. The large black dragon was down by the shore, which meant in order to get there…

Great, Edwin thought. His experience with being carried by dragons hadn't been pleasant so far, and he wasn't hopeful that it would improve. Just the anticipation made him want to heave.

King Clayus pulled himself up onto the green dragon with horns facing forward. Edwin scanned the design of the saddle. It looked very similar to what a horse wears, having a seat, cantle, fender, stirrup, and straps around the dragon's neck, chest, and arms. The only real difference was that the swell was more of a grip and had easy handles built in. The most important feature of the saddle was that it was big enough for two riders. Testing his luck, the young boy strolled over to the back of the saddle as though he owned the beast.

"No, you don't!" the king said, his dragon snorting, causing Edwin to flinch horribly in fear.

"Go out in the middle of the platform, and we'll pick you up," King Clayus shooed Edwin ahead of him. "Try not to move too much, Cerberus isn't so good at grabbing off the ground when he's flying."

"Why cannae he pick me up now and then take aff?" Edwin's voice was shaky.

"He needs the practice. Go and don't run or he might accidentally impale you."

Reluctantly, Edwin made his way out of the archway and to the center of the balcony. He tried not to move his body except for his head. As he looked at the landscape and exterior of the great castle, his jaw gaped. He still couldn't get over how beautiful, how green, how giant everything was! When Cerberus galloped forward, Edwin's jaw went from open to clenched and his muscles tightened as the dragon knocked him down with the wind he created while running past. Jumping off the ledge, the green dragon pumped his legs and wings until he was higher than the towers of the castle. Edwin squinted his eyes, trying to catch sight. Once he did, he realized he had involuntarily moved. Scrambling back into position, Edwin watched as the dragon did a somersault and dove toward him.

Squeezing his eyes shut and holding his breath, he shook as he braced for impact. Extending his talons, Cerberus snatched Edwin and hoisted him into the air, jolting Edwin's bones. The dragon's claws were a little pinchy. However, it was a fair trade to ensure he didn't fall to his death. Suddenly, the dragon tossed Edwin high into the air. Ss the boy yelped in alarm, Cerberus caught him, adjusting a better, firmer grip using both his back and front arms and legs. Loud rumbles came from Cerberus's throat as though he was laughing, saying, "That was a close one!" using a deep masculine voice.

King Clayus laughed along with his dragon as his steed made his way toward the shore, the smell of the saltwater becoming stronger with each wing flap, the other dragons and mothers drawing nearer.

Chapter Seven
Chosen

Skypris sat on the edge of the wet igneous rocks, one arm hugging her knees to her chest and the other tossing loose rocks into the beating waves below, with no dragon egg to call her own. She wandered through the entire thunder of roosting dragons and not one glanced her way for a second! Well, that wasn't entirely true. She ended up approaching some mothers multiple times out of desperation, and they all hissed at her to take their first answer. Skypris chucked another rock into the ocean, a tear of frustration starting to form on her cheek as she felt aches in her chest. Skypris itched her head aggressively and rested her cheek in her free hand. What was she supposed to do now? Perhaps try the Dragon Empress?

No.

No, she would never do that to Terro even if it was a possibility, so she wasn't even going to chance it.

The young girl thought that she could be a palace guard. No, that didn't feel right, as though her shoes were on the wrong feet.

She extended her legs out and over the ledge, wiping another tear from her face, finding it hard not to sob completely as her mind lingered on her parents. Both of them were Dragon Knights, highly ranked Dragon Knights in the king's court. The queen's personal guard. How could she not be one?! How could not a single dragon find her worthy?!

How could she move on, not following in her parents' footsteps like she's always dreamed of? The thing that made her feel connected to them.

Skypris placed a clenched fist over her heart as though someone had punched it. She huffed and stood up, cleaning her face. She decided she couldn't start mourning. Not here, at least. Besides, she was being rude. Surely everyone already had their egg and was waiting for her to arrive. She must have missed Terro receiving his. Facing reality, Skypris began to return to the group. However, with her first step, the igneous rock caught her foot, sending her to the ground, her knee taking most of the blow. She gritted her teeth and rolled over to her back, rubbing her knee as it throbbed. Hissing as she worked through the pain, she focused on her breathing. Forcing herself to recover quickly, she once again stood with a limp, shaking off the tingling. Noticing a hole she'd created in the ground, Skypris examined it with curiosity. What was this, a hidden cave? Back to all fours, she peered into the newly created peephole, making sure to also let in enough light, and there, resting on a ledge, sat an egg.

Doing a double take, Skypris then looked around to see if anyone else was witnessing what she had discovered. But no one had. Peering back in, it was hard to tell, but the egg appeared to be multiple colors of blue. Why was an egg down there?! How could a mother leave it? Did something happen to her? Dragons are immensely maternal. To think one would just allow their egg to go missing from the nest, or to even place it here, was abnormal behavior. Grabbing a loose rock, she started to hit the weakened igneous around the crack, creating a bigger hole until, eventually, an entrance formed that was large enough for the front half of her body to fit. After realizing the cave was about thirty-five feet deep, she was careful. Instead of a there being a floor, she could see water as she heard ocean waves washing in from a hidden entrance as they echoed. She managed to squeeze her torso into the entrance, making it possible to grab the egg that barely fit into her reach after stretching. Almost dropping it into the watery depth below, Skypress used her core strength to exit the cave.

Holding the egg close to her chest for a moment, she let her nerves settle. It was cold. She held it out to examine it—it was about the size of a large cantaloupe. No damage had been done to the unhatched Dragon, not even a single crack. It was blue with a pattern that resembled a flame. Skypris felt eyes on her, making her look up and lock eyes with a dragon mother whose diamond-shaped pupils were dilated with interest. Was she the mother? If that were true, why would she do that to her egg?! The mother didn't deserve it- Skypris shook her bad thoughts away, feeling sick to her stomach as they came and left. That wasn't it. The egg probably got stuck down there somehow. She should return it to the mother, no matter how badly she wanted to keep it. It was the right thing to do. Standing, Skypris took three steps before the dragon mother realized where the girl was heading. Eyes going to slits, she hissed and turned away.

Okay, so not the mother.

Or maybe this was her way of saying she could keep it?

Rotating, Skypris scanned the nests to see if any other dragon took interest. They did not.

She thought about telling Latona and King Clayus about the egg. If she did though, she would never be a Dragon Knight. Skypris rubbed the egg in her arms, taking in how cold the shell was, and the absence of life that there appeared to be. If no one was claiming the egg, then it shouldn't hurt if she took it, right? Skypris reasoned herself into a wide smile as she took the egg back to the group of other teens and guardians.

Approaching, she was finally able to see the full extent of the group. All the knights-to-be held eggs in their arms, except for her friend Terro, who stood next to Latona staring up toward the castle. She furrowed her eyebrows. Why didn't Terro have his egg yet? Was he waiting for her? No, they wouldn't have let him push it off this long. Closer, Skypris was able to notice Cerberus approaching the shore speedily. "Finally!" She saw the young prince throw his arms up.

Instead of getting involved, she decided to wait and watch with the others. She walked a half circle until she was next to Maro, who was staring at the situation in the distance. She wanted to ask what was going on, yet based on everyone's stares, she had a feeling no one else knew what was happening either.

Edwin landed roughly as Cerberus dropped him, wishing there had been something softer than igneous rock under the dragon. Cerberus then gently landed next to the young boy, knocking him back down to the rock with a last powerful wingbeat that Edwin wasn't sure was done on purpose or not. Cerberus smiled playfully as Edwin gave him a challenging stare.

A blond boy around Edwin's age approached King Clayus as he dismounted and grabbed Edwin by the arm. "Father!" he started with a frustrated tone. "Who is this? Don't we have bigger issues at hand with the Empress?"

"This is Edwin. He arrived this morning with the dragons. The Empress brought him."

Clayus yanked Edwin forward until he found himself in front of a curious older woman with a white cloak and long silvery hair. She had a youthful beauty about her despite her age.

"What do you mean?!" the blond boy pressed.

"Terro, please, I will answer questions as soon as I figure out what they are myself." The king gave his son a shooing gesture of his hand.

Terro backed off the pursuit of answers. However, he did not move as he stared Edwin down with anger, as though he had guessed what his father was thinking and not approving.

Edwin found a smile in the older woman. "Not a normal boy, are you?"

"A think am normal." Edwin took a step back.

The woman bobbed her head in a way that indicated she didn't believe the young boy's claim. She turned her gaze to her king. "You want *him* to approach the Dragon Empress?"

"I want to see if she'll give *him* her egg."

The silver-haired woman pointed her finger up at the huge dragon in the distance. Her hand was gnarled, being the only true indicator of her age. "Go to the Empress and see if she will acknowledge you," she instructed.

Edwin looked to the hard-to-miss dragon, then back to King Clayus, who gave him a nod, no longer holding him. The brown-eyed boy found the king's son, who had a face of surprised horror. Facing the dragon, the mist from the water suddenly felt sticky and overwhelmingly hot. If he didn't go, he would more than likely be returned to the dungeon, though he had a feeling he might be returning there anyway. He took one last look behind him, this time at a group of kids his age in the distance with some adults who had large dragons lying down waiting for orders like Cerberus.

Taking a deep breath, he wasn't going to test anyone's patience, so he watched his step, trekking forward. He passed one roosting dragon who hissed at him, then another, until he reached the center of the nests. He looked up at the dragon that was as tall as any guard's watch tower. She was resting, her tail curled in front of her and four-fingered talons intertwined. "Hello, young Edwin." Her voice was filled with a deep calm. "I knew we would meet again soon."

"Why did they bring me tae ye?" he asked, not so scared of her. If anyone was going to kill him just because, they would have done so already, or at least that's what he liked to tell himself.

"I wanted to give you my child."

Edwin's brows furrowed as they raised. He twisted to look at the audience behind him, taking note of the eggs the teens had. Everyone watched him. He had so many questions that, turning back around to face the Empress, he decided to ask the most forward one, "Why me?"

"You are a special young one. Haven't you noticed you're the only one who can understand my speech?"

Edwin stepped back to be closer to the people who had sent him. Confusion on his face, as he called back to them, "Ye cannae understand her?!"

The adults and the blond boy looked puzzled by the question, as though it wasn't normal. The silver-haired woman cuffed a hand on the side of her mouth. "You can?"

"It's not just me, Edwin," Tthe Empress drew back his attention. "You can understand our language. My kin and I talk little with words. Usually, we rely on body movements. However, when we do speak, there are no humans who can understand."

Scratching the top of his head, he could feel the dirt the dungeon and flights had brought to his body. What was he supposed to think of this situation? "Is that why ye brought me here? Tewk me from Gorish. Is this why ye're affering me yer egg?"

She thought long before blinking. "Take care of my child. Let him be your friend, your brother, your dragon."

"Thanks for answerin'," Edwin's brows were narrow.

His expression and attitude shifted, however, when the Empress lifted her tail up over his head and to the back of her. Her talons moved out from the front of her as they revealed an egg with the colors and patterns of fire. Edwin looked at it, to her, to the ones behind him, who had open mouths, then to the egg again. "Go on," the Empress encouraged.

Edwin hesitantly moved towards her and grabbed the egg. It was warm, and he could feel movement under the shell. Hugging it to his core, he walked back to the king, the older woman, and the scowling boy. The king's eyes were wide open. His question came more as an observation. "She gave you her egg."

The king's son stomped his foot, hard enough to damage the igneous rock under his feet. Everyone's attention snapped to him, even the audience in the back. "He's not even of the royal family, let alone a Xolite!" the prince hissed acidly, looking at Edwin. "It's not fair that he gets the Empress's egg—it was supposed to be mine!"

King Clayus neither condoned nor corrected his son's attitude, leading Edwin to think he felt—or at least thought—the same. "Am I to be a Dragonless hier?!"

With that, the king stepped closer to the Dragon Empress as she watched the entire scene play with a hint of annoyance. "Is there no Dragon for my son?" the king asked.

Looking up in thought, the Empress turned her head behind her and scanned the thunder of roosting mothers. She paused and then made a long, low bellow. A couple of seconds later, a feather-winged mother approached the young prince, gently setting one of her eggs before his feet. The egg was smaller and was shaped more sharply than the one Edwin held. Instead of a powerful fire, the egg's coloration was a simple robin's egg blue with the same speckles as one.

Chapter Eight
The New Dragon Knights

On the way to the castle, Edwin was expecting to be thrown back into a prison cell once more. However, instead, King Clayus told him that he was under the protection of the Dragon Empress as her ward; and because it wasn't fit for anyone to be sleeping on rocks, the two rulers had agreed for him to stay at the castle. Where he would be staying exactly, Edwin didn't know, and the king didn't bring it up as he was explaining the situation.

Trekking, Edwin walked behind the trail of teens with their eggs as they took a path through the woods, the city, and up to the castle. Many of them were talking amongst themselves, mainly about what had happened, all surprised as to why Edwin had received the Empress's egg instead of the crown prince as tradition demanded. It got to the point where the prince himself, up in the front, had halted the entire line to yell "Shut up" to those gossiping before continuing in silence.

As the shore got farther away, they entered the city. The adults on their dragons had been waiting for them as they led the parade. The king took the front with the silver-haired woman riding with him. Through the city on a path to the castle, the streets they walked were filled with crowds of citizens on both sides of the roads, cheering for their new "Dragon Knights."

Decorations streamed from building to building, connecting the two halves of the street. Flowers of all sorts were being tossed to them. Edwin wasn't used to attention at all, especially an entire parade's worth. He saw that another boy was having a hard time with the recognition as well, trying to hide from both sides of the crowd with his egg held to his face, his head bowed. He was quite the scrawny fellow. Edwin swore he saw the red-haired girl behind the crown prince staring at him in curiosity. Edwin's face felt warm whenever he would catch her, and she would quickly look away. Now here she was sitting across from him.

The parade had stopped at the end of the city, where a bridge led into the castle's entrance. Edwin followed the teens in front of him, passing by King Clayus, who had stopped at the gate, waving to the crowd of citizens still throwing flowers and streamers at the new knights. The king assisted the older woman off Cerberus, and the other dragon riders dismounted from theirs. The adults walked in behind the teens after the king gave thanks to his subjects. The doors were as tall as the Empress and remained open from what Edwin was able to see. He followed the line of people across many halls of the grand structure. It was as magnificent as he had assumed. Soon, he entered a ballroom that was giant in width and height. The floor was waxed so fine that those who walked across it found their reflections. The walls were drenched in windows or archways that led deeper into the castle, lavishly decorated in vines and grapes carved from gold. A bunch of platforms almost created a second floor with several large beasts as they perched and slept, except for two of them that were conversing loudly, their voices echoing only for the Goreon's ears to hear. However, with the music being played, it was hard to discern their exact words. Cerberus and the rest of the dragons, who were owned by riders, climbed effortlessly onto the second floor. Many tables were laid out across the room, standing vertically except for a shorter table that rested horizontally above the others.

King Clauys took a seat at a wooden throne with red cushions, armrests carved into spirals, and its back designed to be a dragon bowing its head, wings folded. The Crown Prince from the shore sat next to a younger boy who looked identical but had brown hair instead of blond. On the other side of the king was one of the most gorgeous girls Edwin had ever seen, and once he noticed her, it was hard to look away. Her skin was fair, and her brown hair was knotted into a bun with a small single-sided braid pulled back. She shared her father's lips and eyes and nothing more. She looked older than Edwin, only by a year or two. The children all sat in chairs and wore crowns that were extravagant, yet not as extravagant as their father's. King Clayus and his beautiful daughter were laughing at a man who had been talking warmly with both of them. Edwin's eyes caught the crown prince's, who sat on the other side of his father, shooting Edwin daggers.

Many individuals were there in their finer fashion, cleaned up better than he ever could. Children were polished as they ran around the giant space, their parents intermingling. With his rags, Edwin stuck out like a sore thumb. Even the boy who sat next to him with baggy clothes was put together better than he was. Edwin looked at the servants bringing out dishes of lavish foods for the guests to fill their plates with, ensuring the individuals they hosted never had an empty glass or a dirty plate in front of them throughout the night. They all wore similar uniforms, with the castle colors of black and gold and complements of white. The knights, or those of higher class, wore the castle colors as well, except their uniforms had golden capes and a large golden dragon stitched into their chests.

"Any name ideas yet for your dragon?" a young male voice said through a stuffed face.

Edwin focused his attention back to the table, where the teens who were down at the shore all sat together holding their eggs in their arms and laps. One egg rested on the table, which a castle staff member clearly didn't approve of based on her scowl.

"Richard, don't talk with your mouth full, you're going to choke again," a black-haired girl said, her dragon egg in her lap, covered by a napkin.

He ignored her mothering. "For mine, I was planning Zelotes or Jadeite!"

"I don't have any female names picked out yet," the scrawny, baggy-clothed boy next to Edwin mumbled. The other kids continued their conversation, not hearing him, which led him to speak to Edwin and the red-haired, green-eyed girl across from them. "I thought that Hamlet would be a good name, maybe Furwan even."

"Back home, we have a knight ahead of us with a dragon named Zelotes," said a girl two seat down as she leaned over.

"Man, I need to think of something else," said Richard, who finally swallowed his food.

"Why? He's a very skilled fighter."

"'Cause I want mine to be one of a kind."

"What about yours, Skypris? Got any names yet?" a teen on her other side questioned, trying to move the conversation forward.

"I don't know, actually. I'm sure it'll come to me—maybe when I see them, I'll know." The red-haired girl looked at Edwin. "What's your name?"

Edwin had to swallow. He wasn't used to socializing, especially with individuals his age. He nodded and glanced at the teens who sat at the table, "Edwin."

"Hello, I'm Skypris!" she greeted warmly. "What are you going to name your dragon, Edwin?"

The inclusion caught him off guard. He was expecting everyone to give him the silent treatment the rest of the night, especially after the prince himself yelled at everyone. “A dinnae ken. Everythin’ came so unexpectedly a didnae actually have time to plan.”

“Ken?”

“Know.”

“Ah. Don’t worry, Dragon eggs take two months to hatch. I’m sure you’ll think of something sooner or later. Maybe you could choose a name that’s native to Gorish, to help you remember home?” she suggested.

Edwin looked down. He tried not to show how downcast her suggestion made him feel. Thinking about home and his aunt and uncle started to sting his eyes. This land was grand and different, which helped distract him, yet he wondered how his family was faring. Had Aland told the king's guards about how he had behaved with the dragon? Did they find him a traitor? Did his guardian's name get shamed, and they were now beggars on the street, or did his uncle’s name, with slaying, spare them?

“You talk funny,” Richard pointed out. “Does everyone from Gorish pronounce things weird?”

Everyone paused for a moment, not knowing what to say about the comment that came out of nowhere.

“That’s rude!” Skypris snapped.

“He just has an accent like from Ishnia,” said a young boy drenched in freckles.

“No, yours is barely a difference! It's maddening. I can’t understand a word he's saying,” Richard commented, ripping the skin off a chicken leg.

“I can understand him,” one girl said.

“Are you sure it’s his accent and not just a personal issue?” Skypris gave a playful laugh, followed by a few others who joined in.

Richard narrowed his eyes at being turned into a joke. He slammed the fist holding the chicken leg on the table, pointing and looking to Edwin. "Why did the Empress bring you here?! You don't belong."

Everyone was quiet, not wanting to say anything for or against Edwin, or the reasons of the Empress. "She weddnae tell me," answered Edwin, fiddling with the egg in his lap.

"Dragons don't talk!" Richard snapped. "I never heard of anyone being able to talk to them before—not even Latona can hear them!"

Some teens nodded knowingly as though the boy had won them to his side. Some of them, farther away, started to whisper things to each other while glancing. "You must be someone special or else she wouldn't have given you her egg." The scrawny boy tried his best at a smile that soon failed him the moment eyes locked on him.

The sound of a utensil hitting a glass echoed across the ballroom. Edwin followed the crowd's eyes as they placed them on their king, who stood in front of his table. He wore a black jacket with a golden undershirt and black trim and pants. His hair was braided into a small bun as the crown rested. His beard was freshly trimmed and groomed. Edwin couldn't recall when the king had stepped away. Then again, he had been distracted by many things this past day. The dragons on the second floor peered below. The ones that were asleep woke up, and the ones talking grew silent.

"I want to take a few minutes of your time to announce that all the children have received an egg!"

"Hear, hear!" the crowd yelled, raising their glasses.

"There were complications with this batch," King Clayus continued. "Fortunately, everything has been sorted out, and the recruits are well on their way to becoming noble knights. Thank you to the kingdoms Laxor, Exwear, Thirst, and Ryjah for joining us. Let the flames of Xolf and Ishnia's bond never dull and the blood of our noble, loyal, and compassionate knights never run dry! To the Dragon Empress!" King Clayus lifted his goblet and then drank the wine from it.

Everyone else repeated after his salute, then drank from theirs, including the recruits. Edwin's mouth opened, then he realized he was far too slow to speak. Which perhaps was a good thing. He was from a kingdom that was an enemy to this one, after all. He didn't know where his allegiance stood exactly. As everyone clapped, cheered, finished their meal, and socialized, Edwin stared at his untouched chicken, potatoes, and corn that rested on his plate with a roll on a napkin. Don't be fooled, he was starving! However, currently, even the taste of water churned his stomach.

As the evening dawned, all the quests slowly made their descent, either drunk and escorted by friends or returning home with their families. All approached the king and his family to give respect to the crown before departing. Talking and laughing, they shook each of the royal's hands, even the younger prince whom they needed to bend their back for. The teens and their hosts of Ishnia and Laxor's kingdom were some of the first to leave, having to travel a great distance that same night. Edwin watched as servants started to clean up the table at which he sat. Skypris had made her way over to the crown prince, standing and whispering to him as he was smiling and greeting everyone a good night.

Standing, Edwin held the Empress's egg tight to his chest. He decided to seek out the king for information on where to stay instead of waiting for him to come. Edwin hesitated with his next step, knowing he would never approach the King of Gorish. Why would this king be any different? Everyone else seemed to be approaching him with no anxiety, yet they were all supposedly his knights, and Edwin was a peasant boy from an enemy kingdom.

Instead, Edwin headed to a round table where the silver-haired woman with the white robe from the shore was talking with the scrawny boy who had jet-black hair. The teens at the table had referred to her as Latona, saying that before they left, they needed to retrieve a satchel from her. Since she was distracted, the Goreon boy grabbed one off the table himself, not wanting to disturb her. He looked the satchel over, not exactly understanding why they needed one.

Oh wait!

Edwin gently placed the dragon egg into the satchel, noticing as he did that the bottom was a hard leather that kept the shape of the circle, while loose cloth made up a nest to help keep the egg warm.

With no more distractions, Edwin now had to approach King Clayus. Edwin took a deep breath and turned, starting to gradually get closer until he heard a voice behind him, “May I have your name?”

Whipping his head to face the owner of the gentle voice, Edwin saw that it belonged to a young girl, the same young girl who sat next to the king, the princess. Edwin froze, staring at her smile, his ears reddening, butterflies fluttering in his stomach, making him fear he was going to heave the water he’d managed to keep down. She was way more gorgeous up close. Her dress was white with thin straps that exposed her shoulders, with sleeves covering her elbows to her wrists. Her dress’s skirt was flowy and loose. Her waist had a gold divider of vines, and the clips that connected the dress were golden leaves as well. She turned her body as she waited patiently for Edwin to recollect himself, her brows slightly furrowed with amusement.

“Edwin,” he forced out.

“So, you’re the boy who got the Empress’s egg instead of my little brother.”

“Sorry, a didnae mean any harm, trust me it wis no ma intention.” The shock of her beauty was wearing off.

“You don’t need to apologize,” she said, looking down and then back up. “Even if it’s alarming, Terro’s ego was getting too big for him. Besides, the dragon chooses the knight, not the other way around.”

Edwin wondered if he was mishearing her tone when he detected some worry and confusion intertwined with it. She pushed whatever was revealed in her voice away, brushing a loose strand of hair behind her ears. “I’m Princess Circe, by the way.”

“Princess…” Edwin tried to mimic her accent, yet it didn’t sound too good. He rolled and tapped the “R” in her name.

She smiled widely, her eyes just as bright as her lips. She tried to reserve her amusement in the way he spoke her name, which made Edwin shift his weight as he felt as though a crowd was going to start laughing at him. "It is a little difficult to pronounce; I think I like the way you said it though. You can just refer to me as Circe." She winked, and Edwin's heart almost stopped.

"Are ye a Dragon Knight?" Edwin bit his inner cheek, thinking how stupid that question was. Of course, she wasn't. She was a princess, not a knight.

"I am," she said, nodding.

"You have a dragon?!"

Edwin didn't mean to sound so surprised, but he was. Imagining her with a dragon seemed weird to him. She pointed up to the second floor at a reddish-brown dragon staring at Edwin with intense eyes. "My Dragon's name is Rueben, and he's also one of the Empress's children, like my father's and now yours."

Guess a dragon was one of the best bodyguard a princess could have. There was no way anyone would touch her! This explained why the prince, Terro, was so upset that Edwin had gotten the egg instead.

"Do you have a chamber yet?" Princess Circe wondered.

Edwin shook his head. "A wis aboot to ask yer father aboot that. A wis too scared to ask, though."

"No worries, I'll help you find a place."

Chapter Nine

The Old Man In The Tower

Hiking up the stairs of one of the castle's many towers, Edwin followed the spiral staircase as the scrawny boy with baggy clothes and jet-black hair led the way. The princess had introduced him as Maro. Maro reluctantly agreed to allow Edwin to stay with him for, at the very least, a few nights and longer if his father would permit it. Maro seemed like a kind boy. As Princess Circe talked with him, he was very shy and awkward, stammering over his words, some barely audible, yet the Princess didn't seem to mind. Edwin didn't blame him. He had a hard time finding words with her as well.

Finally, the boys, with satchels across their chests, reached the top. There was a heavy wooden door with a carving of a dragon rearing up on it and sword marks on the door as though someone was trying to cut out or scratch out the dragon character. Maro halted, holding the doorknob. "B-before you come in, you have to know my father isn't well—he's mad and can come off too strong. He doesn't mean what he says most times, so please don't repeat anything, especially to the king!"

Edwin blinked. He looked back down the steps, then returned to the boy. "Dae no worry, a wudna repeat anythin'."

Maro exhaled unsteadily in an attempt to prepare himself. Putting the key in the lock, he wasn't surprised to find it already unlocked as he turned the knob, opening it. Edwin followed him into the room.

The tower room was set up like a small cottage. The interior structure was square except for the ceiling, which was arched stone supported by beams that all led to the middle with one pillar implanted into the stone floor. It had a large window that took up almost half the wall and appeared to be boarded up. There was a small fireplace with a large pot hanging over it, a chain hung down from the ceiling above it, with a wooden trap door that acted like a sunroof for ventilation against smoke. There was a small table with two chairs, while pots, pans, utensils, and other kitchen and dining tools were shelved next to a wooden tub. Down a step was a section that had a small bed and a wardrobe. The bed was placed so close to the wall that the individual sleeping there might hit their head on the ceiling because of the incline of the arch. Behind the makeshift kitchen was a door that more than likely led to a back room.

"Father, I'm home!" Maro shuts the door behind them.

"Who is that?!"

A scruffy man limped from the table toward his son with a scowl. He was skinny with sunken cheeks and eyes, almost looking sickly or as though he'd never eaten a meal in his life. His hair was balding, and what did remain was graying, not from age but seemingly from stress. His own clothes were baggy on his body, and the seamstresses were probably only able to go so thin with their designs. The man's cheekbone, jawline, chin, and eye shape all indicated that at one point in time, he had been handsome. "Who is this?!"

"This is Edwin," Maro introduced, stepping in front of his guest, putting a barrier between Edwin and his father. "He will be staying with us until new arrangements are made."

Maro's father shot Edwin a dirty look with one eye lazy. "He's a Dragon Knight, too?"

"Yes."

Maro's father suddenly ripped the satchel away from his son and reached into it, pulling out a dragon egg with a burnt umber shell. Maro reached for it in reflex, then held himself to stop the natural reaction, staring in fear of what his father might do. Edwin tensed, holding his satchel away from the madman. He was certain the Dragon Empress wouldn't like him anymore if he got her egg broken the first night having it. Wearing heavy leather gloves, the scruffy man held the egg up in the light. An undeveloped dragon embryo was tangible as the shell became transparent. It was moving with its heart beating and veins connecting all around it.

"I can't believe they let you have one!" Maro's father tossed the egg back to his son and then placed the satchel on the table. "Where are you from, boy? I've never seen you before."

The crazed man grabbed Edwin's shoulder, looking intently at his face as though trying to recognize something.

"Am..."

Playing with his lips, Edwin wondered if he should tell Maro's father or not. In his condition, would it be fine or dangerous if he knew? Edwin tried to look to Maro for approval. However, the man caught on and gripped Edwin, shaking him to focus. "Don't look at him, look at me!"

"A hail from Gorish!" Edwin yelled, not liking to be shaken.

"A Goreon, you say." Releasing the boy, Maro's father grabbed his chin with a hand. "I wish I lived there. You don't have to deal with these stupid monsters! Not to mention the foolish kings and people who believe they're anything more!"

"Ye dinnae like the dragons?" Edwin's eyes were wide in disbelief.

Oh, he had a traitor's tongue. Did the king know of this, or had Maro been keeping it under wraps? Why would the king have someone like this living in the palace?

"Why would I?! They're untrustworthy beasts that deserve to be put down! Don't trust a dragon. All they do is lie, steal, and do things to satisfy their own needs! Do you trust the dragons?!"

Edwin didn't know what to respond with. He wasn't sure. The Empress was keeping knowledge from him. He knew that for certain. The dragons could rip him apart in a blink, and his entire life he was taught that they were nothing more than unpredictable savage beasts. "No yet?"

"That's good! Never do unless you want to be killed!"

"Alright, Father." Maro stepped back between the boy from Gorish and his father. "It's late, and we had a long day."

"I hear you!" Maro's father nodded, walking away. "Sleep with one eye open, Edwin. And, Maro, sleep with your shirt on!"

"Yes, Father!" Maro said, getting flustered. However, his voice was less shaky while talking with his father. It even had a hint of anger and resentment behind it.

Edwin could only imagine what it would have been like being raised by someone like that, who talked ill about your king, your country. Maro had to have a mother who saw things differently.

"He's no sleepin' close to us, right?" Edwin whispered to Maro.

Maro gave a nervous smile to Edwin before leading the boy over to the bed in the arch's corner. "You can take my bed for the night."

Maro grabbed his satchel from the table and gently set it on the floor in a safe place, his egg on top of the leather bag. He walked over to the wardrobe.

"Where are ye gonnae sleep?" Edwin asked.

"On the floor," Maro answered, grabbing some blankets and starting to make a bed by laying them out on the stone ground.

"No, haud oan, ye sleep on yer bed!" Edwin insisted, setting his satchel down next to Maro's, his egg still inside.

"Oh no, please, you're my guest! It's fine. It's good for my back to sleep on something hard occasionally."

Edwin sucked in his lips, shifting weight between his feet. Honestly, he was too tired to argue. As his eyes got drowsy, he started to become too tired to feel bad about putting his host on the ground. Maro seemed determined as he grabbed two extra pillows and lay them down between the two boys' sleeping spots. He rested his egg on the pillow, wrapping it in towels. "I got one for yours, too!"

Taking his egg out of the satchel and wrapping it in cloth, Edwin placed it delicately on the pillow next to Maro's. He climbed into bed and watched as Maro lay on the stone and pulled the blanket over him, adjusting his back. Edwin had his mind made up that tomorrow he would switch places with his host, giving him back his bed. "Thank ye."

Edwin took off his shirt and shoes and lay down, pulling a wool blanket over him.

"Goodnight." Maro's voice was friendly.

"Night."

Edwin couldn't recall a moment when he was able to rest. It was a very eventful two days. Not even the dungeon allowed him to have peace of mind. Still, now he had questions and anxieties swarming in his head. Why was he given the Empress's egg? Why did she bring him here? Why was he the only one able to understand dragons? Was this his permanent home now? How would he get back? Did he want to go back? What should he name his dragon? He had a dragon! They gave him, someone from an enemy country, a dragon. He could go back home using his dragon. How long did it take for them to be rideable? Maybe he could get his father's sword back? A dragon was fine, but a sword? Now that was too far!

Edwin didn't realize when he fell asleep, though, once he did, it was heavy and dreamless.

Chapter Ten
Training

CLANG!

Edwin jolted awake, almost hitting his head on the stone ceiling. "It's bad enough you're a knight! Now they're stealing you from me!"

Edwin heard the familiar sound of Maro's father's voice as he yelled. A rude awakening from sleep to reassure the Goreon that this wasn't all just a bizarre dream. Looking to the kitchen, Maro stood with his hands gesturing for his father to be calm as his father threw a fit, and a pot of soup broth was drained from a knocked-over pot on the floor. "It's just for this morning, Father! I'll eat dinner with you, I promise."

Worried that the situation might escalate, Edwin sat up, putting his shirt and shoes on. He picked up the dragon egg entrusted to him and placed it back into the satchel, wearing the strap around his chest. Maro's egg was already gone, and as Edwin approached, he saw the satchel crossed on the scrawny boy.

"Whatever, fine. Fine!" His father turned his back to his son, throwing his arms up before folding them. "Go eat with that pig and his slop!"

"Are ye awrite?" Edwin asked Maro, not taking his weary eyes off the madman.

"Yeah, I'll be fine," Maro sighed. "Sorry to have woken you."

"Dinnae worry, a cannae sleep forever."

"Well, since you are up, I guess you can head down to the king's dining hall. All the recruits from our kingdom are having a special breakfast with him before our first day of training." Maro was bent down and started to clean up the pot mess.

Edwin remembered the teens at the table last night talking about training the following morning. Yet the breakfast with the king was a surprise. Would he be invited? Would he want to go? His mind wandered to Prince… what was his name? Terro, right! He imagined Prince Terro eyeing Edwin with a sharp fork in hand.

"Are ye no comin'?" Edwin asked, hoping to get more allies than enemies with him.

Even though he didn't know Maro that well yet, the boy had already shown great kindness. Yet perhaps he would be too timid in front of the crown.

"I…" he started, looking at his father with a downtrodden expression. His father was washing new vegetables for his breakfast. "I'll catch up with you later."

"Alright, though, where is the king's dinin' ha'?"

"It's on the second floor of the castle towards the back. It's the room with the largest doors on the floor. You can ask a servant to direct you if you get lost."

“A shedd be able to find it,” Edwin said with a nod.

“Good, I'll see you later.” Maro picked up the pot and set it back over the fireplace.

Edwin trotted to the door, only slowing down to glance back at the forlorn boy, not wanting Maro's father to see him leave. He exited the room and shut the door behind him softly.

Descending the stairs, Edwin made it to the bottom of the tower, where he began to look for every staircase he could find leading down. Thinking he was on the second level, he went around corners and down hallways, not able to find anything that matched Maro’s description. Turning back on his steps, he did manage to find another set of staircases, however. He descended and started searching the floor.

No luck, only more staircases.

Edwin took a shaky breath. It didn’t help that there weren’t any servants in sight either. Maybe he should go back to Maro? He hated thinking this way, but Maro's father gave him the creeps, so going back was an uncomfortable feeling. After a while spent descending stairs and marching down hallways and rounding corners, Edwin realized that he had gotten turned backwards. He didn’t even know how to get back to Maro’s tower. Just how many floors were in this castle?! Why did they need so much?! Did they have the entire island living with them?!

Finally, Edwin caught sight of a bustling manservant. His shoulders relaxed as he started to trot to meet him. The servant was carrying a stack of heavily folded tapestries. Edwin felt bad for wanting to stop him from his duties because he was able to tell by the man's face that the servant was straining with the mass. As much as the boy from Gorish felt bad, he was also desperate and didn’t want to miss out on the chance to get to his destination.

“Am sorry to interrupt ye, however, a wis wonderin’ if ye ken where King Clayus’s dinin’ ha’ is? A got a wee lost.” Edwin placed his hands under the mass and helped the man hold them up, which made him give a sign of relief. The servant had a sparse black beard to go with his hair. His outfit was well-kept for a servant, yet he wasn't in the palace colors like the staff last night.

The man glanced at the satchel against Edwin's hips. "You passed it," he began. "Go up a floor and go down the fourth corner, then turn down the hallway and it should be straight ahead."

"Thank ye." Edwin slowly gave the man back the entire weight before waving as he took his leave.

Edwin found the stairs, then headed up them and to the fourth corner as he was instructed. Down the fourth hall, he saw the large wooden doors that Maro described. He couldn't believe he had missed them. His footfalls started to become hesitant. What would the King think of him entering alone? Was he allowed to roam by himself or even at all? He didn't know how much King Clayus trusted him. But they had told him he was the Empress's ward, which had to mean something, right? He had an egg and was said to start dragon knight training, whatever that was. He had to find out more to know how to go about it or where it even was at.

Taking a deep breath of courage, Edwin trotted the rest of the way to the doors. Grabbing the ring, he pulled backwards using all of his weight opening the door. The wood was solid, making the entry heavier than he had anticipated.

Looking into the room, he saw a large, fancy, carved dining table with equally decorated chairs, a larger one at the head of the table where the king himself now sat eating as teenagers, whom Edwin recognized from the shore and the banquet last night, surrounded him. There were four of them already there; with he and Maro the total would be six. Terro and Skypris sat closest to the king on opposite ends. Richard and another girl from last night took the seats second down from the king, leaving only the farthest two from him available.

"There you are! For a moment, I thought you weren't coming. Is Maro with you?" King Clayus gave a welcoming smile, unlike his son, who gave an opposite expression in Edwin's direction.

"No, he said he wedd catch up," Edwin answered the king.

"Well, come in and eat before the food gets any colder!" King Clayus waved the boy in.

"Aye, yer majesty," Edwin bowed.

Edwin slowly approached the table. There was an array of all sorts of breakfast foods Edwin had only ever heard of. Fruit like oranges, apples, berries, and some others he didn't recognize. Boiled eggs, fried eggs, ham, sausages, and cheese. Many types of breads and buns and baked breakfast goods that Edwin had made many times in his life. Muffins, herb bread, cheesy bread, and honey cake.

He walked to the closest seat to him, which was on the opposite side where Skypris sat, hoping the boy between him and the young prince would be enough to shield his vision from Terro's scowls.

Clayus gestured a hand to the surrounding food. "I hope you had a good night's rest."

"A did, Maro is a very kind host." Edwin started reaching and grabbing the food he was unfamiliar with, eager to try something new, not caring at all if this was a trick to poison him or not. He would die happy.

"Old man Orff didn't give you a hard time, did he?" King Clayus chuckled, leaning on the table towards Edwin as he continued to peel a boiled egg.

Edwin had a guess who the king was referring to, yet he didn't want to assume, especially with a king. "Who?"

"Orff Paldrous! Maro's father."

"Oh… him." Edwin wondered about his relationship with Orff, knowing how the man talked about everyone. "No at aw."

Clayus gave a knowing nod as though he didn't believe Edwin's answer yet didn't care enough to press it. Edwin wanted to ask why he kept Orff in the castle or anywhere else other than the dungeon because of his traitor-like beliefs. He must know, or he wouldn't be so lenient.

"Why did you bring your dragon egg?" Terro barked, intruding on the boy's thoughts. "You don't need it for training!"

Looking around and glancing under the table, Edwin didn't see any satchels anywhere. A tightening warmth entered his chest. Did he do something wrong? Was he going to get into trouble for bringing the egg? "A-A didnae want to leave it behind."

He didn't want to tell them how he was worried Maro's father would smash it, then they would ask questions, and Edwin promised Maro he wouldn't tell.

"So you're going to get it smashed during training?"

"A-"

"Leave him be, Terro!" Skypris cut in, sending the prince a firm expression. "It's not like he's going to be holding it while training."

Was she allowed to talk like that to the prince?! With such a rough tone? Terro shot her a challenging look and said nothing.

"I see nothing wrong with it," King Clayus said, breaking the tension. "Your sister used to carry Rueden around with her all the time, even before she had a satchel ready, and she never even dirtied his shell. You forget the magic placed on the satchel is supposed to be impenetrable."

"Magic?!" Edwin's tongue lept without his permission.

King Clayus chuckled at the boy's excited tone. "Yes, the satchels are enchanted. As long as your dragon egg is in the bag, it cannot crack even if you drop it off the smallest tower of the castle." He bobbed his head from side to side. "The tallest tower, that might be a bit different."

"Whoa! That's powerful magic!" Edwin's mouth hung open in awe.

All the other teens at the table laughed, except for Terro as he shoved some bread in his mouth. "You're kidding, right?" Richard wiped a tear of laughter.

"It's some of the most basic magic," said the black-haired girl who sat next to Skypris.

Edwin felt his ears heat and he assumed his face was red. How was he supposed to know?! In Gorish, the only source of magic was the king's wizard, and nobody had seen him. He was thought to be just a rumor. Edwin sank in his chair, embarrassed at his own ignorance, hoping no one could see if his face was colored. The laughter died down, and Skypris managed to get his attention. "We're laughing because of your reaction."

Her smile was warm and comforting, though Edwin's heart would feel warm if any pretty girl smiled at him like that.

"Yes," King Clayus agreed. "I bet you weren't exposed to magic in Gorish."

Edwin shook his head simply. "No, yer majesty."

"That's fine. The more you're exposed, the more you learn."

"Are we going to try magic?"

"No. Only people who have it in their blood can properly use it. Like my sorceress, Latona. It is a rare feature in humans, like a unique eye color. Those who have this one-of-a-kind eye color then need to study for years before they can do anything with it."

Edwin thought about the old woman wearing the cloak down by the seashore when everyone was picking their eggs. She didn't seem like a powerful sorcereress.

"Who are our trainers?" Richard turned to his king. "Are you going to be training us because of Terro?"

Clayus wiped his hands with his napkin. "No, Louis will instruct you along with Demmis." He pointed at the group. "I might check up on you all now and again, so behave yourselves."

Edwin finally found the comfort to start eating the food off his plate, without him knowing he had started to stuff his face, even going for another round. He was eating so fast that he couldn't even taste the foreign food. In the back of his mind, he hoped that he didn't seem to be gorging himself. Despite him being the last to arrive, Edwin was the first to be done eating, which was probably a good thing, so he didn't end up heaving during training. Edwin wondered what training was going to be like.

Wait.

They were training him to be a knight, like Knight Lockwood. A hero.

Edwin thought about Knight Lockwood, the hero in the story he'd read. He started to get lost and happily distracted in his own thoughts and daydreams. He imagined himself in polished armor, branding his father's sword. He imagined facing down a dragon before he realized that didn't go with the evidence of his situation. He imagined saving a damsel in distress, her facial features resembling the princess he had met last night. Right now, she was the prettiest girl he had ever seen. He shook his head, thinking that was weird. His daydreams helped him pass the time because before he knew it, the teens had all finished and had been excused from the table. Edwin didn't want to get lost again, so he followed behind the other teens who were being led by Terro. As they passed through the halls, Edwin made sure to be extra observant so he remembered the path. It was hard, though, because everything in the castle looked similar. White polished stone, black rugs, pots, and tapestry. Edwin thought relying on the tapestry for recognition wasn't a good idea, just in case they rotated the decor. He decided to count the turns and the stairs they went down.

Down to the last level of the castle, they rounded many hallways until the teens found their way through an archway that led outside to a canopy of stone connecting one side of the castle to another, acting as a hallway. Vines crept up the pillars, and the few cracks in the stone sprouted grass and weeds. Edwin squinted his eyes to adjust to the new lighting as they stepped out from under the canopy into a large courtyard. The tile of the canopy continued covering half of the yard with a large pool fountain with a golden dragon statue roaring out water. Making up the other half of the courtyard was a lavish forest within the walls.

Two men were watching as they sat on the rim of the fountain's pool. One of the men seemed very young, not in his teens yet not entirely into adulthood either. In his early twenties would be a good guess? His face was very handsome with features people would think only a prince should have, and his eyes were light sea green. His hair was dark brown, thick and curly. The other man was much older, maybe fifties? He had short hair and a thick black beard that possessed strands of white making him resemble a badger. It was hard to tell his facial features with all his hair, yet he had a short nose and kind, lively eyes under his thick eyebrows. They both wore similar outfits with the same armor Edwin has seen other dragon riders wear. It was made of thick leather that only covered the wearer's shoulders, core, knees, and forearms. It was either made for agility or it was a poor design. All the king's knights in Gorish had metal and covered every inch of their body except for their face.

The teens all gathered in front of the men as they rose and took a few steps away from the fountain's rim. "Welcome, new prey!" The older bearded man rubbed his hands together. "I am Louis Archer, your trainer." He pointed to the young man. "And this is Demmis Flanke, my assistant."

Demmis gave a slow nod as his eye grazes the group as though he was trying to know them from appearance alone. He smiled impishly. "Despite Louis here calling you prey, you can rest easy knowing *I* at least will not hunt you down."

Edwin was trying to remember if he saw Demmis at the banquet last night but decided he hadn't seen him. However, he did recognize Louis. He had seen glimpses of the buff man talking with King Clayus. "Since we introduced ourselves, I see it only fitting for you all to do the same." Louis smiled, his eyes following. "Let's start with the prince then make our way down."

"Why do *I* need to introduce myself," Terro began. "Everyone knows who I am, and those who don't are fools and shouldn't belong here anyways." Terro's eyes went to Edwin, making sure he knew the last bit was for him.

Louis put his hand on his beard, making a puzzled expression. "Oh yes, you're Prince Snooty, right?"

Clapping a hand over his mouth, Edwin tried not to laugh as the rest of the group snickered. Terro folded his arms and with a pout, grumbled, "Terro."

"There you go! See, not that hard," Louis said, applauding the blond prince.

At first glance, Louis seemed intimidating, yet seeing him mess around Edwin, he began to feel more comfortable. "Next!" Louis pointed to Richard, who introduced himself.

"Richard Mob."

"Skypris Silviress."

"Fayette Mordune," the black-haired girl established.

"And you?" Louis pointed to Edwin who was last in the group.

Edwin glanced around looking for Maro; however, after not seeing his host, he looked back to his instructor. "Am Edwin."

"Well, Edwin, I heard rumors about you. I'm curious to see how well you do with training. If it's as fluent as your Dragon speaking, I bet your a master!"

"Far from it. A've only held a sword once in ma life."

"Really? With Gorish's culture? I don't believe you," Louis laughed. "Come on, show us what you got."

"Wit?" Edwin exclaimed after a moment of hesitation.

The man smiled brightly. "Demmis, could you hand me two wooden swords from the bunch?"

Demmis nodded with a smile and stepped to a pile of Wooden weapons next to the fountain. Edwin bit his tongue. When did he volunteer?! Did saying he held a sword only once mean he new how to fight in this kingdom? The boy from Gorish slouched his shoulders, and any trace of comfortability vanished as his heart started to race. He didn't want the others watching him. It was bad enough that they judged him for his accent; now they would surely criticize his swordsmanship.

Brilliant.

Edwin cursed his uncle under his breath. Cursed his kingdom. Cursed the Dragon Empress for bringing him here.

"Go set your egg down in the grass area." Louis grabbed a sword from Demmis and pointed with it.

It was hard to move because of the heat in his ears and the thought of everyone's eyes on him. With hesitation, the boy jogged over to the grass, took off his satchel, then returned to the instructors, taking the wooden sword that was offered to him. It was heavier than he expected, meaning this was going to hurt more than just his pride.

A lot more.

"Who wants to join him?" Louis asked, holding out the other sword to the group.

Skypris tried, yet Terro stepped faster with a hand up and a devious grin on his face. "I will."

"Perfect!" Louis said, tossing the prince the weapon.

Catching it one handed, Terro met Edwin halfway to where they had some elbow room away from the audience. Edwin knew—he just knew Terro would be the one to jump at the opportunity to humiliate him. To have an excuse to beat him senseless. The boys faced each other six feet apart and positioned themselves into a fighting stance, or at the very least what Edwin imagined to be one.

"I assume you boys know the basic rules with this; however, I'll remind you. The point is to get the weapon away from your enemy or until they yield. Don't go for the neck or head." Louis thought for a second. "Oh, and let's be mature, there are ladies present, so don't hit below the waist if you catch my drift."

Silence fell. Other than the heartbeat in Edwin's ear, it was almost deafening.

Edwin looked to the other teens then to his opponent, adjusting his stance to match his. Terro had a determined expression, one that was intimidating.

"Begin!" Louis cried.

As the word left the older man's mouth, Terro charged and swatted Edwin in the side, hard. Edwin stumbled backwards, preparing himself for the next blow. Terro wheeled his sword back then swung for the stomach, using the wooden weapon more like a club rather than a sword.

Edwin managed to deflect the strike. When Edwin tried to take a swing, Terro took the opening and pushed Edwin to the ground.

"Are you done?" he mocked.

Instead of bouncing back to action, Edwin just lay there winded and already sore. "A yield," he huffed, then spoke more clearly. "A yield!"

The reality that he had a lot to learn hit him as hard as the blow to his side.

Terro chuckled and removed the sword's tip from Edwin's face. "That was pathetic! I honestly expected you would put up a better fight." His pitch then went hushed. "You're not worthy to have the Empress's egg."

The watchers came forward, and Edwin waited to get up until Terro put more feet between them. "Good job!" Richard slugged Terro's shoulder in a playful manner.

Fayette joined in on the praising.

Edwin's side was hurt, yet his pride felt worse. A slap on the back made Edwin tense. "I guess you were right." Louis smiled reassuringly. "Don't feel so down, it's your first day. You'll have plenty of chances to get even."

That didn't reassure Edwin as much as he thought it should have; it was hard to lift his chin, so he left it hang. Skypris came up with a comforting smile that showed off her dimples. "It's okay, Edwin. He always beats me too, and I think you're even better than I am."

Edwin gave a fake smile. "Thank ye."

"How about you and I fight each other next?"

He blinked. The girls back in Gorish would never be caught dead doing something that was considered to be a man's job, let alone fighting and knighthood. They weren't really permitted to do any hunting or anything involving a weapon more than a butcher's knife and an axe for logs. It wasn't a law or anything, it was just how society worked. It seemed that wasn't the case here, so Edwin felt it would be best to keep his mouth shut on the topic. "I think that's a great idea!"

Thankfully, Louis intervened, raising his voice now to everyone. "Grab a partner and a sword! The two of you go find an area and practice with one another."

The teens followed their trainers' orders and headed to the side of the fountain. Just as they picked up their weapons, Maro came running out in the courtyard. "I'm here. I'm here!" he huffed.

"Where were you?" Demmis wondered.

"S-sorry, I had a hard time getting away from my father."

Noticing the satchel against Maro's hip, Edwin wondered if the scrawny boy didn't trust his father either. "Better late than never," Demmis said. "I won't punish you for being late. Go put your egg next to Edwin's on the grass and get a wooden sword and a partner."

Maro nodded and trotted off to drop off his satchel where the grass and the tile met, then joined in with the other teens. Soon everyone paired off: Maro and Richard, Terro and Fayette, Skypris and Edwin. They each started on their own time, going slow then picking up. Terro was going gentle for Fayette, which made Edwin narrow his brow. Maro wanted to go slower, which made Richard annoyed. Maro was having a hard time with the contact of the weapons; every time they clashed, he flinched.

"Stop it or I'll give you something to freak out about!" Richard growled.

"You want to practice or watch?"

Snapping out of his daze, he turned his head to Skypris whose sword rested on her shoulder with the other hand on her hip. "Sorry about Terro and how he treated you. He's a good person, he just has a bad temper when things don't go as he plans."

"Seems like a spoiled prince!" Edwin retorted.

Skypris closed her eyes. "Not the words I would use, however, yeah. He was worse when he was younger though."

"How dae ye two ken each other?"

"Childhood friends." She shrugged. "Our parents used to be really close. They were the queen's..." Her voice trailed off for a moment before she regained her focus. “That's enough chit-chat! Come on. The more you practice, the faster you can put Terro in his place.”

The sky began to take on the colors of a warm sunset. Edwin couldn't see the horizon from where he was, yet the sight he was able to see helped still his mind. Training took quite a while longer than expected despite the two-hour intermission for food and water. Instead of getting refreshments, the boy had fallen asleep next to his satchel. The grass had been warm and soft. The assistant trainer had explained to the teens that some training days would last longer than others. Today they really wanted to see where everyone was in their skills and stamina. After sparing with wooden swords, they were told to exercise to see their endurance, speed, and overall strength.

The last hour of training stretched in an aching way. Edwin knew he would be sore in the morning. He had to make sure Maro got the bed tonight so that his host didn't have a stiff back for training. Maybe it would be short tomorrow? Edwin always heard that stretching helped prevent any muscle tension. After the trainees were excused, Edwin was left behind on the rim of the fountain's pool, mist from the splashing water dampening the back of his shirt. The egg's satchel rested at his feet, leaned against the stone pool.

Demmis approached him once he returned from putting the wooden sword away. Now where that was, Edwin didn't exactly know. “You bored?”

Edwin watched the young teaching assistant sit next to him. “When I was being trained by Louis, I took off whenever I could. Even skipped a few classes,” Demmis continued. “He's getting softer in his old age.”

Edwin took his time to study the young man. “How auld are ye?”

“I'll be twenty-two in a few months. How about you?”

“Am fourteen.”

“That's lucky; you're the same age as our new recruits. Knights usually start training at fourteen.”

“Ye're a Dragon Knight, right?”

“One of the best,” he said, nodding with pride.

“Wit dae dragon knights dae?”

“Well, we serve the kingdom and our rulers. Standing up for and protecting the innocent is our job, which involves going to the front lines of war. However, when not at war, we are sent on missions to help keep peace in the land.”

“Are ye at war?” Edwin's voice cracked thinking of the other teens from distant kingdoms.

“No. All the kingdoms of Xolf and of Ishnia are allies.”

“Has this kingdom been at war with others?”

Demmis shook his head. “Only once on record. That was caused by a king generations ago. Those were some dark days for this land.”

“How bad wis it?”

“It was grave.”

Gulping, the young boy hoped to never have to fight in a war. His hands shook at the thought of taking someone's life, his stomach clenching. Besides, if he went on the battlefield with his current skills, he wouldn't last a second. “A guess a shedd grow familiar with the history af yer home.”

“That would be good. You should learn as much as you can about Xolf since you'll be staying for a while. It can really come in handy.” Demmis smiled.

Edwin's gaze went to his feet. He had a yearning for home—for familiarity. “A guess this is ma home now. A have no way to return to Gorish unless a dragon takes me, and a dinnae think the Dragon Empress will allow that.”

“Sorry, I know it can't be easy leaving it all behind. I'm sure this place will grow on you, and maybe someday you can return to Gorish. I personally don't know why you would want to go back, but that could be because I didn't grow up there.”

“A mainly miss ma aunt,” Edwin tried; however, he couldn't bring himself to miss his uncle. Maybe a little bit that he wasn't acknowledging.

A groan called the boys' attention to a saddled dragon as it landed on the courtyard's stone wall. The final beat of its wings pumped powerful winds into the forest. Edwin grabbed the rim of the fountain tightly, the loose fabric of his outfit getting dunked; however he didn't fret because it was only the tip.

The creature was a light green with a lime underbelly. Spikes went down its spine single file, with four barbs protruding from its tail. It had no horns on its head or face, but made up for it with a small bony frill. It was smaller than Clayus's dragon, Cerberus, yet larger than the floppy-eared dragon that was attacked in Gorish. Its eyes fell to Edwin. His emotions of eagerness and curiosity waved over him, and he was surprised to realize they weren't his.

Demmis stood. "Looks like it's time for me to go."

"Is he yer dragon?" Edwin stood staring.

The light lime dragon stretched off the wall and slithered through the forest to the tiled area, where Demmis met it.

"She," the dragon corrected through barred teeth that were then covered by its lips. The dragon's voice was feminine sounding.

"Sorry," Edwin replied, bending his head low.

"Did she say something?!" Demmis chimed in with a wide smile.

Edwin nodded.

Pulling himself up by the gullet of the saddle, Demmis swung his leg over and tucked his feet in the stirrups. "This is Gale. Gale this is Edwin."

"I know, the others are talking about him without end," Gale groaned.

"Did she say hi?" Demmis asked the translator.

"She told me that she's heard af me through the other dragons."

"Wow, I didn't realize you liked to gossip, Gale," Demmis said. "Anyways, I have to go. I'll see you tomorrow for training, Edwin."

Gale turned and walked back and climbed the wall, which for her took little to no effort. Edwin waved his goodbye, watching as the dragon flapped her wings once, then twice, before leaping off, continuing to pump her wings in the wind until she got her air. She then circled the courtyard with Demmis yelling down, "And if you want to study, I suggest the castle's library!"

Once Demmis and Gale could be seen no more, Edwin retrieved his satchel, having a little more pep in his step after discovering there was a library. He wished he wasn't so tired from training. He would love to see more than just one book, and the castle's library must be filled with all sorts of collections! Edwin headed inside, deciding that he would look for the library tomorrow.

Chapter Eleven
Skypris

The bright light of the morning sun filled the room. Annoyed by the disturbance of her slumber, Skypris rustled in bed, turning away from the window. She fluttered her eyes, her mind more awake than her body. She wet her lips, getting rid of any crust of drool left behind from last night. Sitting up, she raised her arms to stretch, grabbing an elbow to make sure her arm went the full extent. Walking to her dresser, she picked up a brush and raked through her hair, then continued to get herself ready for the day. She changed out of her nightgown and into something more comfortable for training. Usually, being the king's ward, she had multiple castle staff helping her prepare. However, she sent them all away and asked them not to return unless stated otherwise. She didn't want to risk any of them finding out about the condition of her dragon egg.

Her dragon egg.

Trotting over to her fireplace, she picked up a pile of what looked like dirty laundry at first glance, unravelling the clean clothes and revealing the blue-shelled egg. It was ice cold to the touch. With a frown, Skypris made her way to her sheets, her mind exhausted. She had tried everything except putting the egg in a lit fireplace. That was probably too hot, even for a fire dragon.

What should she do? The baby was sure to die if it hadn't already. What was she doing wrong? Hugging the egg to her chest, she placed it down on her bed and retrieved the warmest cloth she owned, and swaddled the egg, making sure no shell was exposed to air. The egg's temperature remained the same as when she had found it. Maybe she should ask for help. She knew Latona would know what to do. Skypris pushed that idea from her mind, knowing that seeking help would expose her. Kneeling, the girl came eye level with the egg, knitting her brows in worry. What if Latona told her that the Dragon inside was dead? That would mean she couldn't be a Dragon Knight, and she needed to be one!

Standing, Skypris clapped her cheeks, making them red as she tried to drown out all the negative feelings. Splashing the water that was in a porcelain bowl in her bathroom on her face, Skypris tied up her reddish-brown hair and headed out of her room. Strolling through the hallways and rounding corners, she descended stairs, giving the castle staff a "Good morning," or a "How are you," when they crossed paths.

On the final floor, taking a short staircase down, Skypris entered the palace's kitchen, bustling with cooks performing their tasks. Some worked on cleaning pots and dishes, others moved and sorted through ingredients, while others handled prepping the food the royal family would eat for the week. All the chefs and staff greeted her with warm smiles and "hello"s, as she walked their way.

"How are you doing this morning, Skypris?" an older man said, scrubbing a pot in a tub of water.

"A little sore, otherwise I'm doing well, thank you. I loved the appetizer you made for dinner last night, it was to die for!" Skrpris smiled, passing him.

"Aw, you flatter me." The old chef's face beamed.

Skypris walked behind a woman who was cutting and washing fruit. She looked worn, being in her fifties, and had a little heaviness to her body like a baker would. Her graying brown hair was tied into a bun, and her apron was covered in food stains. "Morning Skypris."

"Morning, Mary." Skypris scooted up and onto the clean side of the counter next to the fruit-slicing woman.

"Did you sleep well?" Mary continued to work, not taking a second to look at Skypris.

"Mmhm," the young girl wanted to open up to Mary and tell her about the issue she was having with her dragon egg. Skypris decided not to answer with words, not knowing if she would be able to fight those urges off.

Sliding down, Skypris walked to the right of Mary where a bunch of trays with food were lined up, side by side. Some of them were completed and others still needed some food. Skypris recognized them as the breakfast trays for the Royal family. "Which one's Terro's?"

"Oh no," Mary signed, now moving on to strawberries. "What did the prince do this time?"

"I don't know what you mean," Skypris said and held her chin up.

"Don't play innocent. You ask me which is his only so you can spit into it; you do so every time you are upset with him. Which seems to be often nowadays. So what did he do this time?"

"Nothing to me." Skypris walked in front of them all, trying to pick it out of the group. "He's being a jerk to someone new."

"You mean Edwin?"

"Yes, you heard about him?"

"Well, what rumors I hear around the castle. He's quite popular. He came down here this morning and got lost looking for the library."

Skypris lifted both her eyebrows. "Why would he be looking for the library?"

"Maybe to do some light reading before training," Mary guessed. Skypris walked back next to her slicing friend. "You should help him find it. That place is like your home within your home."

"I'm sure he found it by now," Skypris said and grabbed an apple from a basket of them and took a bite.

"Put that down! I just finished your breakfast dish!" Mary grabbed the apple away from the girl.

Skypris sucked in her lips and tried to hide a guilty smile as she swallowed the bite she took. "My bad."

"How was your first day of training? Was it hard?" Mary sighed, moving on to the next subject.

"Yes, though it was mostly tiring because we did so much in one day and I'm not used to that."

"Have faith. I find that you adjust to things faster than most." Mary cut up the apple and walked over to the breakfast trays, setting it down on a plate that Skype presumed was hers.

"I don't think they held back at all, even for a first day." Skypris found her way back to the trays.

"They are preparing you for battles. Missions aren't the safest, you know. I expect nothing less from their teachings." Mary returned to the counter and started to clean up.

"I guess if you put it that way, they are going easy on us." Skypris smiled before turning her gaze back to the dishes. "So which one's his?"

"The one left of yours."

Holding her ground, Skypris faced Maro with wooden swords at the ready. Training had begun in the courtyard only an hour ago, and so far, the trainers had instructed the teens to do the exercises they performed yesterday. Instead of sparring with her, Edwin was paired up with Fayette to Skypris's relief, making Terro and Richard a pair as they didn't hold their strikes back with each other, making loud echoing clashes of wood. Skypris turned her attention back to her partner, Maro, who shook with nerves. She flinched toward him, faking the boy out. In response, Maro swatted the air with his eyes closed. Skypris stepped back to avoid being hit, waiting until the boy settled. "Maro, you can't be afraid."

"I know." The boy slouched. "I just don't want to get hit."

Skypris understood the fear Maro had. She had it too when she was younger, especially after Terro had accidentally gotten her while playing. She had to push her fear away. Being scared would make her lose focus and eventually lead to her getting hit, and maybe not with a wooden sword. "You're going to get hit! In a real battle, if you get cut with a sword, you can die. That's why you need to learn how to prevent that from happening."

Downtrodden, Maro let the front of his sword hit the ground.

Skypris cocked her head and gave Maro a thoughtful look. "We're not at battle just yet, so you have time."

She stepped closer to Maro and held her sword up. "Let's just do some basic movement practice." She positioned her sword into a clashing pose. "Slow."

Maro nodded, holding his head up. The two teens then began to hit their swords together, steadily, so they made no noise as the wood connected. Skypris swung for Maro's stomach, yet the boy moved back effortlessly because of the slow motion. As Skypris took note of Maro getting comfortable with the weapons and poses, she picked up speed gradually with each attempt at the boy. Soon, they were sword-fighting at the normal speed everyone else was at. Maro didn't flinch or let his fear distract him. He held his own against her.

Skypris decided to push him. She made a strike for his chest—it was blocked. She then tried for his stomach, yet when he went to block, she deviated to his side, hitting him. Maro dropped his weapon in surprise. Skypris smiled at him. “That was amazing, Maro!”

“I lost,” his tone was simple and flat.

“Yes, but you were holding your own really well. You didn't flinch at all during it.”

Maro's frown grew to a wide smile as realization entered his mind. “You're right! I didn't!”

Skypris pushed Maro's shoulder in a friendly way. “With more practice, you could beat Terro.”

“Can you beat him?”

“Not yet,” she said, then defended her pride. “Only because he's physically stronger and has more stamina.”

“Alright!” Everyone looked to the Golden Fountain, where Louis stood waiting with Demmis, his assistant. “Get your rumps over here!” Louis waved.

The trainees finished their last few swings and then headed over to the instructors. “First off, I want to say you're all doing a fine job so far!” Louis started. “I see a lot of potential in each of you—some more than others, yet potential. Now, most of you are aware that the trainee competition is coming up.” This got Terro’s and Richard’s attention the most out of the group. “For those of you who aren’t aware, though, in four weeks you will participate in a tournament all trainers host to see how far you’ve come since starting your training. Each one of you will face the other and fight with a wooden weapon. The victor will move on to the next round until we have one champion from each year.”

All the trainees gave each other a glance as though having a silent conversation, then they turned their attention to their trainers. “Don’t worry, there’s a prize,” Demmis cut in, knowing what they were thinking. “The winner will get a week off from training.”

“This is awesome! I’m going to win for sure,” Richard mocked.

“Don’t bet on it!” Terro challenged.

A mellow noise erupted from the group of teens as banter rose up about the competition and how they might perform. Some were more confident than others, and those who weren't, like Maro, were getting encouragement from their peers.

Demmis clapped his hands to quiet the group. "The competition hasn't happened yet! You all still have four weeks to prepare and train."

"Which brings us back to the present," Louis said. "I want you all to take four laps. GO!"

The unit of trainees took off, everyone slowly pacing themselves into a jog as they moved around the rim of the courtyard where the stone and grass met.

Once she found her rhythm, Skypris kept a steady pace, not speeding up or slowing down like the others. She focused on her breathing, going in with her nose and then out with her mouth. Up ahead, Edwin was jogging with Maro as they decided on a speed together, Edwin going slightly faster. She watched him as she thought, *How could he understand dragons?* She didn't even know an ability like that could exist. Was he taught by dragons, though that wouldn't make sense because Latona couldn't understand them.

Terro jogged to her side, taking Skypris out of her head. He smiled, making sure his eye contact didn't stray from hers. Skypris smiled back, narrowing her brows playfully. Terro then picked up his pace, moving past her. Skypris loved Terro. He was her best friend. Sure, he was snooty and stubborn at times, but he had a good heart. As Terro passed Edwin, he bumped the unsuspecting boy's shoulder, giving him a dirty look. Skypris gave a disapproving stare, even though she knew Terro couldn't see her face anymore.

She understood he was upset, though she didn't understand why he was upset with Edwin. He had no control over what the Empress did. Terro should be mad at her, not Edwin.

After the fourth lap, Skypris caught up with the group as they all surrounded a table in the grass that was being shaded by the largest and closest tree in the landscape. The young girl grabbed one of the many mugs by a wooden water barrel. She drank the refreshing water slowly. Once rejuvenated, Skypris looked to her left to see Edwin isolated from the others as he leaned against a nearby tree, sipping on a mug. Her shoulders slumped as she observed; it couldn't have been easy being taken away from everything and everyone you knew, even if it was a place like Gorish. Edwin seemed like a nice person. It was hard to imagine him being from a land where their culture revolved around slaying dragons. Were all Goreons like him? Or was he different?

She approached him. "How are you this morning, Edwin?"

"Am fairing, a wee sore from yesterday though. Wit aboot ye?" He made sure to give Skypris all his attention.

"I'm pretty much the same. Did you ever find the library?" she questioned.

Edwin studied her, looking a little taken aback. "How did ye ken a wis looking for the library?"

"A little birdie told me. You're not the only one who can talk to another creature, you know?" she said with a wink.

Edwin chuckled, guessing that she must have heard it from one of the castle's servants. He remembered how the women in Gorish would exchange gossip to pass the time while they worked endlessly. He supposed gossip would forever be a universal thing, regardless of what land you were from.

"Did you find it?" Skypris wondered.

"A did actually. After an hour af roaming, A finally swallowed ma embarrassment and asked someone."

"That's good!" She leaned up against the tree next to him. "I usually go in the afternoons. Maybe I'll see you there."

Edwin's felt his face grow warm at her words and her proximity to him. She was so nice to him, and she was far above average looking. He prayed that his face wasn't red, or if it was, that she would assume it was from jogging. As embarrassing as it was, his side hurt, and his breathing was rough when he ran. He never had to run back at home.

Skypris was grateful for the little water break their instructors gave them, especially since they seemed to have stepped up their conditioning now that they understood where their trainees stood with skill and stamina. They did all sorts of exercises that Skypris had done, yet not to the consistent level or quantity they were asking. The routine consisted of push-ups, sit-ups, front planks, crutches, and pull-ups using the low tree branch of a nearby tree. Maro heaved, which allowed everyone to take a break. It was gross and kind of cruel, yet Skypris wished more of them would throw up so she would have more breaks. Now the exercises alone were no problem. However, Louis and Demmis were pushing each of them hard, not counting the action unless their form was perfect.

At least training didn't last as long as it had the day prior. After their conditioning, they took four more laps and were done. Her legs felt like they had no bones, and her arms were so sore it was hard to lift them higher than her chest. She approached the fountain with the other sweaty and tired teens. Everyone stood except for Maro, who sat on the ground and stretched out his legs, Fayette following. Louis sat on the rim with a jolly smile on his face. "Good job!" He shook a fist. "I really like you kids. Even when you're aching and worn, you still try hard and don't give in. I admire that!" Louis pointed to Demmis and chuckled. "Unlike his unit, who were all a pain! Glad I don't have to deal with them anymore."

The group looked to Demmis, who was standing by the instructor. The young man scratched his nose, his eyes looking away with embarrassment. "We weren't as bad as he leads on. I was the best of the bunch."

"That's a lie!" Louis directed his attention back to the teens. "Anyway, just keep it up, and you kids will truly be skilled Dragon Knights. Might even be better than me."

Fayette raised her hand after seeing an opportunity to speak. Once she got permission, she went on, "Are we going to exercise like this again tomorrow?"

"No. Lucky for you, we'll be focusing on self-defense instead. You must know how to defend yourself. It's not good to rely on your dragon to protect you. They are strong creatures. However, they have their limits. It's not fair if the partnership is one-sided." Louis stood and waved the kids off. "That's enough for today. Make sure to go to bed early tonight and stretch before bed and in the morning. With all this training, your body will start to weigh you down if it's not properly taken care of. Dismissed!"

Chapter Twelve
The Library

After taking a bath, Skypris changed into fresh everyday wear. Brushing through her damp hair, she sat on her bed next to the frozen egg. Setting her brush down, she took deep breaths, hyping herself up to feel the shell. It was going to be warm. Everything was going to be alright.

Uncovering the egg, the moment her fingers touched it, her heart stopped, hearing it in her head once it resumed beating.

The egg was still so cold.

The dragon instead was dead. There was no way a baby could survive that long in the cold. None of her dragon anatomy classes ever told her of some form of inner heating.

Skypris looked around her room as though she had misplaced something important. Spotting her eggs' satchel against the wall next to her door, she trotted over to grab it, then returned for the egg, sliding it carefully into the bag. She didn't know what to do, and moreover, she couldn't find the strength to execute the plans in her mind. If she told Clayus or anyone that the egg was dead, she couldn't be a Dragon Knight. However, if she didn't tell and the egg didn't hatch, then the results would be the same. She would just be unlucky. It happened once or twice, not as rare as not receiving an egg, yet it was possible eggs simply didn't hatch. Her stomach's acid was eating away at her heart as guilt consumed her. Yes, she was in denial. She knew she was; the issue though was that she was in denial of being in denial.

Skypris headed out of her room and took her leave down the halls of the enormous white castle that lit up like fresh fallen snow in the sunlight.

What could she do? Steal another egg?

That was wrong!

Skypris cursed herself for feeding such an evil thought.

After fighting with her conscience, the girl decided to come clean to the king when her egg didn't hatch. The king was like a father to her, so he should understand, right?

Lost in thought, Skypris hadn't realized she had made it to her target destination. Large wooden doors decorated in carved wooden vines and olive trees with a dragon rearing its head and roaring as its wings lifted it up into the air, allowing it to hold the sun in its claws, was carved in the center. Leaning all her weight against the doors, she pushed them open into an enormous, towering room filled with bookshelves upon bookshelves. The library had five floors with winding staircases, each level dedicated to a different theme or genre, yet most were dedicated to records of past Dragon Knights. Bookshelves reached all the way to the ceiling. A sunroof with a wooden door hung open, letting in natural light, perfect for reading. Tables and comfortable chairs and couches of fine material littered the spacious areas.

Skypris smiled at the sight as though this was the first time seeing it. She loved it here. When she wasn't with Terro, the library was where she spent her days.

People were scarce in the library, which didn't surprise Skypris during this time of day when everyone was busy executing chores or training. Usually in the late afternoon, a bunch of young kids would be in here to read about fun adventuring books, taking some home and bringing back others that they had borrowed previously.

Skypris noticed an older man waving at her, smiling brightly as he put away a stack of books back on the shelf. Crossing the room, Skypris waved back until she met him at the shelf. He was balding in the middle of his scalp with the remaining hair draping to his shoulders, his glasses rested on his long, sagging nose, and his eyes were filled with wisdom. He always ensured his white shirt with puffy sleeves and brown pants were clean and wrinkle-free.

"Hello, Skypirs, I haven't seen you in a few days. It's unlike you." The man's voice sounded energetic even though he was far older.

"Sorry, Kane, I got busy with training and such. I'm here now, and there's no time like the present, right?" Skypris replied.

Kane chuckled, setting a book on the shelf. "Good to see your love of reading hasn't died."

"I don't think that's possible." Skypris shook her head with eyes that showed complete disbelief.

"So you have proved. Well, I'll leave you to it, you know the rules. Your spot is how you left it."

Skypris headed up to the second floor, where she journeyed through the book aisles that doubled as the next floor's pillars. On the back wall was a deep loft with a bed made from pillows and blankets. Books were stacked or opened, and a particular book was open, the pages facing down, marking where she had left off in the story. Climbing up using a four-step ladder, she sat down, not being able to go any higher than a low kneel without touching the ceiling above. She picked up the book, continuing where she left off as she lay back, resting her head on one of the many pillows. Right now, she was in the middle of reading a Dragon Knight's journal, and she was reading about how the knight and his dragon were fighting a basilisk.

It was required that all Dragon Knights keep a journal and record their lives. She, too, had a journal, yet hadn't written in it as of this moment. It wasn't that she didn't have anything interesting to report. She could write a summary of her childhood and life before her training and knighthood. She could also write about Edwin and the oddity he is. She could talk about her egg. However, that was a horrible idea. What would happen if someone read her journal? It was better for her to wait and see if she was even going to be a Dragon Knight. Her stomach tensed, and her eyes burned from the salt of tears. Wiping her eyes, Skypris realized she had lost her place in the journal. Scanning the knight's handwriting, she found it again.

As time passed, Skypris was in the final chapter of the Dragon Knight journal. The Knight was in his forties, and his last entry was about him getting ready for a mission, which was to help a village fight off bandits. You would have thought the village's guard would be able to handle themselves, and they would have, though the band of bandits' members outnumbered them three to one. At the entry's conclusion, Skypris didn't recognize the handwriting as the original author. It was his wife's. He had managed to save the village. However, he never returned from that mission. His wife wrote a little bit about him and their relationship from her perspective. Skypris's heart dropped—fear and sadness washed over her as she took in the lines of the last sentence:

"I wish I could tell him how much I loved him one last time."

When a Dragon Knight died, their closest loved one finished off the knight's journal by recording how the owner perished. Skypris couldn't imagine losing anyone she loved again. It was just too painful to bear. She closed her eyes, pushing images of the royal family from her mind, them being the closest she had to a family. Sitting up, she set the journal down and picked up another, looking at the cover, which had the author's name engraved in gold. It was another Dragon Knight's journal, this one being thicker and greater in page number than the last she had read. This one probably had a full life. Setting it down, Skypris decided that she should look for a book that could help her with her dragon egg problem. If there was any knowledge that could help, the royal library would have a record of it.

Walking through the small maze of bookshelves, she searched the spines of the books. She took the ones out that caught her eye and looked the covers over. Nothing. Kane might know something that could help her, or at least where to start looking. It'd take her possibly months to find what she was looking for in all this documentation, and by then, it would be pointless. The egg would be long gone. Should she trust Kane, though? Kane was trustworthy. However, he might pressure her to tell the truth, which wasn't wrong, yet she didn't want to do that. She was too scared.

"So you're the boy I've heard so much about!"

Recognizing Kane's voice, she walked up to the railings and looked over. It was out of character for the librarian to have a tone so loud. At the entrance of the library, she saw that Edwin had been the cause of it. She held her breath, trying to eavesdrop on their conversation. She made her way down the stairs so her ears could reach them.

"Wow! You really are from Gorish!" Kane said in astonishment. "That accent is very strong, my friend."

"Am hopin' a can find information aboot Xolf," Edwin said with an unsure smile at the mention of his accent.

"Well, you are free to look around. If you need any help finding or translating anything, please don't hesitate to ask," Kane offered.

Skypris got their attention as she neared. "Skypris," Edwin greeted. "A wis no expectin' ye here."

"I told you we might see each other later, remember?" She chuckled.

"A must have forgotten," Edwin rubbed his neck, his face a little colored.

"Ah, yes. You two train together, correct?" Kane chimed in.

Skypris nodded. “We do.”

“How about you show him around instead? Help him find what he's after, I'm sure he'd prefer you over me anyway,” he said with a wink.

Nodding, Skypris grabbed onto Edwin's arm and pulled him along while Kane carried on with his responsibilities. “Come on. What are you exactly looking for?”

“Am lookin’ to read wit a can on some history af Xolf so am no entirely foreign. A wis thinkin’ aboot this kingdom’s wars,” Edwin explained.

“Not much of a history there. The Kingdom of Alena doesn't go to war.” She lifted an eyebrow. “Why do you want to start there?”

“Demmis brought it up. He said the same thin’ aboot Xolf and wars. It made me curious aboot the ones ye've had. He told me that one wis caused by a former king.”

Walking to a bookshelf on the first floor, Skypris reached up on her tippy toes and started to take out books, then place them back one by one after examining, “He must be talking about King Lupus the Third.”

Skypris pulled out a book and dusting it off, she read the cover: *The Dark Ages of Xolf.* She then handed it to Edwin.

“Thank ye.” He smiled.

“Are there any other books you are interested in? I'm sad to say the history of King Lupis isn't that specific and more of a brief summary,” Skypris questioned.

“How many books can a take?”

“As many as you want. Kane doesn't mind, but you have to return them in perfect condition.”

“A shuidnae take them to Maro's home than. Between us, his father seems… unstable.”

“Very,” she agreed. “I'm sure Clayus would give you one of the rooms in the castle if you're not comfortable staying there.”

“A dinnae want to be a bother.”

“It's no bother at all. They have so many empty rooms in this castle. An entire village could sleep here. You could probably get a room next to mine if you want to be close to someone you know," Skypris suggested.

"A think a like keepin' Maro company for now. Dae ye no live with yer family?" Edwin wondered.

Frown lines appeared on Skypris as she went quiet, staring at the boy, wondering how to reply. A familiar sharp pain struck her heart. Her throat was dry, and her eyes stung with threatening tears. She shivered a breath of composure. "No, I don't. They died when I was younger."

Edwin's eyes widened. "Am so sorry, a didnnae realize!"

"It's fine. I don't mind talking about them. Your question just caught me a little off guard."

She bit the inside of her cheek, driving away the thought of her parents, so she wouldn't be tempted to cry anymore.

"A lost ma father a wee years back." Edwin looked down, his face pained. "Ma uncle said he wis killed by a b-dragon."

Skypris's eyes connected with his when he lifted his gaze to meet hers. It was unusual for a dragon to just kill a human. If Edwin's father was killed by one, it must've had to have been in self-defense. It seemed logical because of their culture. It didn't seem appropriate in this situation to point that out, however. "I'm sorry, what about your mother?"

"A didnnae ken her, she died from childbirth. A wis raised by ma aunt and uncle, they are more like parents to me," he explained.

"Do you hate dragons because of what they did?"

"No, a probably shuid. Yet a see it like hating *aw* dogs for one killed chicken. Though a father is worse than a chicken."

"I'm sorry, Edwin."

"Am sorry for yer loss, too."

The two stood in silence for a moment. Skypris was the first to give a knowing smile. It was a horrible thing to have in common with someone, yet still, it was nice not to endure the emotions that came with it alone. She had hoped nobody would go through the pain of losing both their parents, let alone one. She was happy Edwin was able to still have family. “Have you tried to find out why you can talk to dragons yet?” She hoped the question would brighten up the atmosphere.

“No, no really. Dae ye ken if there is a book that could explain?”

“I'm unsure, though I think if somebody has found something like that, we would have already known about it by now. It's definitely worth mentioning.”

“Have ye read aw these books?” Edwin wondered.

Skypris smiled and closed her eyes. “Not me personally, though I'm sure somebody has. And someone could have overlooked a book, and that's the one that would give us the answers.”

“It's goin’ to take me forever to look through aw af these,” he exclaimed, scanning the books around him.

“Maybe it would go fast with a little help? We could meet back here every day after training and look.”

Edwin smiled at her. “If ye’re okay with givin’ me yer time.”

“It's not a problem. Who knows, it might be really fun, and we could discover something nobody else has,” Skypris said with a shrug.

“So, meet here tomorrow?”

“Same time.” Skypris nodded.

Chapter Thirteen
Fairy Tale

Yawning, Edwin's back made a satisfying pop as he stretched. For the past few weeks, he and Maro had been switching back and forth between sleeping on the cot and the floor. This arrangement seemed to be causing back pain for the two of them, yet they both agreed this coordination was fair.

Edwin sat at the table with Maro and Orff as the three ate breakfast in the father and son's tower. Even though the food wasn't anything fancy, it was still pretty good, far better than any food he had back at home, despite the times it was too salty. Orff would only ever make varieties of soups and stews, or at the very least, that's what Maro had explained to him, and the evidence supported the skinny boy's claim. Soup and stews were all Edwin had eaten with them.

The second week of training had just ended the day prior, and it was exhausting, so Edwin's endurance would have to be built up. Either that or he would break. Since the meeting with Skypris a week ago, they had been meeting at the library every day after training. The two scoured the books diligently, looking for an answer to Edwin's ability to understand dragons, while also taking the opportunity to read stories together. Quickly, Skypris realized that Edwin couldn't fully understand what he was reading, so in addition, she was also helping the boy to learn words he didn't know.

King Clayus had summoned Edwin earlier in the week, and even though he would pass the king in the hall on occasion, the request still ennerved him. The king asked how Edwin was settling into the culture and training. He had also asked if Edwin would like a room in the castle. However, the boy declined, saying he was happy where he was. Overall, the king seemed indifferent about him, as though he didn't know what to think or do with him. Edwin wondered if King Clayus had any resentment toward him for receiving the Empress's egg instead of his son. If he did, he hid it well. After apologizing for his neglect toward Edwin's needs, he had arranged for Edwin to learn about dragons and anything else the boy would need in order to live among the people of Xolf. He would be taught by the king's advisor, Latona. Their first lesson was scheduled for that afternoon after Latona finished her morning duties to the king. To finish up the meeting, Edwin had requested his father's sword back, which had yet to be renamed. The boy withheld frustration after the king denied him, saying, "This sword is a powerful weapon. I shall return it to you once you are capable of wielding such a blade."

It was his sword after all, and who was Clayus to say he wasn't worthy! A king, that's what. Yet on Gorish, he would have a sword at his age despite his status. Edwin had a hunch though that if he won the competition the trainers were hosting that the king would give him back his father's sword, so Edwin tried his best to put his anger away. He should get his father's sword back, hopefully, if he at least put on a good show; he didn't think he could win, though. With each training session, Edwin was getting better. However, so was Terro, and the prince always would beat him whenever they would duel; it was clear the blond boy with anger issues wasn't going to go easy on him. He might even take the opportunity to try and kill him, claiming it was an accident.

Edwin's thoughts circled back into the room. They didn't have training today because of the pouring rain, and he was grateful for that. He wanted—needed—a day off. Earlier, though, he saw other teens his age and older training in the rain on the backs of their barely large enough to ride dragons. He guessed he should enjoy the leniency while it lasted.

Edwin watched Orff gulp down the broth in his bowl with no regard for manners. Wiping his mouth, he looked at Edwin. "How's the soup, boy?"

"Ye outdid yersel, Orff. It tastes wonderful. Far greater than the palace food," Edwin exclaimed.

Living with the crazy man, Edwin had discovered all you had to do in order to get on his good side was to insult the royals and or dragons. "Maybe I should see if I could become a castle cook," Orff smiled with yellowing teeth.

"No!" Maro exclaimed as he slammed his hands on the table to make his point.

"It would be a good chance to get rid of the royal pain."

"Could ye poison Prince Terror or maybe give him food poisonin'?" Edwin chimed, taking a bite of his soup as Maro shot him an unamused glance for letting his grudge get the better of him.

"He would be the first to go!" Orff declared, raising a spoon.

Once Edwin had his fill after his third bowl, he excused himself from the table, placed his egg into its satchel, and headed toward the door, crossing the strap against his chest.

"You're going out?" Orff said, his expression unsure.

"Aye. Am gonnae read more aboot this place," Edwin explained, leaving out the part that he was trying to figure out why he was able to understand dragons. He didn't want Orff to know he could do it. He was too unpredictable.

Nodding, Orff gave a wave and returned to cleaning his bowl.

Closing the door behind him, Edwin was careful as he went down the water-covered steps, as water leaked from the stones above, hitting the steps and his nose on occasion. He made sure his feet's grip was sturdy before taking the next step so he didn't slip on the slick stone. After reaching the bottom safely, he took off running down the castle toward the library. The gray clouds made the castle's atmosphere different from its bright, cheery normal, and instead, it made it dark and gloomy, like how authors described dungeons in fairytales. He didn't like stormy weather. After he had completed his chores, he would always crawl up in his bed and read his storybooks repeatedly until the rains stopped. The only welcoming thing about storms now was that instead of training, he got to spend all morning with Skypris at the library.

Pushing open the library's decorative doors, Edwin walked in on a surprising scene as handfuls of servants ran up and down the stairs with empty and filled buckets. Edwin could feel the raindrops as he got under the sunroof.

The sunroof!

Edwin's heart lurched. It wasn't closed.

He climbed up the stairs until he came to the top floor where Kane was quickly removing book after book from its place on the shelf. "Edwin, my boy, you're here! Quickly, we require your assistance."

"Wit can a dae to help?"

"See the shelves over there?" The man pointed. "Take the books off, they are getting wet, hurry!"

"Why is the sunroof open?" Edwin trotted over to the shelf.

"The Dragon Knight who usually closes it during storms is on a mission. We sent someone not long before you showed up to find someone else to close it."

Edwin made a pile of wet books next to him. "Dae a take the books from the second shelf too?"

Edwin didn't hear Kane, guessing he had moved on from his location. "Yes!" Skypris's voice sounded as though she were on the floor under him. "Take down the first, second, and third!"

By the time the Dragon Knight had closed the sunroof, Edwin had cleared almost all the books on the floor with the help of some other castle servants. With the top floor being closest to the sunroof, it had gotten the most exposure to the rain. However, most of the fourth and third floors were cleared. Kane and a few more scribes were looking at the books that had potential water damage, and drying them off, they did their best to restore most words that had been smudged. Sadly though, there were a few older Dragon Knight journals that were lost to the weather.

Skypris and Edwin were sitting in the loft. With a book in her hand, Skypris closed it, having reached its end. "There's nothing in this one either." Her tone was regretful.

"It's awrite. A wis no expectin' to find anythin'." Edwin bowed his head, his finger saving his place in the book he was in.

"Thank you again for helping us with the books."

"Dinnae mention it. It wedd be awful if they aw got ruined. Am a wee sad aboot the ones we couldnnae save."

"Kane told me he could fix the ones that weren't too smudged."

"That's better than none."

Skypris smiled and gave a slight nod. She looked over at one of the books in a pile. Turning the cover over, she read out loud: "*The Tales of Knight Lockwood?* I thought we were supposed to be looking for an explanation for your ability to speak to dragons, not reading fairy tales?"

"Am, however, a like to escape from reality every once in a while, besides ye read aw those Dragon Knight journals and they are similar to this in a way," Edwin said, taking the book from her.

She smiled, amused at him. "Yes, but what happens in the journals really happened."

"How dae ye ken that the thin's in Knight Lockwood aren't real?"

"You're right, I don't know." She shrugged. "So I'm guessing they have the books in Gorish, too?"

"Aye, they are rare and expensive, as many books are though. No everyone can read either only those who can afford them. A got lucky with the one a have. A remember some words ma father taught me before he passed."

"How did you get it?"

"A found it oan the floor at a trading market. A wish a had more than just the one story, yet a couldnnae afford to get another. Am surprised by all the books this library has."

"A long time ago, a Dragon Knight, the prince, traveled around the world, collecting all the books he could find."

"A guess it's easier to dae so with a dragon."

"Oh yes." Skypris beamed. "I can't wait until I can ride mine."

"A can. A haven't had the best experiences when it comes to flyin' with dragons. A hate bein' carried by one," he explained with a nauseating look.

"Who knows, maybe you'll like *riding* one."

"That wedd be a nice change," he admitted with a forced smile.

"Why do you like the stories so much?" she wondered.

"Am unsure, a guess a fancy the parts of adventure and thinkin' there's more out there than being a simple baker. A wedd imagine masel in the story as the hero, Knight Lockwood. A even imagined the people around me to be a character in the legends too." Edwin chuckled. "It seems childish now that a think aboot it."

Resting her head on her arm, she stared into his eyes. "I don't think it's childish at all. I'll sometimes do that when I read, too. So if you were Lockwood, who was everybody else?"

"A guess ma aunt had been kind of like Avice since Lockwood didnnae actually have an aunt and she raised me like a wis her son. That wedd make ma uncle Benemann. A didnnae have many people in ma life so ma imagination was limited to just two characters."

"So no Merlin?" Skypris wondered.

"Merlin?"

"Yes, Lockwood's best friend? He's the squire that travels with him."

"So ye have read the books," Edwin said with a playful mocking smile.

Skypris grinned. "I like fairy tales too. So who would Merlin be?"

"A dinnae ken," Edwin shrugged. "A never had someone like that, a didnnae have any friends back in Gorish, and so a had none to help with ma *'adventures'*."

"What about me?"

"Ye?" Edwin tilted his head.

"Who do I remind you of?"

He thought for a moment before answering her. "Well, ye're too pretty to be a squire… maybe Eilonwy."

Skypris looked away, trying to hide the goofy smile on her face. "Good pick."

Chapter Fourteen
Dragon Traits

At the top of the tower, Edwin couldn't move his legs over the last step, so he grabbed them, one at a time, and let his arm lift them to the last step for him. He was panting almost as much as he was after his first training day. He had climbed the tower that was said to be Latona's, which is where they had made arrangements for him to have his lessons. Imagining needing to climb these steps every day, more than once, made him sick to his stomach and even more tired. Shaking off the workout, Edwin saw two wooden doors with a golden dragon carved into them, the same as the library's and Maro's door. He hesitated, pushing away the fear that maybe this wasn't her room, out of his mind as he knocked on the doors using the heavy metal ring. Soon he saw the door bob multiple times as though someone on the other side was hitting it. "Augh! They're stuck again!" he heard the advisor spit with annoyance, muffled by the doors.

"Here, let me help." Edwin pushed the doors to no avail. They were heavy and hard to budge, though after putting all his strength into it, he managed to push them open.

Entering into the room, the Goreon's jaw dropped. It was far bigger than Maro's home and a lot more cluttered. However, everything in the room appeared to have an importance. A spiral staircase led up to a second floor that was filled with tall shelves of scrolls and books, with a ladder to help reach the higher literature. The banister going down the stairs and the rim of the second floor was covered in vines and other beautiful, exotic plants that hung down. The first floor's walls were decorated with cabinets and shelving that hosted vials of ingredients. Plants grew in pots and covered her long wooden table, along with mixing tools. Over toward the window, a step down, was a large space occupied by a lime green floppy-eared dragon covered in herbs and bandages. Beyond the doctored creature was a red weighted curtain covering an entrance to what Edwin assumed was a balcony or landing platform. Edwin saw a bed that was hidden in the back of the room, and a small loveseat at the start of the unusual empty space.

Latona walked out of the doorway. "Come in, come in," she urged. "Please close the door behind you."

Edwin complied and walked into the room, heading toward the table where all the herbs and ingredients were being prepared. He wasn't able to identify them. However, he was able to tell that the older woman was making a light green paste from them as she mixed the herbs with oils and water. The injured dragon lifted its head as Latona came closer. When Edwin's eyes lingered on the green dragon, a rush of guilt dried his throat as he recognized it as the one Aland and Bramwell had attacked back in Gorish. Latona petted the large creature as she took the bandages off, taking the time to stroke the dragon's muzzle. Edwin noticed the dragon was tracking him like a predator with its prey. Fire-patterned eyes followed his every move.

Approaching the table, the old advisor picked up a marble mortar and began mixing and crushing plants using the pestle. She finished up by adding water, little by little as she stirred, forming a paste. "Don't be afraid," Latona doted. "You've been around dragons enough to know they won't touch you, even the wild ones."

Was he showing fear? The boy checked his posture and noticed his body language had been stiff. Well, it made sense, though. Why shouldn't he be afraid of the dragon?! What would it do once it realized he was a part of the group that tried to kill it? Take revenge? Self-defense? Laugh at him for being a coward and having his comrades fail? "Are ye a dragon healer?" The boy knew talking would help get his mind off his gruesome thoughts.

"In a way, I am."

"Can ye understand them, too?" Edwin hoped, even though he knew the answer based on others' reactions to him.

"I can read their body language and translate a little. However, it's nowhere close to being word-for-word like it is for you."

"Are ye the only one who can read their body language?"

"Yes and no. It's a lot more complex than a single word can convey. Dragon Knights have a special bond with each other, and you can feel each other's emotions. I am the only one who can understand *wild* dragons without having a bond with them. You'll learn more about the bonds of knights and their dragons in our lessons."

"How can ye understand them, and others cannae?" Edwin wondered, his interest being locked.

"Well, in short, I was raised by dragons." Latona bent and grabbed a bucket of water from under the table, along with some cloths. "At five years of age, a family of dragons took me in after my village was destroyed by drakes. Regretfully, I was the only survivor they could find. The family knew I had a magic lineage and helped me to understand and control my powers."

"Y-ye're a sorceress?!" Edwin was dumbfounded twice over.

"Yes. Keep up!" Latona exclaimed before finishing her story. "I was then discovered by the royal family of the Kingdom of Alena and have been the king's trusted advisor ever since."

"How auld are ye exactly?" Edwin wondered, taking note of her age and how the people of Gorish's life span was no longer than the late fifties.

She took the cleaning equipment to the injured dragon. "One hundred and fifty." She wrung the cloth after soaking it in the water.

Edwin went wide-eyed. "Seriously?"

"Yes," Latona barked, acting like she's been insulted. "Creatures of magic can live for a very long time. I feel I'll perish when I reach two hundred."

"That's extraordinary!" Edwin smiled widely.

"There are a lot of extraordinary things in this world. I am not one of them, I assure you."

"Why isnae there more people with magic?"

"Magic comes from a lineage of people who were given magic by the Dragon Empress of old. I am one of the last descendants of them," she explained before cleaning the old medicine from the dragon's scales. "All magic originates from the Dragon Empress, either a predecessor or the current."

"Is she regarded higher than the king?" Edwin remembered when he first arrived and how submissive King Clayus had been toward her.

"Higher than any king or queen."

Edwin watched as the sorceress cleaned the last of the wounds. His chest tightened and his throat dried, afraid to ask the next question that came to mind. "Wit daes King Clayus think af me? The meetin' we had was the first time since bein' here that he's paid attention to me. Terro hates me because a have the Empress's egg. Daes he hate me, too?"

Latona didn't answer. She completed cleaning the dragon and examining the worst of the wounds. "Can you bring the mortar to me and help apply the remedy to her wounds?"

No, Edwin wanted to say, finding it hard to move forward. He glanced at the dragon, which was staring at him until their eyes met, and it then closed its eyes reverently. He then looked back at Latona. The last thing he wanted to do was get close to a dragon who had almost died because of a tradition of his homeland. Latona waited patiently for him, long enough that he started to get anxious because he hadn't moved or responded yet. Edwin scanned the dragon again, still having its eyes closed. It was probably the most docile-looking predator he'd ever seen, and Latona did say it wouldn't touch him. He was the ward of the Dragon Empress. That had to mean something to the dragons, right?

Holding in a sigh, the boy from Gorish grabbed the bowl filled with paste and walked over to the sorceress, who took it from him with a smile. "Thank you. Just take a good amount on your fingers and apply it to the wounds that look infected. When you do this, make sure it's completely covered and it goes into the wound all the way."

Edwin scooped up some paste, rubbing it between his fingers. He felt the grainy texture. He went around the dragon, opposite to Latona, finding the deep wounds inflicted. The stench of rain and fresh-cut grass helped drown out the scent of infection. The dragon bowed its head for him to reach a deep cut on its neck, the skin around it inflamed, though Edwin saw no pus. Meaning it was draining well. As he put the paste on the dragon, it flinched with a whimper of pain.

Edwin swallowed a lump in his throat, hesitant to continue. He watched the dragon's face as tears streamed down its muzzle. "Am sorry." Compassion overcame him, and the words came out with a breath.

He should have stopped Bramwell and Aland. Wait? No! He should have… he should have…

Edwin tried not to linger on the dragon's face, finishing the task as fast as possible. Thoughts started to spin in his head. He shouldn't have any compassion for a dragon—a beast.

"Now this is how a real man does it!"

The memory of his father with the rabbit came to his mind. He could remember the rabbit's screams and the dads' cheering for their kids to beat the poor defensive animal. Yet the actions that stuck out most to him were his father's kindness toward something he would have usually hunted in the wild. Was he like his father? Did feeling remorse for this injured dragon make him a traitor to his country? He already was a traitor at heart.

"There is no need," a soft female voice soothed.

He froze and slowly looked to meet the dragon's open eyes as they rested on him with a kind expression. A wave of nerves passed over him. "Am sorry, a didnae mean to speak oot loud."

Lowering its scaled eyebrows, she gave a confused look. "You can hear me?"

"Every word."

Her eyes grew wide and her pupils dilated, making her appearance more innocent like a child filled with wonder. "I am Newla. What do the humans call you?"

"Hello, Newla, ma name is Edwin." The boy's interest was piqued. "A dinnae ken how or why a can understand dragons. Dae ye ken how this is possible?"

Her eyes danced all over Edwin, as though she was debating or trying to figure out exactly how much the boy knew, and how much she was able to tell him. "I do," she finally spoke after Edwin had completed dressing the wound. "It's one of our oldest stories."

He failed to hide his excitement. "Actually?! Tell me, please!"

"Most of my kind's stories are not shared with human ears. We prefer to keep them a secret from mankind so they do not become changed or corrupted. Does the Empress know of your gift?"

"Aye, she brought me here from Gorish because af it."

"You hail from Gorish?" Newla's tone was sharp.

Edwin did a hard gulp, cursing himself for getting lost in the conversation. "Aye," he squeaked.

The room went silent as the dragon studied him even more, looking for something she knew was on his body but could no longer find. Finally, she let her eyelids sag. "Has the Empress told you about the story behind your gifts?"

"No, she hasnae. A havae spoken to her since the day she brought me."

"Then I cannot share the legend with you if she has not."

"A wis afraid af that." Edwin looked down at the paste on his fingers before wiping it on his pants.

"Do not be upset, young Monarch. The Empress has her reasons for keeping things from you. You are still young, still growing. I believe when you are ready, she will give you the answers you seek."

Edwin lowered an eyebrow. "Why did ye call me Monarch?"

Newla looked at her claw and then back to Edwin's face.

"Let me guess," Edwin started. "Ye cannae tell me."

"I'm sorry, I must respect my Empress."

Edwin didn't say anything as he wandered back to the table. It was his abilities. The Empress was the one who took him from his home. Shouldn't he have the right to know? When would he be ready? A month? A year?

"Did she answer your questions?" Latona met Edwin at the table, putting the mortar on it.

"No. She willna tell me because the Empress hasnnae yet. She did mention it's a legend they have," he explained, taking off his satchel and setting it on the table. Huffing, he continued, "She called me 'Monarch.' Dae ye ken why she called me that?"

Latona closed her eyes and nodded her head, understanding his frustration. "Dragons are wise, mysterious creatures. Not even I know all their secrets."

"If they keep so many secrets from ye, then why trust them?!"

"Yes, they do keep secrets, yet with good reason. Everyone has their hidden secrets. Maybe to protect the ones they love. Maybe to forget the things they've done in the past. Or maybe to keep something from getting into the wrong hands."

The Goreon calmed his frustration with a deep, controlled breath, knowing that no matter how he asked or who he asked, he wouldn't get the answer from anyone other than the Dragon Empress herself.

"Monarch..."

That meant ruler. Could that be a connection as to why he got the Empress's egg instead of Terro? Edwin didn't like that thought. It made no sense, either. He was born from a hunter, raised by bakers, and there wasn't a drop of royal blood in his body. It had to be because of his abilities. Did they make him as royal as the monarch of this castle? Edwin tried to push the thoughts and anything to do with the word out of his head. There was no point in hurting his mind over something to which he couldn't figure out the answers.

"Now," Latona said as she went and searched through her books and scrolls, "let's get your lessons started."

Edwin took a seat at the table. However, he got up once the elder woman was close enough and pulled out a chair for her. "Ah, thank you."

She sat down, and Edwin helped push the seat in before returning to his own. Herbs and mixing tools were spread out on the table, and she pushed them all to the side to clear a space between her and Edwin.

"Now," the sorceress began, "tell me all you know about dragons."

Edwin blinked, rubbed the back of his neck, then, brushing his bangs back, he began, "Uh… they can fly, have predatory bodies, eat meat, have sharp teeth… and uh…"

Latona sat back in her chair, giving the boy a puzzled look. "They didn't teach you anything in Gorish? Not even the proper way to kill one?"

Edwin shook his head. "It wis against the law to aid us until after we showed our loyalty. A suppose they wanted to ken if we were worth the time or no."

Latona scoffed, "Takes 'loyal till the end' to another height, doesn't it? This is fine, just means more fun for us."

Grabbing one of the many scrolls, Latona untied the yarn and unrolled it, weighing each end down by fancy bricks that were designed for the very task. On the parchment was a dragon. It was a spiky one with a quill mane, horns, and spikes going down its back with a tail full of needles that would pierce your bone on impact. The chest scales were layered like a crocodile's, with a sharp end to each shingle, and the rest of the scales were smooth like that of a garden snake. There were writings and lines pointing to certain areas of the drawing, but Edwin couldn't read the writings from where he was. "I assume since you haven't shattered the Empress's egg yet that we don't need to go over how to properly take care of it," Latona observed.

"Maro told me wit he ken."

"Good!" Latona nodded her head. "He's a sweet boy."

Edwin was more interested in the drawing than the compliment about his friend. He felt excitement surge in his blood. Not only to learn about dragons, but to receive any education at all. Only nobles and the rich could afford to send their children to be taught, and he was getting private lessons! Edwin wondered if she could talk about magic, too. "Are ye gonnae teach me the different species af dragons?"

"Species? No." Latona shook her head. "Types? Yes."

"Wit's the difference?"

"There aren't different species of dragons. It's more like categories of them that each dragon's traits belong to." She thought for a moment to see if she was satisfied with the answer she gave. "Here."

Latona rolled out a few more scrolls, each of which had its own unique dragon on it. "There are many different dragon traits that, over time, we have categorized into these assortments. We have Ashtheir, also known as the furred dragon traits; Karoaress is the finned dragon traits; Kaprisairess is the feathered dragon traits; Zandorious is the quill dragon traits; and Brooktorous are the heavy armored dragon traits. They are traits just like human features. Some humans have a pointy nose, while others have a rounder nose. Here is an example!"

Latona got out her book and flipped to a certain page with a dragon on it, which had quills going down its back with feathered wings, a finned tail, and horns that protruded from its bottom jaw. "This is a dragon that has all the different traits, or for a better term, features," Latona finished. "Does this make sense?"

Edwin looked at the book, then the scrolls. The Ashtheir—or the furred dragon—had well…fur, almost covering its entire body. The other traits it had were a mamalistic ear, like a cow or a deer. Its tail's tip was covered in an enormous tuff of fur. On the top of its head was a crown of horns. Fur covered its shoulders and the base of its wings. It almost reminded him of how hairy his uncle was. Maybe he was a dragon! The boy chuckled at the thought before Edwin remembered Newla and how much she resembled an Ashtheir. The scales of the Ashtheir traits weren't anything too special. They were keeled, and he couldn't see the stomach scales because fur had covered them.

Karoaress—fin dragon—was long and fish-like. It had a large sail going down its neck to its hips, another one on its chest and stomach, jaw and under its tail, forearms, and legs. It even had a fish-like fin for an ear. The back flap of its wings went halfway down its tail, and its muzzle was long and thin like a crocodile. Its tail, which was thin and whip-like, was the longest of all other dragons. According to the scrolls, the two fins on its tail could flatten, turning the heavy bones at the end of each finger into a bludgeoning weapon that made a crack in the air exactly like a whip. Its scales were soft and patterned like a fish.

He skipped over Zandorious, already having read the majority of its description. The last thing he saw about it was that the quills could harden and soften based on the dragon's emotion. Neat.

Kaprisairess—feathered dragon traits—was the smallest of the dragon traits, and was covered in feathers. Its tail was shorter, and it had a beak-shaped nose and a crest on it. There weren't any horns in sight, yet instead a decor of large feathers. Its wings were the most striking of the traits. They had the typical skin yet were also covered in feathers, as though someone took a bird wing and a bat wing, threw them in a jar, and shook it. The second set of wings, located on the hips, was smaller.

And finally, the Brooktorous. It was stocky and had the largest wings. Its tail tip was bulky, looking almost like a mass weapon, and a pinecone decided to become a dragon tail. Edwin's bones ached just imagining getting hit with one. It had larger-scale plates over its nostrils, eyes, and where Edwin guessed the ear holes would be. Its most identifying trait was its horns being on its jaw instead of its head. They grew forward instead of back. Its scales looked more like armor a knight wore.

Edwin glanced back up to the elder woman. "Wit aboot Clayus's and the princess's dragon? From wit a mind they have all the traits of a…" He looked at the names on the different scrolls. "Brooktorous and Karoaress with nothing else mixed in."

"The Dragon Princes and Princess traits all do belong to a single category, so it is theorized that on the Dragons Island are fathers these traits belong to, and only the Empress can breed with them. However, we have no proof to back up this claim."

"Why? Has no human ever gone to the island?"

"Never in recorded history. I'm sure a few have, yet none have ever come forward about it. The Dragon Island is sacred to the Dragons. To bring in an outside species might be forbidden."

The young boy stopped to think about that, stalling by looking at the drawings on the parchment. Why did they trust creatures that kept so many secrets from them? That didn't think humans were worthy enough to set foot on the dragon's sacred ground. They thought humans to be their equal, didn't they? Then again, if the wrong human came to the island, things could take a turn for the worse for the dragons.

Edwin flipped the page as he read and examined. He pointed to a drawing of a dragon that had a bony frill on the back of its head like Gale. "Wit aboot that? A dinnae see that trait from any af the categories?"

“Yes!” Latona gestured back to the feathered dragon, pointing to its skull as it hosted the very same frill. “Many dragons can alter the traits as they mix them. That dragon’s skull is taking traits from Kaprisairess. It just doesn’t have any feathers or fur to cover up the frill, in addition to making it longer and wider.”

Edwin nodded, now looking at the dragon's basic anatomy.

“I will be lending this book and scrolls to you so you can study in your free time,” she assured. “We’ll get you caught up in no time! With me as your teacher, we’ll even make sure that you are past most kids your age with education.”

Edwin smiled at his teacher with a childlike wonder in his eyes. He liked the feeling of learning. He felt empowered by it, especially knowing that he would get more attention with it than any other kid in Gorish. It was starting to make him a little biased, making him favor dragons more than someone from his home country probably should.

As her teachings went on that day, she stopped after giving Edwin a lecture about the bone structure of dragons. The thing he found most interesting and terrifying was that in a dragon's skull, on their bottom jaw, was a hole for muscles to go through to make their bite force stronger.

After thinking it over, Edwin decided Maro’s tower probably wasn't the best place for scrolls and books about dragons, so he stashed them in the library in Skypris's loft.

Chapter Fifteen
Champion

Four weeks were finally up. Edwin and Marro made their way to the courtyard where they normally trained. They arrived early, and they were greeted by a crowd of excited people. Most of them were young and older teens in dragon knight armor. The adults who were gathered were mostly in civilian clothing. However, a few wearing armor could be seen in the crowd. Were they all here to watch the competition, or did he and Maro stumble into an event taking place prior? Edwin then spotted Louis talking with the father of a family, laughing at his own joke. The thought of asking him came to mind, yet Edwin didn't want to disrupt him. Demmis was also busy talking to some other teens who looked quite a bit older than Edwin, to the point where he questioned if they were still in training. Seeing them made Edwin wonder where the other knights in training trained with their instructors. There had to be different locations, but where? In the castle?

"I didn't realize the competition was a public event!" Marro shifted his weight. "I wish I had more time to train."

"Dae no worry, ye'll be fine," Edwin tried to comfort his friend.

"Should we find the others?" Maro questioned, starting to glance around.

"A guess so." Edwin shrugged, scanning the crowd.

He couldn't find Skypris anywhere, though he caught sight of Fayette and Richard. Edwin was looking for Terro's scowling face until he felt someone's hand on his shoulder.

"Are you Edwin?" a young, feminine voice wondered.

Turning, he saw that the voice belonged to a teenage girl. She had black, tight curly hair, deep eyes, and a dark complexion. She wore Dragon Knight armor with a pastel pink undershirt and short pants he would never find on a woman from Gorish.

"How did ye ken?" Edwin nods.

"Ken?"

"Know," Maro translated.

"I heard your accent while passing by," she explained. "Is it true you can understand dragons?"

A bunch of teens around the girl's age, who Edwin assumed were her friends, started to gather. Some seemed mature while others still needed to grow into their features. They all wore the armor Edwin had yet to receive for himself. Edwin realized he was slouching and adjusted his posture, glancing away, uncertain about the eyes on him. "Aye…"

"See, I told you it was true!"

"He could be telling a tale." A boy waved a hand.

"If he were, and the king found out, he would be executed!" another said.

With warmth spreading to his cheeks, Edwin felt offended by their disbelief. He tried not to get too mad since the concept seemed impossible, even to himself. "A could prove it to ye," Edwin told them bravely, his pride taking over. "After the competition, a can tell ye wit one af yer dragons is saying."

"That would be wonderful!" the dark-featured girl smiled. "I'm Civil."

"It's nice to meet ye," Edwin said, clasping hands.

The group finished introducing themselves, and Edwin found out that the training group was one year older than his. After talking, they decided that he would prove himself after the youngest trainees were done with their matches. The teens walked away, leaving Edwin alone. Maro had wandered off to talk with Louis, who Edwin found out recently was his uncle. Once more, Edwin scanned the crowd for any sign of Skypris, and still, he couldn't find her or that snot of a prince.

Terro sniffed, itching under his nose with his forefinger. He stood outside the king's council room, waiting with Skypris beside him. His father had business to take care of before the competition, though the young prince didn't know what, since the meeting was out of earshot.

Even if he could eavesdrop, the butterflies in Terro's stomach were too distracting, along with his shaking hands. He wanted to win—he had to! No future king should lose or show any form of weakness. Terro had already lost one birthright to Edwin. He wasn't about to lose his pride in a sword duel to that nobody. Terro shouldn't have been worried about Edwin. It was Richard whom he needed to worry about. The boy was bigger and stronger than the prince.

Interrupting his thoughts, he felt skin brush against his hand, and looking down, he saw that Skypris's hand was against his. Did she want to hold his hand? Terro moved it away, his cheeks getting warm.

"Don't do that." Terro's voice was low. "It's embarrassing."

"*'Embarrassing'?*" Skypris smiled. "You and I used to take baths together."

"When we were three!" Terro's face grew hotter.

"Sorry, I thought it might help settle your nerves."

"What nerves? I'm not anxious about the competition at all. It'll be an easy win for me!"

"Don't count me and the others out just yet. I've been practicing." She held her head high.

"So have I." His chin went up.

Skypris leaned closer, getting in his face. "So we have a challenge, I hear?"

He held his breath. She was so close. "Maybe," Terro finally breathed.

"Well, now I have to win."

"As if you can," Terro said, leaning closer to her face, their noses less than an inch away.

"Don't underestimate me, Terro."

The teens quickly got out of each other's faces when they heard a throat being cleared. Behind them, King Clayus stood staring, placing his hands reverently behind his back, an amused smile growing on his face. "Am I interrupting something?"

"What took so long? We were supposed to be in the courtyard over ten minutes ago?" Terro's tone was defensive.

"I had to give them a list of eligible Dragon Knights so they could select some to be on their squad for some missions," the king explained.

"Couldn't you have done it later? Or told Archesilaus to do it?"

"Don't worry, I told Louis that we were going to run late because of me. Come, let's not keep them any longer."

Luckily, because the council room was on the second level, the walk to the courtyard was shorter. They exited the canopied hallway onto the tile, everyone parting their way once they realized the king was walking behind them, the noise level dropping profusely. King Clayus stepped up to the fountain rim, Louis weaving through the crowd to his monarch. "Your Majesty!" He bowed with a smile. "It's about time you showed."

"A king's duty is never done." Clayus returned the man's expression.

"Well, you're here now, would you like to conduct or shall I?"

"You may do the honors. The more breaks from being in charge for me, the better."

Louis laughed before cupping his hands against his mouth. "Alright, folks! We're ready to start!"

It took a second. Nevertheless, everyone turned their attention over to the king, not caring that it wasn't he who was speaking. "Thank you all for coming to witness the trainee's progress. Thank you to their trainers for being willing to give their apprentices a day off of training. And thank you to King Clayus for blessing this event with his presence." Louis then decreed, "Now, please step off the tiled parts of the courtyard; that is going to be our arena."

Louis moved to the sides along with the multitude, King Clayus shadowing. Louis placed a hand on Terro's shoulder, bringing the boy to a halt. "Are you nervous?"

"Why should I be?" Terro replied.

"Because you might lose."

"I won't let that happen!"

"That's the spirit!" Louis gave the boy's shoulder a shake. "Take Skypris and find the others. Bring them to the center of the tile. Your group will be the first to start."

Terro nodded and did as instructed. Richard and Fayette were by themselves while Maro and Edwin were together. Terro approached the two of them. "We need to line up," he ordered.

"A-alright," Maro said, his fear shining through his cracking voice.

"Not you!" Terro blocked Edwin from walking forward, eyes narrowed. "You shouldn't even bother trying. Save yourself the embarrassment."

Edwin clenched his jaw. Terro could see the anger build in the Goreon's eyes. "Take yer own advice," he retorted.

"So, you can speak, and here I thought you were a mute. Turns out you're just too much of a coward to talk back."

"Am talking to ye now, are a no?"

Instead of responding, Terro held Edwin's hard gaze with his own. None of them backed down or walked away until they heard Skypris call to them from a distance, her tone sharp. "Boys, come on!"

Finally pulling their eyes from each other, they lined up with the rest of their training group, each boy on opposite sides of the line. Louis took a step forward, raising his voice once the crowd settled. "Starting the event off are our newest recruits! And I'm not biased, but I know you'll be impressed as I am with this group of kids. Out of all the youth I've had over the years, they've been the fastest at improving by far. I know today they won't let anyone down." Everyone applauded him as though he were the one fighting. He then turned his attention to his unit of greenies. "Now, kids, this is just for fun, so it's not the end of the kingdom if you lose. You're just starting your adventure, so trust me, you're days of losing have only begun. I will name off the matches in order. First off is Maro and Skypris, Second will be Richard and Fayette, then…"

Louis didn't need to finish for Terro to know who his opponent was. Terro and Edwin's eyes met with a hard gaze. A small grin grew on Terro's face. This was the opportunity Terro had been wanting. By beating Edwin, he would remind everyone of his place. He had already faced him once before, and the Gorish boy lost horribly. It was pathetic, really.

"Alright, second and third matches, please step off and make room for the first two fighters!"

The other teens ventured off the tile while Demmis handed Skypris and Maro wooden swords. Centering themselves, they took a fighting stance and waited patiently as Demmis raised his hand, slashing it down through the air as he yelled, "NOW!"

An anxiety-inducing silence filled the yard. Demmis trotted out of the swinging zone. Maro lunged for Skypris, who blocked his sword with hers. The movement drew Terro back to the present battle. Terro's grip tightened on his arms, and he watched unblinking, hoping his childhood friend didn't get hurt. She and Maro were evenly matched, so the fight could go either way. Terro thought Skypris was too stubborn to lose, though. She moved out of the way, letting the clashing of their swords end. Maro seized the opportunity to slash at her, aiming for her legs. Jumping high, she avoided contact. Terro smiled while everyone cheered. She was doing fantastically! They had to duel later after the event so he could personally see how far she'd come since their last encounter. Terro heard panting as someone came to a running stop by his side.

"I didn't miss anything, did I?" Circe tried catching her breath.

Terro ignored his sister, not wanting to miss a second of the match. Skypris swiped her sword at Maro repeatedly, forcing him to back up. Skypris was trying to get him off balance. He avoided every single one, only losing his footing once. Maro waited until Skypris left herself open. She drew back, and Maro saw the opportunity and took it. He jabbed his sword in a certain direction, and as she flinched to block, he changed its course, striking her in the side. She fell down from being pushed off balance. Maro held his sword out in front of her, sweat beating from his brow. The crowd of people clapped loudly, talking amongst themselves about the moves they thought were performed well.

"MATCH!" Demmis called over the voices of many.

Maro put the sword to his side and gave Skypris a hand up. "Tell me you didn't let me win." Maro gave a nervous smile.

"Nope, it's all you," she clarified. "You did an amazing job. How were you not nervous? I thought all the people would scare you?"

"Oh, I was terrified, yet I pretended it was only you and me, like when we would train."

"Looks like I need more training," Skypris chuckled.

"We're only just starting."

That was the last of what Terro heard. Finally acknowledging his sister, who was in her Dragon Knight armor with her hair tied in a ponytail, he told her, "They were the first match."

"Oh, good," she said and gave a sigh of relief.

Terro left his sister to go see Skypris. A crowd of young knights swarmed Maro, congratulating him on his victory. Skypris backed away, looking happy to see that the boy was getting attention.

"You did well!" Terro stood next to her.

Skypris tucked away some loose hair. "Thank you. Too bad I didn't win, though."

"Yeah, but you showed everyone not to get on your bad side," Terro assured her. "Do you want to hang out after the competition? Ever since training began, we haven't hung out as much."

She hesitated at his question, frowning her brow with an embarrassed smile. "I was planning on going to the library after this."

"You have been going there for the past four weeks. Can't you put the books down for a day?"

"I…" Skypris thought for a moment.

"Hey, Skypris!" Circe walked up to the two teens. "You did an amazing job! You're better than I was when I first started."

"Thank you." Skypris's smile returned. "I'm excited to watch you duel. I feel bad for anyone who has to go up against you."

"I don't know about that." Circe flushed. "I'm sure I'm no better than anyone else my age."

"I would think you would be," Terro said. "You are getting personally trained by Father."

"Yeah, but he's in a meeting and doing royal duties most of his time."

"Alright, next match!" Demmis called.

Those who came to praise the participants shuffled back to the grass, leaving only Fayette and Richard behind. Demmis walked up to them with the wooden swords he retrieved from the previous match pair.

Skypris and Terro stood next to one another, Circe to Terro's right. He wanted to hang out with Skypris. He was missing his best friend. However, he wouldn't make her do anything she didn't want to do. Glancing at Skypris's hand, Terro went to brush his skin against hers until she moved away, walking over towards Edwin and Maro.

"Now!" Dema's voice echoed across the yard.

Edwin watched the match, deeply invested in his peers' movements, until he heard a voice coming up next to him.

"Hey, Edwin." Skypris settled next to him.

"Hi, Skypris, sorry ye lost the match, ye did brilliantly!" Edwin praised.

Skypris shrugged. "If I won all the time, I wouldn't have room to improve. Besides, I only need to win the important fights."

"That's true," Maro agreed happily, sipping on his water-filled mug.

"Maro's coming to the library with us," Edwin added.

Biting the inside of her cheek, Skypris glanced back at Terro as he and Circe cheered on the current match. "Actually," she began, "I was thinking of skipping the library today."

"Why?" Edwin's disappointment was visible.

"I am going to hang out with Terro after the competition," dhe confessed.

Fayette's sword went flying in the corner of Skypris's eye as she turned her attention back to the battle with the two boys and the audience. The wood banged against the tile. Richard held his weapon out to Fayette's neck as Demmis yelled, "Match!"

As in Skypris and Maro's match, a bunch of the crowd cheered and congratulated the victor while encouraging the loser for their efforts. Everyone quickly ushered the two teens off the tile as they continued their applause.

Edwin felt sick to his stomach. It was his turn to fight.

"Want me to hold your satchel?" Skypris asked.

"Aye." Edwin slid it off, giving it to her, his thoughts distracted.

"Don't give up before the match even starts. Just do your best, it's all right if you lose."

"Thank ye, Skypris." Edwin walked over to Demmis, who was already with Terro as they stood in the center of the yard.

Taking the sword from Demmis, Edwin tightened his grip and took a fighting stance. Terro looked at him with a big smirk and tilted chin. Edwin wished he could beat him, or at the very least be more optimistic about it. Not letting Terro's confidence surpass. It would be good to give the snot prince a piece of his own attitude. "Now!" Demmis shouted, making Edwin jump.

Demmis bolted away faster than he did for the other teens, which didn't make Edwin feel any better. Terro lunged for Edwin once the assistant instructor was safe from harm. Edwin deflected his opponent's strike. Terro's sword clashed with Edwin's, and using all of his weight, the prince leaned on the weapons, hoping it would push the Goreon down. Edwin managed to duck away, almost tripping Terro. Edwin tried to take a swing at him, but Terro had recovered too fast. It was block after block with the boys' attempts to strike each other. Edwin backed up as Terro walked forward. Sweat rested on Edwin's brow. He was too focused on his opponent, and it was only then that he realized the rallying of the audience.

Feeling the rim of the fountain at his heel, Edwin quickly jumped up on the fountain's pool, balancing on its rim. He could hear Louis's distinct laughter of excitement, causing the crowd to venture nearer to the two boys as though they wanted to participate. Surely it couldn't be that exciting? Or was it the fact that an outsider was holding his own against one of their kingdom's princes? Terro followed Edwin up on the rim. Swinging the sword was a little harder to do since it would almost throw the charger's offense off balance as well as the defense. Leaping back to the tile, Edwin ran to get some distance between himself and the prince, only stopping and turning to block an oncoming hit. The boys began a constant blocking and swinging standoff. Edwin didn't know how much longer he could endure until he noticed Terro was starting to get as tired as him. Before Edwin could strategize his next move, Terro swiped for Edwin's legs, forcing him to stumble backwards, where the prince immediately slammed the pommel of the fake sword into Edwin, knocking the wind out of him. The match was over after wood touched Edwin, yet right as the pommel hit Edwin, Terro turned his sword around and used it like a bat and hit Edwin, who fell on his back. His stomach ached where he was delt the blow; how was that allowed?!

The chanting was replaced by surprised gasps that fell silent before the chanting resumed. Terro had the tip of his sword in Edwin's face. "That'll teach you to know your place, lowlife!" Terro panted, spitting on the ground, barely missing his defeated opponent.

"Match!"

Chapter Sixteen

The Clouds Are Gray

Walking away, Terro met up with the crowd who gathered around him to congratulate his victory, talking about the boys' talents and the veracity of the battle. Edwin's fists shook as he clenched them in frustration. "That was the best fight I've seen in a while!" a familiar voice praised.

Looking up, Demmis stood over him, offering a hand. Taking it, Demmis pulled the exhausted boy up. Edwin grabbed his stomach in pain, massaging it softly. "He really hit you hard," Demmis said uneasily.

"S-seriously." Edwin found it difficult to catch his breath. "How is… that no cheatin'?"

"It isn't, he was just playing unnecessarily rough. I think it was because he was threatened by you, so he played dirty because he couldn't think of anything fast enough."

"Ye actually think he saw *me* as a threat?" Edwin asked in disbelief.

Demmis nodded. "You too were equally skilled. He probably thought he wouldn't win unless he pulled a fast one."

Edwin stood up straight, the pain in his gut waning. It never occurred to him that they were equal. Even though Edwin didn't win, he at the very least put up a good fight, one that made the prince sweat. One that he wouldn't forget. Edwin smiled with a strange feeling warming his chest. The feeling of confidence. Edwin searched for Skypris in the crowd, expecting her to come and tell him he did good, yet instead saw her talking to Terro. She wasn't smiling, not even a pitiful one. Her face was neutral. He didn't understand why she was still friends with that jerk.

King Clayus and Circe approached Edwin. "That was a very impressive fight," he began. "You have a lot of potential. You will make a fine Dragon Knight one day."

"Thank ye, yer highness." Edwin gave a slight bow.

Edwin tried, but he found it hard to keep his eyes from wavering to Princess Circe. Her knight's armor wasn't as complementary to her figure as the dress she wore at the dinner, yet she suit it quite well, wearing a purple undershirt, fitted pants, and her brown hair tied in a ponytail with a blue silk ribbon. Her hands and fists were wrapped in white medical cloth with a little dried blood. Edwin wondered if she really trained like the rest of them. She was so beautiful! It was hard to imagine her in battle.

Thankfully, Maro came up to Edwin with a mug of water. "Here," he said handing it to his friend. "I thought you could use some water."

"Thank ye," Edwin said, taking the mug eagerly, gulping down its contents.

"Drink slowly or you're going to get sick," Demmis warned.

"Too late." Edwin revealed the empty mug. "Dinnae worry aboot me, a have a stron' stomach."

He claimed, recalling all the times he's been carried through the air by dragons, and although he got sick, he never lost his stomach. Edwin tried to envision how it would be to have a sensitive stomach and be a Dragon Knight.

"That explains why you didn't puke when Terro hit your gut." The King nodded knowingly. Edwin took a long stare at the King, who returned eye contact, his brows slightly lowering. "You have something on your mind?"

"Actually, a dae." Edwin shied after realizing the stare's intensity. "A wis wonderin' if a could have ma father's sword now? A ken a didnnae win, however, a would really appreciate it."

King Clayus rested his hand on the hilt of the sword at his side. It was then that Edwin recognized the red gem embedded in its pommel. It was with him this entire time? The King looked puzzled, then said, "To give you a sword is to give you a weapon. Can I trust you not to harm anyone with it? No dragons either?"

"If a wanted to hurt someone, a wedd have done so by now, ye've given me free range af the castle."

"That's true." He drummed his fingers on the hilt.

He looked to Demmis, who gave him a nod of encouragement. He then looked to his other side, where his daughter nodded also. "He is the Empress's ward," she reminded him.

The king looked back at the boy, heavily debating on what to do. Finally, he took off a second belt around his waist and held the sword out for Edwin to take. "Alright then, here you are."

Taking it, Edwin grew a wide smile. Holding the sword made him feel closer to his father. He imagined his father saying to him that he had earned it. "Thank ye."

"I wish I had a sword like that," Maro gawked.

"You will, in time, Maro. Once Knights learn how to handle a sword, the royal blacksmith makes them a custom sword." Clayus looked at the sky. "Well, I'll need to excuse myself, I must talk with my son before the next match." He excused himself before taking his leave.

"You did very well, Edwin," Circe said before following her father's lead, splitting off from him once she saw a group of trainees she seemed to know.

Demmis gestured with a hand to the sword. "May I see?"

Nodding, Edwin allowed the young assistant trainer to take the sword and unsheathe it. Demmis studied the sharp black blade. His eyes lingered on the handle, then he weighed and fairness of the sword. "Now this is some fine craftsmanship. Strong materials."

Edwin tilted his head toward Demmis's love for weaponry creation. "Ye seem to ken quite a bit."

"Well, when you come from a lineage of royal blacksmiths, you pick up some things here and there," Demmis said, sheathing the sword and handing it back to Edwin.

"That's stupendous!"

"It is what you make of it," Demmis said with a shrug.

"Haud oan, a thought only heirs af Dragon Knights could become them?" Edwin wondered, remembering what Latona had taught him during one of their lessons.

"My father's side was all blacksmiths, my mother's was all Dragon Knights," Demmis clarified.

"So ye chose to be a Dragon Knight over a smith?"

"I did. I felt that I could be more useful. I've always wanted to help people, and this way I can do just that."

Demmis heard someone loudly clearing his throat behind him. Looking, he saw Louis impatiently waiting for him to start the next match. Demmis excused himself from the teens and met up with the main trainer, making sure to retrieve the wooden swords on his way. Louis stood on the fountain and started to clap loudly, drawing everyone's attention near, his booming voice echoing, "Now I know the last fight has gotten all of us stirred. However, let us continue on with the competition! The next duels will be Maro and Richard, then whoever is victorious will face Terro. Everyone to the grass except for the competitors!"

Once again, everyone retreated to the grass, including Louis. Demmis stayed behind to ready Maro and Richard. Maro had handed his satchel to Edwin. "Good luck," Edwin had told his friends before moving with the crowd.

Skypris had found Edwin and stood next to him, returning his dragon egg satchel. Maro shook as he held his sword at the ready. Richard was a lot stronger than he was physically and much more skilled last Edwin had known. "Now!" Demmis cut through the air before walking off.

Immediately, the two boys lunged in unison. Swords clashed loudly. The fact that Maro had tried to attack first made Edwin's eyebrows go up. That was an unexpected move for a docile boy like him to make, which is what he was probably counting on to get some leverage.

Edwin's gaze was diverted from the battle and into the crowd that surrounded him. Marro's father was nowhere to be seen. Surely, he would have wanted to see his own sons duel? To at least support him? Edwin's shoulders slumped on behalf of his friend. He wondered how Maro felt about his father fighting him in anything except for staying home. To have his father not be proud of him for following in his mother's footsteps. Edwin then wondered if his aunt would be proud and if he would have earned the respect of his uncle. Or would he just say something like, *"At least ye lasted for ten seconds."* Edwin chuckled at the thought before an emotional dagger cut his heart. He wasn't ever going to see them again, was he?

Maro had Richard stumbling backwards, afraid. Edwin's eyes widened as the louder cheering drew his attention back to the cause. Skypris called out to Maro, being his loudest supporter. She looked to Edwin with a proud smile that frowned. "Are you okay?" she asked, her voice raised to be heard over the noise.

Why would she…

Edwin touched his eyes and found tears, his eyes being glassy from the thoughts of dread. "Aye, a wis just thinkin'."

"Want to talk about it?" She placed a hand on his back.

"It's just ma aunt and uncle, that's aw. It's fine, please dinnae worry."

Skypris seemed to have dropped the topic for now, turning her attention back to the match, clapping. Richard had disarmed Maro, waving the sword tip in his face, panting, "Match!" Demmis called.

The usual routine of congratulations took its course. Edwin and Skypris stayed by Maro's side after everyone had left it. Maro flinched in pain when Edwin clasped his shoulder. "Sorry, are ye okay?" Edwin removed his hand immediately.

Holding the sore muscle, Maro moved it around. "I am. Sorry, my shoulder's a little sore. Blocking his hits hurt."

"Well, ye did spectacular!"

Maro blushed with a shy smile. "Not as good as yours."

"At least ye made it to the next round." Edwin returned the compliment.

Skypris stepped in, hugging both the boys. "Stop that, you both did amazing!"

"Thanks, Skypris," Maro said, fighting the discomfort off. "I'm glad I'm improving."

"Dae ye want me to keep yer satchel?" Edwin wondered.

"No, I can take it. It's just the one shoulder. I'm sure it'll be fine by the time the competitions are done."

"Ye sure?"

Maro nodded. Taking off the satchel sling that was on the opposite shoulder to his own, Edwin handed it to its owner. Skypris looked over to see Richard and Louis talking with one another before Louis got up on the rim of the fountain to draw the masses' attention. "Alright! We will have a short break before the final duel for the recruits. After the victor has won, we will have a fifteen-minute intermission before the next year's up begin their duels! Please make sure to get some water and stay so you don't miss out."

Once Louis stopped, the noise level rose again. Edwin could see the group Civil was with, prepping and hyping each other up. Their trainer, a thicker-muscled woman with brown hair and a scarred neck, collected some of the older teens to follow her. As they were gone, Edwin took note of dragons flying and landing on the walls of the courtyard and the castle. Basically, any place they could roost that would give them a good spot to watch. They were smaller, about the size of a donkey or a large dog. Once the teens who followed their trainer returned, they carried some flat metal swords. Edwin was taken aback. Were they going to use real swords to duel? Edwin tapped Skypris on the shoulder to get her attention. "Skypris, those are no actual swords, are they?"

Skypris followed Edwin's pointed finger. She hesitated then looked back at her friend reassuringly. "Oh no, those are feder swords."

"Feder swords."

"You don't know much about weaponry, do you, Lord Gorish?" She smiled.

Edwin shook his head with a nervous smile. "Baker, mind ye?"

"It's a training sword with weight to it."

They watched as the older teens' trainer approached Louis, Demmis, and the King, talking amongst them, when another trainer arrived. "I hope the last training groups dragon's don't want to watch," Maro said regarding the wall-crawling dragons. "I don't know if the architecture could take all that weight."

Skypris chuckled, "The yard is looking a bit cramped, isn't it?"

Terro approached the red-brown-haired girl, smiling brightly. "Hey, Skypris, are you going to wish me luck?"

Edwin, being right next to the girl of Terro's interests, narrowed his eyes toward the prince. He wasn't exactly sure how to define his feelings—maybe it was jealousy or defensiveness—either way, he got miffed when Terro was close to her. Skypris smiled back at him and touched his arm. "Good luck, Terro. Please go easy, you don't need to go for the kill."

Terro glanced at Edwin darkly before responding to Skypris with a light look. "I won't be rough, I promise."

Louis then called for the final match of the first round to start. Clearing the tile, Terro stood facing Richard, both boys holding wooden swords at the ready as Demmis stood between them, arm raised.

Terro should have kept his eyes and mind on his opponent. However, he found himself glancing at the audience, where Edwin and Skypris stood next to one another, being *friendly* with each other. Terro's knuckles were white against the grip on his weapon. His stomach lurched as anger bubbled. Why was she being so nice to the Goreon? He was an enemy! He had stolen Terro's birthright.

Demmis slashed down in the air and gave the order. However, it was Richard's lunge that drew the young prince into the duel. Terro jumped back from Richard's swing. Richard swung his sword repeatedly, yet Terro had dodged each attempt. He was struggling to focus. He hated that Skypris was hanging around a lying thief! The prince got a rude awakening when Richard barely missed his wrist. Terro bolted to the fountain, allowing him to collect his bearings. Once his chaser caught up to him, Terro turned, and their swords clashed.

Both were holding firm with a determination to win, trying not to show signs of wear. Terro needed to act fast if he was going to win. Richard was physically stronger and wasn't shy about throwing his weight around. When they managed to break apart, Terro swatted at the challenger harder and faster, in hopes of overpowering him. Sweat beamed from his brow in the sunlight. He needed to end this now. Suddenly, Richard charged at him, but Terro blocked, taking a bit of a blow because of the force the boy showed. Terro thrust forward and threw the boy back using all his strength. While Richard caught his feet and tried to process what happened, Terro hit the boy's side, causing him to kneel where a wooden tip was held out to his throat. Terro smiled after catching his breath.

He'd won!

"Match!" Demmis declared.

Cheering broke out around Terro as a swarm enveloped him, congratulating the prince and comforting Richard, who, despite being beaten, showed a lot of ego because of making it to the final duel. Multiple people waited their turn to shake Terro's hand. King Clayus was the last to approach his son once the audience went on their way, being very verbal as they did. "Good job, Terro. You've improved drastically since the last time I saw you. Soon you'll have me shaking."

Terro smiled, his father's praise feeding his pride the most. "Better watch out!"

With a simple arch of his eyebrows, Terro's father's expression shifted from happy to concern. Leaning closer to his son, Clayus grabbed his shoulders and whispered, "You can't be so rough with your friends. This was a fun competition; you don't need to be so vicious. These kids are your allies, not enemies."

"I wasn't rough on Richard," Terro protested, pulling away.

"I wasn't referring to Richard." King Clayus bobbed his head past the crowd.

Following the gesture, Terro saw Edwin talking with Demmis and Maro. His eyes narrowed as he faced his father. "He's not my friend!" Terro snapped.

"Maybe not *'friend'* yet; at least he's proven to be a possible ally," the King explained reverently. "One day your life might fall into his hands, and trust me, son, you don't want to make enemies with a fellow Dragon Knight."

Tension consumed Terro's body as an irritation formed. How could he be friends or allies with someone who stole from him? Someone whose culture abhored his? "Aren't you upset with him after what happened?"

Terro's voice was raised so much that it turned a few heads for only a minute. Clayus closed his eyes. "No, I'm not upset with him, and neither should you be."

His cape dragged behind him as Terro's father took his leave to talk with Louis. After watching his father, Terro turned to the audience. His breathing returned to normal after the fight. However, when he found Edwin, the irregular breathing threatened to return. He never asked to have his birthright ripped away. "Are you ready to go?"

Whipping his head forward, he saw Skypris in front of him with a mug of water. She gave it to him with a kind smile. Putting it to his lips, he let it sit for a moment, the cool water helping to chill his temperament. A few swigs later, he looked at her and smiled. "I thought you'd forgotten about me."

"I wish! Too bad I have a good memory!" she exclaimed. "So what did you have in mind?"

"Don't you want to watch the rest of the contest?"

She shrugged. "It would be good for us to study the older trainees. Though if you see one sword fight, you've seen them all. I think I would rather spend my time with you."

Terro smiled brightened and he grabbed her wrist, leading her away from the crowd. "Come on. Let's play a game of chess."

"Edwin!"

Edwin turned when he heard his name. Civil was leading the group of older Dragon Knights to him. "Do you want to talk to my dragon now?"

Edwin blinked. It seemed there was more in their group than last time, maybe fourteen now? "Sheddnnae ye aw be gettin' ready for yer matches?"

"Nah, this is a lot more interesting," Civil said. The rest of the group nodded. "I'll call my dragon and we can do it here."

"With aw these people?"

"Shouln't be too much of a problem, unless you were lying about your ability," a boy said, folding his arms.

"Am no!" Edwin said firmly. "Call yer Dragon."

Civil nodded before locking eyes with a large dog-sized dragon walking across the top of the wall. "Kilo!"

The dragon stopped, crouched, then leaped into the air where it glided down to the yard. The group with Civil stepped back to make room for the landing as the dragon pumped their wings, creating wind to soften the drop. Black talons clicked on the tile as Kilo tucked their wings in and looked to Edwin, then to Civil. Kilo was a dull blue with a lighter underbelly. A darker streak went from their cheek down the sides of the neck all the way to the tip of the tail. Brown scruff fur decorated its spine. Patches of scales were missing from her skin. "This is Kilo," Civil said, introducing her. "Beautiful, isn't she?"

Edwin studied the young dragon with excitement in his eyes before a concern crossed his mind. "She's a bairn,"

"Pardon?" Civil seemed taken aback.

"Young." The accent felt weird coming off his tongue. "Can she even talk yet?"

"Guess you'll find out."

"Wit dae ye want me to ask her?"

"I'll go over to the corner and tell her something," she pointed to the other side of the sideless hallway. "Then we'll return and you'll ask her to repeat it."

Edwin nodded in understanding. Civil and her dragon led the way as the group shadowed them, Maro joining. He tried not to get too offended to see Maro needing proof of his ability, yet he would be curious too if the roles were reversed. Waiting, Edwin watched as the teens gathered in a circle, their backs completely hiding Civil and her dragon. Not long after their circle formed, it was dismantled and Civil led the group back over with her dragon, Maro came and stood by Edwin's side with a shy smile as though suspecting he might have insulted him. Edwin gave him a nod of reassurance.

"Go on, have a nice chat," Civil told Kilo.

As Kilo got closer, Edwin took a knee to her level. "Hiya Kilo. Am Edwin."

Kilo regarded him. "Can ye understand me?" Edwin asked, looking at her intelligent eyes.

"Of course she can!" Civil sounded offended.

"Sorry, she's just no sayin' anythin'."

"Maybe it's being you're delusional," a girl in the group suggested.

Edwin shook away the negative comment. He wasn't! He really heard every dragon he's talked to, or else why would the Dragon Empress bring him? "Please, Kilo, can ye talk with me?" Edwin quietly pleaded.

Blinking, Kilo narrowed her scaled brow. Edwin felt a wave of confusion. "What do you want me to say?" Kilo spoke, her voice sounding like a newly teen girl.

Edwin grinned widely, mainly out of relief. "Could ye tell me wit Civil told ye?"

Kilo's eyes widened, then she jumped up and down, and Edwin could feel her excitement, and he could tell Civil did too, as the girl's eyes grew with her dragon's. "You're the Monarch! The one everyone's talking about."

"Aye." Edwin's smile faltered after hearing that title again, knowing he shouldn't even bother to integrate the young dragon. "Could ye tell me wit Civil told ye?"

"Like what? She tells me everything?!"

"Ye see, am tryin' to prove to them a can understand dragons."

"So if that's the case, then I guess I'm supposed to tell you that *'The clouds are gray.'* Which doesn't make sense because it's a clear day!"

Edwin stroked the dog-sized dragon's head, and Kilo purred. Edwin's eyes went to the sky, taking note that she was right. It was a clear day. Once he looked up, everyone started to murmur, then hushed each other up, waiting intently for the verdict.

"She told me, *'The clouds are gray.'*" Edwin stood.

It was with that the teens allowed themselves to get noisily excited as awed faces and smiles crossed the group.

"So it's true!"

"That's amazing!"

"How is it possible?"

"It's unbelievable!"

Soon, the teens all turned to Edwin with questions, some Edwin even had for himself. *"Can you understand other creatures?"* and *"Is it in your family?"* are two new questions that stuck with him the most. The other questions were more like, *"Could you talk with my Dragon for me,"* or *"Can all people from Gorish do this?"*

Thankfully, the call for the next round of duels made the older training group back off and line up where Edwin's unit had been. Instead of Louis leading, it was the scarred-necked woman. Her voice was deep and intimidating. Edwin soon learned her name was Elena. The matches soon began, and they were intense. The metal Feder swords made a more deafening sound as they clashed compared to the wooden swords. Civil made it almost to the finals until another girl in her group managed to overpower her. The crowd was loud for the knights, yet no one held a candle to how loudly their dragons cheered. To everyone else, they were simply roaring and purring; however, Edwin heard their voices and felt their immense emotions. Some dragons even started dueling themselves because the emotions they felt reflected from their knights' dueling were so rich. Edwin would have to hold himself together and fight the urges to run around or punch something.

Once that level of trainees was over, they moved on to the next, and while the dog-sized dragons were gone, the horse-sized dragons came. Not all the walls could host them, so some found more creative means by chilling on the roof of the low parts of the castle. He found that the older dragons were more restrained with their emotions, so it was easy for Edwin not to let them dictate his.

When it was Circe's turn, Edwin's muscles tensed, and he glanced at the king, thinking how he could stand to let his daughter get hurt. Yet then, her match started, and as soon as the instructor gave the go, they were calling *"Match,"* as Circe took two steps and disarmed her opponent, tip of the sword in the face. The crowd and dragons were silent. King Clayus burst out laughing, breaking the tension, and everyone began applauding. Most of the matches she dueled in ended like that. She ended up being the champion. Edwin found it hard to swallow after so many times of his mouth hanging open in awe.

Chapter Seventeen
Terro

Staring at a two-inch-long crystal, Terro lay on a king-sized bed, lost in a trance as his fingers fidgeted with the precious stone that had been turned into a necklace by a simple black yarn. Sunlight shone through a crack between the two heavy red curtains, hitting one of Terro's eyes, yet he didn't mind.

He was lost in a memory of his mother and Skypris's mother walking along the beach as the childhood best friends played. Skypris's father was there too, though he kept his distance, standing guard with his dragon. As a small child, Terro was always scared of Skypris's father. Maybe it was because the man never seemed to smile, or perhaps it was paranoia, as Terro fancied his daughter.

On the beach, his mother, the former queen, wanted to show him something she claimed was beautiful. A rock. With a scrunched-up face, his younger self thought his mother to be odd, yet she had Skypris's mother's Dragon cut the rock, revealing beautiful crystals inside. Mining one, she gave one to Terro. That was the last thing his mother ever gave him before she died that night.

Terro, as a young boy, didn't understand what his mother was trying to teach him, and even now, he couldn't figure it out. Was it the basic *"inner beauty"* revelation? No, that didn't feel right.

A knock on the door broke the crystal's spell. The staff member's voice was muffled. "Sire, breakfast is served."

The morning staff who helped prepare him for the day had come and gone, leaving Terro in his training outfit as requested. Maybe he could skip breakfast? He didn't really want to leave his room, not because he was tired or lazy. It was just awkward to be around his father ever since the competition yesterday. King Clayus had criticized the prince as if he had done something bad. He hadn't done anything wrong, though! He treated Edwin how the Goreon deserved to be treated! Finally rising, his boots tapped the floor as he made his way over to a large, fancy pillow. On the pillow, he unwrapped his dragon egg to check on it. It was warm, shell strong and smooth, all signs of a healthy baby dragon. His egg was blue with sea green freckles. It was thinner and longer than others he had seen, which was a Kaprisairess trait.

He grabbed the satchel hanging on a peg on the wall closest to the dragon bed. Sticking the egg into the protective bag, he decided to bring it. A lot of the training teens had been doing so lately; with the babies getting so close to entering this world, they all need extra attention. He walked out of his rooms into the halls of the castle, beginning to make his way to breakfast.

The doors were wide open with a sentinel at each side who bowed as Terro passed into the room. Circe, his father, and his younger brother, Roman, were seated, halfway through their meal. Pulling out a chair, Terro sat in his assigned seat between his father and brother. His tray of food still had the cover on in hopes of keeping it warm until he arrived. Cerberus and Circe's Dragon, Rueben, were sitting behind the King's seat, where the flooring was no longer polished marble but instead a large flat, easy-to-clean stone. Cerberus worked on a cow-sized meat pile while Reuben had half that, each meal catering to the Dragon's size and age. Reuben was about the size of an average horse, while Cerberus was at the very least double.

"Nice of you to join us, sleepy princess," Circe teased, working on eating an apple slice.

"Hey, I fought almost constantly yesterday, so if I wanted a few extra minutes of rest, I think I deserved it," Terro defended.

A member of the castle staff approached Terro's spot and filled his goblet with water, then took off the breakfast's cover, exposing Terro's favorite foods. Two hard-boiled eggs, toast and butter, ham, and an orange. It wasn't until he had peeled one of his eggs that he noticed the seat next to Circe was empty. "Where's Skypris?"

After their round of the competition, Skypris and he had hung out for the remainder of the day. They played chess, Skypris winning, of course. She was always a better strategist. Once they had rested from the duels, they decided to find a place where they could fight each other. He had won that fight too, though Skypris had improved a lot since their last duel. It was a lot more fun to kick her butt now! They explored the woods around the castle, which made Terro realize that as they got older, they were starting to have fewer common interests. He would rather train, and she would rather keep to her books. Terro was grateful she would be a Dragon Knight, so they would always have that in common.

"I'm unsure," Circe informed. "She hasn't come in yet."

"Probably still trying to do her hair!" Roman mocked with a mouthful of meat.

"You know she doesn't care for that, Roman," King Clayus corrected, working on peeling a boiled egg. "She'll be here, she always shows up."

As if on cue, Skypris entered, running to her seat. "Hey! Sorry, I-yeah."

"Speak of the devil," Roman grumbled, only loud enough for Terro to hear.

She plopped down as Circe had an amused grin, trying not to look at the tardy girl. She often did that, run late for breakfast, which always puzzled Terro because he had realized she would wake up before him. She would get lost in reading and forget to keep track of time, hanging out with the palace cooks, and helping the castle staff. She liked to do stuff like that. After her parents died and she became his father's ward, she had the hardest time adjusting to being pampered.

The family continued to eat. Terro felt eyes on him, and looking up, for a moment, he saw Skypris staring with a mischievous grin before bowing her head to her food as though trying to hide her stare. "What?" Terro wondered with a mouth full of toast.

"Nothing, nothing." Skypris fought a smirk, starting to eat the multitude of fruit.

Feeling self-conscious, Terro wondered why she had done that. She would do so often, mainly always at breakfast. Was he really that much of a messy eater? Terro stopped for a moment. Surely it couldn't be because she was mad at him, then she wouldn't be smirking. Then it hit him, she was probably thinking about the time they'd spent together yesterday. When he thought about their bonding, a smile grew on his face.

"Are you happy you're getting a week off from training?" King Clayus started.

"It'll be nice. I'm going to get bored though," Terro replied.

"Not like training is any more exciting." Skypris shrugged. "We're going to be revised, and it'll be mainly review."

"At least it's something to do."

"Once your eggs hatch, you'll be doing the next part of training," King Clayus explained.

"Can I get my dragon?!" Roman wondered.

"Yes, when you're fourteen."

"But that's years away!" Roman complained. "I want one now! Can't you change the rules? You're King."

"It's not my law, it's the Empress's, and I fully agree with it."

"That's foolish!"

"Not really," Circe added. "To have a dragon is a huge responsibility. You don't only have your own life in your hands but anothers. It's not some game. A dragon isn't a toy. Be patient, your time will come."

"Maybe I could ask Latona to make me older with her magic!" Roman seemed like he hadn't heard a word from his sister.

"*Or* she could fix that brain of yours," she said, fluttering her eyelashes.

King Clayus leaned toward Terro. "I was wondering if you would like to shadow me during your week off? It would be a good opportunity for you to start gaining experience."

Terro smiled widely then tried to be reverent. "I think that would be reasonable, I am going to be King one day."

"Perfect! After breakfast, we have to prepare for—"

"Actually, Father," Terro interrupted, "I was going to finish out this week because there is only today left. Is that alright?"

"It is! We can begin our work next week." His father nodded approvingly.

"Wow, Terro, shadowing the king?" Skypris's tone was sly. "You're just too high class for me now. Guess this is goodbye."

"We were always too high class for you," Roman spat.

Ignoring his younger brother, Terro played the game. "I know, it's like I'm a different person. You should start calling me *'King Terro'* now."

Skypris laughed, "I don't even call you *'Prince Terro,'* so there's no way I'm calling you *'King'* even when you are."

"So much disrespect!" Terro acted melodramatically. "I should have you thrown in prison for that."

"You have to catch me first."

Dapping the napkin on her mouth, Circe stood with an amused smile. "I should take my leave. I'm going to go warm up with Reuben, I don't want my muscles to be too stiff from yesterday."

"That sounds good, sweetie," Clayus said, watching her. "I have some extra meetings today before I can come train you, so I asked Knight Bassil to take over your exercises until I can give you proper attention."

She curtsied to her father, which wasn't as proper in Dragon Knight armor as it would have been in a dress. Her undershirt used to be white, yet it was easy to tell she used it often with the graying coloration and the weariness of the garment, which made her trousers stand out as they were newer. Her hair was tied up in a braided bun today instead of the typical ponytail. The princess looked over to her dragon as he licked his lips. "Rueben, are you ready?"

Terro never took offense that his father personally trained Circe, mainly because he had promised he would do the same with Terro later on. Since Terro was the heir, his father wanted him to be humble, so he thought socializing and training with the others was the best method for Terro, just as he had done.

Reuben perked, then ripped off a final piece of meat from a carcass and joined his knight. The dragon was a rusted brown with a darker-colored underbelly. He had a crown of horns much like the Empress, and a three-finned spine.

"We should go, too." Terro stood and nodded to Skypris.

"Yes, I don't want to run extra laps for being late," she agreed.

The four walked out of the dining hall. Reuben fell behind as he stopped to toss the meat into his mouth, and bobbing his head, he swallowed the meat whole like a snake with a mouse. Soon, Terro and Skypris split from Circe and her Dragon, heading out of the shaded, sideless hallway and into the courtyard. Fayette, Louis, and Demmis stood by the fountain, waiting to start. "Get your rumps over here!" Louis waved them on.

When they approached, Louis looked exasperated, as though he had just seen a ghost. "Prince Terro? What are you doing here, or did you forget you had a week off from training?"

"I was planning on finishing this week out," Terro explained.

"Fair," Louis nodded. "We'll get started as soon—"

"Here!" Richard yelled through a biscuit halfway out of his mouth. "I'm here!"

The boy ran, only stopping in front of Louis, then grabbed the biscuit out before shoving the rest of it into his mouth and licking the butter off his fingers and wiping them on his pants. "Am I late?" He cleared crumbs from his throat.

"No, you're not," Louis said flatly.

Fayette had a disgusted expression towards Richard's eating behaviors, like a mother scolding her children with a glare.

"Today we're reviewing, right?" Skypris asked.

"Just for the first half. We both know how tired you all must be from yesterday, so we'll be giving a history lesson to give you all the chance to sleep," Demmis winked with a playful smile.

Louis scoffed, "Yeah. I really want to make sure you have the basics down before moving on."

It only took a few minutes for Edwin and Maro to show their faces. Terro glared at Edwin, who looked surprised to see him. His father's words yesterday rang in his ear.

"...proven to be a possible ally." How so?! He stole his birthright, and sure, the Empress chose Edwin. However, he could have denied her. Not to mention, he was from a land that *killed* dragons! That has got to ring some bells. Whatever the reason, Terro didn't trust him. Edwin had everyone else think that he could speak Dragon. That was impossible! Not even Latona, who was raised by dragons, knew their language. Skypris was smart, and she seemed to be fooled, too, which seemed to anger Terro the most.

"Ready?" Louis began once the teens gathered. "Before we started today, I want to let you know I'm proud of each of you. During the competition, you showed true potential—some more than others, yes; yet it was there. I admire the fire in you all. Feed that fire!"

"How many speeches does this guy have?" Richard whispered to Terro.

"Enough," Terro breathed in the same pitch.

"I want each of you to grab a wooden sword and spread out. Demmis and I will come around and talk with you about your matches and instruct you on how we think you can improve," Louis directed.

Grabbing a wooden sword, Terro found a spot close to the canopy hallway. Perhaps he should have skipped this session, after all. He won his training level matches, so he didn't have any skills he was lacking. Terro leaned on the sword and watched while Demmis and Louis made their rounds, talking with the other teens. Louis showed Skypris she needed to readjust her grip on the sword. At first, she seemed annoyed for receiving corrections for such a basic thing, yet she let go of pride and took the instructions, gaining a firmer grip on the handle and therefore more control.

A warm sensation covered Terro's cheeks as he watched her move through fighting stances. His heart stilled once she glanced his way, their eyes meeting. He blinked rapidly and turned away, rubbing his eye as though dirt had gotten into them. Glancing back, she returned her attention to Louis. Terro focused his eyes in the new direction his body faced, which brought him to see Edwin in a fighting stance, readjusting his grip. Terro's chest burned with a tight frustration.

"Louis! LOUIS!" A young man, around Demmis's age, in Dragon Knight armor, ran into the yard.

"What is it?" Louis met the man halfway, abandoning Skypris.

"The king wants to see you, it's urgent!"

Louis followed the knight without another word.

Demmis stood at the center between the hallway and the fountain. "Do you think everything's alright?" Fayette strolled up behind her instructor.

"I'm sure everything will be fine. They have dealt with emergencies before." Demmis then raised his voice to the rest of the group. "Continue practicing!"

Hesitantly, the trainees went on with their critiquing. Terro watched as Demmis looked to the sky, taking note of the dark gray clouds consuming the sun, suggesting a storm was coming.

Then the prince looked at Edwin, who slashed his sword through the air, making himself lose balance and stumble. Terro laughed to himself, shaking his head. The Goreon couldn't even keep his balance when he swung!

"Wit's so funny?!" Edwin's tone was sharp.

He'd heard him. Great. Terro was sure that he'd been subtle. It didn't matter! Why should he try to hide it? The boy was laughable. Terro's anger leveled when he met Edwin's now challenging gaze. "You," the prince said with an equally challenging tone.

Edwin lowered his practice weapon.

"I don't know why you even bother, you'll never improve," Terro added.

"If that's true then why didnae ye beat me within the first five seconds af our match yesterday. If ye didnae see me as a threat then why did ye cheat?"

"I didn't cheat! They said nothing about how hard I can hit."

"Ye ken a wis gonnae beat ye, so ye battle unhonorably and pushed me doon!"

"*'Unhonorably'*?! Me?! You're the one who stole my birthright! You're the one lying about talking to dragons."

"Am no lyin' to anyone! It wisnnae ma choice to be brought here by the Empress, and it's no ma fault she thought a wis worthier than ye!"

Terro's fist clenched. How dare he talk to him like that! As if he were lower than him! He was a prince!

"Ye are a high-strong, Eejit af a prince who's jealous that a got wit he could no have!" Edwin continued, anger building.

Terro's fists were turning white as he started to shake. Edwin drew closer.

"A haven't wronged ye! Didnae ye're mother teach ye—"

"Shut your mouth!" Terro snapped, stepping closer to Edwin. How dare he bring his mother into this!

"Make me!" Edwin's voice deepened with a challenging step.

Terro tossed aside his sword and tackled Edwin to the ground. The two boys fought. Each attempting to overpower the other, pinning them down. Yet all they could manage was to roll around. Standing, they lunged again, arms locked, trying to throw the other. They were so determined that they didn't notice the audience around them or that Demmis was telling them to stop.

"Get him, Terro!" Richard shouted.

"That's enough, you two!" The voice's owner was hard to pinpoint.

Pinning the boy from Gorish down, Terro had his knee on the boy's chest, arm raised to deal the first punch. Skypris came up behind and grabbed Terro's arm right as his elbow flew back, hitting her in the nose. Her cry of pain stopped the two boys in their tracks. Skypris was holding her nose with both hands, bending over, head between her legs. Demmis walked over to her, placing a hand on her back. "Skypris, are you okay?!"

She shook her head.

"Skypris, I'm so sorry!" Terro panicked as he hovered over her.

Edwin stood next to the prince with an equally horrified expression. Blood dripped from between Skypris's fingers. Demmis gave the boys a hard stare. "You two come with me while I take her to Latona! I obviously can't trust you to be unsupervised!"

Terro looked down in shame, hating himself for hurting Skypris. It was an accident! He was just so angry that he couldn't control it. "Can you walk to Latona's?" Demmis's voice was kinder as he talked with Skypris.

She nodded and stood up straight, not removing her hands, allowing Demmis to lead her as her eyes remained mostly closed. The four departed from the courtyard, the girl's hands now scarlet. No one spoke as they journeyed to and up the stairs until they reached Laton's highly decorated doors. It was Edwin who knocked.

Distracted, Latona opened the door, then, returning back to the floppy-eared dragon, she was about halfway before she turned to see Skypris. "What happened?!"

Immediately, she led Skypris to a chair with the help of Demmis. Voiced muffled, Skypris said, "It was an accident."

Demmis glared at Edwin and Terro in a scolding manner. "These two started fighting, and she got hurt trying to break them up!"

Whipping around at the boys, the sorceress had an equally rebuked gaze. "What in the known world were you boys thinking! Tell me what compelled the two of you to do such a savage thing!"

"Can ye help her?" Edwin said gently.

"I'll see." Turning back to the injured girl, Latona took Skypris's hands off her face, exposing her bleeding nose. "Let me see."

"It's fine," Skypris said with glassy eyes.

A knot had formed at the nose's arch, still bleeding like a bad bloody nose. Latona placed her hands carefully on the girl's jaw and moved her head to see the nose from all angles. "I believe your nose is broken," Latona diagnosed. "It's a good thing you brought her to me and not the palace's physician. There is nothing to worry about. It's an easy fix. This will only hurt for a moment."

Terro sighed with relief. If something serious happened to her, he wouldn't be able to live with himself, especially if it was his fault.

"I hope you two learned your lesson." Demmis turned to lecture Edwin and Terro. "You have to be careful, or you'll hurt more people you care about. Also, see if you can talk your way through problems instead of fighting. Understood?"

"Yes," Terro gloomed.

"Aye. Sorry." Edwin bowed his head.

Demmis then turned his attentions to Latona. "Do you have everything in hand?"

"Yes, thank you," Latona replied.

"How about you, Skypris?" Demmis questioned.

"I'm good."

Demmis bowed respectfully to the girls, then, with one last disapproving stare, he departed from the room, closing the door behind him.

Edwin approached Skypris. "Am so sorry ye got hurt because af our stupidity," he apologized.

"Don't worry about it, I should have been more careful," Skypris said, blood in her mouth.

Laton reached out to Skypris and softly touched her nose. "You might feel a quick pinch."

Tightly closing her eyes, the young girl braced herself as Latona whispered, using a word from a lost language. Suddenly, an audible crack alarmed Terro. "Ouch!" Skypris shrieked.

The blood from Skypris's nose had stopped dripping, and the knot faded. Latona retrieved a wet cloth and handed it to Skypris to clean her face. She got almost all of it off. However, because she couldn't see herself, some smudges of faint red remained. Taking the place Latona had left to attend to the green dragon, Terro asked, "Did it hurt?"

"Nope, it was the most pleasant feeling in the world." Skypris's sarcastic tone was cold as she handed the prince the damp cloth.

Terro took it and finished wiping the blood that Skypris had missed. She flinched slightly at the action, not expecting it from him. He withdrew and gave her some space. "I'm really sorry," Terro regretted, his guilt almost suffocating.

"I know you are. You two don't have to apologize for hurting me, just apologize for being stupid!"

"Why me? I'm not the one who started it!"

"Aye, ye did ye ned!" Edwin defended. "Ye're the one who pushed me doon!"

"Because you couldn't keep your mouth shut!"

"Stop it! You two are like animals!" Skypris stood up. "Edwin, can I talk to Terro alone?"

Edwin furrowed his eyebrows. "Aye."

As Edwin went to help Latona with the green dragon, Skypris led Terro to the door facing each other, close so they could hear their lowered voices.

"I already said I was sorry." The prince's tone remained gentle toward her.

"And I already told you, it's fine. Besides, that's not what I wanted to talk to you about," Skypris began. "Why did you start fighting? I know you started it."

"How do you know?"

"Because, Terro, I know you. We grew up together, and I know you better than you know yourself. So why did you do it? Why are you so cruel to Edwin?"

"He stole my birthright, and I don't trust him."

"You're smarter than that. You know that choice was out of his hands! And *'trust him'*? How could you, when you haven't even bothered getting to know him? Ever since he's gotten here, all you've been doing is mocking and bullying him just because you got your pride hurt!"

Their voices gradually got louder as the conversation turned more into a debate.

"That's not—"

"*'Not'* what?!" Skypris snapped. "*'Not it'*? *'Not my fault'*? Because that's what I'm seeing. You're in charge of your own decisions, Terro. No one else. *You!*"

"Why are you defending him?!"

"Because, unlike you, I bothered to get to know him," Skypris continued.

Terro paused, his heart racing. Surely, she wasn't that defensive over just a friend? Unless…

Paranoia ate at his stomach. "Do you have romantic feelings for him?"

He watched as Skypris's face grew flustered, her eyes widened, and she swallowed the taste of iron hard. "What gave you that idea?!"

Her hesitation confirmed it for him. "So, it is true," he accused with an angered expression.

"No! It's not like that at all—he's just a friend!" Skypris growled in frustration. "It doesn't matter if I like him or not! The point is, I think you and Edwin would be good friends if you just gave him a chance."

The two took a moment to slow down their anger and frustration. How could Terro be friends with him now? He bowed his head and stared at the tip of his boot. Hatred clouded his gaze, though he was trying not to let it cloud his judgment.

"I don't want to be friends with someone who thinks being a jerk is justified," Skypris said sorrowfully.

Terro looked up at her with new, worried emotions as she continued. "I'm not going to ask you to be friends with him; but at least stop picking on him—stop being mean."

The prince was silent. He didn't know what to say. What was so special about Edwin that Skypris would throw away the friendship they had had their entire lives? Did Terro mean anything to her anymore? What did Edwin have that he didn't? Should he just lie for the sake of not losing her? Maybe just pretend to be nice? Skypris moved her head to get Terro to look at her, yet he averted his eyes from hers. Dejectedly, Skypris walked off to join Latona and Edwin.

Skypris wiped her eyes that were still watery from the pain she had experienced earlier, or at least that's what she told herself they were from. She met Edwin's and Latona's eyes as they were treating the dragon's wounds. Did they hear? Of course they did! Their conversation had gotten loud. She took some paste from the bowl in Latona's hands and started to help apply it to the scabbing cuts. Latona had returned to her care, yet Edwin couldn't stop looking at Skypris as she tried to put all her attention into what she was doing. She tried to distract herself and choked back a sob. She examined how nicely the dragon's wounds were healing, especially for the more dangerous ones, like those on the neck. "Ye didnae have to stick up for me," Edwin said gently.

"No, I did. I hated how he was treating you. It's unfair. He'll come around, just be patient with him, please." Her eyes were pleading.

Terro claimed the chair that the injured Skypris had sat in. He was staring at his feet, yet his mind was elsewhere. How could he not answer her? Was she truly going to end their friendship over someone from Gorish? Shouldn't he have the right to be mad and hate whomever he wanted? Terro pulled out the crystal necklace from his shirt, examining it. Was he going to let jealousy take away his best friend? Terro thought of the times Skypris and he had laughed together. The thought of losing her felt like a stab wound to his heart, making those wonderful memories turn sour. How could he lose her over some little grudge? Was it little though? In comparison, it was. Realization hit him. He would rather put up with Edwin than lose Skypris. Maybe he could ignore Edwin when he could and secretly give him dirty looks? Maybe. Looking behind the chair, he saw Skypris helping Latona and Edwin. Here went nothing. Walking over, Terro approached Latona, rubbing the back of his head, avoiding eye contact.

"Can I help?" he asked.

Chapter Eighteen
Drake

Newla's head perked as her gaze went to the archway that led to the landing platform. Eyes wide as they darted around the entrance. Wind blew, misting the dragon and the caretakers. "It's okay, Newla," Skypris soothed. "It's just a storm."

"Looks like it's gonnae be dreich," Edwin commented, seeing the rain increasing.

Latona stroked the dragon's neck as she looked around her home suspiciously. It was odd that a wild dragon should be afraid of a little storm. Edwin stopped and watched as Newla's expression was less frightened and more like trying to detect something. Her diamond-shaped pupils slitted. "Wits wrang?" Edwin questioned, his voice low in concern.

"Danger, Monarch!" the dragon spat, standing, forcing everyone to stop applying paste and back away.

"Don't move or you'll reopen your wounds!" Latona's arms were up, trying to calm the animal.

"No haud oan, somethin' wrang!" Edwin informed. "She says there's danger."

Newla backed away from the opening, hissing at the storm.

"What type of danger?" Terro asked as he, Edwin, and Skypris ran to the heavy red curtains.

Terro grabbed one half while Edwin and Skypris grabbed the other, yet before the drapes were even halfway closed, Edwin felt a drop of rain hit his nose. He blinked and looked up, seeing a long bear-like claw curving into the room as it gripped the top of the archway.

Another dragon?

No. That wasn't a dragon's talon.

Full of fear, the boy from Gorish walked forward, not taking his eyes off the claw for an instant. Once he found the owner, he wished he had stayed inside. Edwin locked eyes with a beast covered in thick scales; its snake-shaped head was as big as a sheep, and it had piercing eyes that stabbed horror into his soul. Opened its giant maw, it revealed long sharp fangs. Edwin instinctively tumbled forward onto the platform outside, dodging a bite from the creature. Turning back after recovering and hearing a loud noise, he saw the attacker landing on the platform blocking the entrance.

The creature resembled a dragon without wings, its neck and tail leaner and longer. Its eyes were more animalistic, with a scruff that hid little spikes along its spine, and instead of horns on its head, they were on its shoulder blades and hips.

What was this creature?

No time to think as it opened its maw again and lunged forward at the teen boy.

"Edwin!" Skypris cried.

At the last second, Edwin dodged again, tumbling under the creature and into Latona's home. "Run!"

It charged into the house, changing its target from Edwin to Newla as it tackled the injured dragon. Bitting and scratching, the great beasts fought fiercely. Skypris dragged Latona out of harm's way as Terro prevented the girl from being smashed herself.

"We have to get out of here!" Terro yelled.

Throwing Newla on her back, the creature attempted the death hold as its long fangs acted like the perfect bars to cage in her neck. She kicked the snake-like monster into a wall, then got up and slammed her body into it. It slashed its square-tipped claws at Newla's folded wings, she groans and yet endures the pain and holds the monster back.

"We can't leave her to battle the drake!" Latona snapped. "Her wounds aren't healed enough."

"That's a drake?!" Edwin had only heard rumors and stories about them destroying villages in Gorish; however, he'd been lucky to never see one since his village was so close to the castle. "What is it doing here?"

"They're one of the dragon's natural rivals. They usually go for hatchlings or eggs," Skypris explained. "It must have smelled Newla's blood and didn't want to miss the opportunity—"

"Not the time, Skypris!" Terro took hold of Skypris's hand and led her to the door.

The drake slammed Newla to the ground in front of the path. Newla bellowed in agony as the drake slashed, reopening one of her wounds. Shakily, Latona raised her knotted hand and intoned a single word Edwin couldn't hear over the battle and storm. The moment the last syllable left her lips, a flash of green lightning shot from her hand, hitting the drake in the face. Not liking the pain the sorceress had caused, the monster turned its attentions to the new threat, its eyes slits. Edwin pushed Latona to the floor as the drake lashed at the group. Skypris and Terro did likewise, barely avoiding the massive fangs. As the teens found their feet again, Newla bit the drake's neck and wrapped her body around it, giving the group the opportunity they needed to reach the door. Edwin dragged Latona as they exited the room and descended the stairs.

"Will Newla be fine?!" Edwin cried in fear.

"She's a dragon. She can handle herself a lot better than any of us against that thing!" Terro said, his wet boots squeaking on the stone steps.

They stopped once the tower began to shake, and a dragon roared. Skypris almost slipped while going to the nearest window in the tower. Edwin saw a shadow pass by the window. "She's out!" Skypris cried with excitement.

"Yeah, but where's the drake?" Terro cautioned.

"Who cares!" Edwin began. "We need to hide!"

"Wait!" Horror filled Skypris's eyes as her hand went to her mouth. "We left our eggs in the courtyard!"

Edwin tried yet failed to moisten his throat. He placed his satchel with the rest of the group, somewhere safe as they trained. When Skypris got hurt, they were too distracted to think twice.

"Do you think someone picked them up for us?" Terro wondered with uneasy eyes.

Edwin thought about Maro and how, at the very least, he might have picked his up; however, that wasn't a chance he was willing to make. He didn't want the Empress of Dragons angry at him for losing her baby.

"I'm unsure. I don't want to risk losing my egg!" Skypris verbalized Edwin's fears. "And I don't want you guys to lose yours either."

Edwin continued to help Latona move down the stairs, the roughhousing aching the elder woman's bones. "Skypris, it'll be okay. Let's find a safe place for Latona, then retrieve them."

"Leave me here," Latona said, her voice husky. "You three go on and get your dragon eggs before it's too late."

"No! It's a daftie idea to leave ye alone while the drake is still roamin'," Edwin protested.

"I'll only slow you down. I'll be fine."

"Yeah, and she's not completely defenseless. She has magic," Terro reminded.

"Ye think we shedd leave her?!" Edwin defended.

Groaning in frustration, Skypris grabbed Latona's other arm and started to help her down past Edwin. "We don't have time for this! I'll take her to a safe place and then catch up."

"Are ye certain?" Edwin asked.

"Of course she is!" Terro said, descending the stairs past them. "Let's go, we don't have much time!"

The teenage boys trotted two steps at a time. Only once did Terro almost slip. Edwin wished he could have stayed behind with Latona. She was the only defense they had right now against the drake. Edwin shivered, not just from being soaked, but also from the memory of the drake's predatory gaze. At the very least, he was happy his teacher and Skypris would be safe. His head was screaming in fear. However, he couldn't let Terro face the drake alone, even if he was a jerk.

"Where dae ye think the Dragon Knights are?" Edwin asked.

"It's weird they're not here chasing that thing away," Terro agreed, knowing where Edwin was coming from.

"Dae ye think somethin' happened to them?"

"Not possible." Terro shook his head. "Even though most of them are on missions, we make sure the castle is not completely defenseless. We at least have enough to easily overrun the drake."

Reaching the end of the stairs, the boys bolted down the dim, empty hall as lightning began to flash outside. Their footsteps echoed against the roars of thunder. "Shedd we go to yer father?" Edwin questioned.

It was odd that Edwin felt safer with Terro. Braver? He wasn't sure how to categorize it. Edwin was scared; yet seeing Terro so unafraid and confident with knowing what to do helped put his mind at ease. It was probably pride or a desire to one-up the prince from their earlier rivalry, though Edwin could feel himself faking being brave, for now at least.

"It'll be too late. Why do you think it didn't follow us down the stairs?" Terro asked.

"Shedd we grab weapons?"

"No time!" Terro hissed through gritted teeth.

They ran straight to the courtyard, Edwin stumbling to a halt, too troubled to catch his breath. The rain continued to pour with no sign of softening as they scanned the training area, Terro walking on ahead. Did the others flee because of the drake? Or did the training get canceled once the wind picked up before the drake revealed itself? The weather was muggy and made their damp clothes sticky.

With another flash and thunder, Terro shouted, "I found mine and Skypris's!"

Edwin found his near the fountain by his father's sword, where he had left them for training. The others must have left in a hurry. He couldn't imagine Maro being so thoughtless and not picking up Edwin's things for him. The Goreon armed himself by securing his sword belt, then slinging his egg's satchel around his shoulder, making the bag and sword hang on opposite sides of his hips. Edwin stood.

"Behind you!" Terro called.

Turning toward the open hallway, the drake towered over him. Whipping around quickly, the drake knocked Edwin to the tile with its long, powerful tail. Scrambling to his feet, Edwin tried to put as much distance between himself and the monster as possible. Snapping at Edwin, the drake pursued. The boy turned and brandished his sword. He had to keep the creature at least far enough away that Edwin could escape any swift attacks. Edwin swung his sword, keeping the monster at bay until it got too excited and thrust its head forward, where Edwin then gave the drake a slice on its cheek. Stepping back, it hissed dangerously before jumping and pinning its prey down, disarming Edwin. A scaley palm pushed its weight on the trapped boy, making him gasp for breath. With the sword knocked out of his hand, he struggled in vain. He was powerless.

"Hey, ugly!" Terro hit the drake with a sizable rock.

It fixed its attention on Terro, as he attempted to hit the drake with another rock but missed.

Before Terro could grab another rock, a dragon appeared out of the clouds, diving fast towards the drake. It hit the beast in the back of the head before swooping up into the air like a bird of prey. Roaring in anger, the monster focused solely on the dragon, which would surely be a bigger threat than the two boys. Edwin dashed away from the beast's claw, catching his breath. The downpour was heavy on his eyes. He could see that the dragon was light green with a bony frill and carried a young man riding saddleback. It was Gale and Demmis!

Edwin sighed in relief. There was no way the drake could win against a Dragon Knight. The duo dove again, trying to scare it off. The drake watched the dragon prepare for another dive. Suddenly, the skin between the scales on its neck began to glow as the dragon dove toward it head-on. Opening its mouth, the drake discharged a great gout of sulfuric flame, just hitting Gale's tail as she evaded it at the last moment. Seeing that it put the dragon on the run, the drake advanced fiery attacks, giving Edwin the chance he needed to find his sword. He had to stop the drake before it got a lucky shot!

Tightening his grip against the rain, Edwin forced himself to ignore his paralyzing fear. Drawing back his sword over his head, he stabbed the blade deep into the drake's back leg. Lifting its head to the heavens, it screeched in pain, having no choice but to cease its fire. Gale rammed the creature, and they began to fight—tumbling, biting, clawing. With a bear-like claw to the face, the drake overpowered Gale and slammed her into the courtyard's wall, smashing a dragon-sized hole through it. Edwin and Terro moved closer to help.

Edwin feared for the dragon's rider. There was no way Demmis could have stayed on or endured all that. Surely, he was crushed.

The two beasts made their way into the start of the woods, snapping and slashing at each other. Gale managed to pin the drake by its neck. The drake would bite at Gale's frill and scratch the thick scales of the dragon's stomach, doing everything it could to break her hold. Finally, it found a way out, cutting Gale's achilles with its back claw. Distracted by the pain, the drake smacked her face with sharp nails, one strike after another, pushing her back into a tree that splintered into two.

The trainees came through the hole in the brick wall, in time to see Demmis off his dragon, doing his best to fend off the gigantic foe. "We have to help!" Terro charged, with a piece of rubble in his hand.

As he ran, Edwin watched Gale as she lay on the muddy ground, eyes closed, her chest barely rising. Before the two boys could reach their trainer's assistant, the drake clawed the young man in the head, making him bang into a tree.

"DEMMIS!" Edwin shouted in horror!

Edwin tore at the drake's calf while Terro threw his rubble, hitting the beast in the head once it reacted to the cut Edwin had dealt. As it pursued them, the boys led it deeper into the woods, around the mountain, away from the castle, their friend, and away from the city. With the drake bounding at their heels, the boys ran frantically, not caring about going around the forest's obstacles. Terro ran through thickets where branches left cuts on any exposed skin. Edwin slid on mud, feeling a snap as stabbing pain spread through his leg. He yelled in agony, collapsing to the ground. Terro halted and back tracked, dragging Edwin along until he found his footing again, limping drastically.

"Wits the plan?" Edwin barked, the discomfort making it hard to think.

"Don't get caught," Terro yelled through the rainstorm, out of breath.

"No, seriously, we need a plan."

Terro grabbed Edwin and pulled him to the side, hiding behind a tree. "You go back to Demmis and see if he and his dragon are okay. Afterward, find my father, or Louis, just someone who could help," Terro gushed, continuing to glance over his shoulder.

"Wit are ye gonnae dae?"

"I'm going to lead the drake away from you."

"A could dae that."

Terro nodded at Edwin's offer, yet there was no way he would let him face the drake in his condition. He watched for a moment as Edwin's body shook in either pain or fear.

"Not with that leg of yours!" Terro took off his and Skypris's satchels, being thankful that they had magic to protect the eggs.

"That's exactly why we need to switch. We need to get to Demmis as fast as possible, but a cannae dae that."

"No! I'll give you enough time, just keep running and don't stop, no matter the pain!" Terro got up and took off, running in the other direction, not wanting to argue further with Edwin.

Terro could hear Edwin calling for the prince as his voice disappeared in the distance.

Once Terro was satisfied with the space he had placed between himself and Edwin, he raised his head, cupping his hands around his mouth, and howled with all the remaining air in his lungs. He hoped his voice was audible over the sound of rain hitting the dirt. To make sure, he repeated the lure a few more times as he continued to gain more distance. His voice went hoarse and cracked at the end of his third howl. He took off again, looking over his shoulders only to find himself falling off the edge of a ledge. Landing on his stomach, he lurched in pain. Terro rolled over and sat up, giving himself a second to recover, catching the breath he'd lost. No more than a mile away, he heard the drake's bellowing. It worked!

Using his feet, Terro pushed himself backwards up against the cliffside, trying to hide himself using the roots of the tree that grew on the edge, almost like curtains. Terro held his breath as heavy footsteps stomped above him, then stepped down from the ledge. While the beast sniffed the air, Terro could only pray that the mud and rain would throw off his trail. Silence fell until thunder broke it. Terro noticed his feet were barely poking out of the roots' cover. His heart thumped against his chest as Terro slowly started to bring them closer to his body.

Crack!

Terro stopped.

That was all the monster needed to locate him. The drake snatched the prince's leg and hoisted him out into the open, exposing him completely. Why didn't he take Edwin's sword?! He would have had a chance! He should have kept running!

Terro cursed himself. He had to get away somehow. Using his free leg, the boy started to kick the creature's nostrils with his heel. Shaking him, the drake tossed Terro, who landed hard on his side. Terro rolled to his feet and attempted to flee, yet his desire was interrupted by the drake thumping the boy down with its powerful tail. Seeing Terro wiggle loose and run in the other direction, it pinned him with its claws. As the drake added weight, Terro felt cracking in his body with smarting flushing from his ribs like nothing he'd ever experienced. He gasped, trying to fight off the unbearable sting.

This couldn't be it, could it? How he dies? He couldn't! He still had so much to do—he was going to be king! Terro blinked rapidly, trying to focus his blurring vision, rain pounding on his face.

Right before Terro could start to accept his fate, a dragon flew over, getting the drake's attention, relieving Terro of some of the beast's mass, allowing him to gasp and check to see that his lungs hadn't collapsed. Due to his vision's lack of focus, Terro could only make out a man-sized shape dropping from the dragon as it flew lower. He heard a deep voice call out, though Terro was too disoriented to clearly hear the name that was yelled. Suddenly, he saw Edwin impale his sword into the drake's head. Terro sat up fast, too alarmed to give his aches a strong recognition. The monster jolted back, raking at its own head. Edwin only dug the weapon deeper into the skull, until the blade was no longer visible. The earth shook until finally the drake stopped shriveling like a cockroach and fell over to its side. Dead.

Terro stood, hunched over, grabbing his side as Edwin ripped his bloodied sword from the carcass and limped over to Terro.

Cerberus landed, making Terro realize that he had been the dragon the boy had seen. His father leaped from his dragon and bolted over to his injured son. Soon Princess Circe followed, jumping off of Reuben and running over, not waiting until her dragon was fully grounded, "Terro!"

King Clayus hugged his son tightly. Terro groaned.

"Are you okay?" King Clayus asked with a fearful voice.

"I think my ribs are broken," Terro answered before getting attacked with hugs by his crying sister.

"I'm so glad we got here in time," Circe said, wiping her eyes.

"How did you find me so fast?" Terro winced.

"It was Edwin," Circe said. "We were flying back after we chased the other drake away."

Edwin kept his distance, giving the family some privacy. One of his eyes was closed because of the pouring rain. He held one of his arms with the sword in hand, and all of his balance went into his uninjured leg. Edwin wore his enchanted satchel, and no signs of damage were shown. Terro wasn't too worried, knowing the egg would be fine even after that stunt.

That stunt.

Terro used his sister's shoulder to help him walk over to the injured Gorish boy. "You look terrible!" Terro yelled, revolted.

"No as bad as ye," Edwin retorted, shaking with what Terro assumed to be adrenaline.

It was true, both of them looked terrible. Terro felt terrible. Wet, covered in mud, clothes torn, hair a mess, cuts and bruises all over, along with more severe injuries.

Terro didn't know what to think anymore. He had hated Edwin, didn't trust him, and couldn't stand the sight of him. Yet, Edwin had saved him despite his mutual distaste for Terro. They both risked their lives for one another and worked together. Maybe he was wrong about Edwin. Maybe Skypris was right. He should have gotten to know him first. Did he let his pride get in the way of a potential ally or friend? Should he say, *"Thank you?"* or, *"Sorry I treated you badly, you're actually not so untolerable."*

None of that seemed enough.

He didn't want to admit his faults, especially in front of his father and the other Dragon Knights who surrounded them on the ground and in the sky. Terro counted that there would be seven witnesses total. Way too many for his pride to live with. The more Terro thought, the tighter his knuckles got. Edwin might have saved his life, yet he still had stolen his birthright, and that was something Terro could never forgive.

"I hate you…" Terro's words shocked everyone. "At least, a big part of me does, yet after all this… I owe you my life. I'm thinking that I was wrong about you."

Terro and Edwin held a hard gaze with one another for what felt like hours.

Edwin smiled. His shoulders shook as he couldn't bear the intense moment any longer. Terro followed the boy's lead, it being contagious. Soon they both started to laugh as if the same joke came into their heads, and they were trying to contain themselves. "You dropped onto a drake."

Edwin chuckled, "A guess it wis pretty ridiculous."

Terro walked up to Edwin. "More like stupid brave! I cannot believe my father let you do that! You fell through the air!"

The two boys just stood and took a moment to laugh out of fear and relief. They had survived! They had lived! Terro and Edwin were so close to death, yet they escaped.

King Clayus approached them. "I didn't let him. He was there one minute, then gone the next."

"Oh, good, so only he's the mad one." Terro nodded, getting stabbing pains in his side from the laughter.

"*'Mad'* is one word for it, *'brave'* is another." Clayus smiled at Edwin warmly. "One that we will surely reward for."

"Haud Oan!" Edwin's eyes had horror inside them, as though there was another drake right behind them. "Demmis and Gale!"

Chapter Nineteen
Recovery

Edwin rode with Princess Circe on her dragon, Rueben. Edwin sat on the saddle behind her, holding onto her thin waist. For that reason only, Edwin was glad for the pain. It helped prevent him from blushing. Terro rode with his father on Cerberus as they and the other Dragon Knights flew to the castle. Louis and a few others went to retrieve Demmis and Gale. Edwin wanted to be among them to make sure his friend was alive. However, King Clayus demanded they go to Latona in haste to have their injuries treated. Edwin didn't argue, not only because King Clayus was well… the king, but also because his ankle was throbbing, though not as much as his arm, which was almost unmovable. Terro was hurt badly as well, and the laughing sure didn't help.

The storm had died down to nothing more than a sprinkle. Thunder faded, and lightning was a memory. The air was heavy with the smell of the storm still in the wind. "Thank you for saving my brother," the princess said thankfully.

Edwin blinked. He could hear her fine, yet the ringing in his ears made him hesitate. "It wis ma pleasure, Princess Circe."

"Please, just Circe."

"Am a allowed to caw ye just by name?"

"You don't call Terro his title, right?"

"No. No really. Ye're different, though, ye are…" Edwin stopped, not knowing what to say exactly.

"I'm human like you. Don't worry, I'm giving permission."

"Awrite then. Circe," Edwin said, his accent rolling the 'R' in her name.

She smiled warmly. "Honestly, though, thank you for risking your life. I know Terro probably didn't deserve it for being so mean to you."

"How did ye—"

"Skypris mentioned it to me. Besides, I know my brother."

"Well," Edwin said, adjusting to the information. "We helped each other oot. It wis unavoidable in the situation."

"You could have run away, yet you didn't." She shook her head. "You're a good person, Edwin, a true Dragon Knight. I can see why the Empress brought you here."

"Really? Am still tryin' to figure it oot."

"Has she told you why you can talk with dragons?"

"No, a guess she disnae think am ready."

A young man's voice cracked from Reuben, "You're our Monarch."

"A ken that much. A just dinnae ken entirely wit that means," Edwin replied to the dragon.

Circe looked back at Edwin with confusion. "What?"

Edwin winced with embarrassment. "Sorry, I was talking with Reuben."

"Really?" She perked up. "What does he sound like?"

"A young teen who is just gettin' his deeper voice."

The princess chuckled and patted Reuben's neck. He snorted, insulted by the comment.

Reuben and Cerberus made their descent to a landing platform. Cerberus was the first to land, opening his wings. He glided until he got close, then flapped his wings forward as he arched his body, making sure his back legs were the first to touch the platform before his front claws came. Thanks to his smaller size, Reuben did likewise, except with a little more grace. The two dragons then made their way into the castle through a doorless archway.

Edwin actually enjoyed riding on a dragon. Part of him thought he would hate it since all his other flying experiences were sour; but turns out it's a lot more fun to ride one than to be carried by one. It was very relaxing, a different experience. His senses were clearer and sharper, and he felt the wind on his face as mist from the rain's leftover dew blew at him. A laugh of excitement escaped Edwin as he jumped down from Reuben, making sure to land on his good leg. Circe was surprised by his movement, hopping down herself as if she feared the boy would collapse.

King Clayus was already on the ground while Terro remained in the saddle on Cerberus. "Did you enjoy your flight?" he asked, seeing Edwin's smile.

"Aye, it's a lot more fun ridin' a dragon than bein' carried by one," Edwin limped as he took a step.

Accidentally putting pressure on his bad leg, he fell to his knees, pain scaring his smile away. Circe helped him stand and grabbed Edwin's arm, placing it over her shoulder. It was easier, with them being the same height.

"Why don't you hop back on Rueben?" the king suggested. "I don't want you boys to move around. You might make your injuries worse."

"Understood," Edwin said, allowing the princess to guide him.

Using his good arm and leg, and with the help of Circe, Edwin pulled himself up to Rueben's saddle. The dragons walked along as they continued to search for Latona and Skypris. It didn't take them long to find them in the ballroom with the rest of the castle staff, the guards keeping watch by all the entrances. As they entered the ballroom, Latona approached them. "Clayus! Where have you been? We were attacked by a fire drake!"

"Sorry, Latona. I took the castle's knights with me to chase away a fire drake that had been stalking the city. We chased it all the way around the mountain. I had no idea there was another. That was an error on my part. I should have left a few knights behind," he explained, helping Terro down from Cerberus.

"Oh dear, that's not right!" Latona scrunched her brow. "Drakes are solitary creatures."

"I know, Louis mentioned that they must have been a mating pair."

Latona nodded knowingly, then turned her attention to the two boys. "You two look like you've faced death!" she gasped.

"Maybe a little," Terro chuckled, eyes glassy from torture.

"Come and bring them over so I can take a look at them," Latona said, urging the group to follow her to a table.

Sitting the two boys in chairs, King Clayus excused himself to see some of the Royal Guards and other castle staff, Kane being one of them. Skypris ran up to Terro and Edwin, giving them a big hug, ignoring the groans of soreness. "Skypris, please, I don't need to be more broken than I already am," Terro begged.

Releasing them from her bear hug, she straightened up. "I'm sorry, I just got so scared that you would…" She stopped. "Anyways, I was going to come and help. I wanted to get the castle staff to safety first in case something went wrong."

"Am glad ye didnae come. It wis dangerous. Am surprised Terro and a are alive," Edwin exclaimed.

Latona got between the friends and examined the boys. Her attention first went to Edwin's leg, picking it up, moving it, and feeling the bones. "It's sprained terribly," she diagnosed. "I can't repair it with magic unless I break it. Now, you two boys take off your shirts so I can check your other injuries."

Edwin hesitated, shy to show everyone how scrawny he was. Yet when he complied, he noticed that he had filled out thanks to training and routine meals. He was covered in small bruises, nothing too serious. Terro, however, had a massive growing bruise all around his ribs and along his spine. Skypris gasped in alarm when she saw. Latona's eyes grew wide. "You have a few broken ribs," she said as she traced her finger down the boy's injuries. "This will hurt."

Terro jumped, knowing what she was about to do, "No wait!"

With the same unfamiliar word used to heal Skypris's broken nose earlier, multiple popping sounds went off all at once. Terro howled in pain, bending over and grabbing his sides. Skypris hurriedly placed a hand on his back, remaining close to his side.

Placing a hand on Edwin's arm gently, the sorceress said, "Your turn."

Skypris turned and covered her ears. With the same magical word, Edwin yelped after feeling a surge of pain that was slower to leave than to appear. It had felt as if a nail was being hammered into the bone. With a final snap, Edwin clutched his jaw.

"I need my herbs and time to heal the rest of your injuries. The palace physician should be able to handle you," she explained with a tilted chin and a sly smile as if she was happy Terro and Edwin had felt the pain they had caused Skypris earlier because of their foolishness.

A loud bang drew everyone's attention to the entrance as the large wooden doors burst open, slamming against the stone walls. A dragon was in front, implying that it was the culprit who pushed the doors in. It cleared the path forward for two smaller dragons who dragged Gale. She was drenched in blood and mud.

"HELP!" Louis's voice cracked as he yelled in desperation as he trotted in with Demmis in his arms.

The castle staff watched, giving the injured and their carriers space. Latona rushed over to meet them halfway. Edwin and Terro stood up, shocked by what they saw. From where they stood, Edwin wasn't able to fully see Demmis, though he did catch a lot of red. He limped forward, heart freezing.

No. He couldn't be dead!

"Set him on the floor," Latona demanded.

Louis complied, gently setting his assistant down, and then backed away to let the elder work. She went to her knees and examined Demmis. A bleeding scratch had covered Demmis's face, drenching it in blood. His leather armor remained untouched except for the mud and rain. "I don't know if he's breathing," Louis choked.

Latona placed two fingers to the man's neck, looking desperately for a pulse. For a heartbeat. The room was silent as she did so, all except for Edwin, who finally had reached Gale's side. No, Demmis couldn't be dead! Edwin still had the image of his trainer, his friend, smiling and laughing with an impish smile. The thought of not seeing him again started to hurt worse than his leg.

"He's barely breathing!" Latona shouted. "I need my herbs now!"

Edwin sighed and closed his eyes for a moment, so he was able to just focus on his breath. There was a chance. He would have liked to volunteer to retrieve the remedies needed, but sadly, with his leg, he would just be in the way. Happily, Maro was the first to run out the door. Edwin guessed what his friend's intent was. Three more people—two Royal Guards and a servant—followed Maro out of the ballroom. "We'll bring back as much as we can!" Maro's voice was almost too distant to make out.

"Hurry!" the king yelled after them before turning to a maid servant who stood by his side. "Emma, we need buckets of water with clean rags!"

"Yes, your majesty." Emma bowed her head and led more maids out the door, Fayette and Richard running after them.

"Let me through! Move! MOVE!"

Edwin looked behind him into the crowd. Pushing through, a young girl made it to the front. She looked to be a year younger than Edwin. She wore her black hair in a single braid, with little strands escaping. Her features were similar to Demmis's yet more feminine. She ran into a kneeling position next to the scratched-faced man, tears running down her cheeks like the rainstorm they had just witnessed. Latona moved closer to the girl, her eyebrows furrowed. "You're Demmis's sister, aren't you?"

The young girl nodded her head, sobbing out, "Corythia," as she closed her eyes.

King Clayus advanced to the crying girl along with Circe. "Cory? What are you doing here?"

Corythia wiped away tears. "I was giving Demmis his lunch after he forgot it, then this whole thing happened and-and…" She couldn't get another word out. She buried her face in her hands, crying once more. "Is he going to die?"

Circe knelt next to Cory and hugged her, letting the troubled girl cry in her arms. "I'm going to do everything I can for your brother and his dragon," Latona gently told Corythia.

Standing up, Circe helped Cory to her feet and led her over to Gale. "Let's see how Gale's doing."

"Shouldn't you check on her as well?" King Clayus asked Lataona.

"Gale will be alright, no fatal injuries from what I can tell. I'm more worried about Demmis. If I don't treat him soon, he will die."

Emma, Richard, Fayette, and the rest of the maids who went with her returned carrying big buckets of water and many rags. Other staff came to the doors to help carry the equipment the rest of the way, placing a bucket for Latona next to Demmis, then the rest next to the horse-sized dragon. Dipping one of the cloths in the water, Latona carefully wiped dried mud and blood from Demmis's skin, revealing more clearly the gouge across his once handsome face. Terro, Skypris, Edwin, Circe, and Corythia began to clean up Gale's wounds. Soon after, Maro and those who went with him returned with boxes, their hands filled with vials and plants.

"Quick! Set them by me gently!" Latona directed, waving a hand over a spot near her.

After dropping off the ingredients, Maro and the others gave the sorceress room to work. "This… was the best we could…find. Everything else… was destroyed," a Royal Guard explained, out of breath from his haste.

"This will do," Latona said, nodding before turning to her saved herbs and salves.

Edwin bent down, balancing on his good leg, and dipped his rag in the now muddied water. He wrung it out and was about to continue to clean off Gale yet instead watched Latona work on Demmis. Adjusting his eyes slightly, he noticed that Corythia was watching as well, her body turned to Gale's, and she was mid-wipe with a rag. She sniffled, wiping tears off her cheek. Looking back, she blinked once she realized Edwin was staring. Her eyes were beautiful. They were the colors of bluebell flowers. Guilt tapped his heart. Somehow, he found comfort in them despite the despair of the situation. His friend, Demmis, was gravely injured, yet he had time to think of how pretty his sister's eyes were. The two teens broke away and returned their attention to cleaning the dragon. Edwin hadn't meant to stare at her. She was probably embarrassed by crying in front of everyone. Who could blame her? The girl's brother was just inches away from death, and Edwin himself was holding back tears.

Chapter Twenty
Fire Slayer

Edwin made his way through the castle halls, using a cane as a crutch to help relieve his injured leg.

It's been exactly three days since the attack of the drake. Demmis was stable and resting in a castle room until the repairs for Latona's tower could be completed. He had heard the sorceress murmuring to herself how some of the plants would take years to grow to the potency she needed for certain remedies. So the king was working to get all that she needed imported by merchants.

Training had been put on hold while Terro and Edwin rested. However, they were warned to do warmups and stretches while on hiatus. Edwin was instructed to stay on the cot in Maro's tower, yet

Edwin wasn't fond of lingering with Maro's father too long without a break, so he spent most of his days in the Library with Skypris. Terro was shadowing his father, and they had been busy, especially cleaning up after the drake. Edwin didn't know where he stood with the prince now. He hadn't seen him since the attack.

That morning, Edwin was surprised to find a messenger at Maro's tower doors, and the messenger was surprised to find a pan flying at him. Luckily, the poor informer ducked out of the way. Orff cursed the poor servant for showing his face while wearing a uniform with the King's crest. While Maro tried to calm his father as the man went on a heated rant, Edwin made his way out the door, claiming to chase the messenger away for good. "Are ye awrite?!" Edwin's brows furrowed, closing the door behind him.

The messenger was an older, scrawny gentleman with grayed hair. He was clean-shaven all except for a few hairs he'd missed. He swallowed hard, standing up straight and fixing his outfit from any wrinkles. His chin went high as he took a deep breath. "Um… yes, I am quite alright. I had forgotten how much of a brute that man can be." He cleared his throat. "I take it you're Edwin?"

"Aye," Edwin grabbed the handle of the saucepan.

"The king requests your presence in his council room an hour past noon."

Edwin's lips straightened. Why would the king want to see him? Perhaps to check how he was healing? The boy's mind dived into coming up with negative or dangerous reasons why the king would want to see him, yet for the first time, he couldn't make up any. "Did he say why?"

"He did not." The messenger bowed before descending the steps, eager to get as far away from the madman. "Good day to you."

Now, an hour past noon, Edwin stood in front of the king's counsel room. The doors were closed, and there were guards standing sentinel on both sides. He watched them like he always did. "Let me get that for you," one said, opening the door for the temporarily crippled boy.

"Thank ye." Edwin nodded and walked in.

The room wasn't wide, yet it was very tall. The back wall of the room had two wooden trap doors that touched the ceiling. Edwin guessed they needed to be big enough to host The Dragon Empress if the occasion arose. There were two lengthy windows with open black curtains across from each other. An elongated table, covered in green cloth, took up the entire floor, except for a walkway where attendees could find their seats. All the chairs were the same, fancy decor was carved into the golden frame, soft black cushions on the back, and a slip seat. The room, like the ballroom, had a second level of platforms, big enough to let the dragons roost. Currently, Cerberus slept as his knight sat at the head of the table in the biggest seat, Terro to his right.

Edwin's muscles naturally tensed when he saw the prince. The Royal Guard holding the door open for him bent close to Edwin's ear, "What's your full name?"

"Edwin."

"Full."

"A dinnae have a last name," Edwin shrugged.

The Guard nodded as he straightened, then, in a booming voice, said, "Your majesties, Edwin has entered the room of the king's council."

King Clayus and Terro look up from the mounds of paperwork they were sorting through. "Ah, yes, Edwin. Come in."

With a gesture from the king, the guard closed the door on the way back to his station. Edwin started to make his way to Clayus as the king watched, smiling warmly. Once Edwin was more than halfway, the king stood and met the boy the rest of the way. "How are you doing, Edwin?"

"Am fairin'. Just been restin'."

King Clayus placed a fatherly hand on Edwin's back. "That is good, Latona said you should be fully recovered in six weeks, was it?"

"Aye, Yer Majesty." Edwin bowed his head.

Edwin then looked to Terro, who hadn't taken his eyes off the Dragon Knight reports in front of him. Should he ask how Terro was doing? Edwin noted a bruise on the prince's jaw. "Now, the reason why I summoned you."

The king reached over the table, grabbing the corner of a blue pillow. He pulled it over and placed a hand under it, treating it like a tray. Resting on the pillow was something covered by a golden cloth. King Clayus waved over a scribe who had hidden in the corner of the room. "Winston, make a note of this for the castle's records."

Edwin hadn't realized all the other servants in the room until now. There were two dressed as messengers, two scribes, and a few others Edwin couldn't recognize the positions of. Winston flipped over a new page in his book. He licked his quilled pen before dabbing into an ink foundation that was attached to his hip with a belt. Clayus cleared his throat, "Edwin, for helping aid in defending the castle, for killing the drake, and for your courage in the face of danger, the King of Alena and High King of Xolf gives you his deepest gratitude. For saving the King's heir, Terro Gaius Clayus Dragonsborn, he can never express the amount of gratitude he feels."

Terro had glanced up with a hard gaze before looking down at the paperwork, getting a new stack. Edwin could imagine that this must be hard for him to hear. Guess they weren't best friends after all.

"Deeds such that you have performed are no small feat. They must be recognized," the king went on. "For slaying the drake." He took off the golden cloth, revealing a long, sharp fang. "One of the drake's mighty fangs. This will be a memento of how you slayed the beast. Do with it as you like. The bone is durable."

Edwin picked the tooth up and examined it in awe. The bone was smooth and had a weight to it Edwin wasn't expecting; it was barely longer than his forearm. Knowing how close this tooth had been to ending his life multiple times that day—one wrong move, and it would have all been over—made him shiver. "Thank ye," Edwin said, carefully feeling the sharp tip.

"And for your bravery." King Clayus pointed to Edwin's father's sword. "May I have your sword for the next part?"

Edwin set the fang on the table. *Bravery?* He wasn't brave. He was a coward. Edwin thought back to those moments when he rode on the back of Cerberus as King Clayus cursed that the first attempt to scare the drake from his son didn't work. They had to move fast before it was too late. Edwin still sometimes shook just recalling how much adrenaline coursed through his veins, how mind-numbing the sound of his heartbeat was in his ears. He couldn't remember jumping or falling. All he could remember was sitting on the dragon, then on the ground, his sword embedded in a dead drake's head. That was all. That wasn't bravery, was it?

"Am no brave, though." The words escaped his mouth.

Eyebrows raised, the king regarded the dejected expression on Edwin's face. King Clayus took a second, then turned to Terro, who was staring. "Terro, could you go oversee the progress of Latona's keep? I'll join you once I finish up here."

Terro's eyes threatened to roll, yet they knew better. "Yes, Father."

The prince stood carefully, soreness in his sides making him wince. He departed the room, taking some of the guards and other staff with him. Once the doors closed, Clayus turned his attention back to the self-conscious boy. "Edwin, you faced down a drake and jumped off a flying dragon. You don't consider yourself brave?"

He nodded, looking at the drake tooth. "It wis just adrenaline, a wiznnae thinkin'. Am a coward."

Clayus sat on the table, hand on his knee as he regarded Edwin with a fatherly gaze, one that Edwin hadn't seen in a long time. The king waited patiently until Edwin became aware that the ruler wanted the boy to elaborate. "A've always been afraid to dae the right thin'. A hid instead af aidin' ma group in tryin' to slay Newla…" He winced, looking for any kind of aggression in King Clayus's gaze. He saw none. "And yet a didnae dare to save her either."

Nodding knowingly, King Clayus stood. "All my life, I've seen an array of men and women. What I've learned is that there are brave people who can do acts of cowardice, and also, there are cowards who can do heroic acts of bravery. I think you are the former. Even if so, just because you were a coward then does not mean that you cannot become a hero now."

Edwin was able to look King Clayus in the eyes, his shame leaving him as he took the words to heart. How could he ignore such wisdom? Especially some that was starting to inspire him. Maybe he wasn't a coward after all? He did attack the drake even if he wasn't thinking. He did it naturally, when he could have just frozen in place. He did freeze, or at least he used to. Had he really grown since being that boy in Gorish? Could he be brave? Was it that simple, to just choose to be brave?

"If it makes you feel better, I'm not rewarding you because of what you are. I'm rewarding you because you did an act of courage. Doesn't matter why or how you did it, you took action."

Edwin smiled, trying to stand up straight and puff out his chest. He was going to be brave. Clayus smiled warmly and opened his hand to Edwin's belt. Unsheathing his sword, he gave it to the king, who looked it over. "Kneel."

His anxiety made Edwin hesitate. This would be the perfect opportunity to chop off his head. It would take a few swings and be very painful. Titling those thoughts as foolish, Edwin did as the King of Alena ordered. Edwin knelt on his good knee, relying strongly on the cane to support his weight. "What's the name of this sword?"

"A-"

Edwin thought about it. He had been too distracted, that he had almost forgotten about what his father wanted for his sword. He had told Edwin's aunt to tell him he had to name it for himself, based on the first thing he cut it with. That had been the fire drake. The boy took his time to think of a good name that was related. It would go down in the king's records, be official. The sight of the beast's neck glowing before it breathed fire came to mind, then how Edwin had initially stopped the fire for good by not only killing the drake, yet also by impaling its head close to its bottom jaw, forever closing the beast's mouth and thereby stopping the fire.

"Fire Slayer."

King Clayus nodded, then lifted the sword and tapped each of Edwin's shoulders as he declared, "Edwin, with your sword, Fire Slayer, I hereby give you the title Dragon Translator. With this title, you are granted a position in my court and a seat in my council. With this duty, you will be required to come at my request and translate for the Dragon Empress honorably."

He moved the sword to his side and waved his free hand to the scribe. After Winston finished the king's final words, he bowed and then stepped back into his original spot. King Clayus helped Edwin to his feet and offered back Fire Slayer, where Edwin sheathed it. Edwin felt a little warm in his face, yet he was more concerned that the large smile on his face would seem goofy.

"Thank you again, Edwin, for your mettle," King Clayus nodded respectfully. "I wanted to give you this position earlier, mainly because your ability to communicate with the Empress is valuable. Nevertheless, you are born from a rival nation, so I needed to wait for you to prove your loyalty to us. I think saving the heir to the throne is strong enough."

"Thank ye for believin' and trustin' in me. A Wilnae let ye doon," Edwin bowed once more.

"Of course, you are a future Dragon Knight." the king winked before heading back to his seat. "Now, if you'll excuse me, I must finish these reports before meeting Terro in Latona's tower."

Edwin grabbed the fang from the table and stuffed it into his egg's satchel. Departing, Edwin tried not to let his mind wander as he progressed to the library, where Skypris and he had promised to meet today. He was going to ask her to keep the drake's fang in her chambers. Edwin wasn't sure if Orff would respect the token or not.

Soon, Edwin lost track of reality while walking. A place at the king's court. The thought of him being a Dragon Knight—a noble knight—was finally sinking in. He imagined himself on the back of a dragon, sword raised, decorated in the knight's leather armor. His dragon roared as Edwin lowered his sword, signaling for them to charge as they faced down a drake, courageously.

Chapter Twenty-One
Battle Scars

Two months had passed since the drake's attack. Latona's tower had been restored, minus a few lost scrolls. Afterwards, the masons turned their attentions to repairing the wall of the courtyard that had been demolished during the battle. It took a while to complete, allowing wildlife to leak into the courtyard's gardens and forest. Mostly, deer came in and out. A family of foxes had made the yard their forever home. To Skypris's request, King Clayus instructed the builders to craft a fox-sized hole in the wall so the family could come and go as they pleased. While training, the trainees had stopped to gawk at the fox kits playing.

After returning to training, no more fights broke out between the two boys, yet occasionally Terro would get a little frustrated with Edwin and give him hard stares whenever the Goreon was anywhere near Skypris. Despite Terro's aggression, Skypris and Edwin still remained close friends. Edwin could deal with any stares the prince gave him. Skypris was worth it.

Recently, everyone had been getting excited and congratulating the training group. Edwin thought the behavior was strange until he found out their dragon eggs were supposed to be hatching any day now. Edwin felt a little anxious. Latona had taught him how to take care of a baby dragon, though she also said they were a lot of work. They need constant help grooming, with a balanced diet of fresh raw meat, more than double their body weight. Despite his concern, Edwin was excited and curious to see what traits his dragon would have. He knew it was going to be a male. The Empress only ever had a female for her heir when she prophesied her coming death.

Edwin sat at the table in Maro's tower, staring at his flame-patterned egg. They had given their magic satchels back to Latona for the next group to use when the time came. They also didn't want the trainees to put their eggs in any bags or piles of cloth in case the hatchling started to break the shell. Latona had checked the training group's eggs, giving an estimated time of when they would hatch. Most, if not all, eggs were supposed to hatch today! If not, then two days out, and if they didn't hatch, the dragon inside was likely dead. However, Latona reassured the teens that the chances of that happening were next to nothing. Edwin thought it odd that Skypris didn't want the sorceress touching her egg. She claimed to want the hatching to be a surprise. It seemed a little out of character for her.

With his head on the table, he shifted his gaze up to Maro, who was polishing the shell of his green dragon egg. "Why are ye cleanin' its shell?" Edwin wondered.

"I want to keep a piece of it after my dragon hatches," Maro explained.

Edwin sat up, his attention returning to his egg's shell. It was really epic looking, with it appearing to be a flame straight out of a fireplace. He needed to keep a shard for himself, too!

"Last chance to cook 'em. Are you sure you don't want to find out what the meat of a dragon egg tastes like?" Orff asked as he stirred a simmering stew, his voice filled with an innocent chim.

"No!" Maro snapped.

All Edwin could do was stifle a chuckle.

"Fine," Orff flicked his hand. "I suppose we could always cook them after they hatch."

"We're not cooking them at all!"

A tap silenced the conversation. Maro's attention went to his egg, which also caused Edwin and Orff to examine it. They gathered around listening.

Tap, tap.

"Last chance," Orff pushed.

"Is it hatching?" Maro ignored his father's cruel joke.

"Seems like it," Edwin shrugged.

"It is. The beast inside is awake, yet it will take about an hour for the egg's temperature to build up," Orff explained.

Edwin remembered the lecture Latona gave about how the eggs hatch. The baby is in a hibernative state until they are developed enough to wake, and thereafter, the baby starts tapping the shell, it'll begin to heat it from the inside until the pressure becomes too much and forces the cover apart.

"Shuid we keep the egg warm?" Edwin asked.

"No, just leave it be. It'll do the task itself." Orff straightened and returned to his stew.

Edwin watched Orff, puzzled by the madman. He used to be the King's Ambassador and was married to a Dragon Knight. So he had to have at least respected the dragons at some point. When did he start hating dragons and his own country? Was it because he understood too much? Because of his wife being missing in action? This was a mystery Edwin would never figure out.

The boy stood, picking up his egg, and headed to the door.

"Where are you going?" Maro asked, finishing cleaning the last of his egg.

"Am gonnae Latona's to check up oan Demmis before ma egg begins to hatch," Edwin explained, opening the door.

"Don't you want breakfast?" Orff asked. "It's the most important meal of the day."

"Am no hungry. Thank ye, though." Edwin politely dipped his head, closing the door behind him.

Every other day since Latona gave permission, Edwin had been visiting Demmis as he recovered from his almost fatal injuries. While there, Edwin had met Demmis's family: his father Alexias was the Royal Blacksmith; his mother Alary was a Dragon Knight; his sister was Corythia—or Cory for short; and his younger brother was Hero. Edwin enjoyed their company while visiting his trainer. While they got to know one another, they would tell stories about their lives, especially Alary with her Knight missions.

They were all very nice and reminded Edwin of the family he desperately desired as a kid. Growing up as an only child was lonely. He yearned to know what it was like to have a loving mother and father. Edwin's aunt and uncle cared for him like one of their own, yet still he wondered what it would have been like if his parents were alive.

Strolling down the halls, a maidservant swept remains of a shattered vase. Her hair was dirty blond, and her face worn from age. Coming up the hallway was Skypris carrying a bunch of bundled cloth in her arms. Edwin couldn't stop his smile from growing as their eyes met, and she returned the smile. Skypris and Edwin had stopped going to the library together once their training had started back up. He wasn't meaning to dismiss her, he was just nervous Terro would hate him again if he found out how much time they usually spent together.

Edwin didn't understand why Terro was hostile to him when it came to Skypris. The two had been friends since birth, so maybe it was brotherly love? An excuse to bully Edwin? Could he be jealous of Edwin getting between their friendship? Or was the prince's jealousy driven by more romantic feelings toward her? That must be it; Skypris was not ugly in any way. She was as nearly flawless as Circe. Did Terro see him as romantic competition? Edwin scoffed to himself. Perhaps he was overthinking.

Skypris quickened her pace to reach him. "Edwin!" Her tone showed excitement. "On your way to see Demmis again?"

"Aye, Latona says he shuid be ready to go home tomorrow." Edwin let out a little laugh.

"I regret not being able to see him much. How is his…" Skypris pointed to the right side of her face, wiggling her finger.

"It's healin' well, though Latona said it's gonnae leave a bad scar," Edwin answered, knowing what she was talking about.

She shrugged her shoulders. "At least he's going to be okay."

"Aye," he nodded in agreement. "Dae ye want to come with me?"

"I can't." Skypris looked down at the ground, her facial expression uneasy. "I was going to the library to look up something."

Edwin studied her for a moment. "Wit's with the laundry?"

"Oh, this? It's my dragon egg."

"Is it showin' signs af hatchin'? A dinnae think we're supposed to wrap it in cloth anymore."

"It's okay for right now, it's not showing any signs—I'm sure it'll start any time now!" she corrected herself. "How about yours?"

"Naw," Edwin shook his head. "Maro's is though."

"Really?"

Edwin nodded. "It just started, so it will take a while for it to hatch."

"That's amazing! I wonder if anyone else's is starting?"

"Probably."

"Have you picked out a name yet?" Skypris wondered.

"A have one in mind, wit aboot ye?"

"Same. I'll tell you mine if you tell me yours," her voice becoming playfully sly.

Edwin grinned. "Ye first."

"No, because then you won't tell me yours."

"Guess we'll have to wait," he said with a shrug.

They held one another's gaze for a moment. Skypris chuckled as she stepped to Edwin, patting him on the shoulder as she passed. "I'll see you later."

"Aye, see ye around."

Walking up the many steps of Latona's tower that he has grown accustomed to, Edwin knocked on the decorative door. "Come in," he heard Latona's muffled voice through the thick wood of the door.

He pushed the doors with some extra force. He had expected the doors to be fixed in the reconstruction, yet the workers were probably more focused on the giant hole in Latona's room. Latona sat at Demmis's bedside along with Cory and Hero. The knight was awake and sitting up. A long, freshly scabbed-up wound filled the right side of his face with a gap in between two claw marks that had spared his eye. Latona stood, leaving an available seat for Edwin to take. She limped over to her new table, where her herbs and other mixing ingredients lay ready. The table wasn't the only furniture she'd had to replace. Her cot had been destroyed along with the cots for her patients. Her room wasn't quite the same as before, although it was close. It was a lot less cluttered with plants. Edwin was now able to see more stone and wood. In addition, he was able to recognize the new building materials, which were bright and clean, compared to the older materials, which had been in place for years, possibly decades.

"Morning, Edwin," Demmis greeted. "What brings you here early?"

Edwin walked up to his bedridden friend. "A wanted to come before ma egg hatched."

"It's about time. Training is a lot more fun with dragons."

"Are we no still gonnae dae the same trainin'?"

"Sort of," Demmis shrugged. "You'll be graduating to feders soon enough, and we'll be focusing on hand-to-hand combat. Archery will be addressed, too."

"You'll still be our training assistant, right?" Edwin wondered.

Demmis winked. "Sorry, you're stuck with me."

Edwin smiled at the thought that the injury wasn't going to cost him his trainer's assistant.

The heat from the egg in his arms drew Edwin deeper into his thoughts. He looked down at the shell. Was it starting to hatch?

Cory lay her head on Dema's bed. Grabbing Edwin's attention, her gaze showed uncertainty as it drifted from this reality. Demmis patted his sister on the head. "Still stressing about your decision?"

"Yeah…" her tone seemed constrained.

"Is everything awrite?" Edwin wondered.

His aunt would have smacked him on the lips and said it was none of his business, even though she would gossip with the other women as they did their laundry. Edwin felt the need to see if all the members of Demmis's family were okay, though. He had gotten to know them and even went as far as to say they were friends, and he cared about them.

Demmis scratched his nose, being mindful of the healing wound on his face. "It's fine, Cory is just having a hard time deciding what she's going to do."

"I love blacksmithing," Cory started. "I just don't know… I have this feeling that I need to become a Dragon Knight."

"Why dae ye no dae blacksmithin' if that's wit ye love?" Edwin suggested. "Yer father wedd be glad to have an apprentice."

"That's what I think! It's like I have this guilty feeling telling me I need to become a Dragon Knight." Cory sat up and threw her hands in the air, irritation in her voice.

"Well, I know what I'm going to be!" Hero shared. "I mean, who *wouldn't* want to be a Dragon Knight? You get to go on adventures, fight the bad guys, AND RIDE A DRAGON!"

"Glad *your* mind's made up," Cory said and folded her arms.

Demmis gave an understanding smile to his sister. “Don’t worry, you’ll figure it out.”

Corythia nodded, taking a deep breath to relax. Edwin stared at her for a moment. She had soot on her face. They would often stare, often catching each other in the act. Edwin was embarrassed and cursed himself for his wandering eyes, yet he couldn’t help it. Her eyes were just so unique, and he hadn’t gotten used to seeing them yet. When they would lock gazes, Edwin found her eyes to be intimidating, yet he didn’t know why exactly. They just were.

Edwin continued to stare, focusing on the girl's turmoil instead of the colors of her irises. If Edwin had a choice, would he have chosen to be a Dragon Knight? Or would he eventually have just inherited the bakery from his uncle? A hunter like his father was?

No, he was too much of a coward.

Wait, he wasn’t, though. Not anymore.

The thought of King Clayus’s words rang in his ears. He jumped from a dragon and slayed a drake! That’s brave. Maybe he had been a brave man doing cowardly acts all along.

The heavy doors squeaked an alarm as they opened. Looking, Edwin saw Demmis's parents enter the room with Latona walking up to greet them. Alexias was tall and wide with a buldging belly and large muscles in his upper arms from his career. His face was charming with a clean jawline and chin. His eyes were gentle and light sea green, which was a trait both his sons inherited. Alexis was in his blacksmithing garb with spot stains and gloves in the pocket of his apron.

Alary was a solid woman, and the role of Knighthood was the cause. She wore a simple green and brown dress, one thats fanciness matched the common people. Her hair was long and wavy, as half fell behind her shoulder and the other in front of her chest. She had a few scars on her jaw from close calls with weapons, and her eyes were the same striking blue as her daughter’s.

"Sorry, I didn't clean up. I've been making some new feder swords for the trainees. Those kids do not hold back!" Alexias apologized, his voice softer than expected for his bull-like build.

"I had to drag him away from his work to come here," Alary said to Latona.

Alexias waved a hand. "It's not that big of a deal, he's going home tomorrow."

"That's tomorrow! What about today?" Alary countered.

Latona grinned at the couple, as though she was remembering times long passed. "It's always a pleasure to see parents who care so much for their children. Say 'hello' to your baby. I have medicine to prepare."

The elder sorceress gestured for them to go on before going about one of her many duties. Demmis' parents came to their son's bedside. "How are you doing, Demmis?" Alexias asked.

"Terrible!" Demmis exaggerated. "I can't take another day of resting, I need to run around or I'm going to jump out the window!"

Alary rolled her eyes. "Well, tough! You still have to take it easy. You don't want to overwork yourself and reopen your wounds, do you?"

"If it means getting to fight, maybe," Demmis smiled widely.

Alary huffed and walked towards the entrance of an open-curtain balcony with a landing platform. Gale was resting in the spot Newla once did. Gale's injuries from the drake attack were fully healed, other than some missing scales over some of the closed wounds. She could have been flying and socializing with other dragons, yet she chose to stay by her knight's side always.

Edwin pondered what it would be like to have a creature that committed to him. To fight until death to protect him, to never leave him, even when he fell. His thumb rubbed the egg's warm shell. His imagination took over his mind because of the excitement of having a dragon. How epic would it be to have a deadly predator on his side?

Fighting with him—*for* him. He would be like the great heroes in his story, yet with a twist. In the forest, fighting off bandits, being surrounded—almost defeated—he was saved at the last second by a dragon at his command. The bandits didn't see it coming!

"I'm sure Louis is beating up Edwin and his friends by now," Demmis said, snapping the boy out of his daydreams.

Edwin nodded, not even being self-conscious about the goofy smile on his face. "Aye, he has been pushin' us harder with more conditionin', that's it."

"See, I need to go! Who else can control that tyrant?"

"Never said you couldn't, just that you need to take it easy," Alary clarified, stroking Gale's elegant muzzle. She paused, her expression becoming downtrodden. "Has anyone seen that wild dragon since that night?"

"Newla?" Latona walked over with a bowl of herbs. "No, there hasn't been a sign of her anywhere."

Edwin put his head down, thinking of the young wild dragon. She had helped in the fight against the drake, allowing Latona, Terro, Skypris, and himself to escape. The dragon herself was about to get away, too. However, the possibility of her old wounds reopening and fresh ones from the drake was nerve-racking. The Dragon Empress had been bellowing loudly, calling for her. Some also had claimed to have seen other wild dragons searching for their lost thunder member. King Clayus had sent knights out seeking her as well, to no avail so far. Letters were sent to other kingdoms in Xolf and Ishnia to be on the lookout for her. "What do you suppose happened to her?" Alary questioned.

"I fear I don't have the answer. I pray she didn't attempt to travel back to the Dragon's Island." Latona let Gale eat some of the herbs in the bowl.

"She wouldn't dare in her condition."

"It's an instinct of a wild dragon to return home when they are in severe danger. If she has, I don't think she would make it, considering it is quite the journey. She needs to pass through the lands of Gorish to get there, and considering their traditions…" Latona tried not to glance at

Edwin, though her hesitation was enough. "I don't need to say anymore."

"That's awful," Alary said with sorrow.

"It could have been worse. We could have lost Gale, Demmis, Edwin, Prince Terro, Skrypris, and maybe me."

"That is true. It's a miracle that no one else was severely hurt."

Edwin stayed quiet. It was true that the people from his homeland would kill Newla with certainty. Optimistically, he was assuming the young wild dragon was hiding here in Xolf until her wounds healed. He dared not get his hopes up, though. His chest tightened with guilt. If Newla hadn't gotten those injuries from Gorish, maybe she could have stood a better chance against the drake.

Demmis's family knew who Edwin was on sight, thanks to his accent. Demmis had already been talking to them about Edwin, and it also didn't help that it was the talk of the city that there was a Goreon who was able to talk with dragons. Edwin was happy that the teaching assistant's family was more intrigued by Edwin's ability to communicate perfectly with dragons rather than being from a land that slayed them. During their shared visits to Demmis and Gale, the family would ask Edwin questions about his personal life, yet they didn't ask about Gorish's culture or what it was like to live there. Whenever Cory or Hero asked him about it, their parents would hush them up. Which Edwin appreciated. Waves of shame battered against his stomach to think about his place of origin.

He may not be a coward; however, he was no doubt a traitor to his country.

Alexias bent down, leveling with Edwin's dragon egg. "I'm no Dragon expert, but I think your egg's getting ready to hatch."

His chair made an ear-bleeding squeak as he stood abruptly. "Really?!"

Latona hobbled over, placing a hand on the top of the egg, feeling its warmth. "He's awake. You still have an hour at most before he's out. Might be best if you find a place for him to hatch."

"That's so amazing!" Hero ran over. "I want to see it hatch!"

Ignoring the little boy's eagerness, Edwin tensed, realizing that daydreams are a little less anxiety-inducing than real life. "Where shuid a go?" he asked Latona.

"I would suggest going to the king's throne room. I believe that's where most of the kids are," she explained. "Or that's where all the other generations of Dragon Knights in training have hosted it."

"Where's the throne room?"

"How long have you been here?" Alexias lifted a brow.

"This castle's big. A didnae want to snoop around and accidentally make others think am up to no good." Edwin's face felt warm, and he could hear it in his tone that he was slightly defensive.

"Wise decision," Demmis approved. "You know the courtyard where you train? If you keep going down that hall into the building, it connects to the throne room. You should find it no problem."

"A shuid probably go now then, in case a get lost."

"So soon?" Alary asked in disappointment. "We just got here."

"Hey, I thought you were here to visit me," Demmis smirked.

"Can I come and watch your egg hatch?" Hero followed Edwin to the exit.

Edwin stopped and glanced up at the boy's parents, who showed no signs of protest. "Aye," Edwin shrugged.

"Yah-hoo!" Hero jumped in joy with a fist over his head.

Alary looked at her daughter in a way that silently told Cory to go with her little brother. Cory closed her eyes and gave a little sigh. "Would you like me to show you the way to the throne room?" she asked Edwin.

"If ye dinnae mind." Edwin smiled, mostly out of embarrassment.

Chapter Twenty-Two
Hatching

Walking down the long canopy of the golden dragon fountains courtyard, Edwin and Cory strode next to one another as Hero ran ahead, weaving in between the pillars with his arms out, flapping them as if he were a dragon. With Hero's youth, Edwin was reminded of how he was at that age. He skipped chores and went into the woods to play as Knight Lockwood from his book. Those were distant memories, though; after his father died, his uncle made him help out in the bakery from dawn till dusk. Edwin looked to Cory in hopes of distracting himself with some conversation. Their eyes met.

"Thank ye for showin' me the way," Edwin said smiling.

"No worries!" Cory looked away quickly as though embarrassed. "I'm sure you would have found it on your own."

"Ma dragon egg wedd have hatched by the time a got there, though." Edwin leaned forward, trying to catch her eyes again in the conversation. "Are ye still wonderin' wit to dae? To be a Dragon Knight or a blacksmith a mean."

"The decision is constantly on my mind." She rubbed her arm. "I wonder if seeing your Dragon hatch will help me."

Edwin cocked his head. "Why cannae ye dae both?"

"How? Being a Dragon Knight is a time-consuming duty."

"Daes yer mother no have free time?"

The trio made it to the other half of the castle. They walked under the archway into the structure. The hallways were a little wider than the ones in the part of the castle Edwin was used to, yet the ceiling was the same height. They were decorated by paintings, suits of armor that resembled the castle guards, marble statues of knights with their dragons, and surprisingly large, mounted scales. Edwin approached the first carved face he saw. "Wit are these for?"

"They're monuments of our past kings and queens with their Dragons. There are also ones of those who didn't have royal blood yet were astonishing leaders," Cory explained, coming to a stop next to him.

"Is King Clayus here with Cerberus?"

"No." Cory shook her head. "Only kings who have died get their stature dedicated."

"If they make these after daith, how daes the sculptor ken wit they looked like?"

Cory shrugged. "From portraits and people's descriptions of them."

Edwin chuckled, "So say one af them wis really scrawny in life, then aw people wedd have to dae is claim they were this big, strong person with perfect features, and the sculptor wedd carve them like that?"

Cory blinked, being silent. Edwin tightened his lips. He hoped he didn't unintentionally insult any of their past rulers. Looking down the hall at the statues, it seemed all the men had a strong build and the women a thin one, the typical beauty standards, or at least to those in Gorish. Maybe that's why they were the beauty standards, because the royals who set them looked that way.

"Sorry, bad joke," Edwin said, trying to brush it off.

"That was supposed to be a joke?" Cory looked puzzled.

CLANG!

Cory jumped closer to Edwin as he stiffened. Down the hall, they saw Hero standing over a suit of armor that had toppled over. Edwin signed in relief, glad for the change in topic. Cory didn't seem that approving of Edwin. She seemed hard to impress and serious all the time, not that he was trying to impress her.

"I didn't do it!" Hero let a piece of the armor drop from his hands, and it clashed to the floor as he looked at his sister's deadly gaze with one of guilt.

"Hero! You know you aren't allowed to touch anything!" she snapped, stomping her way over.

"I didn't!" The young boy bent down and picked up the armor's leg, setting it back in place before it fell over.

"So, what, it just fell over? A ghost knocked it?"

Hero looked down, his posture closed. He shrugged, not looking at his sister.

"What happened?" said an authoritative voice from behind, which got their attention. It sounded out of place, however, with the tone coming from a younger owner.

Terro walked up to the group, staring down at the disassembled armor. The prince was a jerk, yet he wasn't honestly going to punish Hero for knocking down a suit of armor, was he? The young boy shouldn't have touched it, yet he was only ten years old.

"I-I didn't do it, I swear!" Hero jumped.

"You're not lying, are you?" Terro resembled his father as he raised his eyebrow at the child.

Shifting the weight between his feet, Hero said nothing and continued looking at the mess of his lapse of judgment.

"It was an accident, Prince Terro," Cory began, her pitch now timid. "I'll clean it up!"

"Don't bother." Terro waved a dismissive hand. "It isn't a big deal. I'll have some of the cleaning staff take it for repairs."

Hero relaxed.

"You're not out of the fire, you know!" Cory told her brother. "I'm telling mother, and she's going to want you to help fix it."

"What?!" Hero pouted. "It wasn't my fault!"

Cory continued to scold her younger brother as the young boy protested. Terro turned to Edwin. "I didn't think I would see your ugly face today."

"And here a wis havin' such a good day," Edwin retorted.

Terro chortled, "Has your egg started hatching?"

"Just a few minutes ago, how aboot yers?" Edwin asked.

"Mine recently started. Fayette and Richard are in the throne room with mine, waiting with theirs." The prince nodded forward down the hallway.

"Are they starting, too?"

"Fayette's is about to hatch, and Richard's has shown close signs. Do you know where Skypris is?"

Edwin hesitated at the venom in Terro's tone as he asked that question. He nodded. "She wis headin' to the library last a checked."

"The library? Of course, that bookworm!" Terro grumbled. "Go ahead and join the others. I'll be right there once I grab her."

Stepping over the guards' scattered armor, Edwin watched as the prince exited under the archway into the canopy-like hallway.

"This way." Cory waved to Edwin as she followed behind Hero, who seemed not to have taken the scolding to heart as he got a little too close to some statues.

Edwin examined the figures as he continued down the statue-filled hallway. He was able to tell the royal dragons apart from the others because of the Dragon Empress trait, which was her arrow-tipped tail. It was interesting how mixed the other dragons were with different traits whereas the royal dragons all had one consistent type of traits. Cerberus was Brookorous, and Reuben is Karartress. Edwin wondered what traits his would all be of. The hatchling's features might be hard to recognize until he became older. He'd be at least able to tell his colors, yet colors didn't belong to any one category of traits.

At the end of the hall, were two very large decorative doors. They were rustic wood with carved grapes, leafs, and vines creating a frame around a golden dragon roaring with its wings wide open. The heavy wooden doors were far easier to push open than Latona's. Entering the room, Edwin saw his training unit on the stone floor with their eggs, including Terro's. They weren't grouped together. Instead, they were set up sporadically throughout the throne room, giving each about ten feet of space in diameter. Suddenly, one of the eggs burst open with so much power that pieces of shell flew everywhere. Fayette stood and ran to the hatched egg, and there, climbing from the leftover shell was a baby dragon, no bigger than a small farm cat.

"Fayette, was that egg yours?!" Cory asked, walking over with Hero and Edwin.

"It was." Fayette bent down on her hands and knees to the hatchling's level.

Taking a second, the baby dragon opened its brilliant, flame-colored eyes. Its wings were tucked as it fell, trying to step out of the shell. Stumbling to its feet, the hatchling made its way to Fayette, who picked it up in her arms, not caring about the slime coating the infant. The hatchling's eyes were big and wide, drawing the most attention. Its body was orange with a few stippled markings that blended in nicely with its red skin. The dragon's spine was a short fin, and at the tip of its tail, showed knobs as if barbs were going to grow there. On its head was also similar nobs where the horns would soon be. Richard joined the group that circled the hatchling.

"That was so epic!" Hero said huskily, barely containing his excitement.

Fayette's dragon sneezed, earning an adoring swoon from the audience. The little creature then tried to sit up in its knights embrace, yet to no avail as it stumbled. "It's a wee little thing," Edwin said.

He didn't expect to see a giant beast come out of the egg, yet he expected something a little bigger. Sizing up the hatchling, it was hard to imagine that this small thing could grow to be as big as the Dragon Empress one day.

"We all have to start somewhere," Fayette said, smiling with pride.

"Do you think it's a boy or a girl?" Hero asked.

"It's hard to tell." Fayette held the baby out to examine it. "We need Latona to check."

Edwin tilted his head as he stared at the hatchling, smiling happily at its knight. An overwhelming feeling of excitement and adoration toward Fayette came from the new dragon. Luckily, the boy was able to discern his own emotions apart from the baby, and it didn't influence him as much as the teen dragons had.

"Do you want to go now?" asked Cory.

Fayette shook her head. "I want to see the others hatch first. That way, we can all go together."

Edwin had a strong intuition that Fayette's dragon was female, yet he kept that hunch to himself, afraid to be wrong.

Hero walked up in front of Fayette with his arms out. "Can I hold it?"

"Sure," the young knight said and gave her dragon to the young boy.

"Eww! It's hot and slimy!" Hero recoiled.

"It did just hatch," Cory said with a smirk at her brother's disgust.

Chapter Twenty-Three
A Late Crack

Terro entered the doors to the library. Kane, the librarian, was at his desk scribbling down notes from books he was reading. Glancing up, he leaped. "Prince Terro—Your Highness!" He bowed. "What brings you to the royal library?"

"I'm here seeking Skypris."

"Then you have come to the right place, Your Majesty. She's on the second floor in her little loft," Kane said, pointing.

"Thank you." Terro headed to the stairs.

"My pleasure, Your Grace."

Taking the final step, Terro made his way across the second floor, walking around the rim of the banister as he glanced down each of the aisles. He found Skypris sitting in a loft built into the wall as a cubby at the end of the shelves. He smiled, watching her lost in her reading. So lost, the girl didn't even notice he was approaching. Should he scare her? The scheme made him grin impishly. Carefully, he crept to the loft, avoiding his childhood friend's vision. He hesitated once he reached her, then jumped. "BOO!"

Skypris threw her book and shrieked in surprise. She glared at Terro, who was smiling up at her, pleased with himself. Grabbing the book she had been reading, she threw it at him. "Holy Dragons Terro!" she spat.

Chuckling, he blocked the book with an arm. "Ouch!" he laughed, still amused by her reaction.

"You know I hate it when you do that!"

"Well, if you don't want me scaring you, then maybe you shouldn't constantly have your nose in a book and pay attention to your surroundings. What if I wasn't a friend and had ill intentions towards you?" The boy put his arms on the loft and lay his head down, almost resembling a begging puppy.

"Dying while reading…" She thought about it. "Doesn't seem so bad, at least then I wouldn't have to deal with you."

"You know, you should consider yourself lucky. Most girls would give anything just to spend one day with me." He flexed his arm and brushed it off.

Skypris smiled. "Yes, yet soon after, they would regret it because they would have gotten to know the real you."

"Skypris, there is no need to be jealous."

"Careful, or they'll also discover you're delusional, too." Skypris tapped his head with a book. "Why are you bothering me?"

"I came to get you because everyone's eggs are hatching."

"Oh." Skypris frowned. "It's fine, I'll just stay here."

Confused, Terro looked down for a moment. "What? You don't want to see them hatch?"

"Not really." She opened a book and turned her back to him.

Terro remembered two years ago when they watched Reuben hatch with Circe. Skypris was even more excited about the event than his sister was, and it wasn't even her dragon. He thought about how happy Skypris was to become a Dragon Knight. Something was wrong.

"Are you okay?"

"Fine, I'm just so into this book I'm reading.'"

Terro smiled and rolled his eyes. "Ah… is that it then? The book will be here when you come back."

But Skypris was silent.

Well, there was only one thing to do.

Terro climbed up on the loft and took the book away from her. "Come on," he encouraged.

"Terro, give that back," she begged, reaching for it.

"Nope, you can put your unhealthy addiction on hold for a few hours," Terro said, moving his arms so she missed.

"I don't want to!"

"Yes, you do."

"No, I—just give me the book!"

"Nope."

Skypris tackled her friend, causing them to start wrestling over the book. She was desperately trying to grab it, yet with each attempt, Terro skillfully held the book out of her grasp. Even weighing his arms down didn't work. He was too strong, and the task needed both her hands. Holding his limbs lowered, she attempted to grab the book with her teeth.

"No, you don't!" Terro laid on top of her, going limp.

"Terro, get off!" she demanded, irritation growing in her tone.

"Are you going to come see the eggs hatch?"

"Yes, now get off! You're crushing me."

Sitting up, Terro allowed Skypris to do likewise. He hopped down, still holding onto her book. "Grab your laundry and let's go."

Skypris grabbed her wrapped egg, frustration heating her cheeks. She held the swaddle of clothes in her arms tightly as she jumped from the hideaway. Once her feet touched the ground, Terro tossed her book back onto the bedding. Skypris winced, knowing it was going to take her a second to find her place in the book again. She desperately didn't want to go, yet she knew Terro would get suspicious and not leave her alone with questions until he figured her out. She also didn't want to be reminded that her egg might be dead and that she would never get that feeling of having a dragon or be like her parents. No, her family's knighthood line would end with her. Fooling herself wasn't a permanent solution, though it was nice to think she could follow her parents' legacies, even if it was only for a short time. Looking at Terro, who was leading their way, they passed Kane on the first floor.

The older man bowed at his desk. "You found her!"

"Indeed, I have."

"Good, you two kids have fun." Kane looked over to Skypris as she walked by. "I'll see you later."

Skypris said goodbye to the librarian under her breath, knowing he probably didn't hear her. Her thoughts became distracting, and feelings of conflict pounded her heart, turning her throat dry. Should she tell Terro? The offer was tempting, as she trusted him the most—well, next to Edwin.

No.

No one must know.

Guilt ate at her like acid. She tried not to think of it. However, she couldn't shake away the feelings. It was sickening.

"What is going on? You haven't said a word since we left." Skypris found Terro beside her. "You're not mad about me forcing you to come, are you? I didn't mean any harm."

Skypris started to become aware of her surroundings. The hallway was completely different from the ones near the library. She must have been lost in her thoughts longer than she had realized. "No, it's not that. I'm fine, I got a lot on my mind."

Terro sucked in his lips, and Skypris couldn't tell if he was trying to moisten them or if he was thinking. Her body threatened to shake with anxiety. He was going to find out. He knew her too well.

No, she just had to hold her ground.

"Does it have anything to do with why you were at the library instead of witnessing the eggs hatch?"

"I was just searching for something."

"What is it? Maybe I can come in and help you?"

"Terro Gaius Clayus Dragonsborn in the library? *Reading?* Is this a dream?" Skypris asked melodramatically, the offer taking her momentarily out of her thoughts.

Terro chuckled, "I'll have you know I read… just not as often."

"What do you read then?"

"Well, I read past King's and Queen's journals, laws of the land, and their relations with us and the other kingdoms, economics, along with reading about dragons."

"So basically, the stuff you need for becoming King?"

"Yes."

Skypris playfully scoffed. Terro stopped and gave her a look as if his pride had been insulted. "Sorry, I'm not a bookworm like you! I think there are better things to do with my time than read."

"I'm not a bookworm!" Skypris's voice squeaked.

"Then what do you call someone who would rather read books all day?"

"I don't read all day!"

"Yeah, that's right. You sleep, too," Terro said animatedly.

"You're such a jerk!"

"Why? Because I'm right?"

"No, because you bully people who don't like what you like or do what you do. And you have this attitude as if you're better than everyone else and can treat others however you want! No matter how crappy!" Skypris got in his face.

"If I'm this ego-centric jerk you make me out to be, then why do you hang around with me?!" Terro snapped back.

Walking up to the two, King Clayus grabbed his son's shoulder. "What are you two fighting about this time?"

"Nothing important, Skypris is just being silly," Terro answered looking at his father.

"*I'm* being silly? Who wouldn't get off me until I agreed to come with him?" Skypris said with attitude.

King Clayus lifted his eyebrows toward his son. Uneasily, Terro scratched the back of his head. "It's not what it sounds like."

"Mhm, I assume not," the king replied with a light smile. "So, I'm guessing you two are on your way to the throne room to join the others?"

"We are."

"Good. I was just heading there myself." King Clayus held up a bucket of water with some rags in it. "I'm bringing this along. I figured it'll come in handy when cleaning the fluids from the hatchlings."

"Skypris and I could take it down for you if you'd like," Terro offered.

"It's quite alright; if I didn't want to, I would have had a maid attend to it. I want to watch the eggs hatch. I usually do it with the trainees, you remember how I was when Circe's hatched. Has your egg started showing signs, Terro?"

"Yes, actually, it is in the throne room right now with the others. I hope it hasn't hatched already."

"What about yours, dear Skypris?"

"Not today." Skypris looked away, afraid that if she made eye contact with the king, it would reveal she was hiding something.

She wasn't really lying to him. She just wasn't bringing it to his attention, right?

"Didn't expect all of them to hatch at once; they have tomorrow and the day after as well." King Clayus led the teens on their way to the throne room.

"Do you think there are any dead ones?" Terro wondered with a concerned tone.

"Doubtful, a dead egg is extremely rare," Clayus reassured his son.

Keeping her distance from the father and son, Skypris hugged her wrapped egg tightly, tears threatening her glassy eyes. It was just her luck to be that one percent—the one with the dead egg!

No. She couldn't linger on this now. She couldn't cry, or she would reveal herself.

She would think of a solution for the situation later. Right now, she should enjoy the other eggs hatching and be happy for her friends.

The doors to the throne room opened, and Terro, Skypris, and King Clayus walked in to see a red and orange hatchling chasing Hero and Fayette around the room, tripping over its own feet and wings as it tried to catch either of the two. Smiling, Clayus walked over to the teens who were sitting and watching with wide smiles plastered on their own faces. "I see one of them has already hatched. Whose is this one playing?"

"Mine, Your Majesty!" Fayette waved her hand as she dodged a leap from her little predator.

"Is it now?" Clayus placed the bucket of water and rags down. "Do you have a name for it?"

"I'm waiting until I know the gender."

The King nodded. "How are the other eggs? Coming close?"

Terro walked up to his egg, bending down to feel the temperature of the shell. He didn't leave his hand on long, and when he took it off, it was quick. "Mine's getting close."

"Same with mine," Richard reported.

King Clayus nodded his head with interest. He then looked to Edwin, who was setting his egg on the ground. "Getting too hot for you?" King Clayus grinned.

"Just aboot." Edwin's eyes smiled.

Approaching, King Clayus placed a hand on Edwin's egg. However, he removed it instantly. "Ah!" Clayus said in shock as he slightly shook his head. "That is burning hot! How are your hands not burned?"

Edwin shrugged. “Am very heat resistant. Must be aw the times a burned masel bakin’ breid.”

“Apparently,” said the king who turned after giving a skeptical look.

King Clayus walked up to the throne and sat down, his smile returning as he watched the trainees interact with the new dragon.

“Hey, Edwin, how’s Demmis?” Skypris approached her friend.

“He’s doin’ good, a wee antsy,” Edwin reported. “He’s gonnae go home tomorrow.”

“That’s good, I’ve missed him at training.”

Edwin nodded in agreement.

“Have you been in here before?” Skypris wondered.

“A have no. It’s astonishin’,” Edwin said as he examined the magnificent room.

Skypris smiled brightly, moving her head to the biggest pedestal behind the king’s throne. “That’s where the Dragon Empress sits.”

“Aye, a kind af figured that. Wit are the others for, more dragons?”

“Yep, they come in with their Empress.”

“And when daes she come in?” Edwin sat on the dais followed by Skypris as she sat her cloth down next to her.

“She comes here usually when the king does, hosts official ceremonies, receives important visitors, to award and grant honors, dispenses laws, or when the kingdom is being inherited by the next monarch.”

“That’s right, she’s the second ruler,” Edwin recalled the lesson Latona gave him about the hierarchy of Xolf.

“Kind of, more like one half. If she doesn’t approve of something, then it cannot happen, and vice versa. The two rulers must come to an agreement.”

“Wit happens if they disagree?”

“They would have to work it out,” said the girl as she shrugged and shook her head.

“So, no wars break out between humans and dragons?”

"No, dragons are wise creatures, so our kings usually respect and take their words to heart."

Terro stood next to his egg, arms folded, watching Edwin and Skypris interact with one another, smiling and laughing. He balled his hand, trapping some of his sleeve in his grip as anger built in him. No, it wasn't anger, but something else. He couldn't place this feeling completely. Was it jealousy? He never got envious until Edwin arrived and started hanging out with Skypris, taking most of her attention.

What did she find so intriguing about him? Was it because he was from another land? It was the accent, wasn't it? Or maybe it was that he could speak to dragons—or so he claimed. Terro looked down, trying to focus on his egg on the floor, tapping his foot in hopes of keeping his temper under control. He didn't want to have this hatred towards Edwin, especially after the drake situation. The boy from Gorish had proven he could be trusted in a fight.

Demmis's little brother led the hatchling that was chasing him into Terro's leg, where the prince turned as the baby dragon got to its feet using its stretched out wings to help balance itself. It took off after the little boy again, nails tapping against the tile. "Be more careful!" Terro called to the boy, his tone sharper than he intended. "The hatchling's still getting used to walking."

Suddenly, Terro heard a tapping sound that wasn't coming from his foot. Looking over, he saw Edwin's egg beginning to shake with cracks appearing. Terro eyed the breaking shell. That dragon was supposed to be his! Terro shook the spiteful thought out of his head.

"Edwin!" He called. "Your egg is hatching!"

Skypris hugged her knees as she sat on her bed across from an unwrapped dragon egg, staring with a broken expression. She sorted through her head on what to do. It was the last day for the eggs to hatch, and all the other trainees had dragons while hers hadn't shown any signs of hatching. Looking out her open curtain window, into the night sky, the stars twinkled with the moonlight. The sky that would usually calm her felt cold. It was a sign that her dreams weren't going to come true, and so the night haunted her. Why hadn't she told the king?! She was his ward. He was like a father to her; Clayus would have understood. She couldn't tell him or anyone else now. It was too late! The egg was dead. It must have been dead all along, with how cold it was. She wasn't meant to be a Dragon Knight. She couldn't be like her parents, no matter how much she wished or prayed.

How could she tell everyone in the morning? Come clean and tell the truth? Act dumb? Flee the kingdom? The young girl placed her hand on the ice-cold egg, moving it around to see if there was even a hint ot life. What did she do wrong? Was it her fault or was she just unlucky? Could Latona have saved the unhatched hatchling if Skypris had brought the egg to the sorceress's attention? Of course, she could have! Latona was a dragon expert and a being of magic!

Skypris lay on her side and pulled the egg to her chest, holding tightly as if scared of it being ripped away from her. Tears streamed onto her bed sheets with each quiet sob. Why was she crying? She had no right! Was it because she was about to get caught in a lie? She'd never lied before, or at the very least, not this big before. It was her fault that she wasn't going to follow her family's lineage. It was her fault a baby dragon was dead before it had a chance to see this world and experience flight.

How could she have been so selfish? Skypris should have taken the egg back. The mother had probably gone looking for food, and the egg somehow fell into the rocks. She messed up so badly, and now it was too late! "I'm sorry," she whipered as her breath escaped her.

Sitting up, she sniffled, wiping her nose with her palm. This was her fault, and now she was going to have to take on the consequences. The truth needed to be accepted. Breathing in deeply, she wiped the last of the tears away. She had to go tell Latona everything—that would be a good start. Reaching for the egg, she was shocked to feel that its shell was burning. Not in a fire sense, but in one where she had been touching snow or ice for too long. The egg was so cold it felt hot. Skypris eyed the shell with confusion as she got off her bed, stepping back as frost began to form, encasing the shell. Was this what happened to dead dragon eggs? The frost in a twisted way was beautiful; it reminded the girl of rime on the windows during winter, being the complex design of snowflakes. Tapping emerged from the egg, making Skypris jump in surprise.

Tap.

Cracks formed.

Tap, tap, tap.

Was it hatching?

Before the girl could examine the anomaly, the shell shattered open. Her eyes widened at the baby dragon emerged from the shell shards with its eyes closed. Its scales were whiter than white with a silver underbelly and a hint of winter blue. Stumbling around, the baby began to sniff the air. It got closer to the edge and fell as Skypris instinctively caught the little creature in her arms.

Her room was silent except for the grunts and chirps of the hatchling. She sat on her bed, staring at the miracle. Opening up its wings, the creature shook off some frozen liquid. It looked to Skypris, then fought to open its eyes. Once open, they were wide with innocence and wonder at the world they had just hatched into. Skypris almost gasped. The hatchling's eyes looked the same as any other dragon—it had the same fire pattern. However, the color of them was blue.

The hatchling's bat wing-shaped ears perked, and its expression grew. It smiled widely at its knight. Skypris smiled back at the newborn as she examined the dragon—her dragon. She laughed with relief. It was alive—the hatchling was alive! Skypris scratched the scruff of the baby dragon. "Hi, little one, you have no idea how happy I am to see you."

Tilting its head, the little dragon made a bird-like reptilian sound in response, its tail swishing in excitement at her voice as though it was happy to see her as well.

Chapter Twenty-Four
Measurements

Lying on his back, Edwin slept on a cot, a baby dragon on his face. Having been there for the past two months, Edwin hadn't requested his own room. However, he had requested another cot so he and Maro didn't have to share the shy boy's bed and floor. Edwin liked staying with Maro, and he seemed to like the company as well. Edwin knew that Orff frustrated his son, so he could imagine Edwin's presence comforting Maro.

The hatchling on Edwin's face covered his forehead and eyes as his small tail curled between Edwin's top lip and nose. The baby dragon was a dull, grayish blue with a striking purple under his wings. Down the dragon's spine, he had three rows of thick quills that resembled a porcupine. On top of his head were two nobs with a set of two more on both sides of his jaw. Finally, at the tip of his tail was the trait of the Dragon Empress to show he was a dragon prince. Twitching his back leg as if he were a dog having a dream of chasing a friend, the hatchling opened his eyes, lifting his head as he yawned and licked his scaled lips. He attempted to scratch his cheek with his back foot yet lost his balance and rolled down to Edwin's chest. Sitting up, Edwin forced his dragon to roll to his lap, where Edwin fluttered and whipped his eyes awake. Staring back at him, the hatchling jumped up with excitement, making a squeaking sound.

Edwin hushed his dragon, glancing to see if anyone else was awake. Seeing it was only him and his dragon, he looked to the sunroof, which revealed a darker, deeper blue. A purring sound got Edwin to look over to where Maro slept. Curled up in a ball on top of Maro's rising and falling side was another hatchling looking at Edwin, however, with scales of red and purple blended in. His friend's dragon stood and tried to climb off Maro, yet instead, it fell to the floor. Scrambling to its talons, the dragon walked to Edwin. "No, Furwan. Go back to sleep," Edwin whispered firmly to the dragon.

In the three days that the hatchlings had been out of their shells, they had been nothing but loud and chaotic, and the behavior only intensified as they got the hang of walking and running. Edwin was grateful they didn't know how to fly. He imagined the chaos they would cause, getting into people's hair. He even imagined they would carry children off. That was an unrealistic thought, though it was an amusing one.

Ignoring Edwin's orders, Furwan called up to Edwin's dragon, who approached over the edge of the bed, peering over. He bounced with his front leg, his back legs never leaving the ground as his tail swayed back and forth. "Merlin, dinnae encourage him." Edwin grabbed his baby dragon and got to his feet, snatching Furwan up as well.

He wanted Maro and Orff to sleep longer if possible. He usually took care of the dragons until the father and son finished their rest. It was the least he could do for them after they took him in and cared for his needs. Besides, when the babies were awake, Edwin too suddenly felt alert and ready for the day. He took the hatchlings over by the front door on the other side of the home. He placed them down, sitting cross-legged, trapping the dragons in a corner with just enough room to play. Merlin and Furwan ran around each other tripping on their talons, tackling one another. Edwin watched them with great amusement, feeling a rise of childish energy. It was weird how the dragons' emotions affected his own. For the first day of the hatchlings' life, Edwin felt like he was acting goofy, wanting to run around and play kid-like games. He was embarrassed by his desires and behaviors until he realized their origin. It wasn't just their emotions Edwin was able to read, but he could almost understand what they were saying to one another despite not being able to talk. Right now, Merlin was taunting Furwan to chase him, and Furwan was gloating at how he was able to catch him last time. When would they start talking? Edwin thought back to Civil's dog-sized dragon. Around then or younger? Edwin would be the first to discover that answer since none of Latona's books talked about how old dragons needed to be to talk.

Edwin risked taking his eyes off them to search the tower. On Orff's desk were some paper and ink. Standing up, Edwin sprinted over, grabbing a piece of paper, a quill, and a well of ink. Returning to his spot, he made it back in time to block Merlin from escaping. Watching the hatchlings return to playing in the area given, Edwin sat and opened the ink well, dipping the point of the quill into the ink. He let the excess drip off before he began to draw. Looking back and forth from the page to the dragons, the boy made notes of their individual features and drew their bodies in different poses the hatchlings made, relying on his memory as he drew. Merlin had complete Zandorous traits despite his mother's features, while Furwan had traits from Karoress and Kaprisairess; however, the dominant traits were those of Ashtheir.

After picking a pose that inspired him, he flipped the paper over to redraw the position larger and add more details. Unfortunately, the ink had bled through to the other side, so he stopped. Merlin ran to him and bit the edge of the paper. "Hoi!" Edwin whispered firmly. "Dinnae dae that. It's no yers."

Once the paper was safely out of the hatchling's jaw, Edwin waved a finger in the dragon's face. Following it with his eyes, Merlin bit the tip, causing Edwin to pull away. Shaking his hand, he then looked at the finger and saw no blood. It was just red. Bouncing with his front arms, a peal of purr-like laughter arose within Merlin. "Aye, ye think that wis funny?" Edwin questioned the small dragon with a smile. "How aboot a bite yer finger, then we'll see whose laughin' ye wee daftie."

"What are you up to?"

Edwin whipped around and met Orff's gaze as the man stood behind him still in his sleep attire, like Edwin, except thankfully, the older man had more of himself covered. "A wis just watchin' the hatchlins. Did they wake ye?" Edwin asked.

The moment Edwin stood, the baby dragons took the opportunity and bolted into the tower's room. "I meant what you're doing with my ink and paper?" Orff corrected, pointing at the page in the boy's hand.

Turning and picking the ink and quill off the ground, Edwin returned it to Orff's desk. "Sorry, a didnae mean to take anythin' withoot permission, a wis only keepin' masel occupied."

Orff snatched the page from Edwin's hand and looked it over. "It's fine. You know, charcoal would work better than ink for drawing that kind of stuff. If you really wanted to do it, they might have some in the royal library."

Nodding, Edwin hunted for the baby dragons again before they woke Maro. "Hey, Edwin, want to help me make some breakfast?" Orff asked.

"Aye, just let me get them before they wake Maro."

Orff cuffed his hands over his mouth, then boomed, "Get your lazy rump up! We're making breakfast!"

Dazingly, Maro turned to his side so he could give his father an annoyed expression. He let out a muffled groan in acknowledgment.

“Come on now, breakfast isn’t going to make itself!” Orff piped, walking over to the fireplace.

Maro’s father picked up a clean pot and set it over a firepit, where he then gathered all the material to make a fire. Edwin wondered which he was going to make for this meal, soup or stew? They must have been Orff’s favorites because that’s all they ever ate, that’s all he ever cooked. It was true there were tons of different types and recipes, yet Edwin would kill for something a little more…solid? Edwin could understand why Maro was so scrawny and would secretly sneak food from the castle's kitchen on occasion. Edwin retrieved vegetables from the storage shelves and laid them out on the table. He started with peeling and cutting the potatoes since they would take the longest to cook, other than the meat. Maro got dressed and dragged his feet over to Edwin. The two hatchlings ran under the tired boy's feet, nearly tripping him.

“Morning, sleepy, did you get all your beauty rest?” Orff chirped to his son.

Ignoring the comment, Maro leaned on the wooden table, “Why don’t I finish so you can get dressed?”

“Thank ye,” Edwin said, switching places with Maro.

“That sounds like a wonderful idea!” Orff took out the wooden spoon he used to mix, giving it to Maro. “Stir the soup every so often. I’ll return shortly.”

Orff ventured back to his room, closing the door behind him. Edwin went over to where the two boys claimed as their space. Opening a dresser near their beds, Edwin had put on one of the pairs of trousers he used for training. Edwin made sure that every night after dinner, he would clean at least one pair, so he never had to wear dirty clothes for training. He was very happy to find out Maro knew how to do lundray as well, despite being a boy. Edwin had guessed his friend had no choice, considering his father's relationship with the castle servants.

Thunk. Thunk.

A knock sounded from the front door.

Both boys stopped in place and looked to one another in surprise. Edwin thought back to the poor messenger and the frying pan incident. He knew Maro did too, as the boy glanced over to his father's door multiple times before he called out, "It's unlocked."

Opening the door was Princess Circe, peeking in, wearing her Dragon Knight's uniform. Realizing who it was, Edwin quickly finished getting dressed by throwing on a shirt and tucking it under his belt. A horrified expression exploded on Maro's face as he charged toward his front door.

"Hey," said the princess, walking in more. "Sorry for the intrusion—"

Maro didn't give her the chance to finish as he gently pushed her out of the tower and closed the door behind him. "Yes-yes! Sorry, princess!" He panicked.

After the front door clicked shut, Orff's door opened, and the old man came out in his daily attire, which was dirty and stained. Edwin headed toward the front door, hopping as his slipped his foot into his second boot. A trail of hatchlings jumping behind him as though to mimicly mock him.

"Where do you think you're going?" Orff wondered sternly.

"We need to go doon to the courtyard early."

"What for?"

"No sure yet, sorry for leavin' ye." Edwin closed the door after the last hatchling was out.

Maro and Princess Circe were waiting for Edwin on the stairs. Reuben was down a few more steps. He looked a bit cramped between the tower walls. Edwin scooped Merlin into his arms, where the hatchling fidgeted to get free from Edwin. Ever since the dragon had hatched, he refused to let anyone handle him, even his knight. He would let people pet him but never hold him. Scratching, Merlin climbed up Edwin's shirt and perched himself on the boy's shoulder. Circe tried not to laugh yet couldn't stop her chuckles from escaping. Edwin hid his blush under his narrowed eyebrows, making Circe cover her mouth. She then cleared her throat before speaking. "Sorry, I didn't mean to mock. Your dragon seems to have an attitude problem."

"That is one way to look at it," Edwin sighed, stroking the dragon on his shoulder, who purred with his chin high in pride. "Maybe this is Terro's dragon after aw."

Furwan scratched at his knight's boot, where Maro then picked him up. "Sorry for being so pushy, Princess. I shouldn't have even laid a finger on you as I did. I just didn't want my father to see you."

A sympathetic expression came across Princess Circe's face. "Your father still hates my family?"

"Yes, though don't get the wrong idea, he's not a traitor to the crown, he wouldn't harm anyone." Maro headed down the tower, forcing Reuben to start backing up as the others followed.

"I'm sorry. I should have had them send someone else instead."

"No, you're good, Princess! Don't be afraid to come to my home!" Edwin could hear the panic in his friend's voice.

"Why did ye come to get us?" Edwin changed the topic to help his host out. "Is there an emergency?"

Princess Circe took the lead, walking down the steps with her hand on the wall. "The Royal Blacksmith is getting your unit's measurements today so he can start building your Dragon Knight armor. They want you in the Golden Statue's courtyard."

Edwin's excitement made Merlin chirp loudly. "That's fantastic! How long daes it normally take to make armor?"

Grabbing her hair, the princess worked it up into a ponytail where she tied it strongly. "He's usually fast, and he has an assistant. Still, it's hard to say, it took mine a few weeks."

They exited the tower's staircase, where Edwin could feel that Reuben was relieved to be out of such a claustrophobic position. He looked to Circe as she adjusted her armor. The overall design seemed to be focusing more on movement than protection. The metal parts were covered in thick leather. He also noticed that there was a chainmail coif. What would that help with? Should he ask her? No, it's probably just for aesthetics, if it were important, he would learn about it. The teens said their goodbyes and parted ways. Edwin took one last look at Circe taking in her beauty before she went out of sight.

When they arrived at the courtyard, the rest of the training group were already there getting their measurements taken. Edwin beamed when he saw Demmis sitting next to Louis on the fountain's rim. The two seemed to be deep in conversation, most likely about training for the day. Looking, he saw the Royal Blacksmith, who was Demmis's father, taking measurements. Edwin was sort of surprised that the man's assistant was Cory.

All the hatchlings were chasing and tackling each other. Maro placed Furwan down so he could play as well. Merlin's tail wagged when he saw the others. Bending down, Edwin lowered his hatchling to the ground, where he took off with Furwan, joining the others. Merlin tackled Junai—Fayette's dragon—as he reached her. The only hatchling who was not playing was Skypris's dragon, Scaltor, who was sitting in the shade watching the other babies eagerly. Her dragon was in some places so white it was almost blinding like the sun in freshly fallen snow, which Edwin had never seen from a dragon's scales before, yet the weirdest thing about him was his blue eyes. Latona had no idea what that had meant. Edwin was supposed to ask the Dragon Empress about it once he had the chance. Until then, the sorceress labeled it a color mutation like melanism or albinoism.

Cory had just gotten done taking Fayette's measurements when she ran over to Maro and Edwin. "Morning, you two," the girl with black hair greeted.

"Mornin', Cory. It's good to see ye," Edwin smiled. "Though, am happier to see yer brother up and gettin' back to work."

"I think everyone's happy about that. He does have the tendency to overdo it sometimes. With that said, would you two look after him for me?"

"A will try, a make no promises."

"I'll take it," Cory shrugged. "You all haven't gotten your measurements done yet, right?"

Both boys shook their heads.

"Well, one of you could go to my father. I need to do Skypris' real quick. After that, I can take over whoever's left," Cory instructed, pointing over to her father, who had just started measuring Terro.

"Okay, thank you," Maro said and walked off.

Edwin stood and watched Cory run back to Skypris. He wondered if she had chosen what she wanted to do already or if she was still undecided.

His attention drifted to Skypris, who was smiling at him. Seeing that she got his attention, the red-and-brown-haired girl waved at him sheepishly. He guessed she didn't feel comfortable about having her measurements taken. Which was odd because she was the king's ward. Who knew how many times in her life she had gotten them taken? Going over to the Golden Fountain, Edwin decided that if he had to wait, he should spend time talking with Demmis to see how he'd been doing.

"Morning," Edwin said, smiling.

"Hello," Louis greeted. "Ready to take the next steps in training?"

"Aye, wit are we doin' for today?"

"Today? Nothing," Demmis said. "Your group will go down to the seashore. It's tradition to introduce the hatchlings to their mothers. It's just a sign of respect."

"And how are ye feelin', Demmis?" Edwin asked.

"Better than the day it happened! The scratch on my face is burning, nothing to worry about though, it's a side effect from the medicine."

"It's still going to scar up badly," Louis reminded.

"I don't mind. I'm still going to be attractive no matter what, and it'll make me seem tougher," Demmis said with a wink.

"Or that you can't handle yourself in a fight," Louis laughed.

"In that case, my enemies will underestimate me!"

Edwin loved that his friend always stayed on the bright side of situations, even if the events had scarred him for life. "How's Gale?"

"Her wounds are healed. I managed to convince her to take a flight and have some time to herself. I feel bad. I think she feels like she failed me. Ever since the drake attacked, I can't seem to shake her. It's like Gale's scared that I'm going to burst into flames the moment she leaves my side."

"It's a dragon's number one job to protect their knight. Give her time, she's still shaken that she almost lost you," Louis explained, grabbing his assistant's shoulder. "On happier news, Edwin, how do you like having a hatchling?"

"In one word… chaotic."

"Perfect!"

Skypris came up behind Edwin and startled him. Turning to face her, he smiled brightly. "Are ye done?" he asked.

"I am, thankfully. Cory told me to tell you she will take your measurements now."

"Thank you, Skypris. Also, a wis wonderin' if we could go to the library after we introduce our dragons to their mothers? Am really tired af the whole *'Dragon Monarch'* mystery."

"Why don't you talk to the Dragon Empress when you go down today?"

"It's a dragon secret. A dinnae think she will tell me if Newla wedd no."

"It wouldn't hurt to try. I mean, it involves you, so shouldn't you have a right to know? If she doesn't, then I'll help you look for the answer."

"Sounds good to me," Edwin said before heading to Cory, who was recording Skypris's measurements.

Standing behind her, Edwin waited for her to acknowledge he was there. When she didn't after a few moments, he leaned over her shoulder and watched as she wrote. She hesitated and must have felt him behind her as she whipped her head back a little too fast, popping Edwin in the mouth. Stumbling back, Edwin covered his mouth and groaned in pain.

"Oh, Edwin! I'm so sorry, I didn't mean to," Cory said, coming to her friend's aid.

"It's fine," Edwin reassured her. "Ye didnae hit me hard."

Edwin checked for blood where he had been hit. Luckily, there wasn't. However, it tingled as it throbbed. "Are you sure? I can take you to—" The young girl stopped for a moment, then lifted an eyebrow while she placed her fisted hands on her hips. "Wait, what were you doing so close behind me anyway?"

Edwin wrinkled his nose, giving himself a second as the burning ended. "A wis curious aboot wit ye were writin' is aw, nothin' more."

She studied him with an expression that rested between regret and weirded out. Looking down, she tucked loose hair from her braid behind her ear. She turned and picked up her measuring tool. "I was just writing Skypris's measurements. You could have just asked me if you wanted to know."

"Aye, a guess…" Edwin rubbed the back of his neck, his face feeling warm. "So are ye gonnae help yer father make our armor?"

Placing her measuring tool in her mouth, she did the stance she wanted Edwin to take, making him form a "T." Edwin replicated, and once he did, she took the tool in her hand and started to measure him. First, his arms. Edwin's muscles tensed at her touch, understanding why Skypris was so shy about the chore. Cory must have felt him because she hesitated before continuing, "You don't have to be so tense."

"Sorry, this is the second time a've had ma measurements taken. A never experienced it before comin' here."

"Why is that?" She moved to the next limb.

"In Gorish ye wedd only dae this if ye could afford somethin' to be made for ye. Those who actually had money were usually nobles and royalty."

"Your family struggled?" She moved to the boy's chest, making Edwin tense up even more.

He'd never had a girl that close before, well, other than his aunt. It was different coming from a girl his age. "Aye, a wis born a commoner.

Although ma family owns a bakery, so we were better aff compared to others. It is kind of funny that am gonnae be a knight."

"Can't commoners become a knight or a guard?"

Edwin shook his head, "No, only those who are af noble lineage could dae so. A noticed that Xolf is more open to common folk."

The young girl moved to his back. "It depends on what you're looking at. Anyone who is qualified can become a Royal Guard to the castle, yet to become a Dragon Knight, you need to have it in your blood." She looked at him. "You seem to be the exception to that rule."

She moved to his stomach and waist.

"Shuidnnae ye be writin' this doon?" he wondered. "Ye might forget the numbers."

"I have a good memory." Once she finished his legs, she walked over to a piece of paper and took her notes in charcoal.

"How good?"

"I've been told one of the best. I am curious to hear more about Gorish in more detail." Cory tapped the butt of her charcoal pen to her chin. "Maybe you could tell me about it sometime?"

"There is nothin' to tell, honestly. A guess a could if that is wit ye want."

"Thank you, and to answer your question: yes, I will be helping my father make your group's armor." Cory gathered her things.

"Daes that mean ye chose to become a blacksmith apprentice?"

Cory thought, then replied, "You can say I have."

"That's good, am happy ye dinnae have the stress af choosin' anymore," Edwin said, as they made their way closer to the fountain where the others waited for him.

Cory's father was over by the hallway and called to her, so she changed direction to go toward him instead, waving goodbye to Edwin. Demmis wrapped an arm around Edwin's shoulders. "You sure took your sweet time. Were you distracting my sister while she worked?"

"Am unsure. She probably got annoyed with me," Edwin said.

"So, is everyone set to go now?" Louis asked, folding his arms. "Yes? Well, then, find your hatchling, and let's get a move on."

"Richard raised his hand. Wait, are we walking all the way there again?"

"Not me, just all of you," Louis chuckled as he pointed his finger around the teens. "Don't be babies. You'll be doing a lot of walking, at least until your dragons are rideable."

Louis looked at Demmis and winked. Nodding in return, Demmis whistled to the sky. The loud noise surprised Edwin and the rest of the teens. Not long after the signal, Edwin's hair began to move in a rhythm as the breeze picked up. Gale and another dragon appeared over the walls, flapping their large wings forward, pumping enough wind to cushion their landing. Edwin recognized Louis's dragon as the one who pushed the doors open in the ballroom the night of the drake attack. They had cleared the way for their injured kin and her knight. They were muscular like a tall bull with thick horns on the back of their head, horns above their eyebrows, and some that sprouted from their lower jaw, yet that curved forward like a brookorous trait, with an underbite. Their wings' back flap stretched to the middle of their tail, spikes protruding like a war mace on the tip of the tail, and along its spine, not in one but three rows. The dragon was gray with a hint of bright yellow.

Gale walked to her knight, resting the top of her head against him. Noisily, all the hatchlings ran to the adult dragons, eagerness showing in their hustle. Stopping to admire them, the hatchlings raised their heads up, eyes wide. Merlin did the usual trick he would do only when he was excited. Bouncing on his front legs, his head bobbing in the same direction with a purr-like laugh. The only baby who didn't seem to be impressed was Scaltor. He looked to Louis's dragon, sizing them up before walking over to Gale's tail, where he then began to bite at it with his sharp teeth. Gale turned to face the little dragon as she curled her tail.

"Blue?" she observed with interest, locking eyes with Scaltor.

While the rest of the teens stood and gawked at their hatchling's cuteness, Edwin ran over to Louis's dragon, feeling the effects of the hatchling's excitement for himself. Louis followed behind the boy. "Oh, that's right! You haven't met Atlas yet."

Atlas turned to both the boy and the older knight. "Hello, young Monarch," the dragon's voice bellowed in a deep grumble.

"Aye, hello, it's nice to meet ye." Edwin smiled.

"Alright, that's enough for now! We're burning daylight!" Louis waved the teens on. "Gather your hatchlings and let's head out."

Edwin grabbed Merlin before he could get away, allowing the small dragon to climb onto his shoulders, yet nothing more. All but two of the other hatchlings came willingly. Richard's had to be chased down by everyone, then tackled to come, while Furwan, Maro's, climbed the top of a tree. Maro had attempted to climb up to get him, however, he was about halfway before Merlin called Furwan down. Once all the hatchlings were gathered, off they went.

Chapter Twenty-Five
Hatchling

The dirt path under Terro's feet soon turned into beach sand. The group of teenagers had been walking for at least an hour, almost two. Terro led the way with Skypris behind him, as Richard and Fayette played with their dragons while Edwin and Maro brought up the rear. Looking, the prince focused on Skypris, and he watched her stare at her steps. Now that he thought about it, Skypris was friendly with Richard and Fayette. However, besides him, Edwin, and Maro, she didn't really go out of her way to socialize. He didn't know what to make of his friend's mood.

Mykale, his dragon, squawked at him, drawing his attention forward. That's when he noticed a large rock in front of him. Stepping over it, he realized he would have tripped over the stone if it hadn't been for the hatchling's warning. Terro lifted his chin, ignoring the hatchling in his arms as she stared at him. He didn't know what to think of his dragon. There was a part of him that resented the hatchling for not being the Empress's. It might have distracted him from the sore wound to his pride if his dragon were a male. However, all she had been to him was a constant reminder. Originally, he had no female names picked out because all the Dragon Empress's hatchlings given were all male. She'd only had one female in her life, and that would be her heir, so Skypris had to name his dragon for him.

Glancing down at Mykale, he looked at her Kaprisairess feathers. She had a thin, lean body that made Terro question if she would be able to handle his weight even when she grew. She had a row of large feathers down her spine, with most of her appearance being of a feathered dragon. However, her back horns were like Ashtheir, and she had a long, whippy tail like a Karoaress trait. The tip of her tail had fanned feathers, and her wings were drenched in them. Did he have a dragon or a chicken? Her snout was skinny, and she had cheeks and lips. Her coloring was beautiful, though, being different shades of blue with her underbelly being the darkest and her markings the lightest.

"She's really pretty." Skypris picked her pace up to match his, finally talking.

"Thank you," he replied, happy to hear her voice. "Are you glad your egg hatched?"

"What kind of question is that?" she scoffed. "Of course."

"He sure took his time. I was getting worried he was a dead egg."

Skypris's lips tightened, and that was the end of their conversation. Soon, the sand turned into wet igneous rocks where the dragons nested. Dragons flew around in the sky, landing, playing, sleeping, or eating prey that they had caught. Some wore saddles and others didn't. The group stopped at the bottom of an elevated plateau. As the teens climbed, their dragons latched onto their backs to stay on—except for Merlin, who refused to move too far from Edwin's shoulder, which he had claimed as his perch. Skypris would have laughed if her mind weren't so numb.

Louis and Demmis waited by Gale as the group made their way up. Atlas was over with a few other dragons as they sunbathed. Gale watched with a smile as though she would have liked to join, yet she dared not leave her knight's side. Louis lifted an eyebrow toward the trainees. "It took you long enough!"

"We would have been here sooner if they didn't take a break every three seconds," Terro said, pointing at the others, who shook their heads.

Demmis smile. "That's fine, it's not a race."

"Yeah, if it were, you would all lose!" Louis added. "Welp, we played long enough, time to start. You all know why we came here, right? Now your job is to introduce your hatchling to its mother. If you don't remember what she looks like, don't worry, because she will recognize her baby. Be aware of the bigger dragons wrestling and playing—I don't want any of my students getting squashed again. The females aren't hostile anymore; plus, if you show her that you didn't smash her child, she'll like you. Now, any questions?"

Edwin raised his hand.

"None? Good. Meet back here a little after noon," Louis said, dismissing them.

Like the others, Skypris made her way forward, with Scaltor right behind her. As the two of them walked, he kept on looking up at every adult dragon they strolled past. Based on his hopeful expression, the hatchling was looking for his mother or any other kind of kin. Going deeper, Scaltor hesitated as he watched other hatchlings play with their siblings and tease—presumably their mother, by biting her snout or tail. Yet, all the troublemakers got in return was an amused purr or loving kiss from their mother's tongue. Catching up to his knight, Scaltor realized they were heading into a space where the rocks were not occupied by dragons, and he called to Skypris with a squeal. Looking over her shoulder, she stopped once she saw Scaltor taking a seat. His blue eyes were confused. Pushing away the feeling of guilt that had dried her throat, she motioned for him to follow.

"Almost there, Scaltor," she reassured him.

Her dragon shadowed her once again as she led him toward a rocky cliff leading out to sea. She kneeled, having reached their destination, patting the wet igneous stone next to her.

Blinking, the baby dragon hesitated with his first step, then he made it to the gestured spot. Curling his tail around his legs as he sat, he looked down a hole in the rocks with wonder. Then he focused his gaze on Skypris. She swallowed the lump in her throat. How was she going to go about this? Her chest tightened, and her shoulders got heavier as the yearning to hide was almost unbearable. Ever since he had hatched, she had thought about how she was going to do this—what she would say. Skypris needed to tell him the truth if no one else. Scaltor was her dragon and deserved to know his origins, even if she only knew probably a quarter of the tale. She opened her mouth, yet no words or sound came out. She stuttered an inhale. How would the little dragon react? No. She couldn't back down.

"Scaltor…" Her voice was hoarse as she started, picking her words. "I…" She sighed, disappointed in herself. "I found you in that hole."

His bat-wing-like ears wiggled as he listened closely to her words. Sniffing around the hole , he was like a hound trying to pick up a scent. With a sneeze, the dragon gave up and looked to her.

"When the rest of the trainees and I came to get our dragon, none of the mothers would acknowledge me. So, I found my way out here, and one thing led to another, and I discovered you as an egg in this crack. I broke you out and decided to take you since no one had claimed you," she explained, the little dragon's full attention to her.

Sniffling, she wiped her nose with her sleeve; stopping, she realized she had begun to cry. Shame washed over her as if she were the rocks that are beaten on by the ocean's tides. Why was *she* crying? She was the one who was lying to everyone! It was she who had taken an innocent hatchling away from being with his family!

Scaltor rested his small head on her thigh, snapping her out of the miserable thoughts. Blinking, she took a composing breath and stroked the dragon's head gently with two fingers. “I'm sorry, I wish I could bring you to your mother, but I just don't know where she is.”

With a weak roar, Scaltor licked Skypris's leg and cuddled up against her, staying in that position as she continued to pet his head. The little hatchling closed his eyes, and Skypris felt a wave of contentment wash over her that was not her own. He didn't need a family or a mother, so long as he had his knight.

Edwin watched as the others wandered to search for their dragon's mothers.

“Now don't tell me you need help locating the Dragon Empress.” Demmis walked up to Edwin with a sly smile, pointing behind him toward the wild dragons. “She's nearly the size of a watch tower!”

The boy looked to see that in the center of the dragons was the Empress lying down. Edwin smiled back at Demmis. “Dae ye think she'll answer ma questions?” Edwin wondered out loud.

“Only one way to find out.”

“Aye then, wish me luck.” Edwin moved toward the towering black dragon with Merlin still on his shoulders, looking prouder than ever.

As Edwin walked, he hoped deep down that the Dragon Empress would answer the questions that had been circling in his head since arriving on the island. Would he finally find out about this whole *Monarch of the Dragons* business, or would she give the same answer as Newla did—that it was a fairytale and she couldn't tell? Preparing his words, he found the Empress talking with a pair of adult dragons. He couldn't make out what exactly they were talking about, though he could tell by their hushed faces and demeanor that it was something private and serious. Edwin felt his throat dry up. He couldn't even gather enough saliva to attempt to moisten it. How should he address her? Would bowing be appropriate? She was royalty, after all.

Whenever he interacted with her, he was either cowering in fear or just *there*. What if he accidentally offended her? No. He was overthinking. Hopefully.

Merlin stood up on Edwin's shoulder, wobbling to keep his balance. Raising his head, Merlin tried to roar, letting out a little squeak instead, getting the Empress to look. Edwin stared at her as their gaze met, not moving. With a smile, the royal dragon turned to the other adult dragons and bobbed her head to dismiss them. They nodded, then stood and took their leave. Bouncing his upper body in excitement, it seemed as if Merlin would explode. The Empress motioned her head up and down in sync with her son's movement.

Some time had passed, and Edwin found the courage to sit and watch Merlin interact with his mother. So far, Edwin and the Empress had only greeted one another. She immediately went to play with Merlin, which Edwin could understand.

The hatchling stopped and rolled playfully on his back. The Empress then lifted one claw and used the end to gently scratch the baby's stomach, making him move around in laughter. Putting her head down, she licked him affectionately as if cleaning the dirt off his underbelly like a mother dog does to her newborn puppies. Merlin let out another purr of laughter as if it tickled. Edwin had been a little worried about the size of the Empress compared to Merlin. She could easily accidentally crush him with the hatchling being about as big as a quarter of the large dragon's face. However, he had been impressed by the control the Empress had over her body, being extremely gentle with her newly hatched baby. The boy found himself smiling as he watched, wondering if he should step away to give the two full privacy, yet decided the Empress would have asked if she wanted some time alone with her son.

Merlin jumped up and began to run around his mother, which took some time before he would complete a lap due to her area, calling out in cheer. Moving her head to watch, the Empress herself let out a laugh in amusement. She then focused on Edwin without him realizing it. "He is one of the most energetic children I have had." Her laughter died down, yet her smile stayed proud. "I don't believe I caught the name you gave him."

"Merlin!" Edwin answered, the hatchling's energy putting a childish grin on the boy's face.

"Merlin, you say? Where did you come up with that name?"

"It's a character's name from some fairytale a liked to read as a wee bairn."

"You don't say. What is the story called?"

Edwin winced, realizing that it might have seemed ridiculous or perhaps insulting to call a Dragon Prince after a character from a children's story.

"*The Tale of Knight Lockwood*," Edwin said, nodding awkwardly.

"Oh, I see! A classic."

"Ye are familiar with the story?"

Merlin stopped running after the Empress moved her tail in his path. "I am over two hundred years old; I have at least heard of all the stories that have been written. The character you named him after is the knight's squire, yes?"

"And best friend," Edwin added, wondering if that would make it sound better.

"I think it suits him," the Empress approved, picking the hatchling up and setting him between her and Edwin. "I do enjoy a good fairytale."

Edwin froze, and his smile dimmed to uncertainty. Now was his chance. Edwin moistened his lip and swallowed, "Speakin' af fairytales…"

Merlin moved to the side of the Empress, where she bent down her wing for him to play with. Biting it, he tugged, causing no real damage. "What do you mean by that?" the Empress questioned as she adored her son.

"Newla called me the *'Monarch of the Dragons'*. When a asked her wit it meant, she told me it wis an auld fairy tale af dragon lore. A legend. When a asked wit it said, she wedd no tell me, sayin' it wiznnae her place."

Upon hearing the title, the Empress whipped her head back to Edwin, her eyes widening. "Did she?"

Edwin said nothing and nodded in reply.

"I suppose the reason you brought this up is because you would like me to tell you?"

"Dae a no have a right to ken if it involves me?"

"You do," the Empress confirmed, closing her eyes and breathing. "However, now is not the time."

"Wit dae ye mean *'now not the time'*?" When wedd the time be?" He tried to mimic the rephrasing in her accent, yet knew he butchered it.

"When you are ready."

"When will a be? Daes this have anythin' to dae with why ye brought me to Xolf?!" Edwin exclaimed, getting ahead of himself.

With her eyes lowered, she slowly closed them and lifted her chin. "When I know that you can handle the truth."

Edwin felt a bit of anger yet kept his tone neutral. "When will ye ken?"

"Patience, young Edwin, you still have a long way to grow, a time for learning understatement and acceptance. When that time comes. Then."

He had to take a deep breath in order to calm himself. He let the feeling of disappointment take control rather than frustration. Why couldn't he know now? How long would he have to wait? He wanted—no, needed to know why he was the only one who could understand the dragon's language. The sorceress who was raised by dragons couldn't even hear them!

Edwin and the Empress let time pass between them, watching Merlin continue to play. The boy's frustration didn't fully go away, though a new emotion crept in as he saw a green dragon pass them. His eyebrows furrowed. "Dae ye ken where Newla is?"

The Empress's expression became downtrodden, and she would not look at him. "Sadly, there has been no news. Clayus reported our Dragon Knights haven't located her, nor have any of my scouts returned with news. I thought maybe you had heard otherwise."

Edwin's heart skipped a beat. It would seem the Empress wasn't able to answer any of his questions today. He had to know Newla was okay and thank her for saving his life, along with Skypris's and Latona's—and Terro's, he supposed. "Dae ye think she's..." He couldn't finish.

"I fear I do not know for sure. Though I believe Newla is a strong dragon, despite her age. I know she can take care of herself. During the drake's attack, she probably thought it wasn't safe here, so she traveled far away and hid."

"Dae ye think she went back to yer island?"

"The Dragons' Island? No, she knows she would not make the journey in her condition. I have faith in her that she is safe and resting and that she will return to us when ready."

"A hope ye are right."

The Empress suddenly tensed up and got a shocked face as if something hurt her. Lifting her tail up and around to the front, where she could see. Merlin was hanging on to her tail with his teeth, refusing to let go. Edwin slipped out a snicker. The Empress looked to her son, her eyebrows lowered as she smiled. "It appears Merlin has found my bold spot."

Chapter Twenty-Six
Maro

Shaking in fury, Maro slammed the door of his tower behind him. That morning, he had gotten into a big fight with his father…again. He was just happy Edwin wasn't there to see this time. The Summer Festival started this week, and he had wanted to go for the past several years. However, his father—no, *Orff*—wouldn't let him go. *"It's all just for show,"* he would say. *"For the royals to trick the stupid people of Xolf into thinking they're caring. It's all an act, I tell you! An act!"*

Maro's entire body got hot whenever Orff was negative toward the royals! His paranoia was almost suffocating at times. Ever since Maro's mother went missing when he was eight years old, Orff had never been the same. He would preach nonstop about how *horrible* the royal family was and spoke in a traitor's tongue. It was a mystery why the king hadn't asked for the old man's head! Maro was grateful to Edwin for taking his father's speeches as a joke rather than a threat to the country. He hesitated—would Edwin care, though? He was from Gorish.

Maro shook his head, thinking back to his father and how he hated dragons! Orff acted as if he had been raised in Gorish. Dragons were the most innocent creatures. Why hate them? A more important question was what did his mother—a Dragon Knight—ever see in Orff?

There were times Maro couldn't sleep at night because the thought of waking up to a dead hatchling in the morning was enough to keep him awake.

Maro looked down at the hatchling, who rubbed his scaly body against Maro's leg like a needy cat. He was glad he was able to become a Dragon Knight, thanks to his mother's lineage. At first, Orff threw the biggest tantrum and was stubborn about his son taking on his mother's mantle until Louis convinced him, thanks to their history. On rare occasions, Louis would come over, and the two men would drink and have a good laugh about the old days while playing cards. Maro assumed the reason Orff's friendship with Louis was still going on was that he was Orff's brother-in-law. If it wasn't for that, Orff would have probably driven Louis away with his madness years ago.

It would be a relief if he could move out and get as far away from Orff as he could. And yet, Maro always hated the idea of his father being alone. Even though the man drove him crazy, he still loved him. He still remembered a time when his father wasn't mad, when he was happy with Maro's mother. Thinking back to a memory of him playing with his parents in a field of wet grass, her dragon watching. What was her dragon's name? Maro had forgotten and dared not ask his father. He let those memories sit with him, allowing himself to take a deep breath, pushing the events of that morning to the back of his mind. At least now, with Edwin, he didn't have to deal with his father's madness alone.

The boy scooped up Furwan and then hurried down the steps. He was already late for training, and even though Louis knew his situation and gave leniency, Maro still wanted to be respectable. The Hatchling squawked, getting the determined boy's attention. Petting and holding the hatchling was very therapeutic.

Reaching the end of the stairs, Maro passed the maids and servants as they worked on cleaning the castle and decorating certain spots for the summer festival's celebration. Taking a moment to look at them, he noticed the decorations were all warm colors with hints of yellows and blues. They were mainly sunflowers or sun patterns, representing the summer blooms. For years, he hadn't had a chance to see them because he wasn't allowed to go out of his tower during the celebration. So, the sight was a nice treat.

Finally, he made it to the Golden Fountain's Courtyard, where the Dragon Knight trainees sat with their trainers. When first coming out, he couldn't stop himself from looking at the Golden Dragon Statue spewing water from the top of the fountain. The sun bounced off it, almost blinding him. He didn't understand why, yet he always got a strange feeling looking at the Golden Dragon symbols throughout the castle, a negative one. His father's hateful words must have been rubbing off on him, after all. It was the crest of the kingdom that his father hated. Once his eyes adjusted, he approached the group sitting in front of the fountains' pool as Louis rested on the rim. Demmis was the only trainer standing.

"Oh! There you are, Maro. For a second, I thought your father finally had enough and cooked you!" he joked, putting everyone's attention on the late knight and his dragon.

With a shy nod, Maro sat down, crisscrossing his legs, hating the attention Demmis placed on him. Furwan launched himself out of his knight's arms as Merlin and Mykale came running to meet him halfway. The chirps and squeals startled Maro for an instant until he watched the hatchlings wrestle.

"You didn't miss much, Maro," Louis reassured. "We did a few warm-ups, then sat down."

"Yeah, lucky you, getting out of the *fun* parts," piped Richard, who didn't glance back at Maro.

Louis smiled and chuckled to himself. "Well, Richard, we could always keep training. I'll even double it for you! How does that sound?"

Richard tightened his lips, saying nothing more. The others around him were trying to hold their laughter in, letting out snorts and snickers. "No?!" Louis acted surprised. "Well then," he stood. "Off we go."

As the group dispersed, Maro stayed behind the group with Demmis. "What exactly are we doing?" Maro wondered.

"We're going into the village to help set up for the summer festival. We'll be doing it today and tomorrow," Demmis answered. "This will be your first one, won't it?"

Maro nodded. "My father doesn't really have much say over me anymore."

"He is still your father. You need to respect him."

"I give him the respect he deserves!" Maro's tone was aggressive, earning a raised eyebrow from the assistant trainer, who seemed taken aback by the boy's unusual tone.

Immediately shying away, Maro quickly collected his dragon and caught up with the other teens.

The city was even grander, seeing it for the second time in the boy's life, the first being when they paraded through the streets when they received their eggs. Even when his mother was alive, he wasn't allowed to go near the city, let alone in it. Thanks to his father's position as the king's ambassador, they lived happily in the castle, not needing to make the trip down. The castle staff used to be welcomed into their tower as they dropped off groceries for the family, but now Orff was so afraid that only Louis could deliver their food. Now Edwin and Maro were able to get a delivery from the kitchen and take it up.

His father's old position in the king's court might have been the reason why he had turned so untrusting. Maybe he went mad because he discovered something he shouldn't have and couldn't bear it mentally? No. The thought of the court hiding anything tyrannical was a foolish idea.

They entered the main street, scoping out the area. Maro wasn't completely sure, but from what he'd read and heard, he was able to guess what the homes were, what the shops were, and what the Dragon Knights' houses were. The smaller cottages were made of wood instead of brick, unlike what he was used to. The bigger homes had a mix of wood and strong brick beams that supported a platform that doubled as their roof and dragon's perch. The shops were all different sizes too, the taller ones being two stories where the top half was living quarters and the bottom was the store, or the shop and owner's cottage were connected side by side. Each building had its own charm or twist to it, custom to its owner's imagination and preferences, making no two cottages the same. He saw signs for bakeries, cobblers, butchers, and an assortment of other craftsmen with their trade. Even though all local shops were walk-ins, many booths were being built and set up along the sides of the street. Looking around, it seemed many people and a few dragons were decorating the roads. Lanterns were ready to light once nightfall came the following day, as they were being hung on roofs with colorful ribbons that connected the tall buildings from above the paths. Dragons were carrying wagons and crates with their knights up and down the roads. Flowers were starting to cover and litter the walls and houses. Maro's attention settled on the ribbons that were intricately woven. Looking up, Maro bumped into someone behind him.

"Sorry!" he sniveled, whipping around to see who it was.

Edwin stood still, gazing at the ornamented city, unfazed by Maro, his mouth slightly hanging. "I'm so excited!" Fayette exclaimed. "My family and I would always go out and trade with the merchants! They always bring intriguing objects from faraway lands; like last year, I got my brother a dagger from Elvous!"

Skypris elbowed Edwin, getting his attention, "I wonder how much trade you're worth."

Smiling, Edwin folded his arms. "More than ye are willin' to trade. A will say am a fine specimen from Gorish."

Prince Terro rolled his eyes, seeming infuriated at Skypris and Edwin's interaction. Maro was surprised the prince didn't start another fight with Edwin because of his jealousy. Maro wasn't afraid of Terro, yet he preferred not to make eye contact when possible, and he never understood how Edwin could act the way he did with the prince.

"Lucky everyone," Demmis said, turning to face them all. "Because you're helping the merchants unload and set up tomorrow, you get the first of the trade, so make sure you bring some goods." He winked.

"At least something good will come out of this," Terro grumbled.

Skypris came up to him and fiddled with his hair. "Don't be like that."

He leaned out of her reach. "Like what?"

"Like you're better than everyone. When we were younger, you used to live for the festival."

"*Used to*," he said, repeating the point. "The only reason I liked it back then was because of the air show my father put on, and now that's ruined thanks to my sister taking over this year. Reuben's barely rideable."

"Air show?" Edwin turned with interest. "Wit is the Summer Festival aboot because am gettin' wee bits and pieces?"

That's right. Edwin hadn't been to one yet either. Maro guessed that they didn't have many festivities in Gorish. What a horrible place to live, especially given what Edwin had talked to him about. Yet Edwin would often express wanting to go back because of his aunt and uncle. Maro felt a little happier because he wasn't the only one his age with a lack of experience with the festival.

"It's basically the announcement for the start of Summer," Louis said and scratched his nose. "Merchants from all across the lands come here with their tradable goods for the entire week. Thinking about it, they'll probably have stuff from your kingdom—Gorish."

"Don't forget about the food!" Richard's mouth watered.

"Right… anyway. The first day, the king would often perform a four-minute air show with his dragon."

"That sounds like a good auld time!" Edwin exclaimed, then his mood dimmed. "A wish a had objects to trade."

"You got that sword of yours. I bet you'd get something valuable, especially if you tell them that you slayed a drake with it," Richard suggested.

"No, a wedd never trade ma sword," Edwin said with a firm tone.

Demmis puts a hand to his chin, where his bandage ends. "Bummer. I would have traded my sister for a sword like yours."

Louis clapped, rubbing his hands together. "These decorations aren't going to hang themselves. Today we're going to help set up the city, then tomorrow we're going to help the merchants unload, so make sure you bring a bag's worth of tradable goods. Everyone but Terro, head to the market square."

"Why can't I go?" Terro snapped.

"I want you to take some food to your sister. The girl left in such a hurry to practice that she forgot to eat," Louis explained. "And your father's busy right now with the festival, so he asked if I could get someone to do it for him."

"So that's why it was so nice at breakfast this morning!" Terro expressed as if he had just figured out the biggest mystery in the world. "Why didn't my father get one of the servants to do it?"

"Because they're all busy with the festival preparations," Louis said. "I was there when the king realized it. He asked me, and I agreed."

"It's not my fault if she's forgetful. Besides, she can go without a meal."

Louis grabbed his face. "Alright, Terro. Maro, take some food down to the princess and her dragon."

Maro lowered his brows in frustration. He didn't want to miss out on anything with the festival, even decorating. Terro didn't even like the festival. It was probably because Skypris was going to help, and the prince was possessive. Maro bowed his head, accepting the task.

"I'se dae it!" Edwin raised a hand, putting the free one on Maro's shoulder.

"Good!" Louis tossed him a sack and some coins. "The castle cooks are either too busy or off, so you'll have to rustle her and her dragon up some food in the markets."

Maro's heart felt pained. Edwin hadn't experienced any of this either, and he didn't want him to miss out.

"A-are you sure?" Maro mumbled.

"Aye!" Edwin nodded. "A dinnae want ye missin' oot. A'll have tomorrow."

As Edwin took his leave, the group of teens went the other direction, their hatchlings staying close to their knight in fear of being lost in the sea of working humans. Maro stayed behind and watched Edwin walk away before he turned to follow the others with Furwan then almost jumped out of his skin to see Louis standing there.

"Are you alright, Maro?" Louis's tone went gentler, which was a rare thing for the rest of the world, but for Maro, he would do so regularly.

The two of them were alone as Demmis continued to lead the trainees to the market square.

"I'm fine," Maro lied, his slumped shoulders probably giving his true feelings away.

"Are you now? You look angry." Louis raised a brow.

"I've just been fighting with him the past few days. He doesn't like the festival," Maro confessed. "I'm going insane, uncle!"

Louis patted him on the back, the man's hand being so large it almost took up the entire upper half of the scrawny boy. "Your father…" He hesitated, clearing his throat. "Has had a rough time."

The boy was silent, his throat dry, his heart thumping, his chest tightening.

"We lost her, too," Maro said with a firm voice as tears stung his eyes.

"I know," Louis said, his voice becoming reverent. "We are all fighting this battle together. Something you will learn out on the field is that every knight and dragon has a breaking point; even though they are exposed to the same things, some are better at handling them than others. For those of us who are lucky enough to recover, it is our job to try to love and help those who aren't so fortunate."

After seeing no response from his nephew, yet tears escaping his hard face, the man continued, "Your father is fighting other battles. He has demons. He's doing his best, so please just be patient with him—love him. It's what your mother wanted."

Maro looked up at his uncle, yet his face retained the same hardness. Louis was right. He had to be kind. It was just so hard and exhausting. The uncle led his nephew toward the others. "Come on! Let's help with some flowers."

Eventually, Maro managed to forget about his father and his negative feelings. It was fun to help decorate, especially rearranging flowers into fun, beautiful patterns or sculptures. Maro helped to finish weaving flowers into a floral sculpture of the Dragon Empress that stood about ten feet tall. That was about all he and the trainees could do before their hatchlings began to go rampant. That afternoon soon evolved from helping set up the decorations to saving them. Furwan played tug of war with the ribbons and ate the flowers after diving into an entire crate of them. Maro had been so busy trying to catch his own that he hadn't seen the demolition the other babies had done; yet when he looked around, it was safe to say they needed to redecorate a quarter of the market square. Finally, they had tied the hatchlings up to a nearby post with some rope. It had taken a while to catch them all. The only hatchling who was allowed to wander was Scaltor, who had done nothing apart from staying close to his knight.

Unfortunately, Edwin hadn't returned from taking food to Princess Circe. Skypris had tried her best to keep Maro included in conversations. He appreciated her and could understand why Terro would get jealous of her attention. The blue sky soon started to turn different pinks and oranges. Maro walked up to Furwan, who was biting and pulling on Richard’s dragon's tail as he tried to run away in vain, thanks to the ropes. Seeing his knight, Furwan let go and squawked.

“If I untie you, do you promise to be good?” Maro scratched the Dragon's nose.

With a purr, Furwan looked up and smiled at him with an expression that told Maro not to trust him.

Chapter Twenty-Seven

The Princess, The Apple, And The Bread

Edwin backtracked to the shops. The scent of the ocean faded as the aroma of baked goods filled his nostrils, reminding him of home. With the castle cooks too busy with the festivities, he needed to ensure he only picked the best quality food for the princess.

Maybe he should have been more disappointed that he would miss the experience of decorating for the festival. However, no matter the ornaments at the celebration, their beauty would be dull compared to Circe's. She was the princess after all. To him, seeing her was the better of the two. Besides, he was more interested in helping the merchants the next day. He was always a better helper than a designer.

He walked over to a shop that had a hanging wooden sign with an apple carved into it. Below the window wall were opened crates full of fruit, apples, mangos, watermelon, and blueberries. Walking into the store, Edwin got hit with a bunch of sweet smells with a hint of ripening vegetables and fruit. The inside was decorated with bright seasonal colors, almost matching the festival ornaments Edwin had seen so far. The building was one floor, and the roof was made entirely of glass, which Edwin was taken aback to see because in Gorish, the material was expensive and rare. The weirdest thing, though, was a long crate under the windowed roof that was filled with dirt as they grew vegetables. He blinked, taking in the odd sight. It was like a personal garden, yet indoors. He looked at a crate of colorful apples, some red, some green, and others yellow.

The woman behind the counter looked to be in her early forties with short black hair. Her build was shaped like the pears she sold. Her clothes were nicely kept as she wore a gardening apron.

"Good morning to you," she greeted.

"Mornin'," he replied with a smile.

"I see you're looking at the apples. They're straight from the tree, just picked them yesterday morning."

"Aye, that'll be perfect, A'll take one." Edwin grabbed the reddest apple he could find and walked to the counter.

"That's a fun accent you got there, don't think I've heard it before." She held out her hand.

Edwin exchanged money with the shop owner before tossing the apple in the sack. "Aye, am from the west."

The shopkeeper stopped for a moment, her eyes widening with enthusiasm. "You wouldn't be the boy from Gorish everyone's gossiping about, would you? The one who can talk with dragons?"

Hesitating, he thought on how to approach this. Should he acknowledge it or deny it? She didn't seem hostile about it, rather intrigued. Maybe not everyone understood the true relationship between the countries. "That a am."

"Oh! How amazing! How do you like it here in Xolf? Is it vastly different than Gorish?"

"It's a lot more welcomin'." Edwin smiled, not really wanting to say more. "Am excited for the festival, it'll be ma first."

"Really? Well then, I hope you enjoy yourself!" Her expression became brighter. "What's it like talking with dragons?"

"It's no different than ye and a talkin'." Edwin was happy no one else seemed to be in the store with them. "A cannae even tell it's a different language. From wit a've heard from others, am talkin' normally."

She nods her head, encouraging the boy to go on.

Edwin's cheeks got warm. "Am so sorry, a must be on ma way."

"Okay, off you go then." She waved to Edwin, not seeming bothered at all.

He gave one last wave before walking out of the store. It didn't take Edwin and Merlin long to collect more food. Edwin tried his best to mimic the local accent to try and avoid interactions like the one with the shopkeeper. Some words were harder than others to say. He found it the hardest to replicate the hard 'R'. He managed to get some cheese and freshly baked buns for her. As silly as it was, he was proud of himself for having a baker's background. It came in handy for telling the best bread apart.

He held it up to his shoulder so Merlin could sniff. "Smell this."

The dragon sniffed.

"Dae ye want to ken how ye can tell af breid is good—"

CRUNCH!

Merlin bit down on the bread, instinctively Edwin called in protest and tried to yank it away from the baby dragon, yet the hatchling wasn't letting go. "That's no for ye!"

The bread tore, leaving the hatchling to lick his lips and Edwin to give him a scowl. He shouldn't have expected anything less if he was being honest with himself. Not wanting the princess to swap spit with the same thing that ate bugs and mice, he tore the bun in half and gave the contaminated portion to Merlin, who enjoyed every crumb. "A thought dragons were carnivores."

Merlin danced his forked tongue around his scaled lips as he looked to his knight, wide-eyed as though he saw Edwin as food.

The knight and dragon in training made their way to the butcher shop. It had three levels too it and was swarmed with people and dragons that came and went fast. It had seemed that the bottom floor was where they processed the meat, the second level was where the common folk got theirs, and the top floor was where the knights would pick up breakfast or lunch for their dragons before setting out on their duties. The top floor had a landing platform made of strong stone and beams. If it wasn't chaotic already, Merlin had leaped for the butcher's table in an attempt to eat the freshly descaled fish. Luckily, though, Edwin caught the little devil. Kindly, the owner gave Merlin some scraps for free. They left with some questionable meat for Reuben. Merlin chewed on scraps as its juices dripped onto Edwin's shoulder. He hadn't realized the mess until it was too late.

He came to the entrance of the village, stopping and looking around. Where was the princess exactly? Going on his tippy-toes, he was barely tall enough to see overhead, noticing that a dragon was flying low to the trees before landing out of sight. Edwin was certain that it had to have been Rueben. They had the same coloring, and it was a dragon with Karoaress traits.

Leaving the path to the castle, Edwin journeyed into the forest following the flying dragon. Edwin hadn't paid much attention to the greenery until now. The forests were very thick and overgrown with tall trees everywhere, with bark covered in spring moss. The two came to a clearing with soft, tall grass that had been patted down by a large weight repeatedly over time. Edwin cupped his hand over his eyes to block out the sun. Merlin squawked as the wind kicked up, making the tops of the trees rustle and the trunks sway. Hearing the wings, Reuben soon came into view, dipping into the clearing, skimming the strands of grass that were brave enough to stand. Rising, he gained momentum before spinning, piercing through the force of the wind like an arrow. Wings folded, he fell back, gaining speed, then opened his wings and soared upwards. Edwin's mouth hung in amazement. He couldn't believe the control shown, not only by the dragon but by his mistress in her guidance with the air trick. Watching the flying dragon, he could see that leaning forward in a saddle was his knight, Princess Circe.

Her hair was tied in a ponytail that flapped in the wind. She wore her Dragon Knight armor. Circe seemed to have noticed her audience as Reuben soared to the ground, giving one last pump to cushion his back legs as they touched the grass. He tucked his wings like a bird and lay his body down until Circe hopped off. He stood once her feet crunched the grass. The dragon looked at Edwin and his younger brother. "Monarch," he greeted.

"Edwin?" Circe smiled.

"Hello, yer—" He caught himself. "Circe."

"What brings you here?"

"I was sent by Louis to bring ye, you and Reuben, breakfast," he said, trying to continue the false accent, wanting her to see him as someone from her home.

"Is that what the sack is for?" She scanned it. "Much thanks. I was just so nervous about the air show, I completely forgot."

"It's myyyy- pleasure." He handed the sack of food to her.

She gave him a nervous smile. "What are you doing? Why are you talking like that?"

His cheeks heated. "Nothing, I just thought a wedd try and talk like the locals here. It seems a-I'm going to be here for a while."

"Oh." She made a downcast expression. "I actually liked your accent."

His face beamed as he reverted to his natural voice. "Really? A dinnae think many dae."

"Don't change for them, I think your accent is rather charming." Her smile was soft.

Edwin had to catch himself from swooning. A princess found something about him charming. He tightened his lips to fight a goofy grin. Reuben turned his head to Edwin, getting the boy's attention. Locking eyes, the boy remembered that his emotions affected other dragons. Was Reuben able to tell that he had a fondness for his knight? What did he think of it? *"Stay away from my knight"*? Or maybe he would approve? Edwin was the monarch of the dragons, whatever that meant. Reuben did nothing more than smile and laugh, where only Edwin was able to understand. Princess Circe opened the bag and grabbed a giant piece of wrapped meat. Unwrapping it, she threw it up to Reuben, who caught it with ease and swallowed it whole, then licked his lips. Reaching in again, she grabbed the bread half, examining it. She lifted her eyebrows and smiled, looking at Edwin.

"Merlin got hungry."

Speaking of the hatchling, he danced on Edwin's shoulder before jumping down and running to his older brother.

"Uhu," she said and nodded before trading the bread for the apple, then tossing the sack back at Edwin.

Not expecting the gesture, he stumbled, managing to catch the bag but not before twirling for it first. His cheeks flushed. Circe giggled, "Sorry."

Heart skipping, Edwin's embarrassment turned into an urgency to make her laugh again. He would volunteer to be the king's jester if he could hear her laugh. He covered his face for a second before smoothing his hand over to the back of his neck. "That trick ye and Reuben did wis brilliant."

"You're just saying that," she said, rotating the apple in her hands.

"Am no." Edwin walked towards Reuben. "Though this is ma first air show, so ma word probably disnae mean much."

Circe scoffed, "I'm glad it's coming along well." She took a bite. "It was so tricky to do the first few times. I almost fell off, Reuben crashed, and we both lost our stomachs. Anyway, do you like festivals?"

"We'll see, this is ma first."

An eyebrow raised as she finished chewing the apple. “They don’t have them in Gorish?”

“To some extent. We have celebrations at times yet none af them are open to the common folk.”

Edwin thought back in his childhood about how they would have parades when someone slew a dragon, or when a lord or nobility was visiting the town. He never took part because he was either too poor or working.

“I’m sorry, it must have been hard to live there. I don’t mean to insult your country.” She took another bite.

“It’s fine, Am here for now so a’ll get to experience one,” Edwin gave a reassuring smile which made hers return. “Am excited to see wit aw the fuss is aboot.”

“Guess we’re going to need to make a good first impression!” Circe gave a giggle, and Edwin’s smile grew a bit goofy. She tilted her head to the side, finishing another bite. “Will you be participating in the trades?”

“Am eager to help the merchants set up.”

The princess turned around to walk back to Reuben. She placed her hand on the saddle’s pommel as if she were thinking of getting back on. Reuben was distracted by Merlin, who was bouncing around, trying to catch a field mouse. “I remember helping when I first started training. It was so interesting that we got a first look at everything.”

“Are ye goin’ to trade?”

“I’m not sure if it’s a good idea. Because of my status as royalty, the merchants target me. It’s not fun when people only see you as someone to get expensive and valuable goods from.”

“Aye, that makes sense.”

“It's for the best, gives me more time to practice.” Circe pulled herself up on the saddle and swung her leg over.

Reuben took his attention off the little hatchling that had a mouse tail dangling from his maw. Standing, Reuben waited for further orders. Circe finished her apple and threw the core off to be taken by some grateful squirrels. Merlin scampered back to Edwin and started to climb him as if his knight was a mountain, not being afraid to use his claws. Edwin flinched every time the hatchling's talons nicked him. Circe laughed, then cleared her throat. Once Merlin returned himself to his perch, he spat out the mouse tail. Edwin chuckled at his dragon's mannerisms, shaking his head then looking back at Circe.

"A weddnnae worry. If ye dae as well as ye did just now, ye'll dae phenomenal. No one will be able to Look away, a certainly cannae," Edwin praised, not caring how excited he sounded. He wanted to make her confident, even if it cost him a little embarrassment.

Circe didn't even try to hide her flattered grin. "You know. If you're not a fan of decorating, and because you've never seen a show before…" She hesitated. "...you could stay and watch me and Reuben practice."

"Am a allowed to?" Edwin grins widdened.

"It'll be our little secret." She winked. "And you could help me perfect my flaws."

What flaws? She was the word 'perfection.' He bowed. "Thank ye, am honored."

"You are," she agreed with a kind smile. "You might want to give us a little more room to take off."

Without another word, Edwin stepped back. Once he was a good distance away, Reuben turned his body toward the center of the clearing and with a, "Let's go," from his knight, the dragon ran, then jumped. Swooping his wings down to project himself into the air. With each ongoing powerful flap, Reuben gained more altitude.

Chapter Twenty-Eight
Art Of Trade

Edwin had stayed up past nightfall, watching Princess Circe and Reuben practice. The team was working so hard, Edwin had to force Circe to eat lunch and supper because she hadn't wanted to stop. Edwin didn't mind returning to the city to grab them food, though. He got to spend the entire day with a princess and eat with her. It had given Merlin and Reuben a chance to bond as brothers, too. It took King Clayus coming down to fetch her to make them stop rehearsals. Edwin was very excited for everyone to see her performance. She deserved all the praise she would surely get.

That morning, Edwin was saddened that his dreams had been interrupted by his friend and his father yelling about Maro joining the festivities again. The jet-black haired boy told Edwin to go along without him, and he would try to catch up. However, Edwin wasn't hopeful he would be lucky enough to get away from his father a second time. It was unfortunate because he thought the summer festival would be fun with a friend or two. At the very least, Maro had enjoyed himself yesterday, or that's what it sounded like when the boys met up to return to the tower as they talked about their days.

After meeting with the trainers and trainees at the Golden Fountain, they all headed toward the seashore, quite a distance away from where the dragons roosted. Now that Edwin was at the docks, he was a little surprised. For some reason, he was expecting more of a naturally built dock than a manmade one. Heavy wood extended out to sea from the beaches for about half a mile before branching into many shorter docks. Edwin had never seen a dock before. However, he guessed that the ones in Gorish weren't this big. Upon arriving this morning, there were already a multitude of boats anchored. Some ships looked newer with fewer barnacles and wear on the wood, while others embraced those age indicators. The vessels were different sizes, ranging from small boats with only a single mast to magnificent ships with tall bunches of them.

Dozens of people were helping carry crates and unload goods. Knights wore their armor, and dragons helped to bring the heavier merchandise to the city that people simply couldn't do without putting a system into play. The boy was glad for how wide the docks were, or he might have fallen off into the water with the tight squeezes as he passed dragons and people. Edwin maneuvered out of the way of a line of older Dragon Knights working together to carry large rectangular crates. The floorboards squeaked to the shifting weight, and he felt another give in. Merlin dug his claws into Edwin's shoulder, catching skin. He hissed against the pain and nothing more. He understood it was overwhelming to the hatchling, so it was hard to get upset.

The group of trainees was behind him with Louis and Demmis. All of them had satchels full of things they were willing to trade, except for him and Terro. He didn't have anything to trade other than Fire Slayer and his book, and he wasn't about to give either of them up. He even left his sword at Maro's place, not wanting merchants to potentially talk him into giving it up with their silver tongues.

Edwin stopped and watched all around him, realizing that he didn't know what exactly to do. Were they assigned to someone specific to help, or did they just jump in wherever they saw the need? Skypris came up next to Edwin, Terro following her. "Is something wrong, Edwin?" Skypris questioned, holding Scaltor in her arms.

"Nothin' is, am just confused with wit we are supposed to dae." Edwin shrugged.

"Uh..." Terro thought for a moment. "Helping?" His tone was sharp, as if the answer was obvious and Edwin was dumb for not knowing it.

Skypris elbowed Terro in the arm. "Just go up to any of the boats, introduce yourself, then see if they need help."

Skypris then walked to the boat with Terro following her, his hatchling lying on his shoulder, Mykale's whip-like tail curled around the prince's neck to help her stay on. Soon, the rest of the group passed him, searching for tasks. Edwin almost tripped over Richard's and Fayette's hatchlings as they raced toward their knights. Catching himself, he continued down the dock, not seeing an opportunity to help arise quite yet.

A dragon the size of Gale elegantly landed on a large crate. The dragon was dark brown with a blue underbelly that reminded him of a bluejay. Edwin watched as the dragon picked up the wooden box using its arms and talons, taking it off the ground as strong wind pumped from its wings. Edwin steadied Merlin until the dragon's wing currents had elevated enough not to affect them. Once Merlin settled back into his throne, he chirped, getting Edwin to look ahead. At the end of the dock was a ship with two masts just about to port.

Moving fast, he turned to the farthest dock branch that had no ships on it yet. Getting into the area where the ship was aiming, Edwin made it in time to see a scrawny man toss a thick rope to him. “Tie it fast, lad!” the man instructed.

Catching it, Edwin looped it around a post, tightening it to make sure it was secure. The boat drifted close to the dock, wood almost touching wood as seawater splashed up, misting Edwin. Merlin scampered down the boy's shoulder and sat next to him. The man stepped out of view, where Edwin heard a splash as he saw what he guessed was an anchor breaking the water's tension. Coming back into view, the man aboard the ship slid out a long wooden plank that connected his vessel to land. Now that the man was close enough, Edwin got a better look at the scrawny boat owner. He had blue eyes that matched the sea he sailed, with long blond hair tied into a ponytail, a short stubbled beard, and his mustache slightly thicker than the rest of his facial hair. He wore a rich blue jacket over a button-up shirt with frayed ends, as the bottom of the shirt was tucked into black pants. The merchant placed a heavy boot on the ramp.

“Ahoy!” His voice had a natural spark.

The merchant threw himself together well, which meant he was a successful one. “Ahoy,” Edwin smiled.

“So you’ll be one of the lads helping us today?” He waved Edwin up.

Ascending the ramp with Merlin behind him, Edwin jumped down onto the ship. “Us?”

“Aye, aye, my family and I,” the man clarified. “They’re below deck right now. They should be up any minute.”

From what Edwin knew of merchants, they often worked with guilds or companies. Rarely did they work independently, and it was odd that he had his family along. Usually, they would leave their families for months at a time. Maybe it was a sailor thing? Or perhaps some of Xolf’s culture.

Edwin began to walk around, Merlin scampering off to check out the rest of the new environment. On the deck were crates and baskets filled with supplies and items of all kinds. Some were foods he didn’t recognize, others he did, knowing they originated from Gorish. He checked to see what other wares the merchant possessed, and coming up to a bunch of barrels, he got hit with the strong scent of mixed spices. Edwin covered his nose and backed away. The man laughed, placing a kind hand on Edwin's shoulder. "Aye, I specialize in spices and textiles! The fruit is my wife's fancy, though, and I'm not apozed to venture from my specials now and then. The name's Israel, what might I call you and your handsome little friend that's scampering about?"

"Am Edwin, and ma dragon is Merlin," Edwin introduced.

"Say, my friend, you're from Gorish, aren't you?" Israel's eyes widened with interest.

Edwin eventually nodded to the merchant. Of course, he would have been able to pinpoint his accent. Some of his merch was from the country, after all. Israel smiled with a hand on his chin, a finger tapping his jaw. "Never thought I would see a Goreon on Xolf, let alone a Dragon Knight. How did you find yourself here, lad?"

"It's a long, weird story," Edwin smiled nervously.

Israel laughed and patted Edwin's shoulder in a reassuring manner. "You'll need to tell my wife and me sometime. She's from Gorish, too, you see."

Edwin's eyes opened more. That would explain why Israel didn't seem too unfriendly toward a Goreon; he shouldn't be too surprised, either. Surely there were a few merchants here with Gorish origins. Knowing how women were seen and treated in his homeland, Edwin wondered how the merchant acquired a wife from the empire. Traded for her? Stole her? The boy tilted his head, showing interest.

Israel nodded, leading Edwin over to some crates farthest from the ramp. "Her parents were going to marry her off for some profitable land you see. We met on the docks, and she begged me to take her away because the man she was betrothed to abused women. She and I were both so young. I took her with me, and on our travels, we fell in love, got married, and started a family together," Israel concluded, aacting out the tale.

The love story had Edwin wondering if he would risk everything for a girl. He hadn't thought of romance till Xolf. Honestly, he didn't know he was going to make it past fourteen because of Gorish's coming-of-age tradition. He had expected himself to be in a dragon's stomach by now, so he tried not to think too much of his own future back then. Hearing Israel's story, he liked the idea of having a family one day. Circe came to mind. She was pretty. However, she was a princess and older than him. True, his fifteenth birthday wasn't too distant yet still, she probably has suitors already, and she would be betrothed before he even had the chance. The reality squeezed his heart, especially after their interaction yesterday. His mind then went to Skypris. He did fancy her, and maybe if things developed, he could have a future with her? The thought made Edwin bashful. Realizing he hadn't acknowledged the merchant's story, he nodded.

"That's quite a courtship," Edwin said, smiling. "Best a've heard so far."

Israel smiled from ear to ear. "Thank you, my friend. I would love to sit here and tell you more stories of our courtship. However, this beautiful merchandise isn't going to unload itself. It's nice to have an extra pair of hands since my wife can't help."

"Is yer wife ill?" Edwin wondered, examining where to grab on a crate.

"Aye, only for a few more months if all goes well."

A wooden door closing distracted Edwin from the conversation. Turning, he saw a young boy who looked like a scruffless Israel, walking toward them across the deck. He was wearing a long-sleeved shirt with a brown vest over it, and he had a red scarf around his neck and a red cloth around his brown trousers. His long, light brown hair was messy and rested just below his ears with some strands braided together. "Jarod, my son! Glad you could join us, how's Mother?" Israel cheered.

Jarod looked at his father and said, "Mama's fine. She's sleeping."

His voice seemed a little off to Edwin. It almost sounded like he had a faded Gorish accent. It must be an effect of being taught to read by someone with an accent. Looking at the boy, he might have been no older than ten years, like Hero. Jarod stood next to his father, looking at Edwin, his face decorated in freckles. “Is this a Dragon Knight?” the boy asked in awe.

“Aye, this is Edwin, and he will be one of the knights helping us.”

“Where’s yer dragon?” Jarod beamed almost cutting his father’s sentence off.

Edwin smiled. He could tell the boy was trying to hide his excitement. “He is around here somewhere.” Edwin looked around. “Merlin?!”

Coming from the ship's starboard bow, the little hatchling tripped over his front feet, continuing after he got back up. Jarod’s smile grew larger as the baby dragon approached. Running to meet him halfway, Jarod knelt, and Merlin stopped to sniff the boy. Merlin started doing his signature bouncing up and down on his front feet move. Jarod giggled, reaching out his hand to pet Merlin.

“My boy loves dragons. He looks forward to our stops at these lands,” Israel explained to Edwin, leaning on a crate. “He’s always dreamed of becoming a Dragon Knight. It’s going to be a blue day when I finally get the heart to tell him his dream will have to stay that way.”

That’s right. Only those with a Dragon Knight lineage can become one. An emotional soreness pulled at Edwin’s heartstrings for the cute little boy. The rule seemed unfair, yet again, he could understand it. If just anyone could have a dragon, then who was stopping a thief or murderer from taming one?

Assuming by the look the merchant gave him, he expected Edwin not to tell Jarod. Picking Merlin up, Jarod held him in his arms as the boy stood and walked to Edwin and his father. The hatchling wiggled out of the boy’s grasp and climbed onto his head, letting out a weak roar. Jarod looked puzzled at the dragon’s new location choice. “He’s no fond af bein’ handled,” Edwin reassured.

“What’s his name?” Jarod questioned.

“Merlin.”

Jarod's eyes widened. "I love Lockwood books! When I get a dragon, am going to name it either Velcor or Eilonwy, depending on its gender!"

Not knowing what to say, Edwin gave the kid an uneasy smile. He didn't like lying to the boy. However, it wasn't his place to tell, so he needed to respect his parents' wishes. "Those are intriguin' names," Edwin agreed. "Are they yer two favorite characters?"

Jarod nodded in response before moving on. "What was it like getting yer dragon?"

"It wis…" Edwin thought of the right words for the experience, "unexpected?"

"Take this conversation on the way, lads, we need to get to work before all the good spots are taken," Israel began, changing the subject. "Grab what you can carry. We'll make our first trip to find a spot."

Edwin did what he was told and picked up a crate that was heavy yet made no sound, so Edwin assumed it was full of clothes. Israel took a crate up on his shoulder in one hand, then a basket in the other, while Jarod struggled to lift a smaller crate on his shoulder like his father. "What have I told you, my son? Only take what you can carry, the village isn't right around the corner," Israel taught.

Nodding, the little boy went for the cloth that was covering some weapons. The only way you could tell was because of the noise they made while knocking together as the boy picked them up.

"Want me to take Merlin aff yer head?" Edwin asked.

"No, I got it! Am stronger than I seem," Jarod hastily declared as if he was desperate to keep the hatchling.

"If yer certain," Merlin was the littlest of the hatchlings, so Edwin didn't push.

"Should I wake Mama before we go?" Jarod asked his father, striding to the ramp.

Israel, in the lead, stopped at the edge of the ship where the ramp leaned. "Let her sleep. This way, she can enjoy the festival with us.

There are plenty of Dragon Knights around. I don't believe anyone is funny enough to try and take anything."

As the father and son headed down the ramp, Edwin started to follow then halted when he saw Richard and a few older knight trainees coming up. One of them was Civil. Walking up the ramp, Richard asked Israel as he passed by, "Can we help?"

"The more the merrier!" Israel replied. "Grab what you can and then follow us to the village."

"On it!" Richard gave two thumbs up and trotted up the rest of the ramp.

Edwin wanted to greet Civil, yet he was in too much of a rush to keep behind Israel. The trio made their way through the docks, with Richard, Civil, and the other two Dragon Knights ten feet behind. Avoiding the other knight helpers, Edwin had to move quickly out of the way as he almost collided with someone carrying a crate that covered their line of sight. Continuing to hike the trail to the city below the castle, Israel called back to Edwin, "I hope you know someone with a bigger dragon. If not, it will be harder with the bigger crates, even with your other friends helping."

"Dinnae worry. A ken a few."

Finally, entering the city, it wasn't as cramped as the docks had been, mainly because there was more space. Multiple booths had been claimed with merch set up, and Dragon Knights continued to help with either carrying goods or helping to place them on display. Already, there were civilians walking by pretending to go about their business when, in reality, they were trying to catch a peek of the merchandise before the festival began. Edwin followed Israel farther back until he found the first empty booth. He set his crate and basket down on the wooden table. Edwin set his crate under it and stretched. A satisfying popping sound cracked from his back. Israel had to call out for his son and the other knights to find them. Edwin saw Merlin on the boy's head before he actually saw Jarod. The hatchling was lying down, enjoying Jarod's soft hair. Jarod awkwardly placed the wrapped weaponry with his father's load. After a few trips from the docks to the city, and with some help from Demmis and Gale, Edwin, Israel, and the others finished unloading. Jarod was asked to stay on the boat until his mother woke. Edwin hadn't seen Israel's wife during any of the trips to the ship. She must be very sick to sleep so long. Dusk would soon fall in an hour or so.

After setting down a barrel, Edwin sat down on a crate and relaxed for a moment. Observing other merchants finishing up their displays and starting to haggle with people joining in the festivities. The lanterns were being lit, and children wore flower crowns as they ran around. Food was being served and eaten as city folk walked about the merchants' booths. Edwin's stomach growled as he saw a man eating some mutton. Israel had stayed behind a few trips back to start setting up. He still seemed to have quite a few crates, barrels, and baskets untouched though. Edwin forced himself to stand. "Let me help ye."

"Aye, thank you, my friend, that's mighty generous of you, however I'm almost done. Besides, you have helped enough already, lad."

The others that were assisting had already moved on without a word, either looking at the merchants' trade, helping them set up, or, in Richard's case, eating.

"If it Wilnae take too much time, wits the harm?"

The merchant smiled. "Very well, my dear lad. Since you're up to it, could you line up the baskets of fruit? They don't all have to be in a straight line."

Edwin did as instructed with the baskets, deciding they would look best in rows of three. Some he had to rock in place because of their weight. Merlin was sunbathing on top of a lid of a basket. His stomach was exposed to the sun's warm rays. "Shoo, Merlin," the boy said, gesturing with a hand.

Not moving, the hatchling's foot twitched, still resting as if he didn't have a care in the world. Annoyed by his command going unnoticed, Edwin pushed Merlin a little. "Move ye ned!"

After not following orders again, Edwin pushed the dragon off the basket, having Merlin land on the ground unfazed by the impact. Now, being able to move the last basket into place, Edwin looked back to Israel, who was laying out some fine cotton. "Is there more ye wedd like me to dae?" he asked.

Merlin climbed to the top of a basket, with his eyes closed and chin high, he curled on the lid like a napping cat.

"That's all for now. I'm not displaying everything. Things are easily looted that way."

"That's wise."

"Trust me, lad, I learned the hard way with that one," the merchant winked.

"Awrite, a shud go," Edwin said, picking up his hatchling, who squawked in protest.

"Hold on a second, my friend! I want you to have something," Israel then rummaged through an open crate next to him. "Now, where is it?" he mumbled to himself.

Waiting patiently, Edwin placed Merlin on his shoulder, knowing the hatchling would prefer it. Digging deeper into the crate, Israel pulled something out, holding a money pouch up in praise. "Aha!"

He wasn't going to pay him, was he? He didn't know if he was allowed to accept any money given for this service, he had enjoyed helping the man and his son. It was nice hearing another person have somewhat of a Gorish accent. Israel untied the pouch and dumped into his hand a single golden coin. Holding it up to where Edwin could see it, Israel said, "This coin is said to be from a treasure lost in time. If I'm honest, it's the most valuable piece in my collection. I would like you to have it, my boy."

Edwin's mouth hung in astonishment at the unique coin. Taking it from Israel, he examined it closely, noting the engraving of a dragon with runes on the edge of the coin. Unlike the money of Xolf, where the dragon in the coin was a sitting empress, this one was a dragon roaring with different features. It was too small to see them. After a good look,

Edwin extended it back to the merchant, gesturing for him to take it with a subtle shake, “A have nothin’ to trade.”

Israel laughed, then closed Edwin's hand. “I don’t expect you to. It’s a gift!”

The boy’s hand came back to his chest. “Ye’re serious?!”

“I’m no king’s jester!”

Not resisting the giant smile growing on his face, Edwin glanced back at the coin. “Thank ye! It’s quite the spectacle.”

“It’s the least I can do for your help. Besides, it’s nice to meet another charming person from Gorish who isn’t my wife. I will say you aren’t nearly as attractive as she is, though. Now go on and enjoy the festival! Please stop by later so I can introduce her to you.”

“A promise!” Edwin turned and took his first step before stopping and looking back at the merchant, with an indecisive look painted on his face.

“What’s troubling you?” he questioned.

“A wis wonderin’. Is Gorish in yer trade route?”

To Edwin’s mind, it would make sense, considering he had been there in Gorish for his wife. Hesitantly, Israel bobbed his head side to side slightly. “Here and there. I visit that place for business only. Even then, I dare not stay long. I dislike how that land is ruled, and my wife doesn’t have fond memories. King Borin is a brute and a tyrant! Forcing children to slay dragons, what a savage thing to do! Not to mention enslaving an entire country after conquering it.” Israel gave Edwin a look over, leaning on his booth. “Are you wondering if I could give you a ride back? You know if I did, you would have to leave this whole Dragon Knight obligation behind, right? Including your little friend there?” Israel twirled a finger at Merlin.

Sadly, that was true. They would kill Merlin and then Edwin for being a traitor to his country, or they wouldn’t recognize them, and he would still be killed because he’s from a rival land. Despite the risk, Edwin wanted to be with his aunt and uncle once more, if anything else, to give a proper goodbye. They were his family. They should know he's alive, for all they knew he was already digested in a beast's stomach.

Could they come here? There was no guarantee they would leave their home just to go with him to the unknown. His uncle wasn't the biggest dragon fan, either. He took sport in slaying them.

Merlin's forked tongue was wet and felt like sandpaper as the baby licked Edwin's cheek, snapping him out of his trance of storming thoughts. He looked into the hatchling's fire-patterned gaze. Sighing, he tried to lighten the weight of the decision. "No, a ken a need to stay here, for now."

"I see, this is where you feel you belong?"

"For no," he repeated. "Wedd ye be willin' to deliver a letter for me?"

Israel grabbed his chin to think. "I could talk with a few buddies of mine."

"That wedd be appreciated." Edwin nodded. "A will see ye later."

"Looking forward to it, dear Edwin!"

Striding away up the road that was now bustling with city folk, buying and trading, Edwin was pondering hard about who he was and what his decision to stay meant. He was a traitor, and he was okay with that?

What of his aunt and uncle? He probably skipped on his only chance to ever see them again until Merlin was old enough to make that trip. However, he could see the Empress forbidding Edwin to risk her son's life on a fool's errand. As much as he missed his origins, staying in Xolf felt right for some reason. He had never belonged in Gorish, right? He was different? A coward? No. He remembered the time he slayed the drake and how Clayus had honored him.

Edwin shook his head to keep all his thoughts and feelings at bay. He should enjoy his first-ever festival and not overthink everything.

What should he do now? He couldn't trade anything, except for the coin he had just been gifted, and that would be disrespectful to trade away a present he had received only moments before.

Maybe he could catch up with Skypris? Though, Terro would probably be with her, and he didn't feel like dealing with that boy's jealousy today. Skypris wouldn't ditch the prince, either. Who else did he know that was here? Edwin was almost halfway up the road when he noticed Skypris at a trader's stand, looking at a book that a woman merchant was selling. He maneuvered in her direction, warily glancing for Prince Terro. Why was he so intimidated by that silver spoon snot? Skypris was his friend, too, and he had as much right to hang out with her as anyone else. Plus, he and Terro were sort of on good terms now… Edwin hoped. "Skypris!" Edwin called out.

No reply.

The young girl's nose was stuck in the book. She was definitely lost in a different land. Smiling, Edwin stood in front of Skypris, keeping track as her eyes moved across the pages, reading the words with ease. She still didn't notice him? Looking down, he caught Scaltor staring at him from between Skypris's feet with his strange blue eyes. It was then that he realized he had forgotten to ask the Empress about the oddity.

Looking back at Skypris, he found her looking at him with a smile. "Hey, were you waiting to see if I would notice you?"

"Basically," Edwin said with a shrug.

Skypris closed the book and set it back on the table with many others in a stack by it, her eyes not leaving Edwin's face. "How are you enjoying the festival so far?"

"A just finished helpin' a merchant."

She nodded. "Oh, did you see anything you liked?"

He shrugged again. "No lookin' to trade. A got a golden coin for helpin', though. It's unique, a think it might have been an auld version af Xolf's currency."

"That's quite a reward. All that the merchants I helped gave me was a scowl. I'm thinking that was mostly because Terro was there."

"Seems right, he disnae get alon' wit people, daes he?"

"Unless he wants to," she said and shrugged.

"Speakin' af the prince, is he around? A wis for sure he wedd be stuck to yer hip."

"He had to go talk with his father. We're supposed to meet back up at the city's entrance right before dusk."

Edwin nodded, trying to fight off his smile. He could spend the rest of the day with Skypris without worrying about the big mouth. Skypris lifted an eyebrow, "Don't try to hide the fact you're happy Terro isn't around."

"A wis no," he denied.

"I don't blame you. He hasn't been the kindest to you, even after the drake."

"Well, there is an improvement. Let us no talk aboot that now, did ye get anythin' fun yet?"

"Not a lot. I got to try a few exotic fruits I didn't have a chance to last year."

"And how did those taste?"

"Different," she said, giving a distasteful look.

Edwin chuckled, and they walked with each other, Scaltor following right at their ankles. "Not all of them were bad, though, one of them tasted a lot like a sweet strawberry," she explained. "I'm just looking for anything that sticks out."

"Really? Oot af aw this, ye have no found anythin' yet, wit aboot the books ye were just readin'?"

"Most of these books they have in the royal library already, and the ones that aren't don't seem that intriguing."

They tried to stay as close together, with the volume level getting so loud it was hard to hear each other through the thicket of voices of adults and merchants animatedly trying to make good deals, along with the sound of children's laughter as they played and men as they drank with friends. Skypris had disappeared into the crowds only to show up again with food for him and her. With a growling stomach, Edwin ate his with little guilt about her buying food for him. It was a large chicken leg that was crispy and moist with a butter-like flavor. Fortunately, Skypris had also kept the baby dragons from trying to steal by buying them their own. Merlin almost choked on his chicken bone.

The trainee duo passed by many stands, and Skypris checked out a few, yet didn't see anything that caught her eye. Edwin, on the other hand, found something that got his attention while Skypris was taking a closer look at decorative bookmarks. He stood by her, watching intently at a gathered audience. Sneaking nearer, the boy went on his tippytoes as he peered over heads to see that in the center was a man standing with an easel holding a canvas. The man's arm moved with grace as he painted a little girl sitting down and posing with a big, toothy smile for the portrait. Edwin stared in amazement at how precise the man's art was to the living thing. In Gorish, any artwork he had seen felt so flat, but this, on the other hand, felt as if the little girl had a twin.

It wasn't until Skypris spoke that he realised she'd walked up next to him. "Are you into art?" she wondered.

"Aye, ye could say that a have been startin' to dabble around a bit while am bored, nothin' serious," he replied, not taking his gaze off the painter's magic.

"You want to make it serious?" Skypris asked.

Her sly tone won his attention. He stared at her for a moment, studying her face like the portraitist did to his client. Her smile shifted to a light-hearted one as she grabbed Edwin's hand and led him away from the crowd and back into the city's main road.

"Come with me!" she ordered.

"Why? Where are we goin'?"

"You need art supplies, right? I don't think you brought any from Gorish when the Empress took you."

He couldn't get art supplies. He had nothing to trade for them or money to use. She knew this, so she must be scheming to do it instead. He hated the idea of Skypris trading her stuff away for him. Despite this, he allowed the girl to drag him wherever she wanted. He didn't mind, especially since she was holding his hand.

The two finally approached a booth after looking around for a couple of minutes. Edwin couldn't believe his eyes. There were lots of various paint brushes of different sizes, lengths, hairs, and charcoal, sketchbooks, and old canvases made from animal skin. "Morning, ma'am," Skypris greeted, taking a previous customer's spot.

Letting go of Edwin's hand, Skypris placed both of hers on the booth. The merchant was a scrawny old lady with large earrings, many bracelets, necklaces, and rings. Her gown was a dull pink, and her hair was covered by red cloth. "Hello, my dear, what can I do for you?"

"I'm interested in your art supplies. My friend here wants to do art." Skypris moved her head, suggesting to him.

"Skypris, a dae no have trade or money," he told her.

The girl stuck a finger in his face, "I know, don't worry about it."

"A will no let ye get anythin' for me." Edwin came closer to Skypris, now able to make eye contact with her.

"I can do what I want. Think of this as a gift of our friendship. It's rude not to accept a gift you know, especially from a lady friend." She sat up straighter.

Edwin stopped. He didn't want to make her feel bad for just wanting to do something nice for him. The situation was not worth the argument. "I have a small but nice collection. Pick out what you want, and we'll see what the trade's worth," the merchant instructed.

"Get what you want," Skypris nudged Edwin.

Selecting a sketchbook, Edwin flipped through the pages, examining them to see if any were damaged. He wasn't really into painting at the moment; besides the painting supplies would be worth a lot more than just the average sketching equipment. He took the sketchbook with the most pages and a couple of charcoal pencils and brought them to Skypris. She looked at them, "Is that all you want?"

"It's aw a need to get started." Edwin scratched the back of his head.

"If you're sure." Skypris got the merchant's attention. "I would like these items, please."

"What do you have to trade?" The old lady's voice was hoarse.

Opening her satchel, Skypris took out a fancy bracelet with rubies decorating it and set it on the table. The women became speechless upon seeing the beautiful wristwear. "You have a nice trinket here, this should be more than a fair trade."

Edwin fought off the feeling of guilt trying to gnaw at him. He convinced himself that she had never worn jewelry or dresses before, and she wouldn't trade away something if she wanted it.

"So it's a deal?" Skypris asked.

"A deal it is!" The merchant seemed more than eager.

Skypris took the sketchbook and charcoal pencils, giving them to Edwin. "Wedd ye accept it if a promised to pay ye back?"

"How about you draw me a picture and we'll call it even," Skypris grinned and led on.

Merlin leaned down and sniffed the charcoal, causing him to build up a sneeze.

Edwin scratched Merlin's chin as a smile grew on the boy's face. Holding art equipment felt exciting, like the entire word was in his hands. He hoped he wasn't putting on too much of a goofy grin at the thought of drawing. Perhaps he could draw himself as a mighty knight riding on Merlin like he often dreamed of; the options were endless yet one thing was for sure, he wanted to practice before making anything for Skypris. She deserved no less than the best.

Chapter Twenty-Nine
Chaos In The Fire

Terro and Mykale ventured to the city entrance where he had promised to rendezvous with his childhood friend. After he made a small detour, the prince made sure to take the path of the city that had the fewest number of people. He didn't like it when others recognized him. They usually always asked for his attention in one way or another, and he didn't have time for that right now. One might argue that his duty was to his people. However, for this evening, he wasn't the crown prince, but rather, Skypris's escort.

Arriving, he found Skypris sitting on a rock with her face in a book. Scaltor was fast asleep until his knight spoke, seeing her friend.

"Look who showed up," Skypris said as Terro approached.

“It took me a while to get away from my father,” Terro excused himself. “How long have you been waiting for me?”

Terro looked up at the sky and noted the sun was just starting to set, creating a gorgeous harmony of pinks.

“Ages,” she replied with sarcasm.

“Wow, I didn’t know I was worth the wait,” he played.

“You’re not. I was mainly here to read a new book in peace. The entrance is the least crowded part of the city at the moment,” she explained, closing her book, standing to face him.

“So I'm a bonus?” he asked, sounding hopeful.

“Don’t fool yourself.” Skypris smiled and rolled her eyes as she turned her back to him.

She picked up the book she had been reading and put her nose in it again. Terro stopped for a moment to look at her unusual reddish-brown hair coloration. It was only one of many things he found beautiful about her. Scaltor jumped off the rock, landing on Mykale, initiating the two to wrestle and chase each other playfully.

Reaching into his trousers pocket, he pulled out a necklace that he had gotten by trading a golden ring. It was the only item he’d brought to trade, promising himself he would only barter for her. It was small so no one had noticed it. Terro glanced at Skypris, pondering how to present this to her. They weren’t old enough to court, so it couldn’t be that kind of a gift.

“How long until your sister’s show?” she questioned as she read.

“Probably soon before it gets too dark—doesn’t matter, we don’t have to watch. We can skip and go off on our own,” Terro said as he strolled over to the rock his friend had made into a chair.

He wasn’t interested in seeing his sister perform. He wished that his father hadn’t insisted on passing the mantle down this year. Now that the best part of the festival had been ruined, Terro wanted to take this opportunity to hang out with Skypris alone. Terro moved the chain behind his back as she turned her head to look at him, marking her spot with a finger. "I'd like to see the air show," she began. "It's your sister's first time. She needs her brother's support."

"My sister doesn't need my support. She has the entire kingdom!" He raised his empty hand.

Skypris narrowed her eyes at Terro's comment, turning back to the book. "Then *you* could skip it. I want to watch your sister," she spat.

"Why? She's not going to be as good as my father, especially on her first try."

Skypris closed her book, turning her attention fully on Terro. "I'm not saying she'll be as good as your father. It's her first time—no one expects it. She's my friend, and I'm going to be there for her whether her little brother is or not. And who knows, maybe she'll surpass the king."

Sliding off the rock, Skypris walked past Terro.

"There's no way she'll surpass my father," Tero clarified. "Though, I guess I could watch her since there's nothing better to do."

Skypris turned around to face him, walking backwards only to say, "Yes, Terro, don't watch your sister to support her, do it because it's your only choice." She did a sarcastic bow before twisting her body forward and walking off.

Terro felt some tightening in his chest like he had done something wrong and was afraid to move and expose it. He didn't mean to appear like a boor, nor did he want Skypris to be annoyed with him. They could always spend time together during and after.

Scaltor went running past the prince, as Mykale chased after the hatchling, stopping at Terro's feet.

Terro saw Skypris disappear into a crowd. Terro stuck the necklace back into his trousers pocket and ran after her. Mykale jumped onto his back and climbed, holding on to his shoulder to help herself stay on, not wanting to get lost in the sea of people her knight dove into. Her claws hurt; however, Terro shrugged it off easily. Terro was able to find Skypris by following Scaltor through the crowds. He spotted his childhood friend examining pottery at a trader's stand. Terro weaved through the citizens, not wanting to bump into any of them, which was a challenge. He came behind Skypris as she was distracted by looking at designs on a teacup. Getting out the necklace, Terro put the golden chain in front of her. She gasped, startled. "Relax!" Terro immediately reassured her. "It's just me."

Terro moved the girl's hair out of the way and worked on clipping the necklace around her neck. "You can't get away from me that easily."

"I wasn't trying to run away from you. I wasn't going to stand there the rest of the evening, though." Skypris's tone was a bit snappy. "What are you doing?" She placed the teacup back.

Terro finished putting on the necklace. "Giving you this."

Grabbing the long chain around her neck, she studied it. She turned, still looking at the fine golden chain. "You know I'm not fond of jewelry."

"I know, that's why it's nothing fancy," Terro said, hoping that this was making up for his behavior earlier. "I thought you could use it to wear your parents' wedding rings."

The mention of Skypris's parents made her look at him with an unsure expression. He then continued, "I thought since you're training to be a Dragon Knight, like them, it would be inspiring to carry their memory with you instead of having the rings rot under your pillow."

Terro looked down, his face feeling warm.

Skypris couldn't help the goofy smile from growing on her face as her friend spoke. It was such a sentimental thought that she would never have imagined the prince to have. She wouldn't have painted Terro to remember that she kept her parents' rings. Thinking of how much they meant to her made the warm emotions intensify. Terro could be self-centered and a real royal pain. However, he had a positive side reflected by moments like these that made him who he was. As she thought more about it, her cheeks got warm, knowing how much someone cared for her. She missed her parents and tried so hard to live up to their names. She looked to Scaltor, who was between her legs, thinking about the egg situation and how relieved she was that everything worked out. "Won't it break in battle?" she questioned.

"What? No! Don't be silly, this chain is made from a unicorn's horn, the merchant said so himself, nothing can break this chain," he said with a little laugh to himself.

"Unicorns aren't real." She laughed at the ridiculous thought.

"Of course, they are! Remember when we would go hunting for them as kids?"

"You mean when you would drag me into the woods to go running after your fantasies? And when you finally realized they weren't real, you cried for two days."

Terro laughed, remembering the situation all too well. "Hey, you're the one who's still reading fairytales!"

"I read them. However, I know they're not real." She laughed in protest.

The two laughed for a second, their eyes locking with each other's. Skypris looked away for a moment, tucking her hair behind her ear.

"Are you still trading?" Terro asked when she looked back.

"No, I was just wasting time by looking," Skypris told him, still smiling.

"Perfect!" he said, grabbing her hand, hesitating to do so only for a moment. "Come on then, let's find a good spot to watch my sister's air show."

Terro led Skypris back to the entrance of the city. Scaltor protested, getting annoyed with all the running he had to do just to keep up with his knight. Skypris didn't fight Terro's new change of heart about supporting his sister by watching her. She knew that, in Terro's way, he was apologizing for how he had behaved earlier. The prince didn't apologize by verbally saying the word *"sorry"* or confessing what he did wrong. Part of her thought he felt shame, though she also knew that he felt the need to put up this big front because he was the prince of a kingdom, so everyone expected him to be perfect. Yes, it was frustrating when he wouldn't swallow his pride and admit when he was wrong.

However, it was one flaw Skypris accepted about him—they were both still young and learning.

After talking it over, the two decided to climb onto a jumble of rocks a little off the path leading up to the castle. On the tallest rock there, the two could see the whole city in front of them and the horizon lines beyond. The sun was setting, and the shadows lengthened, slowly moving further into dusk. Sitting, Skypris and Terro let their legs dangle over the edge. The two hatchlings curled up with each other behind them, drifting into sleep. Looking down, the duo saw a few families and individuals who had the same idea as them, making their way up. She spotted some Dragons and some Dragon Knights in the air for the best view of the show. “How much longer until it starts?” Skypris asked.

“It should be starting about now,” Terro said, looking around.

Then, a Dragon bellowed a roar, signalling that the air show was about to start. Skypris recognized the roar as Reuben’s. Others followed her gaze as she scanned the sky for the two stars to emerge. “There!” A little girl holding her mother's hand pointed towards the forest, bouncing and squealing excitedly.

Everyone strained to see where the girl was pointing and saw Rueben pumping his wings skyward, spinning around like a top to help gain speed and altitude. When he got the level he wanted, his wings spread open as he did a backward somersault, and that’s where Skypris was able to see Circe on the dragon’s back. Reuben glided against a few wind currents as he and his knight took the time to recover from the fast-paced tricks he had done. He flapped his wings and then dove, tucking his wings. Before touching the tops of the trees, he opened his wings again, soaring up before falling into a graceful spiral. Being high in the sky, Reuben performed six connecting loops in a row. After completing the trick, she was able to tell that Reuben had gotten dizzy because his flight pattern had missed its mark.

However, he corrected himself right when he realized he was beginning to mess up. Small laughter arose from the adults in the audience, suggesting that they, too, saw the poor dragon get confused momentarily. Reuben and Circe were able to shake off the hiccup and move on to the next trick.

Despite a nicely performed show in front of her, Skypris's attention was caught out of the corner of her eye. Terro was staring at her with a warm expression. She could feel his eyes on her. He was giving her that look again. She was sure of it. She continued to pretend as though her attention was on the air show as her friend looked down and inched his hand closer to hers.

Was he going to take it?

He retracted it, then looked back at the air show.

She closed her eyes and stealthily sighed to herself. Skypris suspected that Terro had stronger feelings for her. He didn't seem to try and hide them much. Wanting to hold her hand and the necklace today just confirmed it for her. She honestly didn't know how to feel about it. She's never seen him that way, and if she had the same affection for him, they couldn't be anything more than friends until they were of courting age in two more years.

Biting her lip, Skypris secretly prayed to herself that he wouldn't do anything that would put her on the spot. She didn't want a relationship or distractions right now, yet she didn't know how to break it to him, knowing how extreme he could take things. The last thing she wanted was to lose her best friend. Was she leading him on or accidentally giving him mixed signals? Maybe if she just let things alone, he would lose interest on his own. Looking back at the show, she pushed away the thought of what could happen and enjoyed the moment she was in.

Flying in a straight line, Circe stood up in Reuben's saddle. This made everyone gasp! Terro stood instantly, his eyes locked on his sister, who was steadying herself. Skypris gave a small smile at the prince's reaction. She hadn't seen him worry for his sister since the time she had almost died along with their mother and Skypris's parents. It was good seeing this side of him every so often.

"Please don't fall!" Terro thought. Reuben slowly lost altitude. This gave Circe the ability to stand up straight with her arms stretched

out for balance like a pair of dragon wings. Everyone was in awe at the trick, especially since she was able to hold it for such a long time. Reuben continued to get closer to the treetops as he circled his way down. Once, skimming the pines' bristles, Circe sat down, and Reuben flapped his wings, boosting himself. With one last spin, the dragon flew high and opened his wings, then he held still. It was over.

Everyone started to clap and cheer, and Terro and Skypris could hear the city's volume rise in a raucous! Clapping, whistles, cheers, dragons bellowing, children giggling, and others laughing, filled the mountainside and the coast.

"Amazing!"

"She did wonderfully for her first time!"

"Better than her father's first for sure!"

"Again! Again!"

Terro smiled proudly at the sight of everyone's excitement. Skypris stood up next to him, still clapping herself. The young girl nudged him on the shoulder. Terro knew what she was implying. "Alright, fine. You were right."

Skypris's smile vanished as she peered down at the city as though she had heard something urgent. Confused, Terro focused his attention on the cheering coming from the city. Cheering?

No.

Screams, not of joy but fear, sounded and began to be the main instrument of the city's volume. What was going on? After several distant and indistinct sounds around them, the word to the question finally became clear.

"FIRE!"

Terro, like everyone else on the large rock, looked around to see what could be on fire. The forest? The castle? A home? A shop? Just as black smoke revealed its location, someone shouted, "The docks! The ships are on fire!"

The merchants' ships! What happened? How did it start? Was this a revenge scheme to satisfy a petty grudge? This had never happened before. Throughout all the generations of this festival, the merchants' ships had been under special protection by the king. Taking off, Skypris ran down until she reached the ground. Terro followed her with a similar stride, the sounds of commotion seeping out of the city becoming louder as he got closer to the docks. Terro had to avoid a mob of citizens who were pulling and shoving everyone in their path to get down to the shore to see the fire. Chaos consumed the city as others panicked. People were carrying buckets to the shore, Dragon Knights flew overhead to the burning ships, most carrying two or three buckets. Terro, with Mykale safely on his back, desperately looked for Skypris, not liking the state of the crowd. He shoved a man out of his way, preventing both of them from colliding as the man almost trampled the prince. He had lost Skypris in the mob. He decided to hug a building wall as he continued to look for his friend, knowing that if he called her name, it would be lost in the crowd.

Skypris was weaving in and out of fleeing people with Scaltor in her arms, as she got pushed and bumped into. Most of the swarm was heading to the shore so that they could try and help put the fire out. Skypris was trying not to panic herself. What if they didn't save the ships? The merchants would lose their livelihood and homes! As people ran out of the city, Skypris managed to hide behind a wagon until the herds had cleared.

A screeching hatchling caught her attention, and she turned to see a blue, gray, and purple Zandorious dragon attacking someone's head. Wings flapping, Merlin was desperately trying to stay on the man as he scratched, bit, and ripped the man's face and the back of his neck. Skypris couldn't believe what she was seeing! Why was Merlin attacking that man? Did the chaos make him go mad?

Skypris ran to give aid. She didn't get there until it was too late to help. Merlin had let the man go and used his underdeveloped wings to glide to the ground, landing roughly. Jumping to his feet, the hatchling hissed viciously, wings spread out, quills rattling as they stood up hardened. The man ran off, face bleeding as he wailed miserably.

The knight in training approached Merlin in bewilderment. Dragons weren't supposed to attack humans in such a horrible manner unless instructed by their knights or in self-defence. "Merlin!" she scolded in disappointment.

Merlin hopped around to face her, his fury dying into a happy purr as his quills lay flat, softening. "How could you attack that man? What made you do something so horrible?"

Merlin roared weakly, cutting Skypris off as he jumped up and down in earnest. He called again, yet this time Scaltor called back, and Merlin ran off. Scaltor wiggled his way free from his knight's arms and following the dragon. Scaltor stopped and called back for Skypris to come.

Something was wrong.

Skypris shadowed the two hatchlings, grateful that the melee had moved to the docks.

Gasping in alarm and horror, Skypris saw a young girl lying on the ground as still as death. Skypris knelt to her and realized it was Demmis's sister, Corythia, lying on her stomach. Skypris turned the girl to her back so she could examine her better. Moving the hair out of Cory's face, she saw a large gash on her head as if a great force had hit her. Was she dead? Skypris checked the girl's neck and found a pulse. Relief overcame her. "Cory! Cory!"

She seemed to be out cold. Did she get trampled? "Cory, wake up! Please wake up!" Skypris was starting to think that trying to revive the girl was foolish until Cory's eyes fluttered open.

Cory's eyes hung low, then suddenly got wide as she sat up fast, yelling, "EDWIN!" before grabbing her head and wailing in pain.

The injured girl leaned on Skypris for support, her eyes closed. "Cory, are you okay?" Skypris asked fearfully, trying to get the girl to keep her eyes open by tapping her cheeks.

"N-n…no!" Cory spoke out with a slur.

"What happened? How did you get hit in the head, and what's wrong with Edwin? Why did you call out for Edwin?" Skypris feared that something had happened to her dear friend, though she couldn't imagine what it was.

Dazed, Cory gritted her teeth until she managed to sit up without Skypris's help. "They took him!"

Chapter Thirty
The Monarchy

Going their separate ways, Edwin walked from the city entrance after dropping Skypris off, where she and Terro said to meet up. Edwin wished she would watch the air show with him instead. However, he could imagine the dagger look Terro would give him if he intruded.

Down the streets, Edwin wondered if he could find the painter from earlier. He had questions about the man's craft and his life that tied into it. Maybe a mentorship? No, he couldn't because his Dragon Knight duties took too much time and dedication; perhaps after he graduated from training. That is, if he stayed here. Edwin stopped for a moment, which made a herd of people passing him push the young boy around.

He was starting to feel how Corythia did about choosing to be a smith instead of a knight. At least Skypris had gotten him the basics so he could draw for fun in his free time.

Merlin nibbled on Edwin's hair, making pieces stick together with the hatchling's drool. The young Knight wanted to draw his dragon in his new sketch book, making it the first page anyone saw once they opened it. He also wanted to take the little time he had before sundown to check on Israel and Jarod. Edwin wanted to meet another from Gorish who had a more positive experience with dragons like him, despite what they were taught growing up.

Striding up to the family's merchant booth, customers swarmed their merchandise with loud discussions of bartering and interests. Walking over to the crowd, Edwin set Merlin down on a crate and took a seat on the one next to his hatchling. He couldn't even see the family among all the heads. However, he thought he heard little Jarod's voice being the main seller and a laugh from Israel. It would be better to wait for the merchant's business to die down. With the air show starting soon, it shouldn't take much longer for the citizens to finish up their trade.

Resting his sketchbook on his lap, Edwin put his feet on Merlin's crate to elevate his sketchbook. Taking out the charcoal pencils he ordered, "Haud still, Merlin," at the little dragon.

Merlin mostly respected the command yet would randomly get bursts of energy that he had to relieve by running around the crate with glee a few times. Edwin got the basic shape and position down, ready to go back for the details later. The hatchling didn't need to stay still for Edwin to get his scale pattern. The boy remembered that part. Edwin tilted his head, looking at the portrait sketch of Merlin looking off in the distance, then added and adjusted a few changes.

"That's brilliant!" a woman said, looking over Edwin's shoulder.

Looking up, he saw a woman with light brown hair, a thin, beautiful face covered in light freckles. Her olive-green dress was simple and loose. Turning to face her directly, Edwin's eyes widened at the sight of the woman's large belly, which was about the size of a watermelon!

Dumbfounded, Edwin had realized he was staring with his mouth hanging. “Thank ye,” he said and averted his eyes back to the woman’s face, his own being warm from his behavior.

Was she pregnant? Of course she was! She looked very close to being due. Should she be out during the festival like this? What if a mob bumped into her or pushed her over? Edwin looked around himself. Where was her husband? The baby's father shouldn’t be by herself right now.

Israel appeared out of nowhere and embraced the soon-to-be mother from behind, placing a hand gently on her stomach. “Hello again, my friend!”

Edwin gave Israel an alarmed look, as though he didn’t know what to think or do. Should Israel be touching this woman like that? “What’s wrong, lad? Dragon got your tongue?” Israel laughed.

Thinking, Edwin remembered that Israel’s wife had been resting because she was sick—oh!

Edwin huffed out a small laugh and smiled. “Sorry, a wis a wee surprised. She’s yer wife?”

“Yer right! He is from Gorish!” she said with a similar accent to Edwin.

“Aye, this is the one and only love of my life,” Israel cooed, looking lovingly at his wife.

“Dinnae kiss in front of the customers!” Jarod shouted, walking to the crate where Merlin sat. “Ye’ll scare ‘em off!”

“Oh, we wouldn’t want that now, would we?” Israel leaned in to his wife's face.

Instead of completing the motion to make the kiss and cuddle, his wife turned her face away. “No, a feel like am gonnae boke!”

“It’s probably better if you don’t watch the show then.”

“No unless ye want a mess to clean up.” She opened her eyes and looked at Edwin. “Are ye the one a have to thank for helpin’ ma two men?”

"Well, no just me," Edwin said, smiling back. "Other knights and their dragons helped as well."

Israel waved a hand. "He's being modest! The others came and went, yet he stayed from start to finish and made sure we were comfortable."

"In that case, thank ye for yer time and help. Am sorry a didnae mean to startle ye if a have. A saw yer sketch and had to give it praise."

Edwin's cheeks got hot at her words. He didn't expect others to think highly of his art. He was just starting. Israel looked down at the drawing in the book, his eyebrows raised. "You got talent! How long have you been drawing?"

"Am only startin' to get serious with it," Edwin explained, embarrassed from the attention he was getting.

"Serious indeed."

"I want to see it! I want to see it!" Jarod shouted, climbing on the crate that was now getting crowded.

The little boy looked at the drawing and gasped. "It looks just like him! Can ye draw me a dragon too? Please?!"

Edwin nodded. "A dinnae promise it'll be any good."

"If this is yer, *'no any good'* then I'll take ten!"

Israel and his wife chuckled at their little boy's excitement. Edwin heard footsteps get closer to the merchant's booth. Israel left his wife with Edwin and Jarod to go and make trade. "How may I help you, Blue Eyes?" Edwin could hear him greet the customer.

"My brother and I are just looking around." Edwin recognized that voice.

He looked over to Israel's booth to see Cory and her little brother, Hero, looking at a bunch of different trade Israel had.

"You've come to the right place! As a merchant, I have a variety of different goods to look at." The siblings smiled and chuckled. "If you have any questions or find something you do want to trade for, then I'll be at your service!"

"Okay, thank you," Cory smiled.

Cory, being a blacksmith's daughter, went straight for the weaponry. Hero, who was looking bored with his sister, then noticed Edwin and Merlin. With his expression lightening, he checked to see that his sister was distracted before running over to the two. "Edwin! Finally! Someone who isn't boring!"

"Hello, Hero," Edwin greeted, then returned to his sketch.

"What are you doing?" Hero questioned, straining his neck to get a look at the sketchbook.

"He's drawing me a dragon!" Jarod said proudly.

"Drawing? I didn't know you could do that! Why haven't you drawn me anything?" Hero said, acting insulted.

"A only started and a'll give ye one later, let me give Jarod one because his family is only here for the festival," Edwin explained.

"I guess that's a good reason." Hero grabbed his chin, still looking a bit pouty.

Cory strolled up to the crates. "Is he bothering you?"

Not taking his eyes off the paper, Edwin replied, "No, he's fine. How are ye, Cory? Enjoyin' the festival?"

"I'm doing alright, just trading for some rare material to make little knick-knacks from. For practice," Cory said as she took a metal block out of her satchel. She put it away once Edwin took the moment to see it before his eyes drew back to the sketch. "By the looks of it, you're enjoying yourself."

"Stop distracting him!" Hero snapped at his sister. "Can't you see he's working magic?"

Edwin didn't have to see Cory's face to know she was shooting daggers at her brother.

"Aye, are ye excited to see the air show?" Edwin said, his eyes now off the paper onto her face.

"Great. Now look what you did!" Hero threw his arms up, then crossed them.

"I'm curious to see how well the princess will do for her first time, mostly. I love the air shows, it's the main reason I take part in the festivals," Cory explained. "I hope you like it. I would hate for the first one you experience not to be memorable."

A wide smile grew across Edwin's face as he thought back to yesterday and how he had already seen it. However, that was his and Circe's little secret. "Watchin' a dragon performin' tricks in the sky… a think it's safe to say it's gonnae be memorable no matter the ootcome."

"Stop. Distracting. Him!" Hero hissed with gritted teeth.

"Jarod, ye shuid take yer wee friend here and enjoy the festival," Israel's wife said, placing a hand on her son's back. "We'll keep yer drawin' and surprise ye when ye get back." She then looked at Cory. "As long as it's alright with his sister."

"Please take him! Trade him away if you want," Cory said eagerly.

Jarod cheered before getting off the crate, taking Merlin off his head and setting him in the spot he once sat in. "It's been a while since a got to play with someone ma age!"

"I guess I could do that. It would be more fun playing with a friend than my older sister, who's only into rocks!" Hero raised an eyebrow at his sister, who just rolled her eyes in annoyance.

"Just meet back here after the air show is finished!" the pregnant woman shouted to the boys as they disappeared into the streets.

Edwin focused back on his drawing, Cory watching over his shoulder before looking to Jarod's mother. "I'm Corythia, but everyone calls me Cory."

"Hello, Cory, ma name's Quinn," she replied.

"I hope this isn't too personal. How far along are you?"

Quinn sounded bashful. "We are no entirely sure yet, aw we ken is the baby's gettin' close."

"Have you got any names picked yet?" Cory threw another question.

"We had a few. However, a think we finally decided on either Seafae or Poseidon."

"I love those names!" Cory said.

"Thank ye. Me personally am hopin' for a Seafea so am no the only girl in the crew," Quinn explained.

"Are you from Gorish? Yours and Edwin's accents are identical."

"Aye, a left when a was a wee bairn."

"What was it like there?"

Quinn was silent for a second. "No as fun as here a'll tell ye that."

Merlin got off the crate and walked to Cory, who had picked him up, letting the little dragon move to her shoulders to perch. "Well, am gonnae go spend time with ma husband now that our son is busy." Quinn waved bye to Cory and made her way back to the booth where Israel was trying to sell a woman a gown.

Cory sat down on the crate where Merlin once was, and Edwin returned his focus on shading in the details of his image.

"Do you want me to pose with him for you?" she asked.

"No, am almost done," Edwin replied, applying his final pencil stroke.

He tilted the book to Cory so she could take a peek at the finished piece. "You're talented! Did you even look at Merlin that much?"

"Thank ye, and a tried to go more aff memory," Edwin explained. "A think that's why his nose is a little aff though."

"And I thought I had a good memory! It's nothing compared to yours," Cory chuckled. "Are you going to sign the paper?"

"Why wedd a dae that?"

"So that everyone he shows it to will know you did it, and he can remember you by it."

Edwin understood where she was coming from, so off to the side of the page, he wrote his name. She then read:

"Edwin."

Seing it, Cory didn't seem impressed. "What about your last name?"

"Last name?" Edwin asked.

Cory narrowed her eyebrows. "You know, the name you carry through your family?"

Edwin stared. Trying to puzzle together what she ment.

"A last name. Like, mine's *Corythia Flanke*." Cory was still stunned. "Do they not have them in Groish?"

Oh, she was thinking of the names of houses and clans!

"Only the royals and nobles have them. The common folk like me dinnae," he explained. "We're no important enough to carry one, even those who are famous for slayin'—" Edwin didn't want to finish the sentence.

Cory thought for a moment. "Then give yourself one."

"Just like that?"

"Why not? You're starting a new life, aren't you? Why not give yourself a last name, and it could be anything you want!"

"Is Edwin no enough?"

"I guess it could be if that's what you want."

Edwin thought hard. She was right, he could be named whatever he wanted to be named! He could start a family name for himself, something that neither he, nor his family, had back in Gorish. What should it be, though? Should it relate to dragons? *"Gorish"*, as a reminder of where his family originated? He thought for a second, then wrote something after his first name, making his signature:

"Edwin Dragonknight."

He let Cory see the addition to his name. "Isn't that more of a title than a last name?" she asked, seemingly not satisfied.

"Can it no be both?"

"I guess it can, but I've never seen a last name like that before," Cory admitted.

"Have ye ever seen someone from Gorish before me?"

"Can't say I have," Cory sighed. "If that's what you want then that's your new name, *Edwin Dragonknight*."

"Thank you, *Cory Flanke*," Edwin smirked at her.

Once Edwin had finished the drawing of Merlin resting on Jarod's head, which wasn't shown, looking it over, Edwin wished he hadn't worked on the tip of Merlin's tail so much. He couldn't figure out what was throwing it off. Carefully, he tore out the paper in a nearly clean cut and walked to Israel, handing it to him and Quinn. After getting praises from the cute couple, Edwin said his goodbyes and walked off with Cory after deciding they would watch the show together.

"We should find a place to watch, the show's about to start!" Cory said, starting a path through a crowd who were standing and staring up at the sky.

"Dae ye ken any good places to see it?" Edwin asked trying not to lose her.

As the two weaved through people, a tall, hooded figure going the opposite way bumped into Edwin's shoulder, getting his attention. "Sorry," Edwin said, stumbling a bit.

"No worries, young Monarch."

The words made Edwin freeze. He turned around to see the hooded man standing facing the boy. "Wit did ye call me?"

Putting his hood down, the man revealed long blond hair, a slightly crooked jaw, and crystal blue eyes. "I called you by your title, the Dragon's Monarch."

Edwin couldn't fully process what was happening. How did he know? Questions and excitement whirled in the boy's mind. How did he know who Edwin was? How did he recognize him? Did he know about the story behind it, that the dragons weren't telling? Did he know why they weren't?

"A-a," Edwin tried to sort through his questions. "Who are ye? How did ye ken—"

"Please, I'll be more than happy to share what I know with you," the man said, glancing around, before lowering his voice. "Let's talk someplace more private."

Cory came up behind Edwin and grabbed his arm harshly, turning him around to face her. "Edwin, are you sure that's a good idea?"

"Cory, ye dinnae understand, he might ken the answers a have been lookin' for. Dae no worry, ye and Merlin can wait out here and watch the show since yer uncomfortable. Am just gonnae talk with him really fast." Edwin then pointed to a tavern. "We'll be right in there so if anythin' goes wrong, ye can jump in. Besides, with a crowd like this, a dinnae think he'll try anythin'."

Edwin could tell that his attempts to convince her of the safety of the situation had failed. Yet, it wasn't her call to make. Edwin walked in the direction he pointed. "Would this work?" he asked the cloaked, handsome man.

"Excellent choice, Monarch." He nodded before following.

Merlin roared weakly, calling out to Edwin, yet his knight was already out of earshot.

In the tavern, there were a bunch of wooden tables and stools with a long bar. Behind it was the barkeep, and barrels were lined up towards the end of the bar, filled with wine and alcohol. The curtains were red, along with the tablecloths. It wasn't hard to pick a spot since the business wasn't so hot. Everyone was probably enjoying the festival. Edwin only saw five people drinking and eating. They were mostly older folks, those who were sick of seeing the show repeatedly. The young boy and the man picked a table out of the way. An old waitress came over to greet them, taking their orders. Edwin, not liking alcohol, had asked for water, unlike the man across from him.

"I believe introductions are in order," the man said. "You can call me Coner Vain."

Edwin blinked for a moment, excited that he could be getting the answers he was searching for in a matter of minutes. Realizing he hadn't answered, he exclaimed, "Edwin Dragonknight!"

"Dragonknight?!" Coner drummed his fingers. "Now that's a unique name!" he said, making Edwin feel proud he had chosen it.

"So how dae ye ken am the Dragon's Monarch?" Edwin went straight to the point.

Coner looked around with his eyes, suspiciously scanning the room. No one was paying attention. Leaning in, Coner invited Edwin to do so with his hand. Pulling out of his black cloak, the man showed off a glowing glass ball the size of his palm. This intrigued Edwin even more. "Wit's that?"

"It's a little trinket I picked up from an old wizard in Ishnia. I got it so I could find you. Whenever you're near, the glowing gets brighter." Coner moved the glass ball to Edwin, then away from him to demonstrate his words.

Edwin stared at the orb in bewilderment, enchanted to see more magic. After his eyes had their fill of the blue light, he asked, "Ye were lookin' for me, why? Daes it tie into ma title?"

"Indeed."

"Could ye tell me wit it means now?" Edwin wondered.

"I can't go into too much detail, but let's put it this way. King Clayus and his family aren't the true royal family." Coner looked around before leaning in closer. "They were a replacement when the true bloodline was forced to flee the land."

"Wit dae ye mean by that? Why wedd the true monarchy be chased off?" Edwin questioned, starting to see the story as nothing but hearsay. "Weddnae the people ken?"

"Ken?"

"Know," Edwin restated.

Coner nodded before continuing, "Not if it happened over four centuries ago. The monarchy fled because the people of this land were so enraged and didn't respect the king. So, they threatened the lives of the royal family."

Coner took a swig from his mug.

"Wit did he dae to get them—" Edwin was cut off by loud cheering coming from outside.

The air show must have started by now. He felt guilty—not from missing the show because he had already seen it—but because he had promised to watch it with Cory, yet he had been so excited to possibly get some answers, he pushed his friend aside. Edwin scanned the entrance for a quick minute, then turned back to his companion. Coner had removed his hand from under his cloak, implying that he put the orb away.

Coner looked sheepishly at Edwin. "It's uh…" he began. "It's best we put the magic away so that we don't draw the attention of unwanted thugs. Picking up where we left off?"

"Why were the people so angry with the original monarchy?" Edwin asked, thinking of what he was saying before the cheering distracted him.

"The king—Lupis—was young and saw a way for humans and dragons to become closer, and because of the Dragon Empress, the people of this land feared it. For she disapproved."

Edwin didn't know what to think of what he was hearing. He thought the dragons were kind and fair to the humans, and they wanted to live in harmony. If King Lupis had a plan to make them closer, then why would the Dragon Empress at that time turn against him? Was the Empress back then not as good hearted as the current one, or were they the same one? He didn't know exactly how old she was. Was this why he couldn't find alot of history about his reign?

Coner watched the look of confusion linger on Edwin's face for several heartbeats, so he smiled gently. "I know it's hard to believe. The dragons don't like to talk about it or tell any humans the tale because they are ashamed that they messed up. Not all dragons were kind to humans; at first, they treated us like we were lower than them," Coner explained. "It's why Gorish hates them so much. That land used to be the dragons' home; however, to save their race, they needed to move. That's why Gorish and Elvous are between their breeding grounds and Xolf."

Edwin took a sip of water, feeling some sweat start to build on his brow as Coner's story began to make sense. He thought back to his homeland and the stories they told about the history of Gorish and dragons. It never painted the flying beasts in a good light. The questions in his head kept circling, yet the question he had asked thirsted for its conclusion the most. Edwin scratched his head. "So wit daes this have to dae with me? Am a related to the true royal bloodline?"

"You are, my friend! You're a direct descendent of the great King Lupis." Coner nodded his head, excited the young boy was getting it.

Shaking his head, Edwin tried to think of his next question; however, they kept slipping. He felt very sleepy with his mind cloudy. He formed words, yet they slurred. Grabbing his head the young knight in training attempted to steady himself. Was he in shock? Was all the new information too much for him?

"Looks like it kicked in faster than I thought," he heard Coner's voice say in a lower voice. "I'm truly sorry for doing this. However, you are the key to my plans, and I can't risk you not being compliant."

Edwin could only make half of what the man was saying out. He did this to him? Why? What was he planning? Edwin swayed back and forth until his head thudded on the table and everything went black.

Merlin and Blue Eyes were in the spot where Edwin had left them. He liked her. She was very pretty for a human. Not saying all humans were ugly, however, her eyes were what was most appealing to the little dragon. As the two watched Merlin's older brother do tricks with his knight, he dreamed what it would be like to fly already. The taste of the air on his face, the power of the wind currents under his wings. How powerful was that feeling? To be able to create strong winds with just the pump of a wing. Merlin sensed tension with the girl he perched on. He didn't know what it was. However, he knew it lingered in her body. Was she worried about Edwin? Is this what human anxiety felt like? She scratched his chin, which made his quills rattle in delight. The little hatchling purred.

All was well until Merlin realized it hadn't been Blue Eyes' anxiety he was feeling, it was Edwin's. His quills spiked as his eyes widened, looking at the tavern entrance where he had last seen Edwin. Merlin's spikes poked Blue Eyes in the face, getting her attention to the tavern as well.

Edwin and the crystal-eyed man walked out of the tavern. However, something was wrong—horribly wrong. Edwin wasn't walking and was instead being carried by the stranger. Blue Eyes stepped forward, her heart racing, as another man who was bigger came up to the stranger and Merlin's knight and grabbed the boy, tossing him over his shoulders. The two men made their way toward the front of the city.

"Edwin!" Blue Eyes' voice cried out, yet it was overpowered when she heard a man screaming with all his might.

"FIRE!"

Blue Eyes turned her head toward the voice and saw black smoke rising from the shore. Wait, that wasn't right? Humans and fire didn't mix. That's where the little, red-scarved boy came from!

Suddenly, chaos unfolded, and everyone began running to fetch buckets. Merchants were the ones panicking the most, for the ships were their homes and were the obvious source of the fire. Because water couldn't burn, Merlin knew that for sure. Blue Eyes didn't run to help with the fire; instead, she ran to follow the men who had taken his knight.

"HELP!" she screamed in vain against the wails of panic from the other humans.

"Someone, PLEASE! My friend! MY FRIEND!" she screamed as loud as she could.

Merlin was tempted to leap off and go get help himself. However, with the humans running around with no order, he decided to keep to the girl's shoulders so he wouldn't get smashed. Blue Eyes pushed her way through several humans, getting pushed around by the bigger men trying to rush past. "Help! They're taking him!"

Merlin hopped down from his perch onto a crate right next to her, roaring for help with a rasp. Taking a deep breath for another cry for help, Blue Eyes was cut off when a strong force hit her over the head, knocking her to the ground unconscious.

Behind her, a man wearing a black cloak held a rock in his hand, which now had blood on it from the girl's head. The man shadowed over her for a moment before raising the rock up again. No, wait! He was going to hit her again!

Merlin leapt into the air, grabbing onto the man's face with his sharp baby talons. Biting and scratching, he ripped into the man's skin, causing him to cry out in pain. The man stumbled, moving farther away from the unconscious blue-eyed girl.

Chapter Thirty-One
Taken

Edwin's nostrils filled with the scent of rich pine in the breeze, with a slight hint of faded smoke from a fire. His stomach arched as extreme pressure was placed on it, bouncing and swaying. Blood rushed to his head as his body felt somewhat numb and drowsy. His mind was cloudy as his eyelids created slits. He saw nothing but green. He closed his eyes again, hearing horse hooves clipping and crunching rocks and plants of some kind. He opened his eyes wider, his vision still blurry; moving his head around, he realized he was across a horse on the back of a saddle, lying on his stomach. Blinking, his vision focused, yet his mind was still overcast.

He tried lifting his head, yet let himself swing back upside down, his mind throbbing from the rush of the sudden movement, and he groaned in discomfort.

"You're awake!" a familiar voice came from the front of the horse's saddle. "That was a bit earlier than planned. No matter, no one for miles."

Looking at an awkward angle, Edwin saw the back of Coner Vain, urging the steed along an overgrown forest. Behind them were about ten men on horseback following. "Wit dae ye dae to me?" Edwin groaned, drool escaping his mouth.

"Sorry, Edwin, you must speak up. It's hard to understand you with the accent and all," Coner said with an amused tone.

Not being able to get a good look at the other men because of their black hoods, Edwin wheezed a dry cough. This was not a comfortable position to be in, especially with a headache. What could he do, though? He was outnumbered and was in disorder with himself. How long had he been like this? Coner was kidnapping him, right? This all must have had something to do with his title from the dragons.

Suddenly, cheering and yelling arose from the men on horseback, making their mules stand alert. "Not long now, men!" Coner called back to them. "The time is drawing nearer when the *true* king shall rise!"

Edwin decided to wait for an opportunity to escape, preferably when he was right-side up. He closed his eyes and tried his best to relax, yet how could he after being kidnapped and having no idea what they had in store for his fate? Questions such as these were uneasy in his mind, but he ignored them, seeing no use in contemplating them if he couldn't get answers.

He looked up to their approaching destination and saw they were traveling through heavily vegetated wilderness. Edwin managed to see a single tower standing with ruins surrounding it, with moss, trees, and vines growing over and in, hiding the older architecture from the land. Expecting to hear some form of wildlife, Edwin's ears were empty of sound except for hooves clopping. Not even birds or cicada chirping.

The deafening lack of sound stilled Edwin's heart against the urge it had to pump adrenaline because of fear. The horses stopped, and the men dismounted. The largest one of the group picked Edwin up off the horse, only to shoulder him. Edwin was still too numb in body and mind to do anything. Even if he could get away, he wouldn't get far. The structure they were walking into had once been grand in size, almost as big as the castle of Alena. Almost all the brick walls had collapsed, with parts of the ceiling shakily intact in certain locations. Sunlight shone through holes, illuminating the shadows with pillars of green light. The group made it to the throne room, which was the only location that seemed to be still intact, which surprised Edwin because it appeared to be on a cliff. The big man set Edwin down, and that's when the young knight in training tried to flee. The big man grabbed his throat and slammed him to a pillar. Coner laughed, and the man finished tying Edwin up to the post.

Edwin recovered, and the large man moved to reveal that right before Edwin was a large dragon skeleton—not as big as the Empress, but bigger than Cerberus. Edwin couldn't see too much of the dragon's anatomy though. Its skull was…wrong… it was stumpier than a brooktorous snout. The room looked identical to the one in King Clayus's castle. The throne chair was carved from thick wood that was worn and cracked, with splinters protruding from it, its color but a memory.

Glancing up, Edwin saw that the second floor was roughly damaged, with pieces of the platforms gone. Edwin's attention went back to his kidnappers after he heard scratching on the stone floor. Four men were drawing around the skeleton, creating weird runes with ash. Coner was standing closest to him, watching contentedly, occasionally whispering something to the man next to him. The other men who didn't have a task cleared the room of roots and damaged building materials, such as stone and wood.

"Wit are ye dinnae?" Edwin asked in a breath.

Coner stared at his accomplices' work. "You'll see soon enough, young Monarch."

Edwin persisted, "Wit dae ye want with me?"

"You—more so your blood," Coner said. "It's the key to our success. The entire rebellion's lifetime has led to this moment. I can't believe I will be having the honor of bringing back our King!"

Frozen by the man's words, Edwin got a shocking chill down his spine. Coner's tone, once so formal, was now unstable as it shook and jumped from word to word. *"Bring back our King"*? By the conversation in the tavern, Edwin suspected the man was referring to King Lupis. *"The entire rebellion's lifetime..."*? What rebellion?!

Talking about King Lupis in the tavern, Coner had made it seem that the true Monarchy was the victim of the Dragon Empress's unjustified exile and destruction. If these people were in the right, why kidnap him at all? Why not just tell the truth? Why not tell him instead of tying him up like a prisoner now? Edwin's gut turned. He was going to heave.

"Wit are ye sayin' exactly?" Edwin asked, finding the courage to speak.

"I mean what I say. We are resurrecting our King," Coner replied.

"Impossible," Edwin challenged.

"How long have you been in this world? I would think you would know that with magic, anything's possible, especially with the dark arts."

Dark magic didn't sound good at all—the exact opposite.

Edwin passed through his thoughts. How could he have been so stupid for getting kidnapped?! When did Coner even have the time to drug his drink? That had to be it! Thinking back, Edwin remembered that in the tavern, once the cheering started, he had turned away for a moment, and when he looked back, the man had been putting away something. It wasn't the orb he had shown Edwin.

"Ye drugged me," Edwin said to himself more than to the men.

Coner's men snickered and chuckled. Coner laughed, "Wow, you're really slow, aren't you?"

Edwin's chest felt like it had caught on fire, and he felt his hands shaking, knowing it was rage building instead of fear. Feeling foolish for being tricked. The festival had been the perfect cover to sneak him away from the protection of the Dragon Knights. "Why are ye resurrectin' him?!" Edwin snarled. "If the Empress destroyed him, then he is no King! He is a monster—a mink tyrant!"

The room's laughter died into silence, and Coner bent down to Edwin's level, anger gleaming in his eyes. Pulling out a dagger from his boot, Coner held it up to Edwin's face. "If I were you, I would bite my tongue before someone cuts it off." Coner's voice was a whisper to force Edwin to pay close attention to ensure the knight heard every word. "For this to work, we only need your blood. So, understand the only reason you're not dead is because you are his descendant, and it needs to be fresh for the full effect."

Coner stood up, still looking at Edwin with his cold eyes. Suddenly, a man wearing a black cloak ran into the throne room, calling out in anger, "YOU LEFT ME!"

Ripping the hood off, the man revealed his face, which was covered in small, fresh bite marks and scratches. "Bondge, what in the crown's name happened to you?!" Coner said, surprised at the man's appearance.

"I was attacked by a hatchling!" Everyone laughed at the declaration.

"A hatchling?" laughed one man. "A baby dragon?"

Bondge threw his arms up in anger. "Don't make me into a jester! I had to clean up your mess! The girl that boy was with saw you taking him away and was chasing after you, calling for help! If I hadn't stepped in and taken care of her, you all would have been caught! And leaving me behind was how you thank me?!"

A stabbing pain shot through Edwin's chest as he struggled to breathe. The girl the man was referring to must have been Cory, and the hatchling must have been Merlin. Did he kill her? The thought ate at him. He should have listened to her, and now, because of him, Demmis's younger sister was dead! Tears formed in Edwin's eyes.

"How did you take care of her?" Coner enquired. "Did you hide the body?"

"I knocked her out with a rock. Before I could finish her off, though, that beast attacked me!" Bondge pointed at his damaged face.

"WHAT?!" Coner shouted in rage. "You didn't kill her! FOOL! If that girl tells Clayus what happened and mentions our cloaks? Latona, that witch, knows exactly who we are! They're probably looking for him as we speak! Our whole operation will be ruined!"

Edwin sighed with relief. Not only was his friend alive, but he was probably about to be rescued by Dragon Knights. Not to mention, he felt some second-hand pride from his dragon saving Cory's life.

Coner looked down and thought for a moment, anger stirring up in him. "Are the preparations done?" he asked one of the men.

"They are; however, we still need to find a sacrifice to begin," the man informed.

"We can't wait any longer!" Coner said. "We're doing this now."

Bondge tilted his scratched-up head. "What are we going to do for—"

With a blur of blood splattering onto the floor, Bondge dropped, holding his slashed throat. Coner's dagger was covered in blood. "Move him to the circle, quickly! He has the honor of being the next key to King Lupis's resurrection!"

Coner wiped the blood off Bondge's shirt before returning to Edwin. Two men dragged Bondge's corpse into the circle drawn around the dragon skeleton. At first, the men were shocked at Coner's sudden choice of action, yet they got over it and did as they were told. After they all started walking around the circle, staying out of the crown lines and chanting in a language Edwin didn't recognize. It sounded something like Latona's spells. Edwin's stomach couldn't bear seeing someone murdered in front of him. Edwin leaned to his left as much as possible and started to retch. There had been nothing in his stomach but acid that made his throat burn. Coner had just killed an ally! If he did that to a comrade, if he did that to those on his side, Edwin didn't want to know what he did to his enemies.

Coner returned to Edwin. Crouching down, he grabbed the knight-in-training's shoulder. Edwin started to struggle and lash out, attempting to get free. "Fight me and I'll do to you what I did to him," Coner threatened, his voice grim.

Fearfully, Edwin stopped fighting against the man and let him do as he pleased. Coner cut the boy loose from the pillar, keeping hold of him until the large man who had shouldered Edwin came and kept a grip on the boy. Following Coner to the circle, the large man held Edwin firm as he forced his arm out, the underarm up. Coner grabbed Edwin's arm and, with his sharp dagger, he punctured Edwin's skin and drew blood as he went down his arm, not even bothering to lift up the boy's sleeve. Edwin's wails of pain almost muted the chanting as the knife went from his elbow to his wrist. Edwin tried lashing his body to break free from the danger. It was no use. Digging the dagger out of Edwin's skin, Coner started to say words that were unknown, different from the chanting.

The moment Edwin's blood leaked into it, Tthe drawn circle glowed a deep red. Coner took the knife and flicked the blood onto the skeleton. The big man then took hold of Edwin's bleeding arm and squeezed it, making blood ooze out. Edwin howled in agony.

Coner walked around the skeleton in the circle as the effects intensified; the green steam became smoke, which, in time, became slime, sticking to the skeleton, drenching it. Muscles formed. Edwin could do nothing as his arm bled and he looked on in horror. Edwin thought they had wanted to resurrect King Lupis, yet it seemed they were testing it out on his dragon first, and by the size of the beast, he was a powerful one.

Edwin knew he was involved in something horrible. What was happening in front of him was dark and evil. Edwin was hurt and powerless to stop it, so all he could do was watch, terrified, as the scene played out. He watched as muscle completed and skin tissues appeared, covering the dragon's body.

A loud roar echoed from outside, putting an end to the chanting. "NO! We needed more time!" Coner yelled in fury.

Without warning, the wall of the throne room collapsed and toppled inward, making a Clydesdale-sized hole. Edwin's eyes widened as he saw that the dragon was Newla.

Lunging the rest of the way, she was not careful with watching her step, her foot crushing a man who had fallen because of her grand entrance. She bit another man and threw him away, his screaming cut short with a large thud against stone. Still moving in, she looked around and spotted Edwin, who had a smile on his face. Not only was the young dragon alive, but she was also his savior! Her sights were set on the man who held Edwin captive. Drawing a sword from under his cloak, the man pushed Edwin aside and charged Newla. Not holding back as she did in Gorish, Newla closed her wings and swiped the man off his feet with her tipless tail. Grabbing him with both talons, she slammed him to the ground once-twice-thrice. Destruction followed her as she fought off the rest of the men, not afraid to end them in the process.

"EDWIN!" she called out.

Edwin had been lying on his stomach, holding his arm tightly, attempting to stop the bleeding. Hearing her, he used a nearby wall to help himself up to his feet.

"HERE!" he shouted.

Newla took the time to come to him. A man sliced her back thigh with a sword. Newla hissed in pain and kicked the man back with both legs, and that was the end of him. Kneeling, she helped Edwin onto her back. She demanded that he, "Hold on!" as she spread her wings, knocking down the unstable pillars nearby as a result.

With one arm, Edwin grabbed hold of the scruff going down the dragon's back. A man ran toward her, brandishing a sword. However, by the time he had gotten to Newla, she had leaped out of the hole that she'd made, taking off into the sky.

Before they could call it safe, a bolt of powerful electricity zoomed passed them like a lightning strike, barely missing. Turning to face the attacker, Newla was hit by a smaller bolt, roaring in pain as she took it. Edwin struggled to stay on with his one good arm as the dragon's body contorted. Coner had made it to the castle's roof, shooting at them. Another magic bolt of lightning shot out of Coner's fingers. Newla folded her wings and dropped out of the way.

In an attempt to maneuver away from being hit, Newla had to loop upside down, causing Edwin to lose his grip and fall. "NO!" She dived after the boy yet was cut off by a bolt of lightning shot directly at her. She weaved to avoid it, catching Edwin in her arms.

"You can't escape me, Dragon!" Coner cried, unaware of the shadow dropping behind him.

The Dragon Empress had emerged from behind the castle. At the last minute, Coner saw the shadow just as the Empress breathed a powerful flame of burning fire. Large flames of yellows, reds, blues, greens, and purples intensified as she dared not stop the oncoming flames. Newla flew at the young wizard from behind.

Coming close, Newla flew back into the throne room. Everything was moving so fast, Edwin's eyes couldn't keep up as his vision blurred, seeing the skeleton that was once there had been replaced with a large, deformed body of a dragon, still steaming and oozing green pus.

Then everything went dark.

Newla tucked in her head, making sure to shield Edwin before she shot up into the roof, going through brick and wood. Smashing through, she broke out where Coner stood, demolishing the tiles, causing Coner to fall. The Empress had stopped the fire for fear it might touch Newla and, therefore, Edwin. The Dragon Empress took flight, joining her smaller kin. "You found him! Does he breathe?"

Newla couldn't feel his emotions anymore. She looked down at him, fearing she had lost her Monarch. Blood from his arm now covered her scales and her wounds taken today and the ones that had reopened. She twitched her ears, listening contentedly until she heard the sound of a faint human heartbeat. She looked back to her Empress. "He's alive. However, he doesn't have much time! We must head back!" she replied, fear taking over her voice.

Still, he might not even make it back to the castle in his condition. Newla found it hard to keep a grip on him, his blood making her grasp slippery.

"You must take him to the nearest village. He will not make it to the castle!" the Empress explained.

"I'm not leaving you here to face the sorcerer alone! His magic is too strong for your fire!"

"My flames will burn him alive! Now, your Empress is ordering you! GO!" the Empress snarled, snapping to ensure the young dragon was not forgetting her place.

Not even the threat made Newla move. A roar of pain erupted from Newla's jaw when a bolt of lightning shot her in the back. Newla fell on her side, making the remainder of the roof rattle, her tail and legs dangling off the hole she had made. Edwin had been flung from Newla's grasp and was now lying on the other side of the hole, as still as a corpse. Coner was pulling himself back onto the structure, his hands igniting electricity once he got his knee up and could spare a hand.

Once more, lightning shot out at the Empress. She tried to move out of the way but was too large for a fast attack. Landing, despite hitting her underbelly, the electrifying attack didn't have a deadly effect on her. The tiles beneath her claws rattled as she attempted to take a step. Her body weight shifting from one foot to another was not boding well with the weakened architecture. Newla struggled to pull herself up, and pain ached in her bones as her blood mixed with Edwin's as both stained her scales. After all she'd been through, she might become a crimson dragon, after all. Her old wounds throbbed as she finally got to her feet. She looked at the Empress with a pleading expression, her big doe eyes making her eyes almost black.

Wings extended, the Dragon Empress took to the air, hovering to help Newla. Another bolt of lightning shot at her, yet this time missed. The mighty dragon snarled at their attacker, glaring at Coner. The Empress fired her breath at the sorcerer. He changed his tactics from attack to defense to block her fire again. She stopped immediately. "Newla, get ready to fly!" she ordered.

Newla grabbed Edwin at the same time as she pumped her wings up for momentum. The Empress, using all her weight, slammed down on the roof, making it rumble as if an earthquake had struck. The woods and tiles of the surrounding roof began to cave in, having already lost their supporting beams to Newla. Taking off, Coner was too distracted with trying to escape the ground under him. By the time the area of the roof caved in, Newla and the Empress were in the sky, long away from the ruins, leaving Coner and his followers to meet their fate.

Chapter Thirty-Two

Comforting Words

Something wet dabbed Edwin's forehead, yet all he could see was darkness.

He remembered pain, a lot of pain. He looked down, being back at the scene with the dragon skeleton. His arm was cut as Coner looked at him, dagger in hand, as Edwin squirmed. Then his memories went black.

He could hear voices that were distant and muffled. He heard sobs and pleas. He could hear someone reading him a story, or were they just talking?

Yet all he could see was nothing.

He felt something warm on his stomach. It didn't have a lot of weight to it. It was comforting, though, like a warm hug from someone you loved.

And yet nothing.

A wet, cold rag dabbed his forehead, moving down his temple, and then he could see light through his eyelids. He smelled soil and herbs. His mouth felt dry as he tried to moisten it. He twitched his fingers as his eyes started to flutter.

In the light of his eyes, he could see the scene happening again: Coner slashing his comrade's throat, the Empress and Nelwa being attacked, blood and death.

Edwin suddenly sat up, wheezing with his eyes wide open. He had to escape and get somewhere safe! He moved his legs off the cot and was about to stand until he saw Merlin fall off the bed in front of him. The little dragon stood straight up and roared at him. Edwin could feel that he was angry, yet once the little hatchling realized his knight was awake, Edwin felt immense joy radiating from his dragon. "Merlin?"

"You finally woke!" Latona cheered as she left her table and came to Edwin's aid.

"Coner… Newla, wit-wit happened?! Where am a?!" Edwin's words slurred with confusion as he spat them out.

Merlin hopped onto Edwin's lap and climbed the boy's bare skin gently. Once on his knight's shoulders, Merlin started to rub his head and purr.

Latona placed her hand on the boy's back, shooing Merlin off of his shoulder as she guided him back until he once again lay on the cot. "Please Edwin, calm down. You're in shock. Everything will be alright now. The Empress and Newla brought you back to the castle safe and sound."

Edwin's eyes darted around the room as if needing proof that he was back at the castle and secure. Breathing heavily, Edwin felt a sharp pain in his arm and grabbed it, sitting up once again. Tight bandages covered his forearm where Coner had slashed. Merlin jumped down to his knight's lap and licked the wrapping, staring up at his knight with concerned eyes. Edwin began to breathe slowly, Merlin's calmer emotions helping his. He again scanned the room. A lot of plants had grown almost to adulthood. The red heavy curtains that led to the landing platform were wide open, letting in birds and other creatures to make a home out of hers as they enjoyed her inside garden of smells and remedies.

"Am in yer room?" Edwin restated.

"Yes." Latona nodded.

"Wit happened? How long have a been oot?"

"The Dragon Empress and Newla found you. They must have taken you to a village first because by the time they brought you to me, there had already been stitches on your arm. Not a clean job, yet one that will work. Once they returned with you, I fixed your injury properly, and you've been resting here for five days."

"Five?!"

"Five. You are lucky to be alive with how much blood you lost."

"Are the Empress and Newla alright?! A mind them gettin' attacked by Coner's magic."

Latona nodded, her voice calming, "The two of them are fine."

Before Edwin could say anything else, Latona asked, "Do you think you can stand? King Clayus and I need to ask you some questions about what happened."

"A think so."

With a little help from Latona, Edwin got out of bed, his legs overly weak, causing him to collapse. Alarmed, Latona helped him to his feet once more. He then reassured her that he had it this time, now knowing he needed to find his legs again. His entire body was bruised and sore from battle. He knew Newla did what she could to shield him from getting hurt, and she had succeeded. The only major damage he suffered was the cut he had on his arm. Now being able to stand with a little support, Edwin leaned on Latona's table while the sorceress returned with some trousers and a shirt for him. He changed out of his tethered, stained trousers and tucked the shirt over his head, the cloth being loose and baggy. After getting changed, Latona, Merlin, and the knight in training left her tower and descended her staircase. Edwin needed to use the brick wall for support. Merlin stayed uncharacteristically on the ground.

In the halls, most of the servants, including the males, whispered amongst their ranks as they saw Edwin approaching or passing them as they went about their cleaning and duties. Edwin took notice yet was too sore at the moment to care. The news of his disappearance must have spread throughout the entire castle and the city. Latona was just a few paces ahead of him. Edwin was dragging his feet, being in no rush to recall all that had happened to him. He wished it had never happened. The sights he saw were actions that belonged in nightmares. He still remembered how gruesome Coner had been to turn on his ally—to use him as a sacrifice, like it was second nature.

Edwin stopped. All he was able to see was red—red and green. Muscle forming, skin molding, screams numbing. He smelled smoke and tasted the rich iron of blood. His chest tightened as it felt like he was drowning, gasping for air as he wheezed.

"Edwin?!" a young female voice called from ahead of Latona.

The voice snapped Edwin out of the trance that had trapped him. "Edwin!" Skypris ran through the halls, passing Latona as the girl threw her arms around the boy, hugging him tightly.

Scaltor trotted to catch up, he and Merlin squealing at one another in greeting. Edwin was surprised at first then started to laugh with relief as he hugged her back, not wanting her to let go just yet. "I thought you would never wake up! You had a terrible fever, and it wasn't breaking!"

Edwin realized Skypris's eyes were brimming. "Sorry, ye must have been really worried aboot me."

"It doesn't matter anymore. You're awake now and safe," Skypris reassured him and squeezed him one last time.

Latona tapped the girl's shoulder to get her attention. "Latona, I'm so sorry I almost trampled you."

Latona steadied a hand at the girl's apology. "I know how worried you have been about our friend. I must take him to talk with King Clayus now, though."

"Can I come?" Skypris asked hopefully, letting Edwin have some breathing room.

"I think it would be best if it were just the three of us for now. Besides, I know of another girl around your age, who has been just as worried for him."

"I'll go tell Cory," Skypris said, walking off, with Scaltor scampering after.

Latona, Edwin, and Merlin resumed their journey to the king's council room. Entering through large wooden doors, Edwin took in the grand, skinny room again, having only been there once. The red curtains and cushioned chairs at the long table, the green carpeting. Clayus sat at the head of the table and stood once he saw Latona and Edwin enter.

"Entering, Royal Advisor and the king's sorceress, Latona!" the announcer said. "Accompanied by Edwin, Official Translator for the Dragon Empress and King's Court Member!"

Clayus immediately dismissed all the castle staff in the room, including Winston. They all walked out on one side of the table while Latona and Edwin walked to the king with the other. "Edwin!" the king hesitated, surprised to see the young boy awake. "How are you feeling?!"

"Am a wee sore, that's aw."

The king pulled out one of the chairs. "Then sit and rest, there's no point in you standing."

Sitting down, King Clayus took the chair next to Edwin, arranging it so he and the boy faced each other. Edwin looked to the elder woman. She nodded her head at him with a wink. "I'll be standing. It's good for the old bones."

"I know how traumatic this ordeal must have been for you, and I'm sorry to bring up memories, but you need to understand the urgency we are facing if it's what I fear. The night you were taken, the abductors started the merchants' ships on fire as a distraction while they snuck you out. We would have never known this if it wasn't for Corythia and Skypris running to me in great panic."

"The merchants' ships were on fire?!" Edwin said fearfully. What about little Jarod and his parents, Israel and Quinn? Quinn. She was pregnant! "Are they aw okay? Where are they now?! Those boats were their lives!"

The king stilled Edwin's alarm with a hand. "No one was harmed, and though we weren't able to save most of the ships in time, we are making repairs and rebuilding those that were lost. Until they are completed, the merchants are sharing homes with some volunteers in the city. Everything is okay and taken care of."

"Has the process of rebuildin' started?" Edwin asked. "A want to help."

The King laughed. "I appreciate the offer, Edwin. However, I think we both know you're no shipwright. You have other responsibilities, which brings us back to the topic of this conversation. Now, what exactly happened? Cory says you were kidnapped, yet others are suspecting otherwise."

Edwin didn't know how to take that last statement. Who was suspecting otherwise? King Clayus? Surly not Latona. Others on the council? The city? "A dinnae go with them willingly! Am no traitor!"

"I believe you. Now, please tell me what happened at the festival. Why did they want you?"

Edwin's eyes were dazed as he searched for words to begin. "Coner drugged me, and he and his comrades tewk me to the ruins of some ancient castle. In the throne room, a saw a huge dragon skeleton, only there wis somethin' aff aboot it." Edwin wasn't sure how to describe it. Perhaps the bones had warped over time. Edwin continued, "They said they wanted to resurrect the true monarchy—King Lupis."

"NO! They wouldn't—they couldn't!" Latona cut Edwin off in disbelief. "That dark art has been outlawed for years, and any book of that ceremony had been destroyed by the previous Dragon Empress!"

Edwin processed Latona's words. Shaking his head. "Well, she must have missed one! They were not trying to restore Lupis. I think they were practicing it on his dragon first to make sure it worked." He turned to the sorceress. "Latona, he ken the title the dragons called me. He told me it is because ma ancestors are the true royal monarchy af Xolf yet were chased oot on the Empress's orders!"

King Clayus looked puzzled and shared a look with Latona for support. "None of our history books mention a lost Monarchy. My family has been this land's absolute ruler for generations! He must have been filling your head with lies."

Latona looked to Edwin, moistening her lips. "I wish I were able to help you. However, only the Empress can tell. You'll need to ask her for the truth."

"Trust me after this, a plan on it!" Edwin said determined to finally get the answers and not take no for one. "Dae ye ken anythin' aboot King Lupis? A want more information than wit the library's books say. Dae ye ken, or dae a have to ask the dragon for that information, too?"

"He is mentioned in my family's genealogy records. The records started with him. Any knowledge before him has been lost or destroyed for ages. He's known as the '*Corrupted King,*' and he put this kingdom into a war that took years to end. He was defeated finally by the previous Dragon Empress, and his nephew then took over who was my line." King Clayus scratched his chin. "I always assumed that he was one of my tyrannical ancestors, yet I guess his cult followers don't believe what they read in history."

"That's another thin' a wanted to ask," Edwin started. "A ken that Coner Vain and the men wearin' black dragon-scaled cloaks are no friends to the Dragon Empress. They mentioned somethin' aboot bein' a rebellion. Wit dae ye ken?"

King Clayus read with hesitation as he pondered. Edwin couldn't determine if it was because the subject was a secret to everyone or if it was because King Clayus wasn't as trusting of Edwin as he appeared to be. The thought made Edwin's blood rise. He had betrayed his own country for this one, for this culture they had, and that wasn't enough to stop the questions. He couldn't get too mad at him, though. From his point of view, he was a boy taken from Gorish and who didn't really have a say in the fate the Empress had brought him into.

Merlin came out from under Edwin's legs and climbed up on Edwin's shoulder, purring lovingly as he rubbed his scaled head on Edwin's cheek. With everything going on, Edwin had barely acknowledged the hatchling. The poor little dragon had been just as worried for him, if not more than anyone else. Edwin had a proud smile for his dragon. Merlin had saved Cory's life by attacking her attacker's face, and Edwin saw the aftermath. Edwin shook off the image of the men in cloaks dragging Bondge's body into the circle.

"The rebellion has been going on through this land for generations," Latona began, earning a benevolent look from the king. "It's a group of people who do not approve of us working alongside dragons. They have a similar belief as Gorish."

"Why wedd they want to resurrect the Corrupted King?" Edwin wondered, trying to make sense of it.

"We are trying to find that out. It seems their goals over the years have changed or they are scheming something bigger than we thought," King Clayus explained.

"Were ye able to go back to the castle yet? Ye could have captured one af them and questioned him?" Edwin suggested.

Clayus shook his head. "No, Edwin, we tried. Newla and the Empress took too long to return. We sent out our strongest Dragon Knights, and they reported back that there were no signs of the rebellion ever being there besides the destruction Newla and the Empress had caused to the building. No dead bodies, and no dragon skeleton like you mentioned."

Edwin got chills. What did that mean? They moved the skeleton or— "Wis there a drawn circle with magic-lookin' runes? Wit aboot blood? Wis there any blood?" Edwin questioned, hoping there was any evidence behind his story.

"It was hard to find anything because of the damage the dragons caused while rescuing you," King Clayus admitted.

Suddenly, the wooden doors opened fast, and a voice called, "Cory, wait!"

A young blue-eyed girl hesitated only until she spotted Edwin, then she ran to him. One guard tried to grab her while the other told Demmis, Skypris, Terro to wait at the door entrance. Stopping at Edwin's chair, Cory stared at the boy for a moment as if seeing if he truly was awake, her eyes glassy as they filled up with tears. Streams of water escaped as she saw Edwin's injured arm wrapped up. Realizing what was bothering her, Edwin quickly slapped his hand on it to cover it, wincing in pain as he hit it.

"I'm so sorry," she said under her breath.

"Come on! You're coming with me, you're not allowed in here!" the guard who chased her demanded as he went to grab her arm.

King Clayus gave a hand to order the guard to back off.

"Yes, my king." The guard bowed in surprise, then walked back to his station.

Edwin jumped up and let the young girl hug him, returning the action to her. "It's no yer fault," he reassured, hoping the words would comfort her.

King Clayus motioned for the guard at the door to let the others pass, and so the guard stood down, and the others walked as the second guard walked out, leaving the door open until further instructed. "Your majesty, please forgive her!" Demmis bowed.

"It's alright," King Clayus said and stood up smiling. "I know how she must feel. We were done anyway."

"Oh, so you are alive," Terro said as if he had received bad news.

"Sorry to disappoint," Edwin smirked, being released from Cory's arms.

"It's fine. You can't always get what you want." Terro shrugged, earning a hard glare from Skypris.

Demmis put his hand on Edwin's shoulder. "Wow! I think you're the first in your training group to have had field experience twice. First the drake, then getting kidnapped. What's next? Going to war?"

The joking words made everyone in the room chuckle, except for Terro and Cory. "Please, I order you not to give the boy any ideas!" King Clayus mused.

"I'm so sorry," Cory said, fighting the tears. The young girl was holding onto Edwin's shirt as if afraid that if she let go, he would be taken again.

Edwin hated to see her like this. It made him remember the first time they'd met. She had been sobbing because Demmis was so badly hurt by the drake's attack. The young girl kept on breathing *"I'm sorry"* under her breath, where only Edwin could hear it. Merlin jumped down to Cory's head, then stepped to her shoulders as he began licking her cheek.

"Please, Cory, dinnae blame yerself. It wis ma fault and no one else's."

Edwin looked up at everyone, hoping they would take the hint that Cory and he needed a moment to talk. Luckily, Latona was able to read his mind. "Let's give them a moment," the sorceress said.

King Clayus glanced back at his paperwork, then followed everyone else out of the room, leaving the two teens alone. The doors were open, and King Clayus stood at the entrance. He wouldn't be able to hear them, though. Edwin knew he probably didn't want to leave important documents alone.

"I knew that man wasn't a good person! He rubbed me the wrong way. I should have tried harder to stop you, or I should have gone with you!" Cory choked. "I'm so sorry, Edwin."

"Cory, stop. Please." Edwin backed away from her so he could look into her eyes. She was looking down. Edwin gently lifted her head so their eyes met. "A made the choice af goin' by maself. Ye warned me and a didnae listen," Edwin tried to reason with her.

“I could have done something when they took you! I… I just wasn’t strong enough,” Cory said.

“Ye tried! Cory, a ken ye were tryin’ to run after me. Ye got knocked oot. A overheard ma kidnappers talkin’. Ye could have died if it were no for Merlin.”

“There must have been something more I could have done!” Cory whimpered, her guilt fading, realizing what Edwin just said.

“Ye did wit ye could dae at that moment.” Edwin took a breath out, pushing the memories away. “It happened. It’s over. The dragons were able to get to me in time because af ye.”

“I’m sorry you had to go through that! I couldn’t imagine—” Cory stopped once Edwin hugged her again.

“A ken. Am okay and alive. That’s wit matters.” At this point, Edwin couldn’t tell if he was trying to reassure his friend or himself.

Edwin held her in his arms, letting her breathing settle from the tears. He wanted to hold her for as long as it took to make her guilt die. And selfishly, holding her made his mind focus elsewhere instead of on his arm. Like he needed to be a protector instead of a victim, like Lord Lockwood in his books. It wasn’t her fault! She had to know that! He could understand how she must feel. Feeling powerless to help the ones you love was an awful feeling. He thought back to his father and the day he lost him.

His uncle had come home, yet his father was not with him, only his father's sword. His uncle then told his aunt she had lost her brother to a dragon.

Dragons.

“A have to go now,” he said.

“Where are you going?” Cory questioned. “You must be starving! You need to eat and rest.”

“I need to talk to the Dragon Empress,” Edwin said, his tone full of distaste.

Chapter Thirty-Three
The Corrupted Monarchy

Edwin followed the dirt path from the castle all the way down to the shore. He went around the city, not wanting to deal with the crowd of knights and citizens in their busy everyday lives. He also couldn't handle noise right now. It would irritate him further, and he was already heading to the Dragon Empress with a negative temper. Was his anger justified? To him, it was; yet, try telling that to a dragon the size of a tower! Through the forest, he tried to calm himself, but he couldn't. He would need to stop and rest often. He hadn't eaten anything in five days or had much of anything to drink, and he was starting to feel the toll it was taking on his body. He was determined! He had to talk with the Empress *now*!

Merlin didn't ride on his knight's shoulders. He could feel Edwin's fatigue and dared not add to it. Eventually, Edwin had made it to the wet plateau of igneous rocks on which the dragons liked to nest. Dragons flew all above him, enjoying playing and diving into and out of the overcast weather as though they were jumping fish. He found the lowest point of the plateau and began to climb; however, it was hard to do so with an injured arm. If he used it too much, it would ache in pain as he felt the stitches straining. It was hard to climb up with one arm, especially since Merlin needed to hold onto him. Once his head was level with the elevated ground, Merlin hopped onto it and grabbed his knight's shirt sleeve and tried to pull him up. Although it was a nice gesture, it didn't really do anything. Edwin took a moment to catch his breath after the workout, and then he got onto the igneous.

He stood up and watched as the dragons of the shore played, ate, fished, and slept. It wasn't hard to spot the Empress since she was the biggest of the thunder. He moved his way to her, weaving through dragons and stepping over running and wrestling hatchlings. Merlin skipped, wanting to chase some hatchlings down that had invited him to play, yet he declined, following close to his knight. As Edwin passed, dragons would glance at him or watch, soon returning to their own business once it was too much effort to keep their eyes on him.

Once they reached the Empress, Merlin bounced on his front legs as he chirped and cheered, running to his mother, getting her attention. The Empress turned her attention to her son with a welcoming smile.

"Hello, Merlin," she greeted, lowering her head to the ground so her son could nuzzle her.

Edwin approached the large dragon, putting his thoughts in order, trying to make questions out of them. He could feel his anger building. He had calmed down, yet being here in the moment started to bring the emotions back. As if it was her fault he had gone through his traumatic experience. Oh wait! It was.

Despite his anger, he could feel Merlin's overjoyment at seeing his mother. It was almost enough to outweigh the negativity. Suddenly,

Edwin's emotions won, and Merlin's smiles and happy purs turned into confused hums as he tilted his head to his mother, probably not understanding where his joy for her had gone. He scampered back over to his knight and sat down as Edwin stood. The Dragon Empress looked at Edwin, probably reading his emotions.

"Young Edwin, it's good to see you're making a recovery. How are you feeling?" She tilted her head at him.

"Physically or emotionally?" Edwin folded his arms, eyes locked on her.

The front she had put on melted away, and she raised her chin. "You're mad at me," she said, stating the obvious.

"Aye. A want to ken exactly wit is goin' on aboot ma family! Ma ability to understand dragons, the lost Monarchy, King Lupis—everything! And dinnae dare say am no ready, a dae no believe that is a luxury anymore!" Edwin stated firmly, pointing up at the Empress.

The Dragon Empress blinked slowly and inhaled. "What exactly do you know currently?" Her voice was submissive.

He told her everything he knew, even some things he didn't understand. He told her about the conversation he and Coner had in the tavern and his claim about the past Empress chasing the monarchy out, how he was the lost monarchy. He relayed everything he had talked about with King Clayus, had found in the library about the topic, and the events that had happened to him in the ruined castle before Newla and she showed up to save him. Talking about the castle again made him stammer a bit. Gratefully, however, he was too upset for the memories to overwhelm him. Throughout Edwin's whole explanation, the Empress's facial expression stayed the same—content and interested in every word, as though she was taking them and analyzing them further.

After finishing, Edwin stopped for a moment to calm himself. Still trying to catch his breath, Edwin looked back up to the Empress. "Is wit Coner says true? Is that why ye brought me here, because ma bloodline is the rightful heir af the throne? Why did ye brin' me here, if ye ken the rebellion wedd use me to try to resurrect the Corrupted King?" Edwin's questions poured out of his mouth.

"Young Edwin!" she said firmly, her powerful voice halting the boy's rant.

The dragons around them halted what they were doing or woke up from their naps. They looked on, then soon either took flight to somewhere else or went farther away from their ruler and the boy. After Edwin's nerves had settled down, the Empress continued, "If what you say is true, that the Corrupted King's followers are trying to bring him back, then this is a serious problem."

Edwin's eyes danced with the dragon's. He was still a little too scared to talk because of her stern voice that had shut him up moments ago. He had to talk, though. He swallowed painfully and moistened his throat. She readjusted her talons and took a deep breath, looking into the sky. "I suppose you should know the reason for the war before you fight in it."

"They didnae finish resurrecting him, though," Edwin pointed out. "They were practicing on his dragon first, and am even unsure if that ritual wis completed."

The Empress shook her head, before bringing it back down. "The tale I'm about to share with you will reveal all. However, once I do, tell no one who is not worthy of this knowledge. You must understand that we dragons had to hide history from humans because it's so evil we feared for it to be repeated."

Edwin nodded, and the Empress continued. "The founder of this island was the one who brought humans and dragons together to live in peace. Because of his wisdom, he became King, and the original Dragon Empress gave him her blood to show her gratitude for him stopping the war among the species. The chosen King then consumed her blood, giving him a half-dragon bloodline, and with it came some unusual abilities. Understanding our language is just scratching the surface of them. His descendant, Lupis, thirsted for more power. He thought that in order to gain it, he must become a full dragon, so he sought the dark arts that were forbidden because of their malicious nature. Developing his own dark spell, he found a way to merge himself with his dragon.

"However, the spell failed, and they both perished because Lupis did not understand what he had done before doing it. His new body became unstable. In the Empress's rage, Lupis's family line was driven from the throne and fled to the land of Gorish on her orders. That is when King Clayus's ancestors took the crown and their places as rulers. This story is neither a myth nor a fairy tale, as it has been perceived throughout the generations of dragons. I hope you understand why it cannot be told."

Edwin felt his jaw clench. The story he had just heard was unbelievable and so… horrifying. So that dragon was King Lupis, too? The entire concept was confusing. "He did that to his dragon? Why?" Those were all the words he could muster.

"Power, pride, greed," the Dragon Empress ticked off. "The natural flaws of man. He didn't respect the bond that the original Empress and King had made and put forth. Therefore, only certain families can be granted the option to become Dragon Knights. To get a dragon is the highest honor. A dragon is not only your partner or friend but is kin. Lupis and many other greedy humans do not honor this and only see having a dragon as a means of gaining power over others."

Edwin looked down at Merlin, who looked up at his knight with his big, innocent eyes. "A never really thought af Merlin in that way," Edwin admitted.

"How did you think of him?" the Empress asked.

"Honestly, nothin' like a partner or a friend—let alone a brother or equal. A thought af him as ma dragon."

"He is your dragon, Edwin, and you are his knight. Together, you are a Dragon Knight. Together, you are one. We dragons can easily overpower humans, and yet it is against our nature. We don't see how humans see. Our perspective of the world is broader. The first time Merlin hatched—the first time he laid eyes on you—he knew who you were and who you are to become. He loves you for your flaws, weaknesses, and fears. When he sees you, he doesn't see a human, but someone he would die for."

Edwin looked at the Empress as he thought; she could easily take villages, even a small hatchling could damage a man's face. People of Gorish killed dragons for generations, and yet, the dragons didn't retaliate for revenge or anything other than self-defense. When Newla was being attacked and on the brink of death, she refused to harm anyone. He thought back to when the Empress mentioned the humans were at war with the dragons. Were they not evil, then? What about King Lupis's dragon? Did he not know what his knight was doing? "Dae aw the dragons think this way?" Edwin questioned.

"All," the Empress said. "A dragon's bond with their knight is so powerful that it would allow them to hurt others if it pleased them. Everyone has a side to a story, and most believe what they are doing and standing for is right. King Lupis thought that what he was doing was right, and so did his dragon. In times of tyrants, that is for the Dragon Empress to take care of and put a stop to. Only the most foolish of dragons go against my will. In turn, the Empress can't have a knight to persuade her of their beliefs. I must stay neutral for the sake of this land."

"Dae ye get lonly withoot a knight?" Edwin asked.

"Yes, if you see it that way. Yet, no, because how I see it is everyone is my knight."

Edwin's temperature and anxiety mellowed. It felt nice not to have so much anger. She had answered all his questions. All but one. "Why did ye brin' me here? Did ye ken the rebellion could use me to resurrect the Corrupted King?"

"I knew with the dark arts it was possible. However, the thought that they would dare hatch a scheme like they did never crossed my mind. I thought you would be safe in a kingdom filled with dragons and their knights. This fault was mine." She winced with guilt.

"So ye brocht me here because ye thought it wis safer for me?" Edwin wondered.

“I brought you here because even though you hail from Gorish, this is your family's origin. You don’t belong in Gorish. You saw this world differently from others there, and I saw that in you. You were considered a coward, even to yourself, and you begged me for more. You told me you had no other choice, and so I gave you one.”

“Yet ma existence created a problem! King Lupis’s followers ken am here. They can use ma blood to brin’ back the Corrupted King, and who kens, maybe they were successful! A dae no ken wit am suppose to dae or where to go from here!”

“That’s simple,” the Empress began, moving her head so she was eye level with the boy. “Have you made friends here?”

Edwin thought the question was odd to ask at a time like this. “Aye, that a did.”

“Do you fancy this place and how you are perceived by the culture around you?”

Edwin thought about the life he was starting to have here compared to the one in Gorish. As much of a traitor as it made him, he did prefer Xolf’s way of life over his homeland. He thought about Maro, Skypris, Cory, Demmis, Louis—everyone—even Terro was starting to turn around. He liked it here. He wanted to call this place home.

“Aye,” was all he was able to say as his emotions were entangled in his thoughts.

“Then your question has been answered for you. The rebellion is a threat to you and all you care about, and you need to stop them.”

“Why?!” Edwin felt the weight of her words. “Because it’s ma destiny?”

“No, Young Edwin. Because it is the right thing to do.”

Glossery

Ashtheir - (Ash-th-ear)
Karoaress - (Kah-roar-ess)
Zandorious - (Zan-door-ee-ess)
Kaprisairess - (Kah-pree-s-air-ess)
Brooktorous - (Brook-tour-us)

Elvous - (El-vee-us)
Elvin - (El-vee-en)
Gorish - (Gore-ish)
Goreon - (Gore-en)
Xolf - (Reads like 'wolf'; however, replace the 'w' sound with a 'z' sound)
Xolite - (Z-ool-ight)
Alena - (Ah-leen-ah)
Laxor - (L-axe-or)
Ishnia - (Ish-nee-ah)
Thrist - (Th-er-st)
Exwear - (Ex-wee-ear)
Ryjah - (R-eye-jah)

Who Is The Author?

Katelyn Sheddy is a young wife and mother from the red rocks of Utah who has dreams of sharing her stories to the world. Thanks to her time in University and childhood hobby, she's able to not only tell the tales of her characters through the art of words but also has the capability to illustrate them in a visual format on her socials. *Monarch Of The Dragon* is her debut novel and is the first instalment to the *Monarch* series. She has lots of stories to tell and is eager to grow along with the characters.

She posts updates of her stories and shares artwork on her Instagram account, @theartofkatelyn and also YouTube channel, TheArtOfKatelyn.

Edwin  Prince Terro  Skypris  Maro

Corythia Hero Circe

Demmis Louis

The Dragon Empress

Newla

Cerberus

Reuben

Gale

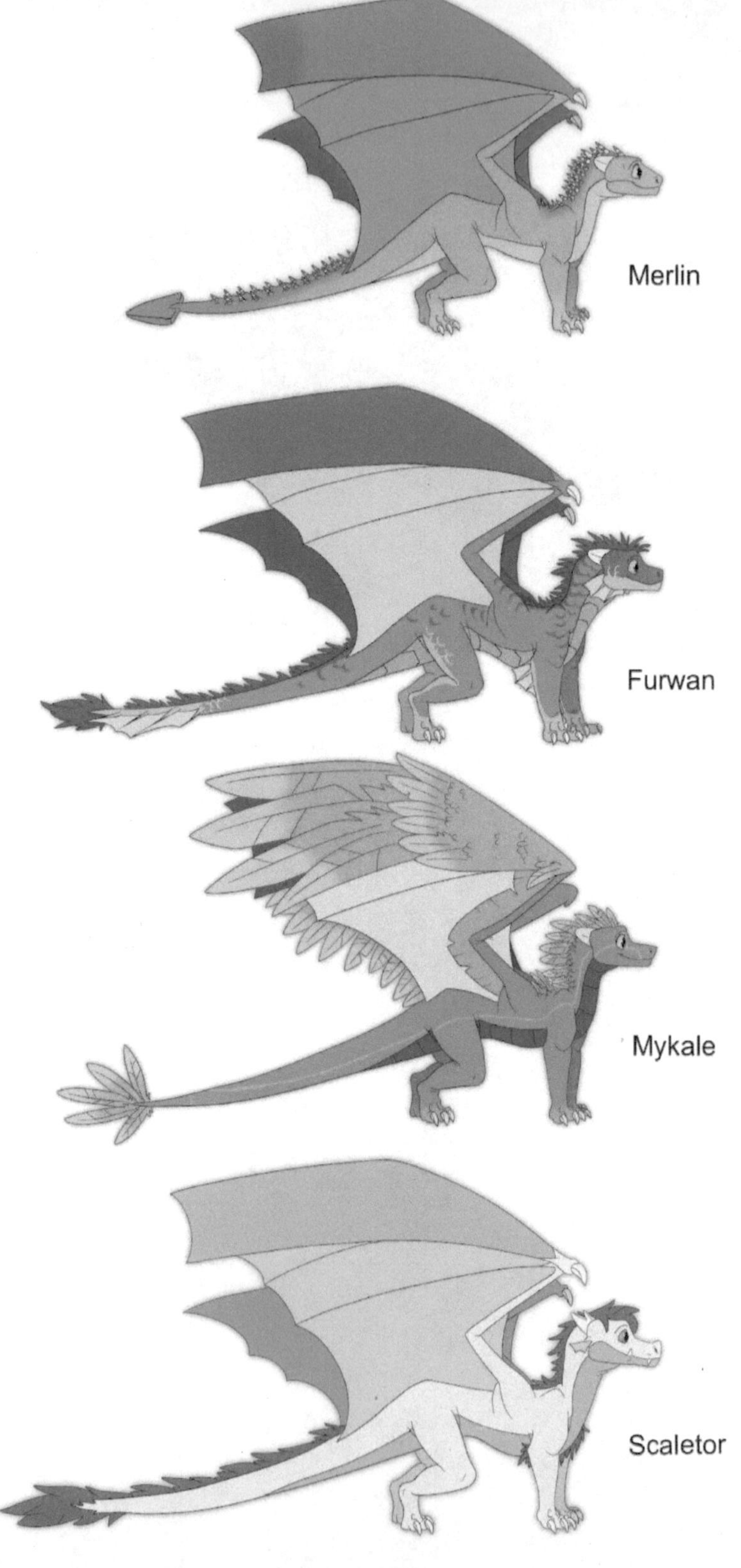
Merlin
Furwan
Mykale
Scaletor

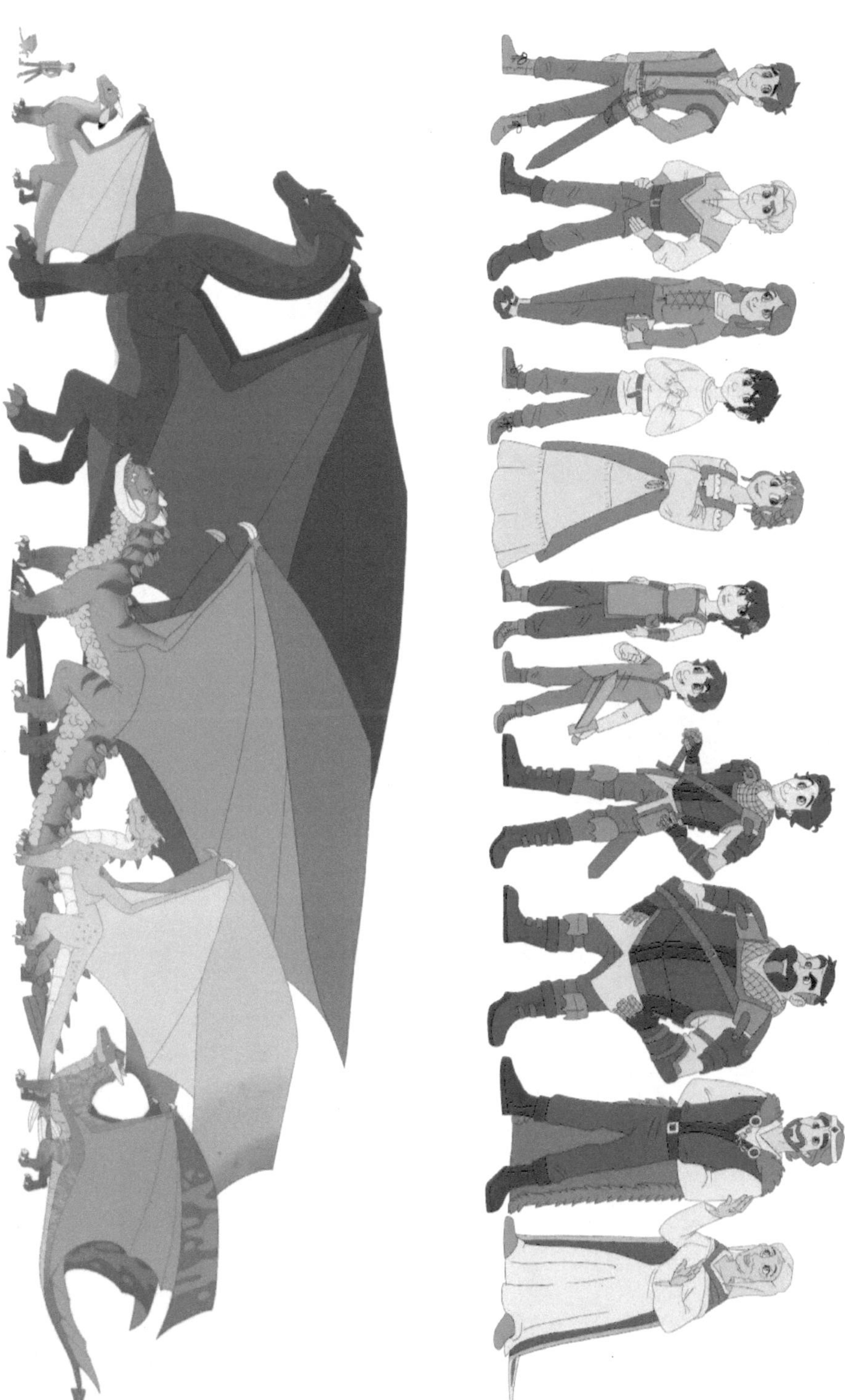

Short Story

My nieces and nephews were a huge part of my inspiration for telling stories, especially in my youth. I became an aunt of seven when I was only eight years old. Of course, the number has increased, so you can imagine how close we all became. With my sisters and brothers happy with their family numbers, the inspiration still grows for telling stories. However, this time in the form of my own children, as my first daughter was just born last year!

The short story that you are about to read is one made by my 15-year-old (2026) nephew, Zander, who I believe has a talent for writing at a young age already! So you bet I want to share some of his work with you all! Praise the kid! Make him blush from all the positive attention! I hope you enjoy his masterpiece as much as I do!

Have fun reading!

Oh!

And… be aware of black goo.

The Black Goo

Written By Zander O'kelley

Entry 1: The Hanging and the Goo.

The air inside Will's Gun Shop hung thick with the metallic scent of oiled steel and gunpowder. Zane, his brother Malcolm, and John stood by the counter, ready to finally make their purchases. Zane, the group's unofficial leader, was lean and wiry with sharp, restless eyes and a buzzed haircut that matched his no-nonsense attitude. He ran a nervous hand over a sleek shotgun. His brother Malcolm was built like a wall, broad-shouldered and heavy set, with a thick beard and a calm, deliberate presence that balanced Zane's intensity. Standing with them was John, the youngest, an athletic man with a quick, nervous energy and a clean-cut look that seemed out of place among the racks of weaponry.

They were finishing their business with the owner, Will, an old friend of John's, a man whose smile didn't quite reach his eyes. "Alright boys, paperwork's done.

Are you ready to walk out of here armed?" Will asked, his voice gravelly.

Before anyone could answer, a bloodcurdling scream tore through the shop's thin walls. It was a woman's scream, sharp and frantic.

Without a word, the four men burst outside. The afternoon street, usually bustling, seemed to hold its breath. A small crowd had gathered, pointing silently at the sign pole bearing the shop's name.

Hanging from the crossbar, dangling horribly, was a body. Zane couldn't tell who it was, only that it was a man, and the way he was strung up was deliberately sickening. But what truly stole their focus was the ground below. A viscous, oily black goo coated the pavement beneath the body, reflecting the harsh sunlight like spilled crude oil.

Zane's hands were already shaking as he pulled out his phone and started dialing. "Jackson," he choked out to his friend, a detective on the city's police force. "Jackson, it's Zane. We're at Will's shop. You need to get down here. There's a body... and something else. Something awful."

Jackson, the seasoned cop, arrived minutes later, his face etched with confusion as he took in the gruesome tableau and the unsettling black substance. The crime scene defied logic. Jackson immediately informed Will that he'd have to come in for questioning—standard procedure since it was his business sign.

"Don't worry about tonight. The party is still happening." Jackson said, putting a comforting hand on Zane's shoulder, his gaze showing the distress of the situation. Jackson told the trio. "You boys go. Vinny and Elijah will be there. Try to clear your heads."

They agreed, the unsettling image of the hanging body and the black goo already burned into their minds.

Entry 2: The Sample.

Later that night, the contrast between the grim scene and Jessica's thumping, crowded house party was jarring. The air was thick with loud music, cheap beer, and nervous energy. Zane, Malcolm, and John joined their friends Vinny and Elijah, attempting to blend in, but the earlier event kept pulling them back.

Elijah, always the observer, was upstairs talking to Jessica. He followed her into her bedroom to check out her new sound system. As he glanced around the big room, his eyes froze on a small shelf tucked into a corner. Three glass jars sat there, filled with a thick, ominous black goo. It was identical to the substance that Zane described at the crime scene. Why does Jessica have the same substance in her room? He thought.

"Hey, I gotta use the bathroom. I'll be right back," Elijah mumbled, his heart hammering against his ribs.

He didn't go to the bathroom. He slipped downstairs, found Jackson talking to John and Malcolm in a quiet corner of the kitchen, and pulled Jackson aside, breathlessly recounting what he'd seen.

Jackson's eyes narrowed. "Okay, we need a sample. We have to be sure it matches."

A plan was quickly devised. Malcolm and John would call Elijah and Jessica downstairs simultaneously, creating a distraction. Jackson would slip upstairs and grab what he needed.

Elijah returned to the bedroom. Seconds later, John's voice boomed from the bottom of the stairs, "Elijah! Jessica! Come down, we need you for a quick second!"

They both descended. As they did, Jackson, a ghost in the chaos of the party, moved swiftly. He entered Jessica's room, found the jars, and used a small kit to take a quick, clean sample of the goo before disappearing back into the crowd.

Meanwhile, across town, Vinny and Zane were at a convenience store, restocking on drinks.

"So, what was all the commotion at Will's shop?" Vinny asked casually as they loaded cases into the trunk.

Zane explained the hanging body and how terrifying black goo was. As they wrapped up the conversation, Zane’s phone buzzed—it was Malcolm.

"Zane! Get here! Now! There was an explosion! Jessica's house—it's ruined, man! And Jessica... she's dead. Black goo is everywhere!"

Entry 3: The Forensics Room and the Warning.

Zane and Vinny raced back to the party. Sirens wailed, and flashing red and blue lights turned the suburban street into a chaotic, terrifying spectacle. The house was partially ruined, black residue seeping from the wreckage. Zane found Malcolm, John, and Elijah standing with Jackson, all staring in stunned disbelief. Jessica's body lay lifeless, covered in the same horrific goo.

The scene was a nightmare of confusion for the responding officers and detectives. Who was this victim? Why the goo? What was the connection to the first body?

Later that night, Jackson, exhausted and covered in ash, drove back to the station. The only hope he had was the small vial of black goo he'd snagged from Jessica's room. He headed straight for the Forensics Lab, expecting to find the two scientists, Lily and Lucas, already hard at work.

He pushed open the door. The sight that greeted him caused him to stumble back.

Lily and Lucas were both dead, sprawled on the floor. And surrounding them, oozing from the shattered equipment and desk surfaces, was the relentless black goo.

Scrawled crudely on the wall in what looked like dried goo was a chilling message:

<YOU'RE NOT FIGURING ME OUT, JACKSON.>

The message was personal. The attacks were escalating, becoming more targeted.

The next day, Jackson had the entire department working overtime, but they had no leads because of the dead forensic scientists. Around nightfall, Vinny told Zane he was planning to crash at John's house, needing a distraction from the horrors of the previous night.

Later, Zane tried calling John to see if he and Vinny were still down to go shooting, but he didn't pick up. Zane then called Vinny to see what they were up to.

"John? Nah, he canceled on me," Vinny replied, sounding genuinely disappointed. "Said he wasn't up to it."

A sick feeling churned in Zane's gut. He called Malcolm. "Let's go to John's. Now."

They arrived and busted the door open. John was gone. Only the familiar, sickening black goo marked the floor. They immediately called Jackson to swarm the house.

Zane then called Vinny to tell him what happened. Vinny feigned shock. As soon as Zane hung up, a dark realization settled in Zane's mind.

Meanwhile, at Vinny's house, the basement lights were dim. Black jars filled with the viscous goo lined shelves. And tied securely to a chair, unconscious, was John. Vinny had lied.

Entry 4: Betrayal and the Explosion.

Panic washed over Vinny after hanging up with Zane. The plan was unraveling too fast.

He dialed a number. "Will! It's Vinny! They're on to us! They went to John's house!"

"Calm down," Will's voice crackled on the line. "I told Malcolm I'd pick him up around five. Everything is set on this end. I'm heading to the station now."

Will, the gun shop owner, was Vinny's partner. The gun shop was the perfect front.

Will and a host of heavily armed men, all equipped with high-powered weapons from the store, arrived at the Police Station. They threw explosives and opened fire immediately. It was an all-out assault.

Inside, Jackson grabbed his AR-15 and started shooting back, shouting orders to get the other officers and staff out the back way. But it was too late. Will and his remaining men placed a massive bomb in the central lobby, the timer ticking down rapidly.

After multiple shots were fired, some of the police department were able to take down nearly all of Will's men, in the process, almost every officer in the station had been killed in the crossfire or gave their lives. Only Jackson remained, alive but exposed. He thought the fight was over, but then Will stepped out of the shadows, a revolver in his hand.

Will fired. Thud. Thud. Jackson staggered as two bullets tore into his shoulder. CRACK. The third struck his stomach.

Will didn't stop there. He aimed the revolver at the bomb and fired. BOOM! The entire police station erupted in a blinding flash of light and a deafening shockwave, collapsing in on itself.

Meanwhile, back at Vinny's house, Vinny had knocked John out again and stuffed him into a cabinet in the basement, just as Zane and Elijah arrived.

The three of them went to the basement to "talk." As they spoke, Zane noticed a streak of black goo near a large cabinet. The sight confirmed his worst suspicion.

"Look, we should go. Head to the station," Zane said, trying to sound natural. "I'll meet you there, I just need the bathroom."

Vinny was suspicious, but he took Elijah with him anyway, not wanting to leave the loose end behind. Once they were gone, Zane rushed to the cabinet, found the goo, and ripped the door open.

There was John. Zane frantically called 911, and then Jackson. No answer. He started nervously trying to wake up John, who was nearly dead.

In the car, Elijah told Vinny “Hey man, find John. I’m not ready to lose another one.”, Vinny looked at him, knowing what will happen and says “Yeah, I’m sure we'll find him.” Then Vinny dropped off Elijah and called Will. "They're onto us. I'll pick up Malcolm instead. Get to the house quick! I think Zane knows."

Entry 5: Desert Showdown and Aftermath.

Back at the house, John finally stirred, confused but awake. He quickly untied his hands, grabbing the shotgun Zane had placed nearby. But the moment John was free, Will burst through the door, his face streaked with soot from the explosion.

Will fired a warning shot, narrowly missing Zane. He commanded Zane to grab the needle next to him—the needle they used to knock out victims—and inject himself. Zane told him "You don't have to do this man! Think of your family!" Will responded "My family had their chance. You're next and after them, your family, then everybody else's."

Zane, realizing this was his only chance, agreed. He stuck the needle into his arm, fell to the floor, and feigned unconsciousness.

Will, satisfied, walked over to the cabinet to check on John. But John had been faking. He opened his eyes, grabbed the shotgun, and slammed the butt of the weapon into Will's face, knocking him back. Before Will could recover, John shot him in the stomach.

Will had mistaken Zane's ordinary medication needle for the actual knockout serum, giving Zane a clear head.

The two friends rushed out, realizing they had to find Vinny. Zane had noted Will's earlier comment about picking up Malcolm, and now assumed Vinny had him. He quickly checked Malcolm's phone location: the middle of the desert, the most random spot possible.

Zane and John sped toward the location in their car.

Meanwhile, Vinny had parked and gotten out of the car. He reached for the back door to get Malcolm, who had only been pretending to be asleep, kicked out while still tied, grabbing Vinny's pistol from the front passenger seat. He tried to fire, but there was no ammo.

"Looking for this?" Vinny mocked, holding up a handful of bullets from his pocket. He grabbed Malcolm, threw him out of the car, and reached for the pistol to reload.

Just then, Zane and John arrived. Vinny quickly aimed the unloaded pistol at them. "Don't try anything!"

They tried to reason with him. Zane said "Vinny please, let's talk about this-"

"Hell no!..." Vinny yelled. "I will complete my mission!" Vinny tells them he has not come all this way to fail. John asks Vinny what he is talking about just as Vinny is about to explain, Malcolm yells "The gun isn't loaded!"

In a fit of rage, Vinny struck Malcolm with a machete. Before he could reload the pistol, Zane fired his shotgun, hitting Vinny right in the shoulder. Vinny crumpled to the ground.

Zane and John rushed to Malcolm, who was bleeding but alive. "The ammo... in his pocket," Malcolm whispered.

Zane's blood ran cold. He looked up at Vinny, who was aiming his pistol while lying on the ground. Vinny laughed like a lunatic and said, "I get the last laugh". CRACK! Vinny shot right at Zane; John jumped right in front of the bullet and was shot right in the heart.

With a primal scream, Zane swung his shotgun and smashed the butt of it directly into Vinny's skull.

Zane was left standing over two bodies—one dead, one his dying brother who he was holding in his arms—screaming in the vast emptiness of the desert.

Fifteen minutes later, the ambulances arrived. Malcolm was rushed to the hospital.

Back at the ruins of the police station, under the heavy debris, three survivors were found: one cop, one of Will's gang members, and Jackson, barely alive. He was taken to the hospital alongside Malcolm.

Both Malcolm and Jackson survived.

After the tragedy, Zane and Malcolm moved away, the terrifying legacy of the black goo and the betrayal of their friends was too much to bear in the city where it all happened.

Entry 6: The New Normal and the Echo.

6 Months after the tragic events. Zane sat on the porch of his cabin, miles from the nearest highway in the high desert of Nevada. The silence was perfect, broken only by the dry rustle of sagebrush. He had traded his shotgun for a fishing rod, but the calm was a lie. Every shadow was a memory, and every unfamiliar car was a threat. Malcolm, his brother, worked on restoring a vintage truck in the garage, the mechanical work a simple, repetitive counterpoint to the complexity they had survived.

They had been rigorous about covering their tracks and using cash only. They thought they were safe.

Then came the "accidents." First, a near-miss car crash where a truck, driven by an aggressive, bland-faced man, tried to run Zane off the road. Then, a power surge that fried their security system, followed by a minor but suspicious gas leak in the cabin's heating system. Zane dismissed the first two as bad luck, but the gas leak felt deliberate. The silence was broken.

Meanwhile, a thousand miles away, Jackson sat in a cramped, windowless office, the only sign of his former life being the persistent stiffness in his shoulder. He was thinner, sharper, running his own cold case on a private retainer. He had dedicated his life to tracing the origin of the Black Goo, a process that yielded nothing but dead ends and heavily redacted corporate documents. He knew Vinny and Will were just middlemen. The person who synthesized the goo was still out there.

Then, his burner phone, reserved for the deepest edges of his network, rang. The number was blocked, the voice on the other end ragged with fear.

"Jackson, it’s me. I know who you are. I saw the jars. That thing... it's back. I saw the logo, Jackson, I remember it. They're coming for me, I know it."

It was Elijah.

Jackson leaned forward, the six months of frustration snapping into focus. "Elijah, slow down. You saw what logo?"

"Omni... Omniscience Bio-Tech. It was on the side of the box those jars came in. I never told you because I was too scared, but they found me. There’s a guy. Tall, pale, drives a rental SUV. He watched my apartment for days. He asked about Zane."

A wave of dread washed over Jackson. He knew this wasn't a coincidence. "Get out of there, Elijah. Now. Don't call me again. I'll find you."

Jackson grabbed a leather travel bag containing his remaining research, a few weapons, and enough cash for a one-way trip. The hunt had just begun, and the first targets were his last surviving friends.

Entry 7: Tracing the Source and The Cleaner.

Jackson drove through the night, his mind calculating angles and routes. He bypassed the city and drove straight into the Nevada desert, knowing the only place Zane and Malcolm would be secure was together.

He found them at the cabin, and the reunion was brief and tense. Malcolm, ever practical, was wary. "Jackson, you bring that mess with you?"

"It found us first, Mal," Zane interjected, pointing to the patched-up gas line. "Jackson, what's going on?"

Jackson spread out his few corporate documents and cross-referenced them with Elijah's frantic call. "The black goo is an asset of a company called Omniscience Bio-Tech. They deal in high-end medical research, but their funding is opaque. Elijah saw their logo on the goo jars."

"Elijah? Where is he?" Malcolm asked.

"He's running. And he has a shadow," Jackson said.

Just then, a vehicle—a nondescript rental SUV—came speeding down the dirt track, kicking up a massive plume of dust.

"The pale guy," Zane muttered, grabbing a rifle. "He's the one who tried to run me off the road." "Hello there, I am Alex Keller."

Agent Keller, operating as a "Cleaner" for Omniscience, screeched to a stop. He was professional, disciplined, and carried no visible goo—only a suppressed automatic weapon. He was here to eliminate the loose ends.

"Final warning, gentlemen. Return what you took and we can make this easy," Keller called out, his voice modulated and flat.

"We took nothing but a bullet!" Malcolm yelled back, firing a warning shot that tore through the SUV's headlight.

A brief, violent firefight erupted. Keller was precise and ruthless, pinning them down. Zane, using his knowledge of the desert terrain, managed to flank Keller. As Malcolm laid down cover fire, Zane disabled Keller's vehicle. Seeing his mission compromised, Keller retreated on foot, disappearing into the vast scrubland, leaving behind a brief case of advanced communication gear.

"He's not like Will," Zane noted, reloading. "He was a pro."

"We can't stay here," Jackson said, examining the briefcase. "They found Elijah, and they found us. If Omniscience is the source, we have to go right to the headquarters. Elijah is the key. We need to find him before they do."

Malcolm looked at Zane, then at Jackson. "Fine. But we do this my way. No more playing cop."

Entry 8: The Facility and Dr. Smith.

The three men tracked Elijah to a rundown motel outside the city where Omniscience Bio-Tech maintained its corporate offices. Elijah, terrified and malnourished, broke down upon seeing them.

"I tried to run, I tried everything. They're everywhere, guys," Elijah wept, clutching Zane's arm.

Elijah insisted he was a liability, but Jackson assured him he was their most valuable asset. The team developed a plan: Omniscience's R&D division was housed in a sprawling, remote campus disguised as a data farm, protected by armed security and biometric scanners.

They infiltrated the campus under the cover of a massive dust storm. Elijah, remembering details of the Omniscience logo and corporate branding, was able to give them the necessary keywords and access codes to bluff their way past the initial security checkpoints.

They found the lower level—the synthesis lab—a sterile, terrifying factory floor. Instead of chemicals, massive, complex robotic arms were assembling tiny, intricate components.

"It's not a chemical weapon," Jackson breathed, watching the process. "It's nanotechnology."

Then, a voice echoed through the sterile chamber. "Ah, the prodigal survivors. I wondered when the residue would finally pool in one place."

Standing calmly on a catwalk above them was Dr. Elias Smith. He was thin, impeccably dressed, with pale, intellectual eyes that held no warmth. He was flanked by two armed guards, silent and efficient, one of the guards being agent Keller.

"I suppose you're here about the cleanup," Smith stated, holding a single glass vial containing a tiny, shimmering droplet of the black goo. "My field operatives, Will and Vinny, were adequate, but crude. They misunderstood the purpose." And did not listen to my orders. "For example Will placing those jars into Jessica's room and a bomb under the house. I did not tell him to do that, what I did tell them to do was take out anybody in the way and Jackson, your police station.

It was a perfect distraction for Vinny to kill Malcolm, but it's obvious that didn't happen."

Smith explained his motivation: "The goo is an advanced nanite swarm. It's not designed for mass destruction, but for perfect biological sterilization. It targets specific DNA markers, dissolves tissue, and leaves only a non-toxic mineral residue—the goo you see. I'm perfecting a solution to manage population growth and 'edit' human error. Your friend John was a regrettable necessity. He saw too much, and his death was required to test the final dispersal methodology."

Smith gestured toward a control panel. "Your visit is timely. I was just about to run a full-scale atmospheric test using a diluted viral strain. You've given me the perfect opportunity to eliminate the last five remaining 'inconsistencies.'"

Entry 9: Chaos and Confrontation.

As soon as Smith finished speaking, Keller and the other armed guard (elite private security, far more skilled than Will's men) descended the stairs. Malcolm, having anticipated the attack, shoved Elijah behind a stack of sealed containers.

"Zane, the mainframe! Jackson, cover us!" Malcolm yelled, firing a coordinated burst that temporarily stunned the Keller and the guards.

The room erupted into chaos. Malcolm and Zane engaged Keller and the other guard in brutal close-quarters combat. Meanwhile, Jackson focused his fire on the controls of the massive synthesis machinery, aiming to destroy the production line.

Elijah, though terrified, noticed a critical detail: a series of interlocking ventilation conduits that led directly toward the power core. "The sub-vents! He's using them to mix the dispersal agent!" Elijah yelled over the noise, pointing toward the ceiling.

Zane knew he couldn't take on the guards alone while Malcolm was pinned down. He broke cover and raced toward the ventilation shafts. Malcolm finally dispatched the first guard, and there was only Keller left. Malcolm and Keller got into a fist fight, and after a moment, Keller got the upper hand on Malcolm. Elijah saw this, looked around, and saw a jar of black goo. He grabbed it and threw it right at Keller, right before he choked out Malcolm. The goo exploded on impact and hit Keller in the back. It brought Keller to the ground, who yelled in agony and pain." It's all doctor Smith's fault!", as he died. Malcolm got up and raced to Zane, yelling, "We need to hit the main cooling valve now, Zane!"

Zane located the main coolant line, but it was protected by a heavy blast door. Elijah saw a remote in Keller's front jacket pocket and yelled out to Malcolm to grab it to open the door. Malcolm carefully grabbed the remote off of Keller's dead body, then remotely unlocked the blast door. Zane kicked open the door, fired into the coolant line, and the whole factory floor was instantly bathed in a freezing vapor, triggering a mechanical failure.

Smith, seeing his life's work dissolved, activated a concealed emergency escape pod on his catwalk. The vapor hit the catwalk, briefly disorienting him. Jackson sprinted toward the pod, ignoring the spray of goo. He tackled Smith just as the pod door began to close. Jackson pinned Smith against the pod, his shoulder screaming in pain.

"It ends here, Smith!" Jackson shouted.

Smith dropped the single glass vial containing the master sample of the black goo. The vial skittered across the wet metal floor. Alarms blared, and the lights failed. The entire facility was going into structural collapse.

Entry 10: Resolution and The End of the Black Goo.

The structural failure was immediate and catastrophic. Zane and Malcolm, with Elijah between them, raced through the crumbling corridor. They emerged onto the desert floor just as the entire Omniscience complex imploded, collapsing into a deep, smoking crater.

Minutes later, Jackson crawled out from the debris field near the edge of the crater, coughing and badly bruised, but alive. He was dragging Dr. Smith, who was clearly dead, with a piece of glass from one of the jars of black goo stabbed into his heart. Next to Smith's body was the shattered master vial. The freezing coolant and the impact of the collapse had neutralized the nanite swarm, leaving only a dark mineral stain. The mastermind and the last trace of the original threat were gone.

They watched from a distance as local authorities, baffled by the strange seismic event, arrived. They knew no one would ever understand the full scope of the nano-technology they had just prevented from being released.

Elijah's Future: The nightmare was finally over for Elijah. Jackson used his remaining resources and contacts to secure Elijah a new identity and an escape path to a quiet life. Elijah left, no longer running from the threat, but walking toward a hard-earned peace.

Zane and Malcolm's Future: The victory was complete. The architect of John's death and the source of the trauma were definitively destroyed. Zane and Malcolm finally felt a burden lift. They realized their path was no longer about paranoid escape or vengeful hunting, but about healing. They sold the cabin and decided to use the money to start a new, simple life, focused on rebuilding their family and honoring John's memory by choosing peace.

Jackson's Peace: Jackson stood on the ridge, watching the smoke rise. His debt to John was paid, and his investigation was closed. The man who synthesized the goo was dead, and the lab was erased. He had no more leads to follow and no reason to run. He sold his office, discarded his burner phone, and drove toward the distant city lights, ready to finally confront his own quiet life.

And that is the end of the black goo.

IN HONOR OF

Audrey Miller Claybrook

A true monarch of her time

www.ingramcontent.com/pod-product-compliance
Lightning Source LLC
LaVergne TN
LVHW100505110826
845146LV00002B/525

* 9 7 9 8 9 9 4 8 6 0 6 0 1 *